Simon t

Simon the Jester

Alpha Editions

This edition published in 2023

ISBN : 9789357934350

Design and Setting By
Alpha Editions
www.alphaedis.com
Email - info@alphaedis.com

Contents

CHAPTER I

I met Renniker the other day at the club. He is a man who knows everything—from the method of trimming a puppy's tail for a dog-show, without being disqualified, to the innermost workings of the mind of every European potentate. If I want information on any subject under heaven I ask Renniker.

"Can you tell me," said I, "the most God-forsaken spot in England?"

Renniker, being in a flippant mood, mentioned a fashionable watering-place on the South Coast. I pleaded the seriousness of my question.

"What I want," said I, "is a place compared to which Golgotha, Aceldama, the Dead Sea, the Valley of Jehoshaphat, and the Bowery would be leafy bowers of uninterrupted delight."

"Then Murglebed-on-Sea is what you're looking for," said Renniker. "Are you going there at once?"

"At once," said I.

"It's November," said he, "and a villainous November at that; so you'll see Murglebed-on-Sea in the fine flower of its desolation."

I thanked him, went home, and summoned my excellent man Rogers.

"Rogers," said I, "I am going to the seaside. I heard that Murglebed is a nice quiet little spot. You will go down and inspect it for me and bring back a report."

He went blithe and light-hearted, though he thought me insane; he returned with the air of a serving-man who, expecting to find a well-equipped pantry, had wandered into a charnel house.

"It's an awful place, sir. It's sixteen miles from a railway station. The shore is a mud flat. There's no hotel, and the inhabitants are like cannibals."

"I start for Murglebed-on-Sea to-morrow," said I.

Rogers started at me. His loose mouth quivered like that of a child preparing to cry.

"We can't possibly stay there, sir," he remonstrated.

"*We* are not going to try," I retorted. "I'm going by myself."

His face brightened. Almost cheerfully he assured me that I should find nothing to eat in Murglebed.

"You can amuse yourself," said I, "by sending me down a daily hamper of provisions."

"There isn't even a church," he continued.

"Then you can send me down a tin one from Humphreys'. I believe they can supply one with everything from a tin rabbit-hutch to a town hall."

He sighed and departed, and the next day I found myself here, in Murglebed-on-Sea.

On a murky, sullen November day Murglebed exhibits unimagined horrors of scenic depravity. It snarls at you malignantly. It is like a bit of waste land in Gehenna. There is a lowering, soap-suddy thing a mile away from the more or less dry land which local ignorance and superstition call the sea. The interim is mud—oozy, brown, malevolent mud. Sometimes it seems to heave as if with the myriad bodies of slimy crawling eels and worms and snakes. A few foul boats lie buried in it.

Here and there, on land, a surly inhabitant spits into it. If you address him he snorts at you unintelligibly. If you turn your back to the sea you are met by a prospect of unimagined despair. There are no trees. The country is flat and barren. A dismal creek runs miles inland—an estuary fed by the River Murgle. A few battered cottages, a general shop, a couple of low public-houses, and three perky red-brick villas all in a row form the city, or town, or village, or what you will, of Murglebed-on-Sea. Renniker is a wonderful man.

I have rented a couple of furnished rooms in one of the villas. It has a decayed bit of front garden in which a gnarled, stunted stick is planted, and it is called The Laburnums. My landlord, the owner of the villas, is a builder. What profits he can get from building in Murglebed, Heaven alone knows; but, as he mounts a bicycle in the morning and disappears for the rest of the day, I presume he careers over the waste, building as he goes. In the evenings he gets drunk at the Red Cow; so I know little of him, save that he is a red-faced man, with a Moustache like a tooth-brush and two great hands like hams.

His wife is taciturn almost to dumbness. She is a thick-set, black-haired woman, and looks at me disapprovingly out of the corner of her eye as if I were a blackbeetle which she would like to squash under foot. She tolerates me, however, on account of the tongues and other sustenance sent by Rogers from Benoist, of which she consumes prodigious quantities. She wonders, as far as the power of wonder is given to her dull brain, what on earth I am doing here. I see her whispering to her friends as I enter the house, and I know they are wondering what I am doing here. The whole village regards me as a humorous zoological freak, and wonders what I am doing here among normal human beings.

And what am I doing here—I, Simon de Gex, M.P., the spoilt darling of fortune, as my opponent in the Labour interest called me during the last electoral campaign? My disciple and secretary, young Dale Kynnersley, the only mortal besides Rogers who knows my whereabouts, trembles for my reason. In the eyes of the excellent Rogers I am horn-mad. What my constituents would think did they see me taking the muddy air on a soggy afternoon, I have no conception. Dale keeps them at bay. He also baffles the curiosity of my sisters, and by his diplomacy has sent Eleanor Faversham on a huffy trip to Sicily. She cannot understand why I bury myself in bleak solitude, instead of making cheerful holiday among the oranges and lemons of the South.

Eleanor is a girl with a thousand virtues, each of which she expects to find in counterpart in the man to whom she is affianced. Until a week or two ago I actually thought myself in love with Eleanor. There seemed a whimsical attraction in the idea of marrying a girl with a thousand virtues. Before me lay the pleasant prospect of reducing them—say, ten at a time— until I reached the limit at which life was possible, and then one by one until life became entertaining. I admired her exceedingly—a strapping, healthy English girl who looked you straight in the eyes and gripped you fearlessly by the hand.

My friends "lucky-dog'd" me until I began to smirk to myself at my own good fortune. She visited the constituency and comported herself as if she had been a Member's wife since infancy, thereby causing my heart to swell with noble pride. This unparalleled young person compelled me to take my engagement almost seriously. If I shot forth a jest, it struck against a virtue and fell blunted to the earth. Indeed, even now I am sorry I can't marry Eleanor. But marriage is out of the question.

I have been told by the highest medical authorities that I may manage to wander in the flesh about this planet for another six months. After that I shall have to do what wandering I yearn for through the medium of my ghost. There is a certain humourousness in the prospect. Save for an occasional pain somewhere inside me, I am in the most robust health.

But this same little pain has been diagnosed by the Faculty as the symptom of an obscure disease. An operation, they tell me, would kill me on the spot. What it is called I cannot for the life of me remember. They gave it a kind of lingering name, which I wrote down on my shirt-cuff.

The name or characteristics of the thing, however, do not matter a fig. I have always hated people who talked about their insides, and I am not going to talk about mine, even to myself. Clearly, if it is only going to last me six months, it is not worth talking about. But the quaint fact of its brief duration is worth the attention of a contemplative mind.

It is in order perfectly to focus this attention that I have come to Murglebed-on-Sea. Here I am alone with the murk and the mud and my own indrawn breath of life. There are no flowers, blue sky, smiling eyes, and dainty faces—none of the adventitious distractions of the earth. There are no Blue-books. Before the Faculty made their jocular pronouncement I had been filling my head with statistics on pauper lunacy so as to please my constituency, in which the rate has increased alarmingly of late years. Perhaps that is why I found myself their representative in Parliament. I was to father a Bill on the subject next session. Now the labour will fall on other shoulders. I interest myself in pauper lunacy no more. A man requires less flippant occupation for the premature sunset of his days. Well, in Murglebed I can think, I can weigh the *pros* and *cons* of existence with an even mind, I can accustom myself to the concept of a Great Britain without Simon de Gex. M.P.

Of course, when I go I shall "cast one longing, lingering look behind." I don't particularly want to die. In fact, having otherwise the prospect of an entertaining life, I regard my impending dissolution in the light of a grievance. But I am not afraid. I shall go through the dismal formality with a graceful air and as much of a smile on my face as the pain in my inside will physically permit.

My dear but somewhat sober-sided friend Marcus Aurelius says: "Let death surprise me when it will, and where it will, I may be *eumoiros*, or a happy man, nevertheless. For he is a happy man who in his lifetime dealeth unto himself a happy lot and portion. A happy lot and portion in good inclinations of the soul, good desires, good actions."

The word *eumoiros* according to the above definition, tickles my fancy. I would give a great deal to be eumoirous. What a thing to say: "I have achieved eumoiriety,"—namely the quintessence of happy-fatedness dealt unto oneself by a perfect altruism!

I don't think that hitherto my soul has been very evilly inclined, my desires base, or my actions those of a scoundrel. Still, the negatives do not qualify one for eumoiriety. One wants something positive. I have an idea, therefore, of actively dealing unto myself a happy lot or portion according to the Marcian definition during the rest of the time I am allowed to breathe the upper air. And this will be fairly easy; for no matter how excellently a man's soul may be inclined to the performance of a good action, in ninety cases out of a hundred he is driven away from it by dread of the consequences. Your moral teachers seldom think of this—that the consequences of a good action are often more disastrous than those of an evil one. But if a man is going to die, he can do good with impunity. He can simply wallow in practical virtue. When the boomerang of his beneficence comes back to hit him on the head—*he won't be there to feel it*. He can thus hoist Destiny with its own petard, and, besides, being eumoirous, can spend a month or two in a peculiarly diverting manner. The more I think of the idea the more am I in love with it. I am going to have a seraph of a time. I am going to play the archangel.

I shall always have pleasant memories of Murglebed. Such an idea could not have germinated in any other atmosphere. In the scented groves of sunny lands there would have been sown Seeds of Regret, which would have blossomed eventually into Flowers of Despair. I should have gone about the world, a modern Admetus, snivelling at my accursed luck, without even the chance of persuading a soft-hearted Alcestis to die for me. I should have been a dismal nuisance to society.

"Bless you," I cried this afternoon, waving, as I leaned against a post, my hand to the ambient mud, "Renniker was wrong! You are not a God-forsaken place. You are impregnated with divine inspiration."

A muddy man in a blue jersey and filthy beard who occupied the next post looked at me and spat contemptuously. I laughed.

"If you were Marcus Aurelius," said I, "I would make a joke—a short life and an eumoiry one—and he would have looked as pained as you."

"What?" he bawled. He was to windward of me.

I knew that if I repeated my observation he would offer to fight me. I approached him suavely.

"I was wondering," I said, "as it's impossible to strike a match in this wind, whether you would let me light my pipe from yours."

"It's empty," he growled.

"Take a fill from my pouch," said I.

The mud-turtle loaded his pipe, handed me my pouch without acknowledgment, stuck his pipe in his breeches pocket, spat again, and, deliberately turning his back, on me, lounged off to another post on a remoter and less lunatic-ridden portion of the shore. Again I laughed, feeling, as the poet did with the daffodils, that one could not but be gay in such a jocund company.

There are no amenities or urbanities of life in Murglebed to choke the growth of the Idea. This evening it flourishes so exceedingly that I think it safe to transplant it in the alien soil of Q 3, The Albany, where the good

Rogers must be leading an idle existence peculiarly deleterious to his morals.

This gives one furiously to think. One of the responsibilities of eumoiriety must be the encouragement and development of virtue in my manservant.

Also in my young friend and secretary, Dale Kynnersley. He is more to me than Rogers. I may confess that, so long as Rogers is a sober, honest, me-fearing valet, in my heart of hearts I don't care a hang about Rogers's morals. But about those of Dale Kynnersley I do. I care a great deal for his career and happiness. I have a notion that he is erring after strange goddesses and neglecting the little girl who is in love with him. He must be delivered. He must marry Maisie Ellerton, and the two of them must bring lots of capable, clear-eyed Kynnersleys into the world. I long to be their ghostly godfather.

Then there's Eleanor Faversham—but if I begin to draw up a programme I shall lose that spontaneity of effort which, I take it, is one of the chief charms of dealing unto oneself a happy lot and portion. No; my soul abhors tabulation. It would make even six months' life as jocular as Bradshaw's Railway Guide or the dietary of a prison. I prefer to look on what is before me as a high adventure, and with that prospect in view I propose to jot down my experiences from time to time, so that when I am wandering, a pale shade by Acheron, young Dale Kynnersley may have not only documentary evidence wherewith to convince my friends and relations that my latter actions were not those of a lunatic, but also, at the same time, an up-to-date version of Jeremy Taylor's edifying though humour-lacking treatise on the act of dying, which I am sorely tempted to label "The Rule and Example of Eumoiriety." I shall resist the temptation, however. Dale Kynnersley—such is the ignorance of the new generation—would have no sense of the allusion. He would shake his head and say, "Dotty, poor old chap, dotty!" I can hear him. And if, in order to prepare him, I gave him a copy of the "Meditations," he would fling the book across the room and qualify Marcus Aurelius as a "rotter."

Dale is a very shrewd fellow, and will make an admirable legislator when his time comes. Although his highest intellectual recreation is reiterated attendance at the musical comedy that has caught his fancy for the moment and his favourite literature the sporting pages of the daily papers, he has a curious feline pounce on the salient facts of a political situation, and can thread the mazes of statistics with the certainty of a Hampton Court guide. His enthusiastic researches (on my behalf) into pauper lunacy are remarkable in one so young. I foresee him an invaluable chairman of committee. But he will never become a statesman. He has too passionate a faith in facts and figures, and has not cultivated a sense of humour at the expense of the philosophers. Young men who do not read them lose a great deal of fun.

Well, to-morrow I leave Murglebed for ever; it has my benison. Democritus returns to London.

CHAPTER II

I was at breakfast on the morning after my arrival in London, when Dale Kynnersley rushed in and seized me violently by the hand.

"By Jove, here you are at last!"

I smoothed my crushed fingers. "You have such a vehement manner of proclaiming the obvious, my dear Dale."

"Oh, rot!" he said. "Here, Rogers, give me some tea—and I think I'll have some toast and marmalade."

"Haven't you breakfasted?"

A cloud overspread his ingenuous countenance.

"I came down late, and everything was cold and mother was on edge. The girls are always doing the wrong things and I never do the right ones—you know the mater—so I swallowed a tepid kidney and rushed off."

"Save for her worries over you urchins," said I, "I hope Lady Kynnersley is well?"

He filled his mouth with toast and marmalade, and nodded. He is a good-looking boy, four-and-twenty—idyllic age! He has sleek black hair brushed back from his forehead over his head, an olive complexion, and a keen, open, clean-shaven face. He wore a dark-brown lounge suit and a wine-coloured tie, and looked immaculate. I remember him as the grubbiest little wretch that ever disgraced Harrow.

He swallowed his mouthful and drank some tea.

"Recovered your sanity?" he asked.

"The dangerous symptoms have passed over," I replied. "I undertake not to bite."

He regarded me as though he were not quite certain, and asked in his pronounless way whether I was glad to be back in London.

"Yes," said I. "Rogers is the only human creature who can properly wax the ends of my moustache. It got horribly limp in the air of Murglebed. That is the one and only disadvantage of the place."

"Doesn't seem to have done you much good," he remarked, scanning me critically. "You are as white as you were before you went away. Why the blazes you didn't go to Madeira, or the South of France, or South Africa I can't imagine."

"I don't suppose you can," said I. "Any news?"

"I should think I have! But first let me go through the appointments."

He consulted a pocket-book. On December 2nd I was to dine with Tanners' Company and reply to the toast of "The House of Commons." On the 4th my constituency claimed me for the opening of a bazaar at Wymington. A little later I was to speak somewhere in the North of England at a by-election in support of the party candidate.

"It will be fought on Tariff Reform, about which I know nothing," I objected.

"I know everything," he declared. "I'll see you through. You must buck up a bit, Simon, and get your name better known about the country. And this brings me to my news. I was talking to Raggles the other day—he dropped a hint, and Raggles's hints are jolly well worth while picking up. Just come to the front and show yourself, and there's a place in the Ministry."

"Ministry?"

"Sanderson's going."

"Sanderson?" I queried, interested, in spite of myself, at these puerilities. "What's the matter with him?"

"Swelled head. There have been awful rows—this is confidential—and he's got the hump. Thinks he ought to be the Chancellor of the Exchequer, or at least First Lord, instead of an Under Secretary. So he's going to chuck it, before he gets the chuck himself—see?"

"I perceive," said I, "that your conversational English style is abominable."

He lit a cigarette and continued, loftily taking no notice of my rebuke.

"There's bound to be a vacancy. Why shouldn't you fill it? They seem to want you. You're miles away over the heads of the average solemn duffers who get office."

I bowed acknowledgment of his tribute.

"Well, you will buck up and try for it, won't you? I'm awfully proud of you already, but I should go off my head with joy if you were in the Ministry."

I met his honest young eyes as well as I could. How was I going to convey to his candid intelligence the fact of my speedy withdrawal from political life without shattering his illusions? Besides, his devotion touched me, and his generous aspirations were so futile. Office! It was in my grasp. Raggles, with his finger always on the pulse of the party machine, was the last man in the world to talk nonsense. I only had to "buck up." Yet by the time Sanderson sends in his resignation to the King of England, I shall have sent in mine to the King of Hosts. I moved slightly in my chair, and a twinge of the little pain inside brought a gasp to my throat. But I felt grateful to it. It was saving me from an unconscionable deal of worry. Fancy going to a confounded office every morning like a clerk in the City! I was happier at peace. I rose and warmed myself by the fire. Dale regarded me uncomprehendingly.

"You look as if the prospect bored you to tears. I thought you would be delighted."

"*Vanitas vanitatum*," said I. "*Omnia vanitas.*"

"Rot!" said Dale.

"It's true."

"I must fetch Eleanor Faversham back from Sicily," said Dale.

"Don't," said I.

"Well, I give you up," he declared, pushing his chair from the table and swinging one leg across the other. I leaned forward and scrutinised his ankles.

"What are you looking at?"

"There must be something radically wrong with you, Dale," I murmured sympathetically. "It is part of the religion of your generation to wear socks to match your tie. To-day your tie is wine-coloured and your socks are green——"

"Good Lord," he cried, "so they are! I dressed myself anyhow this morning."

"What's wrong with you?"

He threw his cigarette impatiently into the fire.

"Every infernal thing that can possibly be. Everything's rotten—but I've not come here to talk about myself."

"Why not?"

"It isn't the game. I'm here on your business, which is ever so much more important than mine. Where are this morning's letters?"

I pointed to an unopened heap on a writing-table at the end of the room. He crossed and sat down before them. Presently he turned sharply.

"You haven't looked through the envelopes. Here is one from Sicily."

I took the letter from him, and sighed to myself as I read it. Eleanor was miserable. The Sicilians were dirty. The Duomo of Palermo did not come up to her expectations. The Mobray-Robertsons, with whom she travelled, quarrelled with their food. They had never even heard of Theocritus. She had a cold in her head, and was utterly at a loss to explain my attitude. Therefore she was coming back to London.

I wish I could find her a nice tame husband who had heard of Theocritus. It would be such a good thing for everybody, husband included. For, I repeat, Eleanor is a young woman of fine character, and the man to whom she gives her heart will be a fortunate fellow.

While I was reading the letter and meditating on it, with my back to the fire, Dale plunged into the morning's correspondence with an air of enjoyment. That is the astonishing thing about him. He loves work. The more I give him to do the better he likes it. His cronies, who in raiment, manners, and tastes differ from him no more than a row of pins differs from a stray brother, regard a writing-chair as a mediaeval instrument of torture, and faint at the sight of ink. They will put themselves to all kinds of physical and pecuniary inconvenience in order to avoid regular employment. They are the tramps of the fashionable world. But in vain do they sing to Dale of the joys of silk-hatted and patent-leather-booted vagabondage and deride his habits of industry; Dale turns a deaf ear to them and urges on his strenuous career. Rogers, coming in to clear away the breakfast things, was despatched by my young friend to fetch a portfolio from the hall. It contained, he informed me, the unanswered letters of the past fortnight with which he had found himself unqualified to deal. He grasped the whole bundle of correspondence, and invited me to follow him to the library and start on a solid morning's work. I obeyed meekly. He sat down at the big table, arranged the pile in front of him, took a pencil from the tray, and began:

"This is from Finch, of the *Universal Review*."

I put my hand on his shoulder.

"Tell him, my boy, that it's against my custom to breakfast at afternoon tea, and that I hope his wife is well."

At his look of bewilderment I broke into a laugh.

"He wants me to write a dull article for his stupid paper, doesn't he?"

"Yes, on Poor Law Administration."

"I'm not going to do it. I'm not going to do anything these people ask me. Say 'No, no, no, no,' to everybody."

"In Heaven's name, Simon," he cried, laying down his pencil, "what has come over you?"

"Old age," said I.

He uttered his usual interjection, and added that I was only thirty-seven.

"Age is a relative thing," I remarked. "Babes of five have been known to die of senile decay, and I have seen irresponsible striplings of seventy."

"I really think Eleanor Faversham had better come back from Sicily."

I tapped the letter still in my hand. "She's coming."

"I'm jolly glad to hear it. It's all my silly fault that she went away. I thought she was getting on your nerves. But you want pulling together. That confounded place you've been to has utterly upset you."

"On the contrary," said I, "it has steadied and amplified my conception of sublunary affairs. It has shown me that motley is much more profitable wear than the edged toga of the senator—"

"Oh, for God's sake, dry up," cried young England, "and tell me what answers I'm to give these people!"

He seemed so earnest about it that I humoured him; and my correspondents seemed so earnest that I humoured them. But it was a grim jest. Most of the matters with which I had to deal appeared so trivial. Only here and there did I find a chance for eumoiriety. The Wymington Hospital applied for their annual donation.

"You generally give a tenner," said Dale.

"This time I'll give them a couple of hundred," said I.

Dale earmarked the amount wonderingly; but when I ordered him to send five pounds apiece to the authors of various begging letters he argued vehemently and quoted the Charity Organisation Society.

"They're frauds, all of them," he maintained.

"They're poor necessitous devils, at any rate," said I, "and they want the money more than I do."

This was a truth whose significance Dale was far from realising. Of what value, indeed, is money to me? There is none to whom I can usefully bequeath my little fortune, my sisters having each married rich men. I shall not need even Charon's obolus when I am dead, for we have ceased to believe in him—which is a pity, as the trip across the Styx must have been picturesque. Why, then, should I not deal myself a happy lot and portion by squandering my money benevolently during my lifetime?

It behooves me, however, to walk warily in this as in other matters, for if my actions too closely resemble those of a lunatic at large, trustees may be appointed to administer my affairs, which would frustrate my plans entirely.

When my part in the morning's work was over, I informed my secretary that I would go out and take the air till lunch-time.

"If you've nothing better to do," said he, "you might run round to Eccleston Square and see my mother."

"For any particular reason?"

"She wants to see you. Home for inebriate parrots or something. Gave me a message for you this morning."

"I'll wait," said I, "on Lady Kynnersley with pleasure."

I went out and walked down the restful covered way of the Albany to the Piccadilly entrance, and began my taking of the air. It was a soft November day, full of blue mist, and invested with a dying grace by a pale sunshine struggling through thin, grey rain-cloud. It was a faded lady of a day—a lady of waxen cheeks, attired in pearl-grey and old lace, her dim eyes illumined by a last smile. It gave an air of unreality to the perspective of tall buildings, and treated with indulgent irony the passing show of humans—on foot, on omnibuses, in cabs and motors—turning them into shadow shapes tending no whither. I laughed to myself. They all fancied themselves so real. They all had schemes in their heads, as if they were going to live a thousand years. I walked westwards past the great clubs, moralising as I went, and feeling the reaction from the excitement of Murglebed-on-Sea. I looked up at one of my own clubs, a comfortable resting-place, and it struck me as possessing more attractions than the family vault in Highgate Cemetery. An acquaintance at the window waved his hand at me. I thought him a lucky beggar to have that window to stand by when the street will be flooded with summer sunshine and the trees in the green Park opposite wave in their verdant bravery. A little further a radiant being, all chiffons and millinery, on her way to Bond Street for more millinery and chiffons, smiled at me and put forth a delicately-gloved hand.

"Oh, Mr. de Gex, you're the very man I was longing to see!"

"How simply are some human aspirations satisfied!" said I.

"Farfax"—that's her husband, Farfax Glenn, a Member on my side of the House—"Farfax and I are making plans already for the Easter recess. We are going to motor to Athens, and you must come with us. You can tell us all about everything as we pass by."

I looked grave. "Easter is late next year."

"What does that matter? Say you'll come."

"Alas! my dear Mrs. Glenn," I said, with a smile, "I have an engagement at Easter—a very important one."

"I thought the wedding was not to take place till June."

"It isn't the wedding," said I.

"Then break the engagement."

"It's beyond human power," said I.

She held up her bracelet, from which dangled some charms.

"I think you're a ——" And she pointed to a little golden pig.

"I'm not," I retorted.

"What are you, then?"

"I'm a gentleman in a Greek tragedy."

We laughed and parted, and I went on my way cheered by the encounter. I had spoken the exact truth, and found amusement in doing so. One has often extracted humour from the contemplation of the dissolution of others—that of the giant in "Jack the Giant-killer" for instance, and the demise of the little boy with the pair of skates in the poem. Why not extract it from the contemplation of one's own?

The only disadvantage of my position is that it give me, in spite of myself, an odd sense of isolation from my kind. They are looking forward to Easters and Junes and summers, and I am not. I also have a fatuous feeling of superiority in being in closer touch than they with eternal verities. I must take care that I do not play too much to the gallery, that I do not grow too conceited over the singularity of my situation, and arrive at the mental attitude of the criminal whose dominant solicitude in connection with his execution was that he should be hanged in his dress clothes. These reflections brought me to Eccleston Square.

Lady Kynnersley is that type of British matron who has children in fits of absent-mindedness, and to whom their existence is a perpetual shock.

Her main idea in marrying the late Sir Thomas Kynnersley was to associate herself with his political and philanthropic schemes. She is the born committee woman, to whom a home represents a place where one sleeps and eats in order to maintain the strength required for the performance of committee duties. Her children have always been outside the sphere of her real interests, but, afflicted, as such women are, with chronic inflammation of the conscience, she had devoted the most scrupulous care to their upbringing. She formed herself into a society for the protection of her own children, and managed them by means of a committee, which consisted of herself, and of which she was the honorary secretary. She drew up articles of association and regulations. If Dale contracted measles, she applied by-law 17. If Janet slapped Dorothy, by-law 32 was brought into play. When Dale clamoured for a rocking-horse, she found that the articles of association did not provide for imaginative equitation. As the children grew up, the committee had from time to time to revise the articles and submit them to the general body for approval. There were many meetings before the new sections relating to a University career for the boy and the coming out for the girls were satisfactorily drafted. Once given the effect of law, however, there was no appeal against these provisions. Both committee and general body were powerless. Dale certainly owed his methodical habits to his mechanical training, but whence he derived and how he maintained his exuberance and spontaneity has often puzzled me. He himself accounts for it on the score of heredity, in that an ancestress of his married a highwayman who was hanged at Tyburn under William and Mary.

In person Lady Kynnersley is lean and blanched and grey-haired. She wears gold spectacles, which stand out oddly against the thin whiteness of her face; she is still a handsome, distinguished woman, who can have, when she chooses, a most gracious manner. As I, worldling and jester though I am, for some mysterious reason have found favour in the lady's eyes, she manifests this graciousness whenever we foregather. Ergo, I like Lady Kynnersley, and would put myself to much inconvenience in order to do her a service.

She kept me waiting in the drawing-room but a minute before she made her appearance, grasped my hand, proclaimed my goodness in responding so soon to her call, bade me sit down on the sofa by her side, inquired after my health, and, the gods of politeness being propitiated, plunged at once into the midst of matters.

Dale was going downhill headlong to Gadarene catastrophe. He had no eyes or ears or thoughts for any one in the world but for a certain Lola Brandt, a brazen creature from a circus, the shape of whose limbs was the common knowledge of mankind from Dublin to Yokohama, and whose path by sea and land, from Yokohama to Dublin, was strewn with the bodies of her victims. With this man-eating tigress, declared Lady Kynnersley, was Dale infatuated. He scorched himself morning, noon, and night in her devastating presence. Had cut himself adrift from home, from society. Had left trailing about on his study table a jeweller's bill for a diamond bracelet. Was committing follies that made my brain reel to hear. Had threatened, if worried much longer, to marry the Scarlet One incontinently. Heaven knew, cried Lady Kynnersley, how many husbands she had already—scattered along the track between Dublin and Yokohama. There was no doubt about it. Dale was hurtling down to everlasting bonfire. She looked to me to hold out the restraining hand.

"You have already spoken to Dale on the subject?" I asked, mindful of the inharmonious socks and tie.

"I can talk to him of nothing else," said Lady Kynnersley desperately.

"That's a pity," said I. "You should talk to him of Heaven, or pigs, or Babylonic cuneiform—anything but Lola Brandt. You ought to go to work on a different system."

"But I haven't a system at all," cried the poor lady. "How was I to foresee that my only son was going to fall in love with a circus rider? These are contingencies in life for which one, with all the thought in the world, can make no provision. I had arranged, as you know, that he should marry Maisie Ellerton, as charming a girl as ever there was. Isn't she? And an independent fortune besides."

"A rosebud wrapped in a gold leaf," I murmured.

"Now he's breaking the child's heart——"

"There was never any engagement between them, I am sure of that," I remarked.

"There wasn't. But I gave her to understand it was a settled affair—merely a question of Dale speaking. And, instead of speaking, he will have nothing to do with her, and spends all his time—and, I suppose, though I don't like to refer to it, all his money—in the society of this unmentionable woman."

"Is she really so—so red as she is painted?" I asked.

"She isn't painted at all. That's where her artful and deceitful devilry comes in——"

"I suppose Dale," said I, "declares her to be an angel of light and purity?"

"An angel on horseback! Whoever heard of such a thing?"

"It's the name of a rather fiery savoury," said I.

"In a circus!" she continued.

"Well," said I, "the ring of a circus is not essentially one of the circles in Dante's Inferno."

"Of course, my dear Simon," she said, with some impatience, "if you defend him—"

I hastened to interrupt her. "I don't. I think he is an egregious young idiot; but before taking action it's well to get a clear idea of the facts. By the way, how do you know she's not painted?"

"I've seen her—seen her with my own eyes in Dale's company—at the Savoy. He's there supping with her every night. General Lamont told me. I wouldn't believe it—Dale flaunting about in public with her. The General offered to take me there after the inaugural meeting of the International Aid Society at Grosvenor House. I went, and saw them together. I shall never forget the look in the boy's eyes till my dying day. She has got him body and soul. One reads of such things in the poets, one sees it in pictures; but I've never come across it in real life—never, never. It's dreadful, horrible, revolting. To think that a son of mine, brought up from babyhood to calculate all his actions with mathematical precision, should be guilty of this profligacy! It's driving me mad, Simon; it really is. I don't know what to do. I've come to the end of my resources. It's your turn now. The boy worships you."

A wild appeal burned in her eyes and was refracted oddly through her near-sighted spectacles. I had never seen her betray emotion before during all the years of our friendship. The look and the tone of her voice moved me. I expressed my sympathy and my readiness to do anything in my power to snatch the infatuated boy from the claw and fang of the syren and hale him to the forgiving feet of Maisie Ellerton. Indeed, such a chivalrous adventure had vaguely passed through my mind during my exalted mood at Murglebed-on-Sea. But then I knew little beyond the fact that Dale was fluttering round an undesirable candle. Till now I had no idea of the extent to which his wings were singed.

"Hasn't Dale spoken to you about this creature?" his mother asked.

"Young men of good taste keep these things from their elders, my dear Lady Kynnersley," said I.

"But you knew of it?"

"In a dim sort of way."

"Oh, Simon—"

"The baby boys of Dale's set regard taking out the chorus to supper as a solemn religious rite. They wouldn't think themselves respectable if they didn't. I've done it myself—in moderation—when I was very young."

"Men are mysteries," sighed Lady Kynnersley.

"Please regard them as such," said I, with a laugh, "and let Dale alone. Allow him to do whatever irrational thing he likes, save bringing the lady here to tea. If you try to tear him away from her he'll only cling to her the closer. If you trumpet abroad her infamy he'll proclaim her a slandered and martyred saint. Leave him to me for the present."

"I'll do so gladly," said Lady Kynnersley, with surprising meekness. "But you *will* bring him back, Simon? I've arranged for him to marry Maisie. I can't have my plans for the future upset."

By-law 379! Dear, excellent, but wooden-headed woman!

"I have your promise, haven't I?" she said, her hand in mine.

"You have," said I nobly.

But how in the name of Astaroth I'm going to keep it I haven't the remotest conception.

CHAPTER III

Some letters in Dale's round handwriting lay on the library table awaiting my signature. Dale himself had gone. A lady had called for him, said Rogers, in an electric brougham. As my chambers are on the second floor and the staircase half-way down the arcade, Rogers's detailed information surprised me. I asked him how he knew.

"A chauffeur in livery, sir, came to the door and said that the brougham was waiting for Mr. Kynnersley."

"I don't see how the lady came in," I remarked.

"She didn't, sir. She remained in the brougham," said Rogers.

So Lola Brandt keeps an electric brougham.

I lunched at the club, and turned up the article "Lola Brandt" in the living encyclopaedia—that was my friend Renniker. The wonderful man gave me her history from the cradle to Cadogan Gardens, where she now resides. I must say that his details were rather vague. She rode in a circus or had a talking horse—he was not quite sure; and concerning her conjugal or extra-conjugal heart affairs he admitted that his information was either unauthenticated or conjectural. At any rate, she had not a shred of reputation. And she didn't want it, said Renniker; it would be as much use to her as a diving suit.

"She has young Dale Kynnersley in tow," he remarked.

"So I gather," said I. "And now can you tell me something else? What is the present state of political parties in Guatemala?"

I was not in the least interested in Guatemala; but I did not care to discuss Dale with Renniker. When he had completed his sketch of affairs in that obscure republic, I thanked him politely and ordered coffee.

Feeling in a gregarious, companionable humour—I have had enough solitude at Murglebed to last me the rest of my short lifetime—I went later in the afternoon to Sussex Gardens to call on Mrs. Ellerton. It was her day at home, and the drawing-room was filled with chattering people. I stayed until most of them were gone, and then Maisie dragged me to the inner room, where a table was strewn with the wreckage of tea.

"I haven't had any," she said, grasping the teapot and pouring a treacly liquid into a cup. "You must have some more. Do you like it black, or with milk?"

She is a dainty slip of a girl, with deep grey eyes and wavy brown hair and a sea-shell complexion. I absently swallowed the abomination she handed me, for I was looking at her over the teacup and wondering how an exquisite-minded gentleman like Dale could forsake her for a Lola Brandt. It was not as if Maisie were an empty-headed, empty-natured little girl. She is a young person of sense, education, and character. She also adores musical comedy and a band at dinner: an excellent thing in woman—when she is very young.

"Why are you looking at me like that?" she asked.

"Because, my dear Maisie," said I, "you are good to look upon. You are also dropping a hairpin."

She hastily secured the dangling thing. "I did my hair anyhow to-day," she explained.

Again I thought of Dale's tie and socks. The signs of a lover's "careless desolation," described by Rosalind so minutely, can still be detected in modern youth of both sexes. I did not pursue the question, but alluded to autumn gaieties. She spoke of them without enthusiasm. Miss Somebody's wedding was very dull, and Mrs. Somebody Else's dance manned with vile and vacuous dancers. At the Opera the greatest of German sopranos sang false. All human institutions had taken a crooked turn, and her cat could not be persuaded to pay the commonest attention to its kittens. Then she asked me nonchalantly:

"Have you seen anything of Dale lately?"

"He was working with me this morning. I've been away, you know."

"I forgot."

"When did you last see him?" I asked.

"Oh, ages ago! He has not been near us for weeks. We used to be such friends. I don't think it's very polite of him, do you?"

"I'll order him to call forthwith," said I.

"Oh, please don't! If he won't come of his own accord—I don't want to see him particularly."

She tossed her shapely head and looked at me bravely.

"You are quite right," said I. "Dale's a selfish, ill-mannered young cub."

"He isn't!" she flashed. "How dare you say such things about him!"

I smiled and took both her hands—one of them held a piece of brown bread-and-butter.

"My dear," said I, "model yourself on Little Bo-Peep. I don't know who gave her the famous bit of advice, but I think it was I myself in a pastoral incarnation. I had a woolly cloak and a crook, and she was like a Dresden china figure—the image of you."

Her eyes swam, but she laughed and said I was good to her. I said:

"The man who wouldn't be good to you is an unhung villain."

Then her mother joined us, and our little confidential talk came to an end. It was enough, however, to convince me that my poor little Ariadne was shedding many desperate tears in secret over her desertion.

On my way home I looked in on my doctor. His name is Hunnington. He grasped me by the hand and eagerly inquired whether my pain was worse. I said it was not. He professed delight, but looked disappointed. I ought to have replied in the affirmative. It is so easy to make others happy.

I dined, read a novel, and went to sleep in the cheerful frame of mind induced by the consciousness of having made some little progress on the path of eumoiriety.

The next morning Dale made his customary appearance. He wore a morning coat, a dark tie, and patent-leather boots.

"Well," said I, "have you dressed more carefully today?"

He looked himself anxiously over and inquired whether there was anything wrong. I assured him of the impeccability of his attire, and commented on its splendour.

"Are you going to take Maisie out to lunch?"

He started and reddened beneath his dark skin. Before he could speak I laid my hand on his shoulder.

"I'm an old friend, Dale. You mustn't be angry with me. But don't you think you're treating Maisie rather badly?"

"You've no right to say so," he burst out hotly. "No one has the right to say so. There was never a question of an engagement between Maisie and myself."

"Then there ought to have been," I said judicially. "No decent man plays fast and loose with a girl and throws her over just at the moment when he ought to be asking her to marry him."

"I suppose my mother's been at you. That's what she wanted to see you about yesterday. I wish to God she would mind her own business."

"And that I would mind mine?"

Dale did not reply. For some odd reason he is devotedly attached to me, and respects my opinion on worldly matters. He walked to the window and looked out. Presently, without turning round, he said:

"I suppose she has been rubbing it in about Lola Brandt?"

"She did mention the lady's name," said I. "So did Renniker at the club. I suppose every one you know and many you don't are mentioning it."

"Well, what if they are?"

"They're creating an atmosphere about your name which is scarcely that in which to make an entrance into public life."

Still with his back turned, he morosely informed me in his vernacular that he contemplated public life with feelings of indifference, and was perfectly prepared to abandon his ambitions. I took up my parable, the same old parable that wise seniors have preached to the deluded young from time immemorial. I have seldom held forth so platitudinously even in the House of Commons. I spoke as impressively as a bishop. In the midst of my harangue he came and sat by the library table and rested his chin on his palm, looking at me quietly out of his dark eyes. His mildness encouraged me to further efforts. I instanced cases of other young men of the world who had gone the way of the flesh and had ended at the devil.

There was Paget, of the Guards, eaten to the bone by the Syren—not even the gold lace on his uniform left. There was Merridew, once the hope of the party, now living in ignoble obscurity with an old and painted mistress, whom he detested, but to whom habit and sapped will-power kept him in thrall. There was Bullen, who blew his brains out. In a generous glow I waxed prophetic and drew a vivid picture of Dale's moral, mental, physical, financial, and social ruin, and finished up in a masterly peroration.

Then, without moving, he calmly said:

"My dear Simon, you are talking through your hat!"

He had allowed me to walk backwards and forwards on the hearthrug before a blazing fire, pouring out the wealth of my wisdom, experience, and rhetoric for ten minutes by the clock, and then coolly informed me that I was talking through my hat.

I wiped my forehead, sat down, and looked at him across the table in surprise and indignation.

"If you can point out one irrelevant or absurd remark in my homily, I'll eat the hat through which you say I'm talking."

"The whole thing is rot from beginning to end!" said he. "None of you good people know anything at all about Lola Brandt. She's not the sort of woman you think. She's quite different. You can't judge her by ordinary standards. There's not a woman like her in the wide world!"

I made a gesture of discouragement. The same old parable of the wise had evoked the same old retort from the deluded young. She was quite different from other women. She was misunderstood by the cynical and gross-minded world. A heart of virgin purity beat beneath her mercenary bosom. Her lurid past had been the reiterated martyrdom of a noble nature. O Golden Age! O unutterable silliness of Boyhood!

"For Heaven's sake, don't talk in that way!" he cried (I had been talking in that way), and he rose and walked like a young tiger about the room. "I can't stand it. I've gone mad about her. She has got into my blood somehow. I think about her all day long, and I can't sleep at night. I would give up any mortal thing on earth for her. She is the one woman in the world for me! She's the dearest, sweetest, tenderest, most beautiful creature God ever made!"

"And you honour and respect her—just as you would honour and respect Maisie?" I asked quietly.

"Of course I do!" he flashed. "Don't I tell you that you know nothing whatever about her? She is the dearest, sweetest——" etc., etc. And he continued to trumpet forth the Olympian qualities of the Syren and his own fervent adoration. I was the only being to whom he had opened his heart, and, the floodgates being set free, the torrent burst forth in this tempestuous and incoherent manner. I let him go on, for I thought it did him good; but his rhapsody added very little to my information.

The lady who had "houp-la'd" her way from Dublin to Yokohama was the spotless queen of beauty, and Dale was frenziedly, idiotically in love with her. That was all I could gather. When he had finished, which he did somewhat abruptly, he threw himself into a chair and took out his cigarette-case with shaky fingers.

"There. I suppose I've made a damn-fool exhibition of myself," he said, defiantly. "What have you got to say about it?"

"Precisely," I replied, "what I said before. I'll repeat it, if you like."

Indeed, what more was there to say for the present about the lunatic business? I had come to the end of my arguments.

He reflected for a moment, then rose and came over to the fireplace.

"Look here, Simon, you must let me go my own way in this. In matters of politics and worldly wisdom and social affairs and honourable dealing and all that sort of thing I would follow you blindly. You're my chief, and a kind of elder brother as well. I would do any mortal thing for you. You know that. But you've no right to try to guide me in this matter. You know no more about it than my mother. You've had no experience. You've never let yourself go about a woman in your life. Lord of Heaven, man, you have never begun to know what it means!"

Oh, dear me! Here was the situation as old as the return of the Prodigal or the desertion of the trusting village maiden, or any other cliche in the melodrama of real life. "You are making a fool of yourself," says Mentor. "Ah," shrieks Telemachus, "but you never loved! You don't know what love is."

I looked at him whimsically.

"Don't I?"

My thoughts sped back down the years to a garden in France. Her name was Clothilde. We met in a manner outrageous to Gallic propriety, as I used to climb over the garden wall to the peril of my epidermis. We loved. We were parted by stern parents—not mine—and Clothilde was packed off to the good Sisters who had previously had care of her education. Now she is fat and happy, and the wife of a banker and the mother of children.

But the romance was sad and bad and mad enough while it lasted; and when Clothilde was (figuratively) dragged from my arms I cursed and swore and out-Heroded Herod, played Termagant, and summoned the heavens to fall down and crush me miserable beneath their weight. And then her brother challenged me to fight a duel, whereupon, as the most worshipped of all She's had not received a ha'porth of harm at my hands, I called him a silly ass and threatened to break his head if he interfered any more in my legitimate despair. I smile at it now; but it was real at two-and-twenty—as real, I take it, as Dale's consuming passion for the lady of the circus.

There was also, I remembered, a certain —— But this had nothing to do with Dale. Neither had the tragedy of my lost Clothilde. The memories, however, brought a wistful touch of sympathy into my voice.

"You soberly think, my dear old Dale," said I, "that I know nothing of love and passion and the rest of the divine madness?"

"I'm sure you don't," he cried, with an impatient gesture. "If you did, you wouldn't—"

He came to an abrupt and confused halt.

"I wouldn't—what?"

"Nothing. I forgot what I was going to say. Let us talk of something else."

"It was on the tip of your impulsive tongue," said I cheerfully, "to refer to my attitude towards Miss Faversham."

"I'm desperately sorry," said he, reddening. "It was unpardonable. But how did you guess?"

I laughed and quoted the Latin tag about the ingenuous boy of the ingenuous visage and ingenuous modesty.

"Because I don't feverishly search the postbag for a letter from Miss Faversham you conclude I'm a bloodless automaton?"

"Please don't say any more about it, Simon," he pleaded in deep distress.

A sudden idea struck me. I reflected, walked to the window, and, having made up my mind, sat down again. I had a weapon to hand which I had overlooked, and with the discovery came a weak craving for the boy's sympathy. I believe I care more for him than for any living creature. I decided to give him some notion of my position.

Sooner or later he would have to learn it.

"I would rather like to tell you something," said I, "about my engagement—in confidence, of course. When Eleanor Faversham comes back I propose to ask her to release me from it."

He drew a long breath. "I'm glad. She's an awfully nice girl, but she's no more in love with you than my mother is. But it'll be rather difficult, won't it?"

"I don't think so," I replied, shaking my head. "It's a question of health. My doctors absolutely forbid it."

A look of affectionate alarm sprang into his eyes. He broke into sympathy. My health? Why had I not told him before? In Heaven's name, what was the matter with me?

"Something silly," said I. "Nothing you need worry about on my account. Only I must go *piano* for the rest of my days. Marriage isn't to be thought of. There is something else I must tell you. I must resign my seat."

"Resign your seat? Give up Parliament? When?"

"As soon as possible."

He looked at me aghast, as if the world were coming to an end.

"We had better concoct an epistle to Raggles this morning."

"But you can't be serious?"

"I can sometimes, my dear Dale. This is one of the afflicting occasions."

"You out of Parliament? You out of public life? It's inconceivable. It's damnable. But you're just coming into your own—what Raggles said, what I told you yesterday. But it can't be. You can hold on. I'll do all the drudgery for you. I'll work night and day."

And he tramped up and down the room, uttering the disconnected phrases which an honest young soul unaccustomed to express itself emotionally blurts out in moments of deep feeling.

"It's no use, Dale," said I, "I've got my marching orders."

"But why should they come just now?"

"When the sweets of office are dangling at my lips? It's pretty simple." I laughed. "It's one of the little ironies that please the high gods so immensely. They have an elementary sense of humour—like that of the funny fellow who pulls your chair from under you and shrieks with laughter when you go wallop on to the floor. Well, I don't grudge them their amusement. They must have a dull time settling mundane affairs, and a little joke goes a long way with them, as it does in the House of Commons. Fancy sitting on those green benches legislating for all eternity, with never a recess and never even a dinner hour! Poor high gods! Let us pity them."

I looked at him and smiled, perhaps a little wearily. One can always command one's eyes, but one's lips sometimes get out of control. He could not have noticed my lips, however, for he cried:

"By George, you're splendid! I wish I could take a knock-out blow like that!"

"You'll have to one of these days. It's the only way of taking it. And now," said I, in a businesslike tone, "I've told you all this with a purpose. At Wymington it will be a case of 'Le Roi est mort. Vive le Roi!' The vacancy will have to be filled up at once. We'll have to find a suitable candidate. Have you one in your mind?"

"Not a soul."

"I have."

"Who?"

"You."

"Me?" He nearly sprang into the air with astonishment.

"Why not?"

"They'd never adopt me."

"I think they would," I said. "There are men in the House as young as you. You're well known at Wymington and at headquarters as my right-hand man. You've done some speaking—you do it rather well; it's only your private conversational style that's atrocious. You've got a name familiar in public life up and down the country, thanks to your father and mother. It's a fairly safe seat. I see no reason why they shouldn't adopt you. Would you like it?"

"Like it?" he cried. "Why I'd give my ears for it."

"Then," said I, playing my winning card, "let us hear no more about Lola Brandt."

He gave me a swift glance, and walked up and down the room for a while in silence. Presently he halted in front of me.

"Look here, Simon, you're a beast, but"—he smiled frankly at the quotation—"you're a just beast. You oughtn't to rub it in like that about Lola until you have seen her yourself. It isn't fair."

"You speak now in language distinctly approaching that of reason," I remarked. "What do you want me to do?"

"Come with me this afternoon and see her."

My young friend had me nicely in the trap. I could not refuse.

"Very well," said I. "But on the distinct understanding—"

"Oh, on any old understanding you like!" he cried, and darted to the door.

"Where are you going?"

"To ring her up on the telephone and tell her you're coming."

That's the worst of the young. They have such a disconcerting manner of clinching one's undertakings.

CHAPTER IV

My first impression of Lola Brandt in the dimness of the room was that of a lithe panther in petticoats rising lazily from the depths of an easy chair. A sinuous action of the arm, as she extended her hand to welcome me, was accompanied by a curiously flexible turn of the body. Her hand as it enveloped, rather than grasped, mine seemed boneless but exceedingly powerful. An indoor dress of brown and gold striped Indian silk clung to her figure, which, largely built, had an appearance of great strength. Dark bronze hair and dark eyes, that in the soft light of the room glowed with deep gold reflections, completed the pantherine suggestion. She seemed to be on the verge of thirty. A most dangerous woman, I decided—one to be shut up in a cage with thick iron bars.

"It's charming of you to come. I've heard so much of you from Mr. Kynnersley. Do sit down."

Her voice was lazy and languorous and caressing like the purr of a great cat; and there was something exotic in her accent, something seductive, something that ought to be prohibited by the police. She sank into her low chair by the fire, indicating one for me square with the hearthrug. Dale, so as to leave me a fair conversational field with the lady, established himself on the sofa some distance off, and began to talk with a Chow dog, with whom he was obviously on terms of familiarity. Madame Brandt make a remark about the Chow dog's virtues, to which I politely replied. She put him through several tricks. I admired his talent. She declared her affections to be divided between Adolphus (that was the Chow dog's name) and an ouistiti, who was confined to bed for the present owing to the evil qualities of the November air. For the first time I blessed the English climate. I hate little monkeys. I also felt a queer disappointment. A woman like that ought to have caught an ourang-outang.

She guessed my thought in an uncanny manner, and smiled, showing strong, white, even teeth—the most marvellous teeth I have ever beheld— so even as to constitute almost a deformity.

"I'm fonder of bigger animals," she said. "I was born among them. My father was a lion tamer, so I know all the ways of beasts. I love bears—I once trained one to drive a cart—but"—with a sigh—"you can't keep bears in Cadogan Gardens."

"You may get hold of a human one now and then," said Dale.

"I've no doubt Madame Brandt could train him to dance to whatever tune she played," said I.

She turned her dark golden eyes lazily, slumberously on me.

"Why do you say that, Mr. de Gex?"

This was disconcerting. Why had I said it? For no particular reason, save to keep up a commonplace conversation in which I took no absorbing interest. It was a direct challenge. Young Dale stopped playing with the Chow dog and grinned. It behooved me to say something. I said it with a bow and a wave of my hand:

"Because, though your father was a lion-tamer, your mother was a woman."

She appeared to reflect for a moment; then addressing Dale:

"The answer doesn't amount to a ha'porth of cats'-meat, but you couldn't have got out of it like that."

I was again disconcerted, but I remarked that he would learn in time when my mentorship was over and I handed him, a finished product, to society.

"How long will that be?" she asked.

"I don't know. Are you anxious for his immediate perfecting?"

Her shoulders gave what in ordinary women would have been a shrug: with her it was a slow ripple. I vow if her neck had been bare one could have seen it undulate beneath the skin.

"What is perfection?"

"Can you ask?" laughed Dale. "Behold!" And he pointed to me.

"That's cheap," said the lady. "I've heard Auguste say cleverer things."

"Who's Auguste?" asked Dale.

"Auguste," said I, "is the generic name of the clown in the French Hippodrome."

"Oh, the Circus!" cried Dale.

"I'll be glad if you'll teach him to call it the Hippodrome, Mr. de Gex," she remarked, with another of her slumberous glances.

"That will be one step nearer perfection," said I.

The short November twilight had deepened into darkness; the fire, which was blazing when we entered, had settled into a glow, and the room was lit by one shaded lamp. To me the dimness was restful, but Dale, who, with the crude instincts of youth, loves glare, began to fidget, and presently asked whether he might turn on the electric light. Permission was given. My hostess invited me to smoke and, to hand her a box of cigarettes which lay on the mantelpiece, I rose, bent over her while she lit her cigarette from my match, and resuming an upright position, became rooted to the hearthrug.

With the flood of illumination, disclosing everything that hitherto had been wrapped in shadow and mystery, came a shock.

It was a most extraordinary, perplexing room. The cheap and the costly, the rare and the common, the exquisite and the tawdry jostled one another on walls and floor. At one end of the Louis XVI sofa on which Dale had been sitting lay a boating cushion covered with a Union Jack, at the other a cushion covered with old Moorish embroidery. The chair I had vacated I discovered to be of old Spanish oak and stamped Cordova leather bearing traces of a coat-of-arms in gold. My hostess lounged in a low characterless seat amid a mass of heterogeneous cushions. There were many flowers in the room—some in Cloisonne vases, others in gimcrack vessels such as are bought at country fairs. On the mantelpiece and on tables were mingled precious ivories from Japan, trumpery chalets from the Tyrol, choice bits of Sevres and Venetian glass, bottles with ladders and little men inside them, vulgar china fowls sitting on eggs, and a thousand restless little objects screeching in dumb agony at one another.

The more one looked the more confounded became confusion. Lengths of beautifully embroidered Chinese silk formed curtains for the doors and windows; but they were tied back with cords ending in horrible little plush monkeys in lieu of tassels. A Second Empire gilt mirror hung over the Louis XVI sofa, and was flanked on the one side by a villainous German print of "The Huntsman's Return" and on the other by a dainty water-colour. Myriads of photographs, some in frames, met the eye everywhere—on the grand piano, on the occasional tables, on the mantelpiece, stuck obliquely all round the Queen Anne mirror above it, on the walls. Many of them represented animals—bears and lions and pawing horses. Dale's photograph I noticed in a silver frame on the piano. There was not a book in the place. But in the corner of the room by a further window gleamed a large marble Venus of Milo, charmingly executed, who stood regarding the welter with eyes calm and unconcerned.

I was aroused from the momentary shock caused by the revelation of this eccentric apartment by an unknown nauseous flavour in my mouth. I realised it was the cigarette to which I had helped myself from the beautifully chased silver casket I had taken from the mantelpiece. I eyed the thing and concluded it was made of the very cheapest tobacco, and was what the street urchin calls a "fag." I learned afterwards that I was right. She purchased them at the rate of six for a penny, and smoked them in enormous quantities. For politeness' sake I continued to puff at the unclean thing until I nearly made myself sick. Then, simulating absentmindedness, I threw it into the fire.

Why, in the sacred name of Nicotine, does a luxurious lady like Lola Brandt smoke such unutterable garbage?

On the other hand, the tea which she offered us a few minutes later, and begged us to drink without milk, was the most exquisite I have tasted outside Russia. She informed us that she got it direct from Moscow.

"I can't stand your black Ceylon tea," she remarked, with a grimace.

And yet she could smoke "fags." I wondered what other contradictious tastes she possessed. No doubt she could eat blood puddings with relish and had a discriminating palate for claret. Truly, a perplexing lady.

"You must find leisure in London a great change after your adventurous career," said I, by way of polite conversation.

"I just love it. I'm as lazy as a cat," she said, settling with her pantherine grace among the cushions. "Do you know what has been my ambition ever since I was a kid?"

"Whatever of woman's ambitions you had you must have attained," said I, with a bow.

"Pooh!" she said. "You mean that I can have crowds of men falling in love with me. That's rubbish." She was certainly frank. "I meant something quite different. I wonder whether you can understand. The world used to seem to me divided into two classes that never met—we performing people and the public, the thousand white faces that looked at us and went away and talked to other white faces and forgot all about performing animals till they came next time. Now I've got what I wanted. See? I'm one of the public."

"And you love Philistia better than Bohemia?" I asked.

She knitted her brows and looked at me puzzled.

"If you want to talk to me," she said, "you must talk straight. I've had no more education than a tinker's dog."

She made this peculiar announcement, not defiantly, not rudely, but appealingly, graciously. It was not a rebuke for priggishness; it was the unpresentable statement of a fact. I apologized for a lunatic habit of speech and paraphrased my question.

"In a word," cried Dale, coming in on my heels with an elucidation of my periphrasis, "what de Gex is driving at is—Do you prefer respectability to ramping round?"

She turned slowly to him. "My dear boy, when do you think I was not respectable?"

He jumped from the sofa as if the Chow dog had bitten him.

"Good Heavens, I never meant you to take it that way!"

She laughed, stretched up a lazy arm to him, and looked at him somewhat quizzically in the face as he kissed her finger-tips. Although I could have boxed the silly fellow's ears, I vow he did it in a very pretty fashion. The young man of the day, as a general rule, has no more notion how to kiss a woman's hand than how to take snuff or dance a pavane. Indeed, lots of them don't know how to kiss a girl at all.

"My dear," she said. "I was much more respectable sitting on the stage at tea with my horse, Sultan, than supping with you at the Savoy. You don't know the deadly respectability of most people in the profession, and the worst of it is that while we're being utterly dull and dowdy, the public think we're having a devil of a time. So we don't even get the credit of our virtues. I prefer the Savoy—and this." She turned to me. "It is nice having decent people to tea. Do you know what I should love? I should love to have an At Home day—and receive ladies, real ladies. And I have such a sweet place, haven't I?"

"You have many beautiful things around you," said I truthfully.

She sighed. "I should like more people to see them."

"In fact," said I, "you have social ambitions, Madame Brandt?"

She looked at me for a moment out of the corner of her eye.

"Are you skinning me?" she asked.

Where she had picked up this eccentric metaphor I know not. She had many odd turns of language as yet not current among the fashionable classes. I gravely assured her that I was not sarcastic. I commended her praiseworthy aspirations.

"But," said I innocently, "don't you miss the hard training, the physical exercise, the delight of motion, the excitement, the——?"—my vocabulary failing me, I sketched with a gesture the equestrienne's classical encouragement to her steed.

She looked at me uncomprehendingly.

"The what?" she asked.

"What are you playing at?" inquired Dale.

"I was referring to the ring," said I.

They both burst out laughing, to my discomfiture.

"What do you take me for? A circus rider? Performing in a tent and living in a caravan? You think I jump through a hoop in tights?"

"All I can say," I murmured, by way of apology, "is that it's a mendacious world. I'm deeply sorry."

Why had I been misled in this shameful manner?

Madame Brandt with lazy good nature accepted my excuses.

"I'm what is professionally known as a *dompteuse*," she explained. "Of course, when I was a kid I was trained as an acrobat, for my father was poor; but when he grew rich and the owner of animals, which he did when I was fourteen, I joined him and worked with him all over the world until I went on my own. Do you mean to say you never heard of me?"

"Madame Brandt," said I, "the last thing to be astonished at is human ignorance. Do you know that 30 per cent of the French army at the present day have never heard of the Franco-Prussian War?"

"My dear Simon," cried Dale, "the two things don't hang together. The Franco-Prussian War is not advertised all over France like Beecham's Pills, whereas six years ago you couldn't move two steps in London without seeing posters of Lola Brandt and her horse Sultan."

"Ah, the horse!" said I. "That's how the wicked circus story got about."

"It was the last act I ever did," said Madame Brandt. "I taught Sultan— oh, he was a dear, beautiful thing—to count and add up and guess articles taken from the audience. I was at the Hippodrome. Then at the Nouveau Cirque at Paris; I was at St. Petersburg, Vienna, Berlin—all over Europe with Sultan."

"And where is Sultan now?" I asked.

"He is dead. Somebody poisoned him," she replied, looking into the fire. After a pause she continued in a low voice, singularly like the growl of a wrathful animal, "If ever I meet that man alive it will go hard with him."

At that moment the door opened and the servant announced:

"Professor Anastasius Papadopoulos!"

Whereupon the shortest creature that ever bore so lengthy a name, a dwarf not more than four feet high, wearing a frock coat and bright yellow gloves, entered the room, and crossing it at a sort of trot fell on his knees by the side of Madame Brandt's chair.

"Ah! Carissima, je vous vois enfin, Ach liebes Herz! Que j'ai envie de pleurer!"

Madame Brandt smiled, took the creature's head between her hands and kissed his forehead. She also caressed his shoulders.

"My dear Anastasius, how good it is to see you. Where have you been this long time? Why didn't you write and let me know you were in England? But, see, Anastasius, I have visitors. Let me introduce you."

She spoke in French fluently, but with a frank British accent, which grated on a fastidious ear. The dwarf rose, made two solemn bows, and declared himself enchanted. Although his head was too large for his body, he was neither ill-made nor repulsive. He looked about thirty-five. A high forehead, dark, mournful eyes, and a black moustache and imperial gave him an odd resemblance to Napoleon the Third.

"I arrived from New York this morning, with my cats. Oh, a mad success. I have one called Phoebus, because he drives a chariot drawn by six rats. Phoebus Apollo was the god of the sun. I must show him to you, Madonna. You would love him as I love you. And I also have an angora, my beautiful Santa Bianca. And you, gentlemen"—he turned to Dale and myself and addressed us in his peculiar jargon of French, German, and Italian—"you must come and see my cats if I can get a London engagement. At present I must rest. The artist needs repose sometimes. I will sun myself in the smiles of our dear lady here, and my pupil and assistant, Quast, can look after my cats. Meanwhile the brain of the artist," he tapped his brow, "needs to lie fallow so that he can invent fresh and daring combinations. Do such things interest you, messieurs?"

"Vastly," said I.

He pulled out of his breast pocket an enormous gilt-bound pocket-book, bearing a gilt monogram of such size that it looked like a cartouche on an architectural panel, and selected therefrom three cards which he gravely distributed among us. They bore the legend:

PROFESSOR ANASTASIUS PAPADOPOULOS GOLD AND SILVER MEDALLIST THE CAT KING LE ROI DES CHATS DER KATZEN KONIG

London Agents: MESSRS. CONTO & BLAG,

172 Maiden Lane, W.C.

"There," said he, "I am always to be found, should you ever require my services. I have a masterpiece in my head. I come on to the scene like Bacchus drawn by my two cats. How are the cats to draw my heavy weight? I'll have a noiseless clockwork arrangement that will really propel the car. You must come and see it."

"Delighted, I'm sure," said Dale, who stood looking down on the Liliputian egotist with polite wonder. Lola Brandt glanced at him apologetically.

"You mustn't mind him, Dale. He has only two ideas in his head, his cats and myself. He's devoted to me."

"I don't think I shall be jealous," said Dale in a low voice.

"Foolish boy!" she whispered.

During the love scene, which was conducted in English, a language which Mr. Papadopoulos evidently did not understand, the dwarf scowled at Dale and twirled his moustache fiercely. In order to attract Madame Brandt's attention he fetched a packet of papers from his pocket and laid them with a flourish on the tea-table.

"Here are the documents," said he.

"What documents?"

"A full inquiry into the circumstances attending the death of Madame Brandt's horse Sultan."

"Have you found out anything, Anastasius?" she asked, in the indulgent tone in which one addresses an eager child.

"Not exactly," said he. "But I have a conviction that by this means the murderer will be brought to justice. To this I have devoted my life—in your service."

He put his hand on the spot of his tightly buttoned frock-coat that covered his heart, and bowed profoundly. It was obvious that he resented our presence and desired to wipe us out of our hostess's consideration. I glanced ironically at Dale's disgusted face, and smiled at the imperfect development of his sense of humour. Indeed, to the young, humour is only a weapon of offence. It takes a philosopher to use it as defensive armour. Dale burned to outdo Mr. Papadopoulos. I, having no such ambition, laid my hand on his arm and went forward to take my leave.

"Madame Brandt," said I, "old friends have doubtless much to talk over. I thank you for the privilege you have afforded me of making your acquaintance."

She rose and accompanied us to the landing outside the flat door. After saying good-bye to Dale, who went down with his boyish tread, she detained me for a second or two, holding my hand, and again her clasp enveloped it like some clinging sea-plant. She looked at me very wistfully.

"The next time you come, Mr. de Gex, do come as a friend and not as an enemy."

I was startled. I thought I had conducted the interview with peculiar suavity.

"An enemy, dear lady?"

"Yes. Can't I see it?" she said in her languorous, caressing voice. "And I should love to have you for a friend. You could be such a good one. I have so few."

"I must argue this out with you another time," said I diplomatically.

"That's a promise," said Lola Brandt.

"What's a promise?" asked Dale, when I joined him in the hall.

"That I will do myself the pleasure of calling on Madame again."

The porter whistled for a cab. A hansom drove up. As my destination was the Albany, and as I knew Dale was going home to Eccleston Square, I held out my hand.

"Good-bye, Dale. I'll see you to-morrow."

"But aren't you going to tell me what you think of her?" he cried in great dismay.

The pavement was muddy, the evening dark, and a gusty wind blew the drizzle into our faces. It is only the preposterously young who expect a man to rhapsodise over somebody else's inamorata at such a moment. I turned up the fur collar of my coat.

"She is good-looking," said I.

"Any idiot can see that!" he burst out impatiently. "I want to know what opinion you formed of her."

I reflected. If I could have labelled her as the Scarlet Woman, the Martyred Saint, the Jolly Bohemian, or the Bold Adventuress, my task would have been easy. But I had an uncomfortable feeling that Lola Brandt was not to be classified in so simple a fashion. I took refuge in a negative.

"She would hardly be a success," said I, "in serious political circles."

With that I made my escape.

CHAPTER V

I wish I had not called on Lola Brandt. She disturbs me to the point of nightmare. In a fit of dream paralysis last night I fancied myself stalked by a panther, which in the act of springing turned into Lola Brandt. What she would have done I know not, for I awoke; but I have a haunting sensation that she was about to devour me. Now, a woman who would devour a sleeping Member of Parliament is not a fit consort for a youth about to enter on a political career.

The woman worries me. I find myself speculating on her character while I ought to be minding my affairs; and this I do on her own account, without any reference to my undertaking to rescue Dale from her clutches. Her obvious attributes are lazy good nature and swift intuition, which are as contrary as her tastes in tobacco and tea; but beyond the obvious lurks a mysterious animal power which repels and attracts. Were not her expressions rather melancholy than sensuous, rather benevolent than cruel, one might take her as a model for Queen Berenice or the estimable lady monarchs who yielded themselves adorably to a gentleman's kisses in the evening and saw to it that his head was nicely chopped off in the morning. I can quite understand Dale's infatuation. She may be as worthless as you please, but she is by no means the vulgar syren I was led to expect. I wish she were. My task would be easier. Why hasn't he fallen in love with one of the chorus whom his congeners take out to supper? He is an aggravating fellow.

I have declined to discuss her merits or demerits with him. I could scarcely do that with dignity, said I; a remark which seemed to impress him with a sense of my honesty. I asked what were his intentions regarding her. I discovered that they were still indefinite. In his exalted moments he talked of marriage.

"But what has become of her husband?" I inquired, drawing a bow at a venture.

"I suppose he's dead," said Dale.

"But suppose he isn't?"

He informed me in his young magnificence that Lola and himself would be above foolish moral conventions.

"Indeed?" said I.

"Don't pretend to be a Puritan," said he.

"I don't pretend to like the idea, anyhow," I remarked.

He shrugged his shoulders. It was not the time for a lecture on morality.

"How do you know that the lady returns your passion?" I asked, watching him narrowly.

He grew red. "Is that a fair question?"

"Yes," said I. "You invited me to call on her and judge the affair for myself. I'm doing it. How far have things gone up to now?"

He flashed round on me. Did I mean to insinuate that there was anything wrong? There wasn't. How could I dream of such a thing? He was vastly indignant.

"Well, my dear boy," said I, "you've just this minute been scoffing at foolish moral conventions. If you want to know my opinion," I continued, after a pause, "it is this—she doesn't care a scrap for you."

Of course I was talking nonsense.

I did not condescend to argue. Neither did I dwell upon the fact that her affection had not reached the point of informing him whether she had a husband, and if so, whether he was alive or dead. This gives me an idea. Suppose I can prove to him beyond a shadow of doubt that the lady, although flattered by the devotion of a handsome young fellow of birth and breeding, does not, as I remarked, care a scrap for him. Suppose I exhibit her to him in the arms, figuratively speaking, of her husband (providing one is lurking in some back-alley of the world), Mr. Anastasius Papadopoulos, a curate, or a champion wrestler. He would do desperate things for a month or two; but then he would wake up sane one fine morning and seek out Maisie Ellerton in a salutary state of penitence. I wish I knew a curate who combined a passion for bears and a yearning for ladylike tea-parties. I would take him forthwith to Cadogan Gardens. Lola Brandt and himself would have tastes in common and would fall in love with each other on the spot.

Of course there is the other time-honoured plan which I have not yet tried—to arm myself with diplomacy, call on Madame Brandt, and, working on her feelings, persuade her in the name of the boy's mother and sweetheart to make a noble sacrifice in the good, old-fashioned way. But this seems such an unhumourous proceeding. If I am to achieve eumoiriety I may as well do it with some distinction.

"Who doth Time gallop withal?" asks Orlando.

"With a thief to the gallows," says Rosalind. It is true. The days have an uncanny way of racing by. I see my little allotted span of life shrinking visibly, like the *peau de chagrin*. I must bestir myself, or my last day will come before I have accomplished anything.

When I jotted down the above not very original memorandum I had passed a perfectly uneumoirous week among my friends and social acquaintances. I had stood godfather to my sister Agatha's fifth child, taking upon myself obligations which I shall never be able to perform; I had dined amusingly at my sister Jane's; I had shot pheasants at Farfax Glenn's place in Hampshire; and I had paid a long-promised charming country-house visit to old Lady Blackadder.

When I came back to town, however, I consulted my calendar with some anxiety, and set out to clear my path.

I have now practically withdrawn from political life. Letters have passed; complimentary and sympathetic gentlemen have interviewed me and tried to weaken my decision. The great Raggles has even called, and dangled the seals of office before my eyes. I said they were very pretty. He thought he had tempted me.

"Hang on as long as you can, for the sake of the Party."

I spoke playfully of the Party (a man in my position, with one eye on Time and the other on Eternity, develops an acute sense of values) and Raggles held up horrified hands. To Raggles the Party is the Alpha and Omega of things human and divine. It is the guiding principle of the Cosmos. I could have spoken disrespectfully of the British Empire, of which he has a confused notion; I could have dismissed the Trinity, on which his ideas are vaguer, with an airy jest; in the expression of my views concerning the Creator, whom he believes to be under the Party's protection, I could have out-Pained Tom Paine, out-Taxiled Leo Taxil, and he would not have winced. But to blaspheme against the Party was the sin for which there was no redemption.

"I always thought you a serious politician!" he gasped.

"Good God!" I cried. "In my public utterances have I been as dull as that? Ill-health or no, it is time for me to quit the stage."

He laughed politely, because he conjectured I was speaking humourously—he is astute in some things—and begged me to explain.

I replied that I did not regard mustard poultices as panaceas, the *vox populi* as the *Vox Dei*, or the policy of the other side as the machinations of the Devil; that politics was all a game of guess-work and muddle and compromise at the best; that, at the worst, as during a General Election, it was as ignoble a pastime as the wit of man had devised. To take it seriously would be the course of a fanatic, a man devoid of the sense of proportion. Were such a man, I asked, fitted to govern the country?

He did not stop to argue, but went away leaving me the conviction that he thanked his stars on the Government's providential escape from so maniacal a minister. I hope I did not treat him with any discourtesy; but, oh! it was good to speak the truth after all the dismal lies I have been forced to tell at the bidding of Raggle's Party. Now that I am no longer bound by the rules of the game, it is good to feel a free, honest man.

Never again shall I stretch forth my arms and thunder invectives against well-meaning people with whom in my heart I secretly sympathise. Never again shall I plead passionately for principles which a horrible instinct tells me are fundamentally futile. Never again shall I attempt to make mountains out of mole-hills or bricks without straw or sunbeams out of cucumbers.

I shall conduct no more inquiries into pauper lunacy, thank Heaven! And as for the public engagements which Dale Kynnersley made for me during my Thebaid existence on Murglebed-on-Sea, the deuce can take them all—I am free.

I only await the stewardship of the Chiltern Hundreds, for which quaint post under the Crown I applied, to cease to be a Member of Parliament. And yet, in spite of all my fine and superior talk, I am glad I am giving up in the recess. I should not like to be out of my seat were the House in session.

I should hate to think of all the fascinating excitement over nothing going on in the lobbies without me, while I am still hale and hearty. When Parliament meets in February I shall either be comfortably dead or so uncomfortably alive that I shall not care.

Ce que c'est que de nous! I wonder how far Simon de Gex and I are deceiving each other?

There is no deception about my old friend Latimer, who called on me a day or two ago. He is on the Stock Exchange, and, muddle-headed creature that he is, has been "bearing" the wrong things. They have gone up sky-high. Settling-day is drawing near, and how to pay for the shares he is bound to deliver he has not the faintest notion.

He stamped up and down the room, called down curses on the prying fools who came across the unexpected streak of copper in the failing mine, drew heart-rending pictures of his wife and family singing hymns in the street, and asked me for a drink of prussic acid. I rang the bell and ordered Rogers to give him a brandy and soda.

"Now," said I, "talk sense. How much can you raise?"

He went into figures and showed me that, although he stretched his credit to the utmost, there were still ten thousand pounds to be provided.

"It's utter smash and ruin," he groaned. "And all my accursed folly. I thought I was going to make a fortune. But I'm done for now." Latimer is usually a pink, prosperous-looking man. Now he was white and flabby, a piteous spectacle. "You are executor under my will," he continued. "Heaven knows I've nothing to leave. But you'll see things straight for me, if anything happens? You will look after Lucy and the kids, won't you?"

I was on the point of undertaking to do so, in the event of the continuance of his craving for prussic acid, when I reflected upon my own approaching bow and farewell to the world where Lucy and the kids would still be wandering. I am always being brought up against this final fireproof curtain. Suddenly a thought came which caused me to exult exceedingly.

"Ten thousand pounds, my dear Latimer," said I, "would save you from being hammered on the Stock Exchange and from seeking a suicide's grave. It would also enable you to maintain Lucy and the kids in your luxurious house at Hampstead, and to take them as usual to Dieppe next summer. Am I not right?"

He begged me not to make a jest of his miseries. It was like asking a starving beggar whether a dinner at the Carlton wouldn't set him up again.

"Would ten thousand set you up?" I persisted.

"Yes. But I might as well try to raise ten million."

"Not so," I cried, slapping him on the shoulder. "I myself will lend you the money."

He leaped to his feet and stared at me wildly in the face. He could not have been more electrified if he had seen me suddenly adorned with wings and shining raiment. I experienced a thrill of eumoiriety more exquisite than I had dreamed of imagining.

"You?"

"Why not?"

"You don't understand. I can give you no security whatsoever."

"I don't want security and I don't want interest," I exclaimed, feeling more magnanimous than I had a right to be, seeing that the interest would be of no use to me on the other side of the Styx. "Pay me back when and how you like. Come round with me to my bankers and I'll settle the matter at once."

He put out his hands; I thought he was about to fall at my feet; he laughed in a silly way and, groping after brandy and soda, poured half the contents of the brandy decanter on to the tray. I took him in a cab, a stupefied man, to the bank, and when he left me at the door with my draft in his pocket, there were tears in his eyes. He wrung my hand and murmured something incoherent about Lucy.

"For Heaven's sake, don't tell her anything about it," I entreated. "I love Lucy dearly, as you know; but I don't want to have her weeping on my door-mat."

I walked back to my rooms with a springing step. So happy was I that I should have liked to dance down Piccadilly. If the Faculty had not made their pronouncement, I could have no more turned poor Latimer's earth from hell to heaven than I could have changed St. Paul's Cathedral into a bumblebee. The mere possibility of lending him the money would not have occurred to me.

A man of modest fortune does not go about playing Monte Cristo. He gives away a few guineas in charity; but he keeps the bulk of his fortune to himself. The death sentence, I vow, has compensations. It enables a man to play Monte Cristo or any other avatar of Providence with impunity, and to-day I have discovered it to be the most fascinating game in the world.

When Latimer recovers his equilibrium and regards the transaction in the dry light of reason, he will diagnose a sure symptom of megalomania, and will pity me in his heart for a poor devil.

I have seen Eleanor Faversham, and she has released me from my engagement with such grace, dignity, and sweet womanliness that I wonder how I could have railed at her thousand virtues.

"It's honourable of you to give me this opportunity of breaking it off, Simon," she said, "but I care enough for you to be willing to take my chance of illness."

"You do care for me?" I asked.

She raised astonished eyes. "If I didn't, do you suppose I should have engaged myself to you? If I married you I should swear to cherish you in sickness and in health. Why won't you let me?"

I was in a difficulty. To say that I was in ill-health and about to resign my seat in Parliament and a slave to doctor's orders was one thing; it was another to tell her brutally that I had received my death warrant. She would have taken it much more to heart than I do.

The announcement would have been a shock. It would have kept the poor girl awake of nights. She would have been for ever seeing the hand of Death at my throat. Every time we met she would have noted on my face, in my gait, infallible signs of my approaching end. I had not the right to inflict such intolerable pain on one so near and dear to me.

Besides, I am vain enough to want to walk forth somewhat gallantly into eternity; and while I yet live I particularly desire that folks should not regard me as half-dead. I defy you to treat a man who is only going to live twenty weeks in the same pleasant fashion as you would a man who has the run of life before him.

There is always an instinctive shrinking from decay. I should think that corpses must feel their position acutely.

It was entirely for Eleanor's sake that I refrained from taking her into my confidence. To her question I replied that I had not the right to tie her for life to a helpless valetudinarian. "Besides," said I, "as my health grows worse my jokes will deteriorate, until I am reduced to grinning through a horse-collar at the doctor. And you couldn't stand that, could you?"

She upbraided me gently for treating everything as a jest.

"It isn't that you want to get rid of me, Simon?" she asked tearfully, but with an attempt at a smile.

I took both hands and looked into her eyes—they are brave, truthful eyes—and through my heart shot a great pain. Till that moment I had not realised what I was giving up. The pleasant paths of the world—I could leave them behind with a shrug. Political ambition, power, I could justly estimate their value and could let them pass into other hands without regret. But here was the true, staunch woman, great of heart and wise, a helper and a comrade, and, if I chose to throw off the jester and become the lover in real earnest and sweep my hand across the hidden chords, all that a woman can become towards the man she loves. I realised this.

I realised that if she did not love me passionately now it was only because I, in my foolishness, had willed it otherwise. For the first time I longed to have her as my own; for the first time I rebelled. I looked at her hungeringly until her cheeks grew red and her eyelids fluttered. I had a wild impulse to throw my arms around her, and kiss her as I had never kissed her before and bid her forget all that I had said that day. Her faltering eyes told me that they read my longing. I was about to yield when the little devil of a pain inside made itself sharply felt and my madness went from me. I fetched a thing half-way between a sigh and a groan, and dropped her hands.

"Need I answer your question?" I asked.

She turned her head aside and whispered "No."

Presently she said, "I am glad I came back from Sicily. I shouldn't have liked you to write this to me. I shouldn't have understood."

"Do you now?"

"I think so." She looked at me frankly. "Until just now I was never quite certain whether you really cared for me."

"I never cared for you so much as I do now, when I have to lose you."

"And you must lose me?"

"A man in my condition would be a scoundrel if he married a woman."

"Then it is very, very serious—your illness?"

"Yes," said I, "very serious. I must give you your freedom whether you want it or not."

She passed one hand over the other on her knee, looking at the engagement ring. Then she took it off and presented it to me, lying in the palm of her right hand.

"Do what you like with it," she said very softly.

I took the ring and slipped it on one of the right-hand fingers.

"It would comfort me to think that you are wearing it," said I.

Then her mother came into the room and Eleanor went out. I am thankful to say that Mrs. Faversham who is a woman only guided by sentiment when it leads to a worldly advantage, applauded the step I had taken. As a sprightly Member of Parliament, with an assured political and social position, I had been a most desirable son-in-law. As an obscure invalid, coughing and spitting from a bath-chair at Bournemouth (she took it for granted that I was in the last stage of consumption), I did not take the lady's fancy.

"My dear Simon," replied my lost mother-in-law, "you have behaved irreproachably. Eleanor will feel it for some time no doubt; but she is young and will soon get over it. I'll send her to the Drascombe-Prynnes in Paris. And as for yourself, your terrible misfortune will be as much as you can bear. You mustn't increase it by any worries on her behalf. In that way I'll do my utmost to help you."

"You are kindness itself, Mrs. Faversham," said I.

I bowed over the delighted lady's hand and went away, deeply moved by her charity and maternal devotion.

But perhaps in her hardness lies truth. I have never touched Eleanor's heart. No romance had preceded or accompanied our engagement. The deepest, truest incident in it has been our parting.

CHAPTER VI

Dale's occupation, like Othello's, being gone, as far as I am concerned, Lady Kynnersley has despatched him to Berlin, on her own business, connected, I think, with the International Aid Society. He is to stay there for a fortnight.

How he proposes to bear the separation from the object of his flame I have not inquired; but if forcible objurgations in the vulgar tongue have any inner significance, I gather that Lady Kynnersley has not employed an enthusiastic agent.

Being thus free to pursue my eumoirous schemes without his intervention, for you cannot talk to a lady for her soul's good when her adorer is gaping at you, I have taken the opportunity to see something of Lola Brandt.

I find I have seen a good deal of her; and it seems not improbable that I shall see considerably more. Deuce take the woman!

On the first afternoon of Dale's absence I paid her my promised visit. It was a dull day, and the room, lit chiefly by the firelight, happily did not reveal its nerve-racking tastelessness. Lola Brandt, supple-limbed and lazy-voiced, talked to me from the cushioned depths of her chair.

We lightly touched on Dale's trip to Berlin. She would miss him terribly. It was so kind of me to come and cheer her lonely hour. Politeness forbade my saying that I had come to do nothing of the sort. To my vague expression of courtesy she responded by asking me with a laugh how I liked Mr. Anastasius Papadopoulos.

I replied that I considered it urbane on his part to invite me to see his cats perform.

"If you were to hurt one of his cats he'd murder you," she informed me. "He always carries a long, sharp knife concealed somewhere about him on purpose."

"What a fierce little gentleman," I remarked.

"He looks on me as one of his cats, too," she said with a low laugh, "and considers himself my protector. Once in Buda-Pesth he and I were driving about. I was doing some shopping. As I was getting into the cab a man insulted me, on account, I suppose, of my German name. Anastasius sprang at him like a wild beast, and I had to drag him off bodily and lift him back into the cab. I'm pretty strong, you know. It must have been a funny sight." She turned to me quickly. "Do you think it wrong of me to laugh?"

"Why shouldn't you laugh at the absurd?"

"Because in devotion like that there seems to be something solemn and frightening. If I told him to kill his cats, he would do it. If I ordered him to commit Hari-Kari on the hearthrug, he would whip out his knife and obey me. When you have a human soul at your mercy like that, it's a kind of sacrilege to laugh at it. It makes you feel—oh, I can't express myself. Look, it doesn't make tears come into your eyes exactly, it makes them come into your heart."

We continued the subject, divagating as we went, and had a nice little sentimental conversation. There are depths of human feeling I should never have suspected in this lazy panther of a woman, and although she openly avows having no more education than a tinker's dog, she can talk with considerable force and vividness of expression.

Indeed, when one comes to think of it, a tinker's dog has a fine education if he be naturally a shrewd animal and takes advantage of his opportunities; and a fine education, too, of its kind was that of the vagabond Lola, who on her way from Dublin to Yokohama had more profitably employed her time than Lady Kynnersley supposed. She had seen much of the civilised places of the earth in her wanderings from engagement to engagement, and had been an acute observer of men and things.

We exchanged travel pictures and reminiscences. I found myself floating with her through moonlit Venice, while she chanted with startling exactness the cry of the gondoliers. To my confusion be it spoken, I forgot all about Dale Kynnersley and my mission. The lazy voice and rich personality fascinated me. When I rose to go I found I had spent a couple of hours in her company. She took me round the room and showed me some of her treasures.

"This is very old. I think it is fifteenth century," she said, picking up an Italian ivory.

It was. I expressed my admiration. Then maliciously I pointed to a horrible little Tyrolean chalet and said:

"That, too, is very pretty."

"It isn't. And you know it."

She is a most disconcerting creature. I accepted the rebuke meekly. What else could I do?

"Why, then, do you have it here?"

"It's a present from Anastasius," she said. "Every time he comes to see me he brings what he calls an *'offrande''*. All these things"—she indicated, with a comprehensive sweep of the arm, the Union Jack cushion, the little men mounting ladders inside bottles, the hen sitting on her nest, and the other trumpery gimcracks—"all these things are presents from Anastasius. It would hurt him not to see them here when he calls."

"You might have a separate cabinet," I suggested.

"A chamber of horrors?" she laughed. "No. It gives him more pleasure to see them as they are—and a poor little freak doesn't get much out of life."

She sighed, and picking up "A Present from Margate" kind of mug, fingered it very tenderly.

I went away feeling angry. Was the woman bewitching me? And I felt angrier still when I met Lady Kynnersley at dinner that evening. Luckily I had only a few words with her. Had I done anything yet with regard to Dale and the unmentionable woman? If I had told her that I had spent a most agreeable afternoon with the enchantress, she would not have enjoyed her evening. Like General Trochu of the Siege of Paris fame, I said in my most mysterious manner, "I have my plan," and sent her into dinner comforted.

But I had no plan. My next interview with Madame Brandt brought me no further. We have established telephonic communications. Through the medium of this diabolical engine of loquacity and indiscretion, I was prevailed on to accompany her to a rehearsal of Anastasius's cats.

Rogers, with a face as imperturbable as if he was announcing the visit of an archbishop, informed me at the appointed hour that Madame Brandt's brougham was at the door. I went down and found the brougham open, as the day was fine, and Lola Brandt, smiling under a gigantic hat with an amazing black feather, and looking as handsome as you please.

We were blocked for a few minutes at the mouth of the courtyard, and I had the pleasure of all Piccadilly that passed staring at us in admiration. Lola Brandt liked it; but I didn't, especially when I recognised one of the starers as the eldest Drascombe-Prynne boy whose people in Paris are receiving Eleanor Faversham under their protection. A nice reputation I shall be acquiring. My companion was in gay mood. Now, as it is no part of dealing unto oneself a happy life and portion to damp a fellow creature's spirits, I responded with commendable gaiety.

I own that the drive to Professor Anastasius Papadopoulos's cattery in Rosebery Avenue, Clerkenwell, was distinctly enjoyable. I forgot all about the little pain inside and the Fury with the abhorred shears, and talked a vast amount of nonsense which the lady was pleased to regard as wit, for she laughed wholeheartedly, showing her strong white, even teeth. But why was I going?

Was it because she had requested me through the telephone to give unimagined happiness to a poor little freak who would be as proud as Punch to exhibit his cats to an English Member of Parliament? Was it in order to further my designs—Machiavellian towards the lady, but eumoirous towards Dale? Or was it simply for my own good pleasure?

Professor Anastasius Papadopoulos, resplendently raimented, with the shiniest of silk hats and a flower in the buttonhole of his frock-coat, received us at the door of a small house, the first-floor windows of which announced the tenancy of a maker of gymnastic appliances; and having kissed Madame Brandt's hand with awful solemnity and bowed deeply to me, he preceded us down the passage, out into the yard, and into a ramshackle studio at the end, where his cats had their being.

There were fourteen of them, curled up in large cages standing against the walls. The place was lit by a skylight and warmed by a stove. The floor, like a stage, was fitted up with miniature acrobatic paraphernalia and properties. There were little five-barred gates, and trapezes, and tight-ropes, and spring-boards, and a trestle-table, all the metal work gleaming like silver. A heavy, uncouth German lad, whom the professor introduced as his pupil and assistant, Quast, was in attendance. Mr. Papadopoulos polyglotically acknowledged the honour I had conferred upon him. He is very like the late Emperor of the French; but his forehead is bulgier.

With a theatrical gesture and the remark that I should see, he opened some cages and released half a dozen cats—a Persian, a white Angora, and four commonplace tabbies, who all sprang on to the table with military precision. Madame Brand began to caress them. I, wishing to show interest in the troupe, prepared to do the same; but the dwarf scurried up with a screech from the other end of the room.

"Ne touchez pas—ne touchez pas!"

I refrained, somewhat wonderingly, from touching. Madame Brandt explained.

"He thinks you would spoil the magnetic influence. It is a superstition of his."

"But you are touching."

"He believes I have his magnetism—whatever that may be," she said, with a smile. "Would you like to see an experiment? Anastasius!"

"Carissima."

"Is that the untamed Persian you were telling me of?" she asked, pointing to a cage from which a ferocious gigantic animal more like a woolly tiger than a tom-cat looked out with expressionless yellow eyes. "Will you let Mr. de Gex try to make friends with it?"

"Your will is law, meine Konigin," replied Professor Papadopoulos, bowing low. "But Hephaestus is as fierce as the flames of hell."

"See what he'll do," laughed Lola Brandt.

I approached the cage with an ingratiating, "Puss, puss!" and a hideous growl welcomed me. I ventured my hand towards the bars. The beast bristled in demoniac wrath, spat with malignant venom, and shot out its claws. If I had touched it my hand would have been torn to shreds. I have never seen a more malevolent, fierce, spiteful, ill-conditioned brute in my life. My feelings being somewhat hurt, and my nerves a bit shaken, I retreated hastily.

"Now look," said Lola Brandt.

With absolute fearlessness she went up to the cage, opened it, took the unresisting thing out by the scruff of its neck, held it up like a door-mat, and put it on her shoulder, where it forthwith began to purr like any harmless necessary cat and rub its head against her cheek. She put it on the floor; it arched its back and circling sideways rubbed itself against her skirts.

She sat down, and taking the brute by its forepaws made it stand on its hind legs. She pulled it on to her lap and it curled round lazily. Then she hoisted it on to her shoulder again, and, rising, crossed the room and bowed to the level of the cage, when the beast leaped in purring thunderously in high good humour. Mr. Papadopoulos sang out in breathless delight:

"If I am the King of Cats, you, Carissima, are the Queen. Nay, more, you are the Goddess!"

Lola Brandt laughed. I did not. It was uncanny. It seemed as if some mysterious freemasonic affinity existed between her and the evil beast. During her drive hither she had entered my own atmosphere. She had been the handsome, unconventional woman of the world. Now she seemed as remote from me as the witches in "Macbeth."

If I had seen her dashing Paris hat rise up into a point and her umbrella turn into a broomstick, and herself into one of the buxom carlines of "Tam O'Shanter," I should not have been surprised. The feats of the mild pussies which the dwarf began forthwith to exhibit provoked in me but a polite counterfeit of enthusiasm. Lola Brandt had discounted my interest. Even his performance with the ferocious Persian lacked the diabolical certainty of Lola's handling. He locked all the other cats up and enticed it out of the cage with a piece of fish. He guided it with a small whip, as it jumped over gates and through blazing hoops, and he stood tense and concentrated, like a lion-tamer.

The act over, the cat turned and snarled and only jumped into its cage after a smart flick of the whip. The dwarf did not touch it once with his hands. I applauded, however, and complimented him. He laid his hand on his heart and bent forward in humility.

"Ah, monsieur, I am but a neophyte where Madame is an expert. I know the superficial nature of cats. Now and then without vainglory I can say I know their hearts; but Madame penetrates to and holds commune with their souls. And a cat's soul, monsieur, is a wonderful thing. Once it was divine—in ancient Egypt. Doubtless monsieur has heard of Pasht? Holy men spent their lives in approaching the cat-soul. Madame was born to the privilege. Pasht watches over her."

"Pasht," I said politely in French, in reply to this clotted nonsense, "was a great divinity. And for yourself, who knows but what you may have been in a previous incarnation the keeper of the Sacred Cats in some Egyptian temple."

"I was," he said, with staggering earnestness. "At Memphis."

"One of these days," I returned, with equal solemnity, "I hope for the privilege of hearing some of your reminiscences. They would no doubt be interesting."

On the way back Lola thanked me for pretending to take the little man seriously, and not laughing at him.

"If I hadn't," said I, "he would have stuck his knife into me."

She shook her head. "You did it naturally. I was watching you. It is because you are a generous-hearted gentleman."

Said I: "If you talk like that I'll get out and walk."

And, indeed, what right had she to characterise the moral condition of my heart? I asked her. She laughed her low, lazy laugh, but made no reply. Presently she said:

"Why didn't you like my making friends with the cat?"

"How do you know I didn't like it?" I asked.

"I felt it."

"You mustn't feel things like that," I remarked. "It isn't good for you."

She insisted on my telling her. I explained as well as I could. She touched the sleeve of my coat with her gloved hand.

"I'm glad, because it shows you take an interest in me. And I wanted to let you see that I could do something besides loll about in a drawing-room and smoke cigarettes. It's all I can do. But it's something." She said it with the humility of the Jongleur de Notre Dame in Anatole Frances's story.

In Eaton Square, where I had a luncheon engagement, she dropped me, and drove off smiling, evidently well pleased with herself. My hostess was standing by the window when I was shown into the drawing-room. I noted the faintest possible little malicious twinkle in her eye.

During the afternoon I had a telephonic message from my doctor, who asked me why I had neglected him for a fortnight and urged me to go to Harley Street at once. To humour him I went the next morning. Hunnington is a bluff, hearty fellow who feeds himself into pink floridity so as to give confidence to his patients. In answer to his renewed inquiry as to my neglect, I remarked that a man condemned to be hanged doesn't seek interviews with the judge in order to learn how the rope is getting on. I conveyed to him politely, although he is an old friend, that I desired to forget his well-fed existence. In his chatty way he requested me not to be an ass, and proceeded to put to me the usual silly questions.

Remembering the result of my last visit, I made him happy by answering them gloomily; whereupon he seized his opportunity and ordered me out of England for the winter. I must go to a warm climate—Egypt, South Africa, Madeira—I could take my choice. I flatly refused to obey. I had my duties in London. He was so unsympathetic as to damn my duties. My duty was to live as long as possible, and my wintering in London would probably curtail my short life by two months. Then I turned on him and explained the charitable disingenuousness of my replies to his questions. He refused to believe me, and we parted with mutual recriminations. I sent him next day, however, a brace of pheasants, a present from Farfax Glenn. After all, he is one of God's creatures.

The next time I called on Lola Brandt I went with the fixed determination to make some progress in my mission. I vowed that I would not be seduced by trumpery conversation about Yokohama or allow my mind to be distracted by absurd adventures among cats. I would clothe myself in the armour of eumoiriety, and, with the sword of duty in my hand, would go forth to battle with the enchantress. All said and done, what was she but a bold-faced, strapping woman without an idea in her head save the enslavement of an impressionable boy several years her junior? It was preposterous that I, Simon de Gex, who had beguiled and fooled an electorate of thirty thousand hard-headed men into choosing me for their representative in Parliament, should not be a match for Lola Brandt. As for her complicated feminine personality, her intuitiveness, her magnetism, her fascination, all the qualities in fact which my poetical fancy had assigned to her, they had no existence in reality. She was the most commonplace person I had ever encountered, and I had been but a sentimental lunatic.

In this truly admirable frame of mind I entered her drawing-room. She threw down the penny novel she was reading, and with a little cry of joy sprang forward to greet me.

"I'm so glad you've come. I was getting the blind hump!"

Did I not say she was commonplace? I hate this synonym for boredom. It may be elegant in the mouth of a duchess and pathetic in that of an oyster-wench, but it falls vulgarly from intermediate lips.

"What has given it to you?" I asked.

"My poor little ouistiti is dead. It is this abominable climate."

I murmured condolences. I could not exhibit unreasonable grief at the demise of a sick monkey which I had never seen.

"I'm also out of books," she said, after having paid her tribute to the memory of the departed. "I have been forced to ask the servants to lend me something to read. Have you ever tried this sort of thing? You ought to. It tells you what goes on in high society."

I was sure it didn't. Not a duchess in its pages talked about having a blind hump. I said gravely:

"I will ask you to lend it to me. Since Dale has been away I've had no one to make out my library list."

"Do turn Adolphus out of that chair and sit down," she said, sinking into her accustomed seat. Adolphus was the Chow dog before mentioned, an accomplished animal who could mount guard with the poker and stand on his head, and had been pleased to favour me with his friendship.

"I miss Dale greatly," said I.

"I suppose you do. You are very fond of him?"

"Very," said I. "By the by, how did you first come across Dale?"

She threw me a swift glance and smiled.

"Oh, in the most respectable way. I was dining at the Carlton with Sir Joshua Oldfield, the famous surgeon, you know. He performed a silly little operation on me last year, and since then we've been great friends. Dale and some sort of baby boy were dining there, too, and afterwards, in the lounge, Sir Joshua introduced them to me. Dale asked me if he could call. I said 'Yes.' Perhaps I was wrong. Anyhow, *voila!* Do you know Sir Joshua?"

"I sat next to him once at a public dinner. He's a friend of the Kynnersleys. A genial old soul."

"He's a dear!" said Lola.

"Do you know many of Dale's friends?" I asked.

"Hardly any," she replied. "It's rather lonesome." Then she broke into a laugh.

"I was so terrified at meeting you the first time. Dale can talk of no one else. He makes a kind of god of you. I felt I was going to hate you like the devil. I expected quite a different person."

The diplomatist listens to much and says little.

"Indeed," I remarked.

She nodded. "I thought you would be a big beefy man with a red face, you know. He gave me the idea somehow by calling you a 'splendid chap.' You see, I couldn't think of a 'splendid chap' with a white face and a waxed moustache and your way of talking."

"I am sorry," said I, "not to come up to your idea of the heroic."

"But you do!" she cried, with one of her supple twists of the body. "It was I that was stupid. And I don't hate you at all. You can see that I don't. I didn't even hate you when you came as an enemy."

"Ah!" said I. "What made you think that? We agreed to argue it out, if you remember."

She drew out of a case beside her one of her unspeakable cigarettes. "Do you suppose," she said, lighting it, and pausing to inhale the first two or three puffs of smoke, "do you suppose that a woman who has lived among wild beasts hasn't got instinct?"

I drew my chair nearer to the fire. She was beginning to be uncanny again.

"I expected you were going to be horrified at the dreadful creature your friend had taken up with. Oh, yes, I know in the eyes of your class I'm a dreadful creature. I'm like a cat in many ways. I'm suspicious of strangers, especially strangers of your class, and I sniff and sniff until I feel it's all right. After the first few minutes I felt you were all right. You're true and honourable, like Dale, aren't you?"

Like a panther making a sudden spring, she sat bolt upright in her chair as she launched this challenge at me. Now, it is disconcerting to a man to have a woman leap at his throat and ask him whether he is true and honourable, especially when his attitude towards her approaches the Machiavellian.

I could only murmur modestly that I hoped I could claim these qualifications.

"And you don't think me a dreadful woman?"

"So far from it, Madame Brandt," I replied, "that I think you a remarkable one."

"I wonder if I am," she said, sinking back among her cushions. "I should like to be for Dale's sake. I suppose you know I care a great deal for Dale?"

"I have taken the liberty of guessing it," said I. "And since you have done me the honour of taking me so far into your confidence," I added, playing what I considered to be my master-card, "may I venture to ask whether you have contemplated"—I paused—"marriage?"

Her brow grew dark, as she looked involuntarily at her bare left hand.

"I have got a husband already," she replied.

As I expected. Ladies like Lola Brandt always have husbands unfit for publication; and as the latter seem to make it a point of honour never to die, widowed Lolas are as rare as blackberries in spring.

"Forgive my rudeness," I said, "but you wear no wedding ring."

"I threw it into the sea."

"Ah!" said I.

"Do you want to hear about him?" she asked suddenly. "If we are to be friends, perhaps you had better know. Somehow I don't like talking to Dale about it. Do you mind putting some coals on the fire?"

I busied myself with the coal-scuttle, lit a cigarette, and settled down to hear the story. If it had not been told in the twilight hour by a woman with a caressing, enveloping voice like Lola Brandt's I should have yawned myself out of the house.

It was a dismal, ordinary story. Her husband was a gentleman, a Captain Vauvenarde in the French Army. He had fallen in love with her when she had first taken Marseilles captive with the prodigiosities of her horse Sultan. His proposals of manifold unsanctified delights met with unqualified rejection by the respectable and not too passionately infatuated Lola. When he nerved himself to the supreme sacrifice of offering marriage she accepted.

She had dreams of social advancement, yearned to be one of the white faces of the audience in the front rows. The civil ceremony having been performed, he pleaded with her for a few weeks' secrecy on account of his family. The weeks grew into months, during which, for the sake of a livelihood, she fulfilled her professional engagements in many other towns. At last, when she returned to Marseilles, it became apparent that Captain Vauvenarde had no intention whatever of acknowledging her openly as his wife. Hence many tears. Moreover, he had little beyond his pay and his gambling debts, instead of the comfortable little fortune that would have assured her social position. Now, officers in the French Army who marry ladies with performing horses are not usually guided by reason; and Captain Vauvenarde seems to have been the most unreasonable being in the world. It was beneath the dignity of Captain Vauvenarde's wife to make a horse do tricks in public, and it was beneath Captain Vauvenarde's dignity to give her his name before the world. She must neither be Lola Brandt nor Madame Vauvenarde. She must give up her fairly lucrative profession and live in semi-detached obscurity up a little back street on an allowance of twopence-halfpenny a week and be happy and cheerful and devoted. Lola refused. Hence more tears.

There were scenes of frantic jealousy, not on account of any human being, but on account of the horse. If she loved him as much as she loved that abominable quadruped whose artificial airs and graces made him sick every time he looked at it, she would accede to his desire. Besides, he had the husband's right—a powerful privilege in France. She pointed out that he could only exercise it by declaring her to be his wife. Relations were strained. They led separate lives. From Marseilles she went to Genoa, whither he followed her. Eventually he went away in a temper and never came back. She had not heard from him since, and where he was at the present moment she had not the faintest idea.

"So you went cheerfully on with your profession?" I remarked.

"I returned to Marseilles, and there I lost my horse Sultan. Then my father died and left me pretty well off, and I hadn't the heart to train another animal. So here I am. Ah!"

With one of her lithe movements she rose to her feet, and, flinging out her arms in a wide gesture, began to walk about the room, stopping here and there to turn on the light and draw the flaring chintz curtains. I rose, too, so as to aid her. Suddenly as we met, by the window, she laid both her hands on my shoulders and looked into my face earnestly and imploringly, and her lips quivered. I wondered apprehensively what she was going to do next.

"For God's sake, be my friend and help me!"

The cry, in her rich, low notes, seemed to come from the depths of the woman's nature. It caused some absurd and unnecessary chord within me to vibrate.

For the first time I realised that her strong, handsome face could look nobly and pathetically beautiful. Her eyes swam in an adorable moisture and grew very human and appealing. In a second all my self-denying ordinances were forgotten. The witch had me in her power again.

"My dear Madame Brandt," said I, "how can I do it?"

"Don't take Dale from me. I've lived alone, alone, alone all these years, and I couldn't bear it."

"Do you care for him so very much?"

She withdrew her hands and moved slightly. "Who else in the wide world have I to care for?"

This was very pathetic, but I had the sense to remark that compromising the boy's future was not the best way of showing her devotion.

"Oh, how could I do that?" she asked. "I can't marry him. And if I do what I've never done before for any man—become his mistress—who need know? I could stay in the background."

"You seem to forget, dear lady," said I, "that Captain Vauvenarde is probably alive."

"But I tell you I've lost sight of him altogether."

"Are you quite so sure," I asked, regaining my sanity by degrees, "that Captain Vauvenarde has lost sight of you?"

She turned quickly. "What do you mean?"

"You have given him no chance as yet of recovering his freedom."

She passed her hand over her face, and sat down on the sofa. "Do you mean—divorce?"

"It's an ugly word, dear Madame Brandt," said I, as gently as I could, "but you and I are strong people and needn't fear uttering it. Don't you think such a scandal would ruin Dale at the very beginning of his career?"

There was a short silence. I was glad to see she was feminine enough to twist and tear her handkerchief.

"What am I to do?" she asked at last. "I can't live this awful lonely life much longer. Sometimes I get the creeps."

I might have given her the sound advice to find healthy occupation in training crocodiles to sit up and beg; but an idea which advanced thinkers might classify as more suburban was beginning to take shape in my mind.

"Has it occurred to you," I said, "that now you have assumed the qualifications imposed by Captain Vauvenarde for bearing his name?"

"I don't understand."

"You no longer perform in public. He would have no possible grievance against you."

"Are you suggesting that I should go back to my husband?" she gasped.

"I am," said I, feeling mighty diplomatic.

She looked straight in front of her, with parted lips, fingering her handkerchief and evidently pondering the entirely new suggestion. I thought it best to let her ponder. As a general rule, people will do anything in the world rather than think; so, when one sees a human being wrapped in thought, one ought to regard wilful disturbance of the process as sacrilege. I lit a cigarette and wandered about the room.

Eventually I came to a standstill before the Venus of Milo. But while I was admiring its calm, mysterious beauty, the development of a former idea took the shape of an inspiration which made my heart sing. Fate had put into my hands the chance of complete eumoiriety.

If I could effect a reconciliation between Lola Brandt and her husband, Dale would be cured almost automatically of his infatuation, and I should be the Deputy Providence bringing happiness to six human beings—Lola Brandt, Captain Vauvenarde, Lady Kynnersley, Maisie Ellerton, Dale, and Mr. Anastasius Papadopoulos, who could not fail to be delighted at the happiness of his goddess.

There also might burst joyously on the earth a brood of gleeful little Vauvenardes and merry little Kynnersleys, who might regard Simon de Gex as their mythical progenitor. It might add to the gaiety of regiments and the edification of parliaments. Acts should be judged, thought I, not according to their trivial essence, but by the light of their far-reaching consequences.

Lola Brandt broke the silence. She did not look at me. She said:

"I can't help feeling that you're my friend."

"I am," I cried, in the exultation of my promotion to the role of Deputy Providence. "I am indeed. And a most devoted one."

"Will you let me think over what you've said for a day or two—and then come for an answer?"

"Willingly," said I.

"And you won't——?"

"What?"

"No. I know you won't."

"Tell Dale?" I said, guessing. "No, of course not."

She rose and put out both her hands to me in a very noble gesture. I took them and kissed one of them.

She looked at me with parted lips.

"You are the best man I have ever met," she said.

At the moment of her saying it I believed it; such conviction is induced by the utterances of this singular woman. But when I got outside the drawing-room door my natural modesty revolted. I slapped my thigh impatiently with what I thought were my gloves. They made so little sound that I found there was only one. I had left the other inside. I entered and found Lola Brandt in front of the fire holding my glove in her hand. She started in some confusion.

"Is this yours?" she asked.

Now whose could it have been but mine? The ridiculous question worried me, off and on, all the evening.

CHAPTER VII

The murder is out. A paragraph has appeared in the newspapers to the effect that the marriage arranged between Mr. Simon de Gex and Miss Eleanor Faversham will not take place. It has also become common knowledge that I am resigning my seat in Parliament on account of ill-health. That is the reason rightly assigned by my acquaintances for the rupture of my engagement. I am being rapidly killed by the doleful kindness of my friends. They are so dismally sympathetic. Everywhere I go there are long faces and solemn hand-shakes. In order to cheer myself I gave a little dinner-party at the club, and the function might have been a depressed wake with my corpse in a coffin on the table. My sisters, dear, kind souls, follow me with anxious eyes as if I were one of their children sickening for chicken-pox. They upbraid me for leaving them in ignorance, and in hushed voices inquire as to my symptoms. They both came this morning to the Albany to see what they could do for me. I don't see what they can do, save help Rogers put studs in my shirts. They expressed such affectionate concern that at last I cried out:

"My dear girls, if you don't smile, I'll sit upon the hearthrug and howl like a dog."

Then they exchanged glances and broke into hectic gaiety, dear things, under the impression that they were brightening me up. I am being deluged with letters. I had no idea I was such a popular person. They come from high placed and lowly, from constituents whom my base and servile flattery have turned into friends, from Members of Parliament, from warm-hearted dowagers and from little girls who have inveigled me out to lunch for the purpose of confiding to me their love affairs. I could set up as a general practitioner of medicine on the advice that is given me. I am recommended cod-liver oil, lung tonic, electric massage, abdominal belts, warm water, mud baths, Sandow's treatment, and every patent medicament save rat poison. I am urged to go to health resorts ranging geographically from the top of the Jungfrau to Central Africa. All kinds of worthy persons have offered to nurse me. Old General Wynans writes me a four-page letter to assure me that I have only to go to his friend Dr. Eustace Adams, of Wimpole Street, to be cured like a shot. I happen to know that Eustace Adams is an eminent gynecologist.

And the worst of it all is that these effusions written in the milk of human kindness have to be answered. Dale is not here. I have to sit down at my desk and toil like a galley slave. I am being worn to a shadow.

Lola Brandt, too, has heard the news, Dale in Berlin, and the London newspapers being her informants. Tears stood in her eyes when I called to learn her decision. Why had I not told her I was so ill? Why had I let her worry me with her silly troubles? Why had I not consulted her friend, Sir Joshua Oldfield? She filled up my chair with cushions (which, like most men, I find stuffy and comfortless), and if I had given her the slightest encouragement, would have stuck my feet in hot mustard and water. Why had I come out on such a dreadful day? It was indeed a detestable day of raw fog. She pulled the curtains close, and, insisting upon my remaining among my cushions, piled the grate with coal half-way up the chimney. Would I like some eucalyptus?

"My dear Madame Brandt," I cried, "my bronchial tubes and lungs are as strong as a hippopotamus's."

I wish every one would not conclude that I was going off in a rapid decline.

Lola Brandt prowled about me in a wistful, mothering way, showing me a fresh side of her nature. She is as domesticated as Penelope.

"You're fond of cooking, aren't you?" I asked suddenly.

She laughed. "I adore it. How do you know?"

"I guessed," said I.

"I'm what the French call a *vraie bourgeoise.*"

"I'm glad to hear it," said I.

"Are you? I thought your class hated the *bourgeoisie.*"

"The *bourgeoisie,*" I said, "is the nation's granary of the virtues. But for God's sake, don't tell any one that I said so!"

"Why?" she asked.

"If it found its way into print it would ruin my reputation for epigram."

She drew a step or two towards me in her slow rhythmic way, and smiled.

"When you say or do a beautiful thing you always try to bite off its tail."

Then she turned and drew some needlework—plain sewing I believe they call it—from beneath the Union Jack cushion and sat down.

"I'll make a confession," she said. "Until now I've stuffed away my work when I heard you coming. I didn't think it genteel. What do you think?"

I scanned the shapeless mass of linen or tulle or whatever it was on her lap.

"I don't know whether it's genteel," I remarked, "but at present it looks like nothing on God's earth."

My masculine ignorance of such mysteries made her laugh. She is readily moved to mild mirth, which makes her an easy companion. Besides, little jokes are made to be laughed at, and I like women who laugh at them. There was a brief silence. I smoked and made Adolphus stand up on his hind legs and balance sugar on his nose. His mistress sewed. Presently she said, without looking up from her work:

"I've made up my mind."

I rose from my cushioned seat, into which Adolphus, evidently thinking me a fool, immediately snuggled himself, and I stood facing her with my back to the fire.

"Well?" said I.

"I am ready to go back to my husband, if he can be found, and, of course, if he will have me."

I commended her for a brave women. She smiled rather sadly and shook her head.

"Those are two gigantic 'ifs.'"

"Giants before now have been slain by the valiant," I replied.

"How is Captain Vauvenarde to be found?"

"An officer in the French Army is not like a lost sparrow in London. His whereabouts could be obtained from the French War Office. What is his regiment?"

"The Chasseurs d'Afrique. Yes," she added thoughtfully. "I see, it isn't difficult to trace him. I make one condition, however. You can't refuse me."

"What is that?"

"Until things are fixed up everything must go on just as at present between Dale and me. He is not to be told anything. If nothing comes of it then I'll have him all to myself. I won't give him up and be left alone. As long as I care for him, I swear to God, I won't!" she said, in her low, rich voice—and I saw by her face that she was a woman of her word. "Besides, he would come raving and imploring—and I'm not quite a woman of stone. It isn't all jam to go back to my husband. Goodness knows why I am thinking of it. It's for your sake. Do you know that?"

I did not. I was puzzled. Why in the world should Lola Brandt, whom I have only met three or four times, revolutionise the whole of her life for my sake?

"I should have thought it was for Dale's," said I.

"I suppose you would, being a man," she replied.

I retorted, with a smile: "Woman is the eternal conundrum to which the wise man always leaves her herself to supply the answer. Doubtless one of these days you'll do it. Meanwhile, I'll wait in patience."

She gave me one of her sidelong, flashing glances and sewed with more vigour than appeared necessary. I admired the beautiful curves of her neck and shoulders as she bent over her work. She seemed too strong to wield such an insignificant weapon as a needle.

"That's neither here nor there," she said in reference to my last remark. "I say, I don't look forward to going back to my husband—though why I should say 'going back' I don't know, as he left me—not I him. Anyhow, I'm ready to do it. If it can be managed, I'll cut myself adrift suddenly from Dale. It will be more merciful to him. A man can bear a sudden blow better than lingering pain. If it can't be managed, well, Dale will know nothing at all about it, and both he and I will be saved a mortal deal of worry and unhappiness."

"Suppose" said I, "it can't be managed? Do you propose to keep Dale ignorant of the danger he is running in keeping up a liaison with a married woman living apart from her husband?"

She reflected. "If my husband says he'll see me damned first before he'll come back to me, then I'll tell Dale everything, and you can say what you like to him. He'll be able to judge for himself; but in the meanwhile you'll let me have what happiness I can."

I accepted the compromise, and, dispossessing Adolphus, sat down again. I certainly had made progress. Feeling in a benevolent mood, I set forth the advantages she would reap by assuming her legal status; how at last she would shake the dust of Bohemia from off her feet, and instead of standing at the threshold like a disconsolate Peri, she would enter as a right the Paradise of Philistia which she craved; how her life would be one continual tea-party, and how, as her husband had doubtless by this time obtained his promotion, she would be authorised to adopt high and mighty airs in her relations with the wives of all the captains and lieutenants in the regiment. She sighed and wondered whether she would like it, after all.

"Here in England I can say 'damn' as often as I choose. I don't say it very often, but sometimes I feel I must say it or explode."

"There are its equivalents in French," I suggested.

She laughed outright. "Fancy my coming out with a *sacre nom de Dieu* in a French drawing-room!"

"Fancy you shouting 'damn' in an English one."

"That's true," she said. "I suppose drawing-rooms are the same all the world over. I do try to talk like a lady—at least, what I imagine they talk like, for I've never met one."

"You see one every time you look in the glass," said I.

Her olive face flushed. "You mustn't say such things to me if you don't mean them. I like to think all you say to me is true."

"Why in the world," I cried, "should you not be a lady? You have the instincts of one. How many of my fair friends in Mayfair and Belgravia would have made their drawing-rooms unspeakable just for the sake of not hurting the feelings of Anastasius Papadopoulos?"

She put aside her work and, leaning over the arm of the chair, her chin in her hands, looked at me gratefully.

"I'm so glad you've said that. Dale can't understand it. He wants me to clear the trash away."

"Dale," said I, "is young and impetuous. I am a battered old philosopher with one foot in the grave."

Quick moisture gathered in her eyes. "You hurt me," she said. "You'll soon get well and strong again. You must!"

"*Ce que femme veut, Dieu le veut,*" I laughed.

"*Eh bien, je le veux,*" she said with an odd expression in her eyes which burned golden. They fascinated me, held mine. For some seconds neither of us moved. Just consider the picture. There among the cushions of her chair she sprawled beneath the light of a shaded lamp on the further side, and in front of the leaping flames, a great, powerful, sinuous creature of sweeping curves, clad in a clinging brown dress, her head crowned with superb bronze hair, two warm arms bare to the elbow, at which the sleeve ended in coffee-coloured lace falling over the side of the chair, and her leopard eyes fixed on me. About her still hung the echo of her last words spoken in deep tones whose register belongs less to human habitations than to the jungle. And from her emanated like a captivating odour—but it was not an odour—a strange magnetic influence.

I have done my best to write her down in my mind a commonplace, vulgar, good-natured mountebank. But I can do so no longer.

There is something deep down in the soul of Lola Brandt which sets her apart from the kindly race of womankind; whether it is the devil or a touch of pre-Adamite splendour or an ancestral catamount, I make no attempt to determine. At any rate, she is too grand a creature to fritter her life away on a statistic-hunting and pheasant-shooting young Briton like Dale Kynnersley. He would never begin to understand her. I will save her from Dale for her own sake.

All this, ladies and gentlemen, because her eyes fascinated me, and caused me to hold my breath, and made my heart beat.

And will Captain Vauvenarde understand her? Of course he won't. But then he is her husband, and husbands are notoriously and *cum privilegio* dunder-headed. I make no pretensions to understand her, but as I am neither her lover nor her husband it does not matter. She says nothing diabolical or eerie or fantastic or feline or pre-Adamite or uncanny or spiritual; and yet she *is*, in a queer, indescribable way, all these things.

"*Je le veux*," she said, and we drank in each other's souls, or gaped at each other like a pair of idiots just as you please. I had a horrible, yet pleasurable consciousness that she had gripped hold of my nerves of volition. She was willing me to live. I was a puppet in her hands like the wild tom-cat. At that moment I declare I could have purred and rubbed my head against her knee. I would have done anything she bade me. If she had sent me to fetch the Cham of Tartary's cap or a hair of the Prester John's beard, I would have telephoned forthwith to Rogers to pack a suit-case and book a seat in the Orient express.

What would have happened next Heaven alone knows—for we could not have gone on gazing at each other until I backed myself out at the door by way of leave-taking—had not Anticlimax arrived in the person of Mr. Anastasius Papadopoulos in his eternal frock-coat. But his gloves were black.

As usual he fell on his knees and kissed his lady's hand. Then he rose and greeted me with solemn affability.

"*C'est un privilège de rencontrer den gnadigsten Herrn*," said he.

Confining myself to one language, I responded by informing him that it was an honour always to meet so renowned a professor, and inquired politely after the health of Hephaestus.

"Ah, Signore!" he cried. "Do not ask me. It is a tragedy from which I shall never recover."

He sat down on a footstool by the side of Madame Brandt and burst into tears, which coursed down his cheeks and moustache and hung like drops of dew from the point of his imperial.

"Is he dead?" asked Madame.

"I wish he were! No. It is only the iron self-restraint that I possess which prevented me from slaying him on the spot. But poor Santa Bianca! My gentle and accomplished Angora. He has killed her. I can scarcely raise my head through grief."

Lola put her great arm round the little man's neck and patted him like a child, while he sobbed as if his heart would break.

When he recovered he gave us the details of the tragic end of Santa Bianca, and wound up by calling down the most ingeniously complicated and passionate curses on the head of the murderer. Lola Brandt strove to pacify him.

"We all have our sorrows, Anastasius. Did I not lose my beautiful horse Sultan?"

The professor sprang to his full height of four feet and dashed away his tears with a noble gesture of his black-gloved hand.

Base slave that he was to think of his own petty bereavement in the face of her eternal affliction. He turned to me and bade me mark her serene nobility. It was a model and an example for him to follow. He, too, would be brave and present a smiling face to evil fortune.

"Behold! I smile, carissima!" he cried dramatically.

We beheld—and saw his features (smudged with tearstains and the dye from the black gloves which he obviously wore out of respect for the deceased Santa Bianca) contorted into a grimace of hideous imbecility.

"Monsieur," said he, assuming his natural expression which was one of pensive melancholy, "let us change the conversation. You are a great statesman. Will you kindly let me know your opinion on the foreign policy of Germany?"

Whereupon he sat down again upon his stool and regarded me with earnest attention.

"Germany," said I, with the solemnity of a Sir Oracle in the smoking-room of one of the political clubs, "has dreams of an empire beyond her frontiers, and with a view to converting the dream into a reality, is turning out battleships nineteen to the dozen."

The Professor nodded his head sagaciously, and looked up at Lola.

"Very profound," said he, "very profound. I shall remember it. I am a Greek, Monsieur, and the Greeks, as you know, are a nation of diplomatists."

"Ever since the days of Xenophon," said I.

"You're both too clever for me," exclaimed our hostess. "Where did you get your knowledge from, Anastasius?"

The Professor, flattered, passed his hand over his bulgy forehead.

"I was a great student in my youth," said he. "Once I could tell you all the kings of Rome and the date of the battle of Actium. But pressure of weightier concerns has driven my erudition from me. Pardon me. I have not yet asked after your health. You are looking sad and troubled. What is the matter?"

He sat bolt upright, fingering his imperial and regarding her with the keen solicitude of a family physician. To my amazement, Lola Brandt told him quite simply:

"I am thinking of living with my husband again."

"Has the traitor been annoying you?" he asked with a touch of fierceness.

"Oh, no! It's my own idea. I'm tired of living alone. I don't even know where he is."

"Do you want to know where he is?"

"How can I communicate with him unless I do?"

Anastasius Papadopoulos rose, struck an attitude, and thumped his breast.

"I will seek him for you at the ends of the earth, and will bring him to prostrate himself at your feet."

"That's very kind of you, Anastasius," said Lola gently; "but what will become of your cats?"

The dwarf raised his hand impressively.

"The Almighty will have them in His keeping. I have also my pupil and assistant, Quast."

Lola smiled indulgently from her cushions, showing her curious even teeth.

"You mustn't do anything so mad, Anastasius, I forbid you."

"Madame," said he in a most stately manner, "when I devote myself, it is to the death. I have the honour to salute you!"—he bowed over her hand and kissed it. "Monsieur." He bowed to me with the profundity of a hidalgo, and trotted magnificently out of the room.

It was all so sudden that it took my breath away.

"Well I'm——" I didn't know what I was, so I stopped. Lola Brandt broke into low laughter at my astonishment.

"That's Anastasius's way," she explained.

"But the little man surely isn't going to leave his cats and start on a wild-goose chase over Europe to find your husband?"

"He thinks he is, but I shan't let him."

"I hope you won't," said I. "And will you tell me why you made so hot-headed a person your confidant?"

I confess that I was wrathful. Here had I been using the wiles of a Balkan chancery to bring the lady to my way of thinking, and here was she, to my face, making a joke of it with this caricature of a Paladin.

"My dearest friend," she replied earnestly, "don't be angry with me. I've given the poor little man something to think of besides the death of his cat. It will do him good. And why shouldn't I tell him? He's a dear old friend, and in his way was so good to me when I was unhappy. He knows all about my married life. You may think he's half-witted; but he isn't. In ordinary business dealings he's as shrewd as they make 'em. The manager who beats Anastasius over a contract is yet to be born."

By some extraordinary process of the contortionist's art, she curled herself out of her chair on to the hearthrug and knelt before me, her hands clasped on my knee.

"You're not angry with me, are you?" she asked in her rich contralto.

I took both her hands, rose, and assisted her to rise. I was not going to be mesmerised again.

"Of course not," I laughed. Indeed my wrath had fallen from me.

Her bosom heaved with a sigh. "I'm so glad," she said. Her breath fanned my cheek. It was aromatic, intoxicating. Her lips are ripe and full.

"You had better find your husband as soon as possible," said I.

"Do you think so?" she asked.

"Yes, I do. And it strikes me I had better go and find him myself."

She started. "You?"

"Yes," I said. "The Chasseurs d'Afrique are probably in Africa, and the doctors have ordered me to winter in a hot climate, and I shall go on writing a million letters a day if I stay here, which will kill me off in no time with brain fag and writer's cramp. Your husband will be what the newspapers call an objective. Good-bye!" said I, "I'll bring him to you dead or alive."

And without knowing it at the time, I made an exit as magnificent as that of Professor Anastasius Papadopoulos.

CHAPTER VIII

I do not know whether I ought to laugh or rail. Judged by the ordinary canons that regulate the respectable life to which I have been accustomed, I am little short of a lunatic. The question is: Does the recognition of lunacy in oneself tend to amusement or anger? I compromise with myself. I am angry at having been forced on an insane adventure, but the prospect of its absurdity gives me a considerable pleasure.

Let me set it down once and for all. I resent Lola Brandt's existence. When I am out of her company I can contemplate her calmly from my vantage of social and intellectual superiority. I can pooh-pooh her fascinations. I can crack jokes on her shortcomings. I can see perfectly well that I am Simon de Gex, M.P. (I have not yet been appointed to the stewardship of the Chiltern Hundreds), of Eton and Trinity College, Cambridge, a barrister of the Inner Temple (though a brief would cause me as much dismay as a command to conduct the orchestra at Covent Garden), formerly of the Foreign Office, a man of the world, a diner-out, a hardened jester at feminine wiles, a cynical student of philosophy, a man of birth, and, I believe, breeding with a cultivated taste in wine and food and furniture, one also who, but for a little pain inside, would soon become a Member of His Majesty's Government, and eventually drop the "Esquire" at the end of his name and stick "The Right Honourable" in front of it—in fact, a most superior, wise and important person; and I can also see perfectly well that Lola Brandt is an uneducated, lowly bred, vagabond female, with a taste, as I have remarked before, for wild beasts and tea-parties, with whom I have as much in common as I have with the feathered lady on a coster's donkey-cart or the Fat Woman at the Fair. I can see all this perfectly well in the calm seclusion of my library. But when I am in her presence my superiority, like Bob Acres's valour, oozes out through my finger-tips; I become a besotted idiot; the sense and the sight and the sound of her overpower me; I proclaim her rich and remarkable personality; and I bask in her lazy smiles like any silly undergraduate whose knowledge of women has hitherto been limited to his sisters and the common little girl at the tobacconist's.

I say I resent it. I resent the low notes in her voice. I resent the cajolery of the supple twists of her body. I resent her putting her hands on my shoulders, and, as the twopenny-halfpenny poets say, fanning my cheek with her breath. If it had not been for that I should never have promised to go in search of her impossible husband. At any rate, it is easy to discover his whereabouts. A French bookseller has telegraphed to Paris for the

Annuaire Officiel de l'Armee Francaise, the French Army List. It locates every officer in the French army, and as the Chasseurs d'Afrique generally chase in Africa, it will tell me the station in Algeria or Tunisia which Captain Vauvenarde adorns. I can go straight to him as Madame Brandt's plenipotentiary, and if the unreasonable and fire-eating warrior does not run me through the body for impertinence before he has time to appreciate the delicacy of my mission, I may be able to convince him that a well-to-do wife is worth the respectable consideration of a hard-up captain of Chasseurs. I say I may be able to convince him; but I shrink from the impudence of the encounter. I am to accost a total stranger in a foreign army and tell him to return to his wife. This is the pretty little mission I have undertaken. It sounded glorious and eumoirous and quixotic and deucedly funny, during the noble moment of inspiration, when Lola's golden eyes were upon me; but now—well, I shall have to persuade myself that it is funny, if I am to carry it out. It is very much like wagering that one will tweak by the nose the first gentleman in gaiters and shovel-hat one meets in Piccadilly. This by some is considered the quintessence of comedy. I foresee a revision of my sense of humour.

This afternoon I met Lady Kynnersley again—at the Ellertons'. I was talking to Maisie, who has grown no happier, when I saw her sailing across to me with questions hoisted in her eyes. Being particularly desirous not to report progress periodically to Lady Kynnersley, I made a desperate move. I went forward and greeted her.

"Lady Kynnersley," said I, "somebody was telling me that you are in urgent need of funds for something. With my usual wooden-headedness I have forgotten what it is—but I know it is a deserving organisation."

The philanthropist, as I hoped, ousted the mother. She exclaimed at once:

"It must have been the Cabmen and Omnibus Drivers' Rheumatic Hospital."

"That was it!" said I, hearing of the institution for the first time.

"They are martyrs to rheumatic gout, and of course have no means of obtaining proper treatment; so we have secured a site at Harrogate and are building a comfortable place, half hospital, half hotel, where they can be put up for a shilling a day and have all the benefits of the waters just as if they were staying at the Hotel Majestic. Do you want to become a subscriber?"

"I am eager to," said I.

"Then come over here and I'll tell you all about it."

I sat with her in a corner of the room and listened to her fairy-tale. She wrung my heart to such a pitch of sympathy that I rose and grasped her by the hand.

"It is indeed a noble project," I cried. "I love the London cabby as my brother, and I'll post you a cheque for a thousand pounds this evening. Good-bye!"

I left her in a state of joyous stupefaction and made my escape. If it had not fallen in with my general scheme of good works I should regard it as an expensive method of avoiding unpleasant questions.

Another philanthropist, by the way, of quite a different type from Lady Kynnersley, who has lately benefited by my eleemosynary mania is Rex Campion. I have known him since our University days and have maintained a sincere though desultory friendship with him ever since. He is also a friend of Eleanor Faversham, whom he now and then inveigles into weird doings in the impossible slums of South Lambeth. He has tried on many occasions to lure me into his web, but hitherto I have resisted. Being the possessor of a large fortune, he has been able to gratify a devouring passion for philanthropy, and has squandered most of his money on an institution—a kind of club, school, labour-bureau, dispensary, soup-kitchen, all rolled into one—in Lambeth; and there he lives himself, perfectly happy among a hungry, grubby, scarecrow, tatterdemalion crowd. At a loss for a defining name, he has called it "Barbara's Building," after his mother. His conception of the cosmos is that sun, moon and stars revolve round Barbara's Building. How he learned that I was, so to speak, standing at street corners and flinging money into the laps of the poor and needy, I know not. But he came to see me a day or two ago, full of Barbara's Building, and departed in high feather with a cheque for a thousand pounds in his pocket.

I may remark here on the peculiar difficulty there is in playing Monte Cristo with anything like picturesque grace. Any dull dog that owns a pen and a banking-account can write out cheques for charitable institutions. But to accomplish anything personal, imaginative, adventurous, anything with a touch of distinction, is a less easy matter. You wake up in the morning with the altruistic yearnings of a St. Francois de Sales, and yet somehow you go to bed in the evening with the craving unsatisfied. You have really had so few opportunities; and when an occasion does arise it is hedged around with such difficulties as to baffle all but the most persistent. Have you ever tried to give a beggar a five-pound note? I did this morning.

She was a miserable, shivering, starving woman of fifty selling matches in Sackville Street. She held out a shrivelled hand to me, and eyes that once had been beautiful pleaded hungrily for alms.

"Here," said I to myself, "is an opportunity of bringing unimagined gladness for a month or two into this forlorn creature's life."

I pressed a five-pound note into her hand and passed on. She ran after me, terror on her face.

"I daren't take it, sir; they would say I had stolen it, and I should be locked up. No one would believe a gentleman had given it to me."

She trembled, overwhelmed by the colossal fortune that might, and yet might not, be hers. I sympathised, but not having the change in gold, I could do no more than listen to an incoherent tale of misery, which did not aid the solution of the problem. It was manifestly impossible to take back the note; and yet if she retained it she would be subjected to scandalous indignities. What was to be done? I turned my eyes towards Piccadilly and beheld a policeman. A page wearing the name of a milliner's shop on his cap whisked past me. I stopped him and slipped a shilling into his hand.

"Will you ask that policeman to come to me?"

The boy tore down the street and told the policeman and followed him up to me, eager for amusement.

"What has the woman been doing, sir?" asked the policeman.

"Nothing," said I. "I have given her a five-pound note."

"What for, sir?" he asked.

"To further my pursuit of the eumoirous," said I, whereat he gaped stolidly; "but, be that as it may, I have given it her as a free gift, and she is afraid to present it anywhere lest she should be charged with theft. Will you kindly accompany her to a shop, where she can change it, and vouch for her honesty?"

The policeman, who seemed to form the lowest opinion of my intellect, said he didn't know a shop on his beat where they could change it. The boy whistled. The woman held the box of matches in one hand, and in the other the note, fluttering in the breeze. Idlers paused and looked on. The policeman grew authoritative and bade them pass along. They crowded all the more. My position was becoming embarrassing. At last the boy, remembering the badge of honour on his cap, undertook to change the note at the hatter's at the corner of the street. So, having given the note to the boy and bidden the policeman follow him to see fair play, and encouraged the woman to follow the policeman, I resumed my walk down Sackville Street.

But what a pother about a simple act of charity! In order to repeat it habitually I shall have to rely on the fortuitous attendance of a boy and a policeman, or have a policeman and a boy permanently attached to my person, which would be as agreeable as the continuous escort of a jackdaw and a yak.

Poor Latimer is having a dreadful time. Apparently my ten thousand pounds have vanished like a snowflake on the river of liabilities. How he is to repay me he does not know. He wishes he had not yielded to temptation and had allowed himself to be honestly hammered. Then he could have taken his family to sing in the streets with a quiet conscience.

"My dear fellow," said I through the telephone this morning. "What are ten thousand pounds to me?"

I heard him gasp at the other end.

"But you're not a millionaire!"

"I am!" I cried triumphantly. And now I come to think of it, I spoke truly. If a man reckons his capital as half a year's income, doubles it, and works out the capital that such a yearly income represents, he is the possessor of a mint of money.

"I am," I cried; "and I'll tell you what I'll do. I'll settle five thousand on Lucy and the children, so that they needn't accompany you in your singing excursions. I shouldn't like them to catch cold, poor dears, and ruin their voices."

In tones more than telephonically agonised he bade me not make a jest of his misery. I nearly threw the receiver at the blockhead.

"I'm not jesting," I bawled; "I'm deadly serious. I knew Lucy before you did, and I kissed her and she kissed me years before she knew of your high existence; and if she had been a sensible woman she would have married me instead of you—what? The first time you've heard of it? Of course it is—and be decently thankful that you hear it now."

It is pleasant sometimes to tell the husbands of girls you have loved exactly what you think of them; and I had loved Lucy Latimer. She came, an English rose, to console me for the loss of my French *fleur-de-lis*, Clothilde. Or was it the other way about? One does get so mixed in these things. At any rate, she did not marry me, her first love, but jilted me most abominably for Latimer. So I shall heap five thousand pounds on her head.

I have been unfortunate in my love affairs. I wonder why? Which reminds me that I made the identical remark to Lucy Latimer a month or two ago. (She is a plump, kind, motherly, unromantic little person now.) She had the audacity to reply that I had never had any.

"*You*, Lucy Crooks, dare say such a thing!" I exclaimed indignantly.

She smiled. "Are there many more qualified than I to give the opinion?"

I remember that I rose and looked her sternly in the face.

"Lucy Crooks or Lucy Latimer," said I, "you are nothing more or less than a common hussy."

Whereupon she laughed as if I had paid her a high compliment.

I maintain that I have been unfortunate in my love affairs. First, there was an angel-faced widow, a contemporary of my mother's, whom I wooed in Greek verses—and let me tell the young lover that it is much easier to write your own doggerel and convert it into Greek than to put "To Althea" into decent Anacreontics. I also took her to the Eton and Harrow match, and talked to her of women's hats and the things she loved, and neglected the cricket. But she would have none of me. In the flood tide of my passion she married a scorbutic archdeacon of the name of Jugg. Then there was a lady whose name for the life of me I can't remember. It was something ending in "-ine." We quarrelled because we held divergent views on Mr. Wilson Barrett. Then there was Clothilde, whose tragical story I have already unfolded; Lucy Crooks, who threw me over for this dear, amiable, wooden-headed stockjobbing Latimer; X, Y and Z—but here, let me remark, I was the hunted—mammas spread nets for me which by the grace of heaven and the ungraciousness of the damsels I escaped; and, lastly, my incomparable Eleanor Faversham. Now, I thought, am I safe in harbour? If ever a match could have been labelled "Pure heaven-made goods, warranted not to shrink"—that was one. But for this rupture there is an all-accounting reason. For the others there was none. I vow I went on falling in love until I grew absolutely sick and tired of the condition. You see, the vocabulary of the pastime is so confoundedly limited. One has to say to B what one has said to A; to C exactly what one has said to A and B; and when it comes to repeating to F the formularies one has uttered to A, B, C, D and E one grows almost hysterical with the boredom of it. That was the delightful charm of Eleanor Faversham; she demanded no formularies or re-enactment of raptures.

The *Annuaire Officiel de l'Armee Francaise* has arrived. It is a volume of nearly eighteen hundred pages, and being uncut both at top and bottom and at the side it is peculiarly serviceable as a work of reference. I attacked it bravely, however, hacking my way into it, paperknife in hand. But to my dismay, the more I hacked the less could I find of Captain Vauvenarde. I sought him in the Alphabetical Repertory of Colonial Troops, in the list of officers *hors cadre*, in the lists of seniority, in the list of his regiment, wherever he was likely or unlikely to be. There is no person in the French army by the name of Vauvenarde.

I went straight to Lola Brandt with the hideous volume and the unwelcome news. Together we searched the pages.

"He *must* be here," she said, with feminine disregard of fact.

"Are you quite certain you have got the name right?" I asked.

"Why, it is my own name!"

"So it is," said I; "I was forgetting. But how do you know he was in the army at all?"

He might have been an adventurer, a Captain of Kopenick of the day, who had poured a gallant but mendacious tale into her ears.

"I hardly ever saw him out of uniform. He was quartered at Marseilles on special duty. I knew some of his brother officers."

"Then," said I, "there are only two alternatives. Either he has left the army or he is——"

"Dead?" she whispered.

"Let us hope," said I, "that he has left the army."

"You must find out, Mr. de Gex," she said in a low voice. "I took it for granted that my husband was alive. It's horrible to think that he may be dead. It alters everything, somehow. Until I know, I shall be in a state of awful suspense. You'll make inquiries at once, won't you?"

"Did you love your husband, Madame Brandt?" I asked.

She looked at the fire for some time without replying. She stood with one foot on the fender.

"I thought I did when I married him," she said at last. "I thought I did when he left me."

"And now?"

She turned her golden eyes full on me. It is a disconcerting trick of hers at any time, because her eyes are at once wistful and compelling; but on this occasion it was startling. They held mine for some seconds, and I caught in them a glimpse of the hieroglyphic of the woman's soul. Then she turned her head slowly and looked again into the fire.

"Now?" she echoed. "Many things have happened between then and now. If he is alive and I go to him, I'll try to think again that I love him. It will be the only way. It will save me from playing hell with my life."

"I am glad you see your relations to Dale in that light," said I.

"I wasn't thinking of Dale," she said calmly.

"Of what, then, if I may ask without impertinence?"

She broke into a laugh which ended in a sigh, and then swung her splendid frame away from the fireplace and walked backwards and forwards, her figure swaying and her arms flung about in unrestrained gestures.

"You are quite right," she said, with an odd note of hardness in her voice. "You're quite right in what you said the other day—that it was high time I went back to my husband. I pray God he is not dead. I have a feeling that he isn't. He can't be. I count on you to find him and ask him to meet me. It would be better than writing. I don't know what to say when I have a pen in my hand. You must find him and speak to him and send me a wire and I'll come straight away to any part of the earth. Or would you like me to come with you and help you find him? But no; that's idiotic. Forget that I have said it. I'm a fool. But he must be found. He must, he must!"

She paused in her swinging about the room for which I was sorry, as her panther-in-a-cage movements were exceedingly beautiful, and she gazed at me with a tragic air, wringing her hands. I was puzzled to find an adequate reason for this sudden emotional outburst. Hitherto she had accepted the prospect of a resumption of married life with a fatalistic calm. Now when the man is either dead or has vanished into space, she pins all her hopes of happiness on finding him. And why had her salvation from destruction nothing to do with Dale? There is obviously another range of emotions at work beneath it all; but what their nature is baffles me. Although I contemplate with equanimity my little corner in the Garden of Proserpine, and with indifference this common lodging-house of earth, and although I view mundane affairs with the same fine, calm, philosophic, satirical eye as if I were already a disembodied spirit, yet I do not like to be baffled. It makes me angry. But during this interview with Lola Brandt I had not time to be angry. I am angry now. In fact I am in a condition bordering on that of a mad dog. If Rogers came and disturbed me now, as I am writing, I would bite him. But I will set calmly down the story of this appalling afternoon.

Lola stood before me wringing her hands.

"What are you going to do?"

"I can get an introduction to the *Chef de bureau* of the information department of the *Ministere de la Guerre* in Paris," I replied after a moment's reflection. "He will be able to tell me whether Captain Vauvenarde is alive or dead."

"He is alive. He must be."

"Very well. But I doubt whether Captain Vauvenarde keeps the office informed of his movements."

"But you'll go in search of him, won't you?"

"The earth is rather a large place," I objected. "He may be in Dieppe, or he may be on top of Mount Popocatapetl."

"I'm sure you'll find him," she said encouragingly.

"You'll own," said I, "that there's something humourous in the idea of my wandering all over the surface of the planet in search of a lost captain of Chasseurs. It is true that we might employ a private detective."

"Yes!" she cried eagerly. "Why not? Then you could stay here—and I could go on seeing you till the news came. Let us do that."

The swiftness of her change of mood surprised me.

"What is the particular object of your going on seeing me?" I asked, with a smile.

She turned away and shrugged her shoulders and took up her pensive attitude by the fire.

"I have no other friend," she said.

"There's Dale."

"He's not the same."

"There's Sir Joshua Oldfield."

She shrugged her shoulders.

I lit a cigarette and sat down. There was a long silence. In some unaccountable way she had me under her spell again. I felt a perfectly insane dismay at the prospect of ending this queer intimacy, and I viewed her intrigue with Dale with profound distaste. Lola had become a habit. The chair I was sitting in was *my* chair. Adolphus was *my* dog. I hated the idea of Dale making him stand up and do sentry with the fire shovel, while Lola sprawled gracefully on the hearthrug. On the other hand the thought of remaining in London and sharing with my young friend the privilege of her society was intolerable.

I smoked, and, watching her bosom rise and fall as she leaned forward with one arm on the mantelpiece, argued it out with myself, and came to the paradoxical conclusion that I could pack her off without a pang to Kamtchatka and the embraces of her unknown husband, but could not hand her over to Dale without feelings of the deepest repugnance. A pretty position to find myself in. I threw away my cigarette impatiently.

Presently she said, not stirring from her pose:

"I shall miss you terribly if you go. A man like you doesn't come into the life of a common woman like me without"—she hesitated for a word—"without making some impression. I can't bear to lose you."

"I shall be very sorry to give up our pleasant comradeship," said I, "but even if I stay and send the private inquiry agent instead of going myself, I shan't be able to go on seeing you in this way."

"Why not?"

"It would be scarcely dignified."

"On account of Dale?"

"Precisely."

There was another pause, during which I lit another cigarette. When I looked up I saw great tears rolling down her cheeks. A weeping woman always makes me nervous. You never know what she is going to do next. Safety lies in checking the tears—in administering a tonic. Still, her wish to retain me was very touching. I rose and stood before her by the mantelpiece.

"You can't have your pudding and eat it too," said I.

"What do you mean?"

"You can't have Captain Vauvenarde for your husband, Dale for your *cavaliere servente*, and myself for your guide, philosopher and friend all at the same time."

"Which would you advise me to give up?"

"That's obvious. Give up Dale."

She uttered a sound midway between a sob and a laugh, and said, as it seemed, ironically:

"Would you take his place?"

Somewhat ironically, too, I replied, "A crock, my dear lady, with one foot in the grave has no business to put the other into the *Pays du Tendre*."

But all the same I had an absurd desire to take her at her word, not for the sake of constituting myself her *amant en titre*, but so as to dispossess the poor boy who was clamouring wildly for her among his mother's snuffy colleagues in Berlin.

"That's another reason why I shrink from your going in search of my husband," she said, dabbing her eyes. "Your ill-health."

"I shall have to go abroad out of this dreadful climate in any case. Doctor's orders. And I might just as well travel about with an object in view as idle in Monte Carlo or Egypt."

"But you might die!" she cried; and her tone touched my heart.

"I've got to," I said, as gently as I could; and the moment the words passed my lips I regretted them.

She turned a terrified look on me and seized me by the arms.

"Is it as bad as that? Why haven't you told me?"

I lifted my arms to her shoulders and shook my head and smiled into her eyes. They seemed true, honest eyes, with a world of pain behind them. If I had not regarded myself as the gentleman in the Greek Tragedy walking straight to my certain doom, and therefore holding myself aloof from such vain things, I should have yielded to the temptation and kissed her there and then. And then goodness knows what would have happened.

As it was it was bad enough. For, as we stood holding on to each other's shoulders in a ridiculous and compromising attitude, the door opened and Dale Kynnersley burst, unannounced, into the room. He paused on the threshold and gaped at us, open-mouthed.

CHAPTER IX

We sprang apart, for all the world like a guilty pair surprised. Luckily the room was in its normal dim state of illumination, so that to one suddenly entering, the expression on our faces was not clearly visible; on the other hand, the subdued light gave a romantic setting to the abominable situation.

Lola saved it, however. She rushed to Dale.

"Do you know what Mr. de Gex was just telling me? His illness—it is worse than any one thought. It's incurable. He can't live long; he must die soon. It's dreadful—dreadful! Did you know it?"

Dale looked from her to me, and after a slight pause, came forward.

"Is this true, Simon?"

A plague on the woman for catching me in the trap! Before Dale came in I was on the point of putting an airy construction on my indiscreet speech. I had no desire to discuss my longevity with any one. I want to keep my miserable secret to myself. It was exasperating to have to entrust it even to Dale. And yet, if I repudiated her implied explanation of our apparent embrace it would have put her hopelessly in the wrong. I had to support her.

"It's what the doctors say," I replied, "but whether it's true or not is another matter."

Again he looked queerly from me to Lola and from Lola back to me. His first impression of our attitude had been a shock from which he found it difficult to recover. I smiled, and, although perfectly innocent, felt a villain.

"Madame Brandt is good enough to be soft-hearted and to take a tragic view of a most commonplace contingency."

"But it isn't commonplace. By God, it's horrible!" cried the boy, the arrested love for me suddenly gushing into his heart. "I had no idea of it. In Heaven's name, Simon, why didn't you tell me? My dear old Simon."

Tears rushed into his eyes and he gripped my hand until I winced. I put my other hand on his shoulder and laughed with a contorted visage.

"My good Dale, the moribund are fragile."

"Oh, Lord, man, how can you make a jest of it?"

"Would you have me drive about in a hearse, instead of a cab, by way of preparation?"

"But what have the doctors told you?" asked Lola.

"My two dear people!" I cried, "for goodness' sake don't fall over me in this way. I'm not going to die to-morrow unless my cook poisons me or I'm struck by lightning. I'm going to live for a deuce of a time yet. A couple of weeks at least. And you'll very much oblige me by not whispering a word abroad about what you've heard this afternoon. It would cause me infinite annoyance. And meanwhile I suggest to you, Dale, as the lawyers say, that you have been impolite enough not to say how-do-you-do to your hostess."

He turned to her rather sheepishly, and apologised. My news had bowled him over, he declared. He shook hands with her, laughed and walked Adolphus about on his hind legs.

"But where have you dropped from?" she asked.

"Berlin. I came straight through. Didn't you get my wire?"

"No."

"I sent one."

"I never got it."

He swung his arms about in a fine rage.

"If ever I get hold of that son of Satan I'll murder him. He was covered up to his beastly eyebrows in silver lace and swords and whistles and medals and things. He walked up and down the railway station as if he owned the German navy and ran trains as a genteel hobby. I gave him ten marks to send the telegram. The miserable beast has sneaked the lot. I'll get at the railway company through the Embassy and have the brute sacked and put in prison. Did you ever hear of such a skunk?"

"He must have thought you a very simple and charming young Englishman," said I.

"You've done the same thing yourself!" he retorted indignantly.

"Pardon me," said I. "If I do send a telegram in that loose way, I choose a humble and honest-looking porter and give him the exact fee for the telegram and a winning smile."

"Rot!" said Dale, and turning to Lola—"He has demoralised the whole railway system of Europe with his tips. I've seen him give a franc to the black greasy devil that bangs at the carriage wheels with a bit of iron. He would give anybody anything."

He had recovered his boyish pride in my ridiculous idiosyncracies, and was in process of illustrating again to Lola what a "splendid chap" I was.

Poor lad! If he only knew what a treacherous, traitorous, Machiavelli of a hero he had got. For the moment I suffered from a nasty crick in the conscience.

"Wouldn't he, Adolphus, you celestial old blackguard?" he laughed. Then suddenly: "My hat! You two are fond of darkness! It gives me the creeps. Do you mind, Lola, if I turn on the light?"

He marched in his young way across to the switches and set the room in the blaze he loved. My crick of the conscience was followed by an impulse of resentment. He took it for granted that his will was law in the house. He swaggered around the room with a proprietary air. He threw in the casual "Lola" as if he owned her. Dale is the most delightful specimen of the modern youth of my acquaintance. But even Dale, with all his frank charm of manner, has the modern youth's offhand way with women. I often wonder how women abide it. But they do, more shame to them, and suffer more than they realise by their indulgence. When next I meet Maisie Ellerton I will read her a wholesome lecture, for her soul's good, on the proper treatment a self-respecting female should apply to the modern young man.

Dale filled the room with his clear young laugh, and turned on every light in the place. Lola and I exchanged glances—she had adopted her usual lazy pantherine attitude in the armchair—and her glance was not that of a happy woman to whom a longed-for lover had unexpectedly come. Its real significance I could not divine, but it was more wistful than merely that of a fellow-conspirator.

"By George!" cried Dale, pulling up a chair by Lola's side, and stretching out his long, well-trousered legs in front of the fire. "It's good to come back to civilisation and a Christian language and a fireside—and other things," he added, squeezing Lola's hand. "If only it had not been for this horrible news about you, dear old man——"

"Oh, do forget it and give me a little peace!" I cried. "Why have you come back all of a sudden?"

"The Wymington people wired for me. It seems the committee are divided between me and Sir Gerald Macnaughton."

"He has strong claims," said I. "He has been Mayor of the place and got knighted by mistake. He also gives large dinners and wears a beautiful diamond pin."

"I believe he goes to bed in it. Oh, he's an awful ass! It was he who said at a public function 'The Mayor of Wymington must be like Caesar's wife—all things to all men!' Oh, he's a colossal ass! And his conceit! My word!"

"You needn't expatiate on it," said I. "I who speak have suffered much at the hands of Sir Gerald Macnaughton."

"If he did get into Parliament he'd expect an armchair to be put for him next to the Speaker. Really, Lola, you never saw such a chap. If there was any one else up against me I wouldn't mind. Anyway, I'm running down to Wymington to-morrow to interview the committee. And if they choose me, then it'll be a case of 'Lord don't help me and don't help the b'ar, and you'll see the derndest best b'ar fight that ever was.' I'll make things hum in Wymington!"

He went on eagerly to explain how he would make things hum. For the moment he had forgotten his enchantress who, understanding nothing of platforms and planks and electioneering machinery, smiled with pensive politeness at the fire. Here was the Dale that I knew and loved, boyish, impetuous, slangy, enthusiastic. His dark eyes flashed, and he threw back his head and laughed, as he enunciated his brilliant ideas for capturing the constituency.

"When I was working for you, I made love to half the women in the place. You never knew that, you dear old stick. Now I'm going in on my own account I'll make love to the whole crowd. You won't mind, Lola, will you? There's safety in numbers. And when I have made love to them one by one I'll get 'em all together and make love to the conglomerate mass! And then I'll rake up all the prettiest women in London and get 'em down there to humbug the men—"

"Lady Kynnersley will doubtless be there," said I; "and I don't quite see her—"

He broke in with a laugh: "Oh! the mater! I'll fix up her job all right. She'll just love it, won't she? And then I know a lot of silly asses with motor-cars who'll come down. They can't talk for cob-nuts, and think the Local Option has something to do with vivisection, and have a vague idea that champagne will be cheaper if we get Tariff Reform—but they'll make a devil of a noise at meetings and tote people round the country in their cars holding banners with 'Vote for Kynnersley' on them. That's a sound idea, isn't it?"

I gravely commended the statesmanlike sagacity of his plan of campaign, and promised to write as soon as I got home to one or two members of the committee whom I suspected of pro-Macnaughton leanings.

"I do hope they'll adopt you!" I cried fervently.

"So do I," murmured Lola in her low notes.

"If they don't," said Dale, "I'll ask Raggles to give me an unpaid billet somewhere. But," he added, with a sigh, "that will be an awful rotten game in comparison."

"I'm afraid you won't make Raggles hum," said I.

He laughed, rose and straddled across the hearthrug, his back to the fire.

"He'd throw me out if I tried, wouldn't he? But if they do adopt me—I swear I'll make you proud of me, Simon. I'll stick my soul into it. It's the least I can do in this horrid cuckoo sort of proceeding, and I feel I shall be fighting for you as well as for myself. My dear old chap, you know what I mean, don't you?"

I knew, and was touched. I wished him God-speed with all my heart. He was a clean, honest, generous gentleman, and I admired, loved and respected him as he stood there full of his youth and hope. I suddenly felt quite old and withered at the root of my being, like some decrepit king who hands his crown to the young prince. I rose to take my leave (for what advantage was there in staying?) and felt that I was abandoning to Dale other things beside my crown.

Lola's strong, boneless hand closed round mine in a more enveloping grip than ever. She looked at me appealingly.

"Shall I see you again before you go?"

"Before you go?" cried Dale. "Where are you off to?"

"Somewhere south, out of the fogs."

"When?"

"At once," said I.

He turned to our hostess. "We can't let him go like that. I wonder if you could fix up a little dinner here, Lola, for the three of us. It would be ripping, so cosy, you know."

He glowed with the preposterous inspiration. Lola began politely:

"Of course, if Mr. de Gex——"

"It would be delightful," said I, "but I'm starting at once—to-morrow or the day after. We will have the dinner when I come back and you are a full-blown Member of Parliament."

I made my escape and fled to my own cheerful library. It is oak-panelled and furnished with old oak, and the mezzo-tints on the walls are mellow. Of the latter, I have a good collection, among them a Prince Rupert of which I am proud. I threw myself, a tired man, into an armchair by the fire, and rang the bell for a brandy and soda. Oh, the comfort of the rooms, the comfort of Rogers, the comfort of the familiar backs of the books in the shelves! I felt loth to leave it all and go vagabonding about the cold world on my lunatic adventure. For the first time in my life I cursed Marcus Aurelius. I shook my fist at him as he stood on the shelf within easy reach of my hand. It was he who had put into my head this confounded notion of achieving eumoiriety. Am I dealing to myself, I asked, a happy lot and portion? Certainly not, I replied, and when Rogers brought me my brandy and soda I drank it off desperately. After that I grew better, and drew up a merry little Commination Service.

A plague on the little pain inside.

A plague on Lady Kynnersley for weeping me into my rash undertaking.

A plague on Professor Anastasius Papadopoulos for aiding and abetting Lady Kynnersley.

A plague on Captain Vauvenarde for running away from his wife; for giving up the army; for not letting me know whether he is alive or dead; for being, I'll warrant him, in the most uncomfortable and ungetatable spot on the globe.

A plague on Dale for becoming infatuated with Lola Brandt. A plague on him for beguiling me to her acquaintance; for bursting into the room at that unfortunate moment; for his generous, unsuspecting love for me; for his youth and hope and charm; for asking me to dine with Lola and himself in ripping cosiness.

A plague on myself—just to show that I am broad-minded.

And lastly, a plague, a special plague, a veritable murrain on Lola Brandt for complicating the splendid singleness of my purpose. I don't know what to think of myself. I have become a common conundrum—which provides the lowest form of intellectual amusement. It is all her fault.

Listen. I set out to free a young man of brilliant promise, at his mother's earnest entreaty, from an entanglement with an impossible lady, and to bring him to the feet of the most charming girl in the world who is dying of love for him. Could intentions be simpler or more honourable or more praiseworthy?

I find myself, after two or three weeks, the lady's warm personal friend, to a certain extent her champion bound by a quixotic oath to restore her husband to her arms, and regarding my poor Dale with a feeling which is neither more nor less than green-eyed jealousy. I am praying heaven to grant his adoption by the Wymington committee, not because it will be the first step of the ladder of his career, but because the work and excitement of a Parliamentary election will prohibit overmuch lounging in *my* chair in Lola Brandt's drawing-room.

Is there any drug I wonder which can restore a eumoirous tone to the system?

Of course, Dale came round to my chambers in the evening and talked about Lola and himself and me until I sent him home to bed. He kept on repeating at intervals that I was glorious. I grew tired at last of the eulogy, and, adopting his vernacular, declared that I should be jolly glad to get out of this rubbishy world. He protested. There was never such a world. It was gorgeous. What was wrong with it, anyway? As I could not show him the Commination Service, I picked imaginary flaws in the universe. I complained of its amateurishness of design. But Dale, who loves fact, was not drawn into a theological disputation.

"Do you know, I had a deuce of a shock when I came into Lola's this afternoon?" he cried irrelevantly, with a loud laugh. "I thought—it was a damnable and idiotic thing to come into my head—but I couldn't help thinking you had cut me out! I wanted to tell you. You must forgive me for being such an ass. And I want to thank you for being so good to her while I was away. She has been telling me. You like her, don't you? I knew you would. No one can help it. Besides being other things, she's is such a good sort, isn't she?"

I admitted her many excellencies, while he walked about the room.

"By Jove!" he cried, coming to a halt. "I've got a grand idea. My little plan has succeeded so well with you that I've a good mind to try it on my mother."

"What on earth do you mean?" I asked.

"Why shouldn't I take the bull by the horns and bring my mother and Lola together?"

I gasped. "My dear boy," said I. "Do you want to kill me outright? I can't stand such shocks to the imagination."

"But it would be grand!" he exclaimed, delighted. "Why shouldn't mother take a fancy to Lola? You can imagine her roping her in for the committee!"

I refused to imagine it for one instant, and I had the greatest difficulty in the world to persuade him to renounce his maniacal project. I am going to permit no further complications.

I have been busy for the past day or two setting my house in order. I start to-morrow for Paris. All my little affairs are comfortably settled, and I can set out on my little trip to Avernus via Paris and the habitat of Captain Vauvenarde with a quiet conscience. I have allayed the anxiety of my sisters, whispered mysterious encouragement to Maisie Ellerton, held out hopes of her son's emancipation to Lady Kynnersley, played fairy godmother to various poor and deserving persons, and brought myself into an enviable condition of glowing philanthropy.

To my great relief the Wymington committee have adopted Dale as their candidate at the by-election. He can scarcely contain himself for joy. He is like a child who has been told that he shall be taken to the seaside. I believe he lies awake all night thinking how he will make things hum.

The other side have chosen Wilberforce, who unsuccessfully contested the Ferney division of Wiltshire at the last general election. He is old and ugly. Dale is young and beautiful. I think Dale will get in.

I have said good-bye to Lola. The astonishing woman burst into tears and kissed my hands and said something about my being the arbiter of her destiny—a Gallic phrase which she must have picked up from Captain Vauvenarde. Then she buried her face in the bristling neck of Adolphus, the Chow dog, and declared him to be her last remaining consolation. Even Anastasius Papadopoulos had ceased to visit her. I uttered words of comfort.

"I have left you Dale at any rate."

She smiled enigmatically through her tears.

"I'm not ungrateful. I don't despise the crumbs."

Which remark, now that I come to think of it, was not flattering to my young friend.

But what is the use of thinking of it? My fire is burning low. It is time I ended this portion of my "Rule and Example of Eumoiriety," which, I fear, has not followed the philosophic line I originally intended.

The die is cast. My things are packed. Rogers, who likes his British beef and comforts, is resigned to the prospect of Continental travel, and has gone to bed hours ago. There is no more soda water in the siphon. I must go to bed.

Paris to-morrow.

CHAPTER X

"Ay!" says Touchstone; "now am I in Arden; the more fool I; when I was at home I was in a better place."

Now am I in Algiers; the more fool I; et cetera, et cetera.

It is true that from my bedroom window in the Albany I cannot see the moon silvering the Mediterranean, or hear the soft swish of pepper-trees; it is true that oranges and eucalyptus do not flourish in the Albany Court-yard as they do in this hotel garden at Mustapha Superieur; it is true that the blue African sky and sunshine are more agreeable than Piccadilly fogs; but, after all, his own kennel is best for a dying dog, and his own familiar surroundings best for his declining hours. Again, Touchstone had not the faintest idea what he was going to do in the Forest of Arden, and I was equally ignorant of what would befall when I landed at Algiers. He was bound on a fool adventure, and so was I. He preferred the easy way of home, and so do I. I have always loved Touchstone, but I have never thoroughly understood him till now.

It rained persistently in Paris. It rained as I drove from the Gare du Nord to my hotel. It rained all night. It rained all the day I spent there and it rained as I drove from my hotel to the Gare de Lyon. A cheery newspaper informed me that there were torrential rains at Marseilles. I mentioned this to Rogers, who tried to console me by reminding me that we were only staying at Marseilles for a few hours.

"That has nothing to do with it," said I. "At Marseilles I always eat bouillabaisse on the quay. Fancy eating bouillabaisse in the pouring rain!"

As usual, Rogers could not execute the imaginative exercise I prescribed; so he strapped my hold-all with an extra jerk.

Now, when homespun London is wet and muddy, no one minds very much. But when silken Paris lies bedraggled with rain and mud, she is the forlornest thing under the sky. She is a hollow-eyed pale city, the rouge is washed from her cheeks, her hair hangs dank and dishevelled, in her aspect is desolation, and moaning is in her voice. I have a Sultanesque feeling with regard to Paris. So long as she is amusing and gay I love her. I adore her mirth, her chatter, her charming ways. But when she has the toothache and snivels, she bores me to death. I lose all interest in her. I want to clap my hands for my slaves, in order to bid them bring me in something less dismal in the way of fair cities.

I drove to the Rue Saint-Dominique and handed in my card and letter of introduction at the *Ministere de la Guerre*. I was received by the official in charge of the *Bureau des Renseignements* with bland politeness tempered with suspicion that I might be taking a mental photograph of the office furniture in order to betray its secret to a foreign government. After many comings and goings of orderlies and underlings, he told me very little in complicated and reluctant language. Captain Vauvenarde had resigned his commission in the Chasseurs d'Afrique two years ago. At the present moment the Bureau had no information to give as to his domicile.

"Have you no suggestion, Monsieur, to offer?" I asked, "whereby I may obtain this essential information concerning Captain Vauvenarde?"

"His old comrades in the regiment might know, Monsieur."

"And the regiment?"

He opened the *Annuaire Officiel de l'Armee Francaise*, just as I might have done myself, and said:

"There are six regiments. One is at Blidah, another at Tlemcen, another at Constantine, another at Tunis, another at Algiers, and another at Mascara."

"To which regiment, then, did Captain Vauvenarde belong?" I inquired.

He referred to one of the dossiers that the orderlies had brought him.

"The 3rd, Monsieur."

"I should get information, then, from Tlemcen?"

"Evidently, Monsieur."

I thanked him and withdrew, to his obvious relief. Seekers after knowledge are unpopular even in organisations so far removed from the Circumlocution Office as the French *Ministere de la Guerre*. However, he had put me on the trail of my man.

During my homeward drive through the rain I reflected. I might, of course, write to the Lieutenant-Colonel of the 3rd Regiment at Tlemcen, and wait for his reply. But even if he answered by return of post, I should have to remain in Paris for nearly a week.

"That," said I, wiping from my face half a teacupful of liquid mud which had squirted in through the cab window—"that I'll never do. I'll proceed at once to Algiers. If I can get no news of him there, I'll go to Tlemcen myself. In all probability I shall learn that he is residing here in Paris, a stone's throw from the Madeleine."

So I started for Algiers. The next morning, before the sailing of the *Marechal Bugeaud*, one of the quaint churns styled a steamship by the vanity of the French Company which undertakes to convey respectable folk across the Mediterranean, I ate my bouillabaisse below an awning on the sunny quay at Marseilles. The torrential rains had ceased. I advised Rogers to take equivalent sustenance, as no lunch is provided on day of sailing by the Compagnie Generale Transatlantique. I caught sight of him in a dark corner of the restaurant—he is too British to eat in the open air on the terrace, or perhaps too modest to have his meal in my presence—struggling grimly with a beefsteak, and, as he is a teetotaller, with an unimaginable, horrific liquid which he poured out from a vessel vaguely resembling a teapot.

My meal over, and having nearly an hour to spare, I paid my bill, rose and turned the corner of the quay into the Cannebiere, thinking to have my coffee at one of the cafes in that thoroughfare of which the natives say that, if Paris had a Cannebiere, it would be a little Marseilles. I suppose for the Marseillais there is a magic in the sonorous name; for, after all, it is but a commonplace street of shops running from the quays into the heart of the town. It is also deformed by tramcars. I strolled leisurely up, thinking of the many swans that were geese, and Paradises that were building-plots, and heroes that were dummies, and solidities that were shadows, in short, enjoying a gentle post-prandial mood, when my eyes suddenly fell on a scene which brought me down from such realities to the realm of the fantastic. There, a few yards in front of me, at the outer edge of the terrace of a cafe, clad in his eternal silk hat, frock coat, and yellow gloves, sat Professor Anastasius Papadopoulos in earnest conversation with a seedy stranger of repellent mien. The latter was clean-shaven and had a broken nose, and wore a little round, soft felt hat. The dwarf was facing me. As he caught sight of me a smile of welcome overspread his Napoleonic features. He rose, awaited my approach, and, bareheaded, made his usual sweeping bow, which he concluded by resting his silk hat on the pit of his stomach. I lifted my hat politely and would have passed on, but he stood in my path. I extended my hand. He took it after the manner of a provincial mayor receiving royalty.

"*Couvrez-vous, Monsieur, je vous en prie,*" said I.

He covered his head. "Monsieur," said he, "I beseech you to be seated, and do me the honour of joining me in the coffee and excellent cognac of this establishment."

"Willingly," said I, mindful of Lola's tale of the long knife which he carried concealed about his person.

"Permit me to present my friend Monsieur Achille Saupiquet—Monsieur de Gex, a great English statesman and a friend of that *gnadigsten Engel*, Madame Lola Brandt."

Monsieur Saupiquet and I saluted each other formally. I took a seat. Professor Anastasius Papadopoulos moved a bundle of papers tied up with pink ribbon from in front of me, and ordered coffee and cognac.

"Monsieur Saupiquet also knows Madame Brandt," he explained.

"*Bien sur*," said Monsieur Saupiquet. "She owes me fifteen sous."

Papadopoulos turned on his sharply. "Will you be silent!"

The other grumbled beneath his breath.

"I hope Madame is well," said Papadopoulos.

I said that she appeared so, when last I had the pleasure of seeing her. The dwarf turned to his friend.

"Monsieur has also done my cats the honour of attending a rehearsal. He has seen Hephaestus, and his tears have dropped in sympathy over the irreparable loss of my beautiful Santa Bianca."

"I hope the talented survivors," said I, "are enjoying their usual health."

"My daily bulletin from my pupil and assistant, Quast, contains excellent reports. *Prosit*, Signore."

It was only when I found myself at the table with the dwarf and his broken-nosed friend that I collected my wits sufficiently to realise the probable reason of his presence in Marseilles. The grotesque little creature had actually kept his ridiculous word. He, too, had come south in search of the lost Captain Vauvenarde. We were companions in the Fool Adventure. There was something mediaeval in the combination; something legendary. Put back the clock a few centuries and there we were, the Knight and the Dwarf, riding together on our quest, while the Lady for whose sake we were making idiots of ourselves was twiddling her fair thumbs in her tower far beyond the seas.

Professor Anastasius Papadopoulos broke upon this pleasing fancy by remarking again that Monsieur Saupiquet was a friend of Madame Brandt.

"He was with her at the time of her great bereavement."

"Bereavement?" I asked forgetfully.

"Her horse Sultan."

He whispered the words with solemn reverence. I must confess to being tired of the horse Sultan and disinclined to treat his loss seriously.

"Monsieur Saupiquet," said I, "doubtless offered her every consolation."

"He used to travel with her and look after Sultan's well-being. He was her——"

"Her Master of the Horse," I suggested.

"Precisely. You have the power of using the right word, Monsieur de Gex. It is a great gift. My good friend Saupiquet is attached to a circus at present stationed in Toulon. He came over, at my request, to see me—on affairs of the deepest importance"—he waved the bundle of papers—"the very deepest importance. *Nicht wahr*, Saupiquet?"

"*Bien sur*," murmured Saupiquet, who evidently did not count loquacity among his vices.

I wondered whether these important affairs concerned the whereabouts of Captain Vauvenarde; but the dwarf's air of mystery forbade my asking for his confidence. Besides, what should a groom in a circus know of retired Captains of Chasseurs? I said:

"You're a very busy man, Monsieur le Professeur."

He tapped his domelike forehead. "I am never idle. I carry on here gigantic combinations. I should have been a lawyer. I can spread nets that no one sees, and then—pst! I draw the rope and the victim is in the toils of Anastasius Papadopoulos. *Hast du nicht das bemerkt*, Saupiquet?"

"*Bien sur*," said Saupiquet again. He seemed perfectly conversant with the dwarf's polyglot jargon.

"To the temperament of the artist," continued the modest Papadopoulos, "I join the intellect of the man of affairs and the heart of a young poet. I am always young; yet as you see me here I am thirty-seven years of age."

He jumped from his chair and struck an attitude of the Apollo Belvedere.

"I should never have thought that you were of the same age as a bettered person like myself," said I.

"The secret of youth," he rejoined, sitting down again, "is enthusiasm, the worship of a woman, and intimate association with cats."

Monsieur Saupiquet received this proposition without a gleam of interest manifesting itself in his dull blue eyes. His broken nose gave his face a singularly unintelligent expression. He poured out another glass of cognac from the graduated carafe in front of him and sipped it slowly. Then he gazed at me dully, almost for the first time, and said:

"Madame Brandt owes me fifteen sous."

"And I say that she doesn't!" cried the dwarf fiercely. "I send for him to discuss matters of the deepest gravity, and he comes talking about his fifteen sous. I can't get anything out of him, but his fifteen sous. And the *carissima signora* doesn't owe it to him. She can't owe it to him. *Voyons*, Saupiquet, if you don't renounce your miserable pretensions you will drive me mad, you will make me burst into tears, you will make me throw you out into the street, and hold you down until you are run over by a tramcar. You will—you will"—he shook his fist passionately as he sought for a climactic menace—"you will make me spit in your eye."

He dashed his fist down on the marble table so that the glasses jingled. Saupiquet finished his cognac undisturbed.

"I say that Madame Brandt owes me fifteen sous, and until that is paid, I do no business."

The little man grew white with exasperation, and his upper lip lifted like an angry cat's, showing his teeth. I shrank from meeting Saupiquet's eye. Hurriedly, I drew a providential handful of coppers from my pocket.

"Stop, Herr Professor," said I, eager to prevent the shedding of tears, blood, or saliva, "I have just remembered. Madame did mention to me an unaquitted debt in the South, and begged me to settle it for her. I am delighted to have the opportunity. Will you permit me to act as Madam's banker?"

The dwarf at once grew suave and courteous.

"The word of *carissima signora* is the word of God," said he.

I solemnly counted out the fifteen halfpence on the table and pushed them over to Saupiquet, who swept them up and put them in his pocket.

"Now we can talk," said he.

"Make him give you a receipt!" cried Papadopoulos excitedly. "I know him! He is capable of any treachery where money is concerned. He is capable of re-demanding the sum from Madame Brandt. He is an ingrate. And she, Monsieur le Membre du Parlement Anglais, has overwhelmed him with benefits. Do you know what she did? She gave him the carcass of her beloved Sultan to dispose of. And he sold it, Monsieur, and he got drunk on the money."

The mingled emotions of sorrow at the demise of Sultan, the royal generosity of Madame Brandt, and the turpitude of his friend Saupiquet, brought tears to the little man's eyes. Monsieur Saupiquet shrugged his shoulders unconcernedly.

"A poor man has to get drunk when he can. It is only the rich who can get drunk when they like."

I looked at my watch and rose in a hurry.

"I'm afraid I must take an unceremonious leave of you, Monsieur le Professeur."

"You must wait for the receipt," cried the dwarf.

"Will you do me the honour of holding it for me until we meet again? Hi!" The interpellation was addressed to a cabman a few yards away. "Your conversation has made me neglect the flight of time. I shall only just catch my boat."

"Your boat?"

"I am going to Algiers."

"Where will you be staying, Monsieur? I ask in no spirit of vulgar curiosity."

I raised a protesting hand, and with a smile named my hotel.

"I arrived here from Algiers yesterday afternoon," he said, "and I proceed there again to-morrow."

"I regret," said I, "that you are not coming to-day, so that I could have the pleasure of your company on the voyage."

My polite formula seemed to delight Professor Anastasius Papadopoulos enormously. He made a series of the most complicated bows, to the joy of the waiters and the passers-by. I shook hands with him and with the stolid Monsieur Saupiquet, and waving my hat more like an excited Montenegrin than the most respectable of British valetudinarians, I drove off to the Quai de la Joliette, where I found an anxious but dogged Rogers, in the midst of a vociferating crowd, literally holding the bridge that gave access to the *Marechal Bugeaud.*

"Thank Heaven, you've come, sir! You almost missed it. I couldn't have held out another minute."

I, too, was thankful. If I had missed the boat I should have had to wait till the next day and crossed in the embarrassing and unrestful company of Professor Anastasius Papadopoulos. It is not that I dislike the little man, or have the Briton's nervous shrinking from being seen in eccentric society; but I wish to eliminate mediaevalism as far as possible from my quest. In conjunction with this crazy-headed little trainer of cats it would become too preposterous even for my light sardonic humour. I resolved to dismiss him from my mind altogether.

Yet, in spite of my determination, and in spite of one of Monsieur Lenotre's fascinating monographs on the French Revolution, on which I had counted to beguile the tedium of the journey, I could not get Anastasius Papadopoulos out of my head. He stayed with me the whole of a storm-tossed night, and all the next morning. He has haunted my brain ever since. I see him tossing his arms about in fury, while the broken-nosed Saupiquet makes his monotonous claim for the payment of sevenpence halfpenny; I hear him speak in broken whispers of the disastrous quadruped on whose skin and hoofs Saupiquet got drunk. I see him strutting about and boasting of his intellect. I see him taking leave of Lola Brandt, and trotting magnificently out of the room bent on finding Captain Vauvenarde. He haunts my slumbers. I hope to goodness he will not take to haunting this delectable hotel.

I wonder, after all, whether there is any method in his madness—for mad he is, as mad as can be. Why does he come backwards and forwards between Algiers and Marseilles? What has Saupiquet to do with his quest? What revelation was he about to make on the payment of his fifteen sous? It is all so grotesque, so out of relation with ordinary life. I feel inclined to go up to the retired Colonels and elderly maiden ladies, who seem to form the majority of my fellow-guests, and pinch them and ask them whether they are real, or, like Papadopoulos and Saupiquet, the gentler creatures of a nightmare.

Well, I have written to the Lieutenant-Colonel of the 3rd Regiment of Chasseurs at Tlemcen, which is away down by the Morocco frontier. I have also written to Lola Brandt. I seem to miss her as much as any of the friends I have left behind me in England. I cannot help the absurd fancy that her rich vitality helps me along. I have not been feeling quite so robust as I did when I saw her daily. And twinges are coming more frequently. I don't think that rolling about in the Mediterranean on board the *Marechal Bugeaud* is good for little pains inside.

CHAPTER XI

When I began this autobiographical sketch of the last few weeks of my existence, I had conceived, as I have already said, the notion of making it chiefly a guide to conduct for my young disciple, Dale Kynnersley. Not only was it to explain to him clearly the motives which led to my taking any particular line of action with regard to his affairs, and so enable me to escape whatever blame he might, through misunderstanding, be disposed to cast on me, but also to elevate his mind, stimulate his ambitions, and improve his morals. It was to be a Manual of Eumoiriety. It was to be sweetened with philosophic reflections and adorned with allusions to the lives of the great masters of their destiny who have passed away. It was to have been a pretty little work after the manner of Montaigne, with the exception that it ran of its own accord into narrative form. But I am afraid Lola Brandt has interposed herself between me and my design. She had brought me down from the serene philosophic plane where I could think and observe human happenings and analyse them and present them in their true aspect to my young friend. She has set me down in the thick of events—and not events such as the smiling philosopher is in the habit of dealing with, but lunatic, fantastic occurrences with which no system of philosophy invented by man is capable of grappling. I can just keep my head, that is all, and note down what happens more or less day by day, so that when the doings of dwarfs and captains, and horse-tamers and youthful Members of Parliament concern me no more, Dale Kynnersley can have a bald but veracious statement of fact. And as I have before mentioned, he loves facts, just as a bear loves honey.

I passed a quiet day or two in my hotel garden, among the sweet-peas, and the roses, and the geraniums. There were little shady summer-houses where one could sit and dream, and watch the blue sky and the palms and the feathery pepper trees drooping with their coral berries, and the golden orange-trees and the wisteria and the great gorgeous splash of purple bougainvillea above the Moorish arches of the hotel. There were mild little walks in the eucalyptus woods behind, where one went through acanthus and wild absinthe, and here and there as the path wound, the great blue bay came into view, and far away the snow-capped peaks of the Atlas. There were warmth and sunshine, and the unexciting prattle of the retired Colonels and maiden ladies. There was a hotel library filled with archaic fiction. I took out Ainsworth's "Tower of London," and passed a happy morning in the sun renewing the thrills of my childhood. I began to forget the outer world in my enchanted garden, like a knight in the Forest of Broceliande.

Then came the letter from Tlemcen. The Lieutenant-Colonel commanding the 3rd Regiment of Chasseurs d'Afrique had received my honoured communication but regretted to say that he, together with all the officers of the regiment, had severed their connection with Captain Vauvenarde, and that they were ignorant of his present address.

This was absurd. A man does not resign from his regiment and within a year or two disappear like a ghost from the ken of every one of his brother officers. I read the letter again. Did the severance of connection mean the casting out of a black sheep from their midst? I came to the conclusion that it did. They had washed their hands of Captain Vauvenarde, and desired to hear nothing of him in the future.

So I awoke from my lethargy, and springing up sent not for my shield and spear, but for an "Indicateur des Chemins de Fer." I would go to Tlemcen and get to the bottom of it. I searched the time-table and found two trains, one starting from Algiers at nine-forty at night and getting into Tlemcen at noon next day, and one leaving at six-fifty in the morning and arriving at half-past ten at night. I groaned aloud. The dealing unto oneself a happy life and portion did not include abominable train journeys like these. I was trying to decide whether I should travel all night or all day when the Arab chasseur of the hotel brought me a telegram. I opened it. It ran:

"Starting for Algiers. Meet me.—LOLA."

It was despatched that morning from Victoria Station. I gazed at it stupidly. Why in the world was Lola Brandt coming to join me in Algiers? If she had wanted to do her husband hunting on her own account, why had she put me to the inconvenience of my journey? Her action could not have been determined by my letter about Anastasius Papadopoulos, as a short calculation proved that it could not have reached her. I wandered round and round the garden paths vainly seeking for the motive. Was it escape from Dale? Had she, womanlike, taken the step which she was so anxious to avoid—and in order to avoid taking which all this bother had arisen—and given the boy his dismissal? If so, why had she not gone to Paris or St. Petersburg or Terra del Fuego? Why Algiers? Dale abandoned outright, the necessity for finding her husband had disappeared. Perhaps she was coming to request me, on that account, to give up the search. But why travel across seas and continents when a telegram or a letter would have sufficed? She was coming at any rate; and as she gave no date I presumed that she would travel straight through and arrive in about forty-eight hours. This reflection caused a gleam of sunshine to traverse my gloom. I was not physically capable of performing the journey to Tlemcen and back before her arrival. I could, therefore, dream among the roses of the garden for another couple of days. And when she came, perhaps she would like to go to Tlemcen herself and try the effect of her woman's fascinations on the Lieutenant-Colonel and officers of the 3rd Regiment of Chasseurs d'Afrique.

In any case, her sudden departure argued well for Dale's liberation. If the rupture had occurred I was quite contented. That is what I had wished to accomplish. It only remained now to return to London, while breath yet stayed in my body, and lead him diplomatically to the feet of Maisie Ellerton. Then I would have ended my eumoirous task, and my last happy words would be a paternal benediction. But all the same, I had set forth to find this confounded captain and did not want to be hindered. The sportsman's instinct which, in my robust youth, had led me to crawl miles on my belly over wet heather in order to get a shot at a stag, I found, somewhat to my alarm, was urging me on this chase after Captain Vauvenarde. He was my quarry. I resented interference. Deer-stalking then, and man-stalking now, I wanted no petticoats in the party. I worked myself up into an absurd state of irritability. Why was she coming to spoil the sport? I had arranged to track her husband down, reason with him, work on his feelings, telegraph for his wife, and in an affecting interview throw them into each other's arms. Now, goodness knows what would happen. Certainly not my beautifully conceived *coup de theatre.*

"And she has the impertinence," I cried in my wrath, "to sign herself 'Lola'! As if I ever called her, or could ever be in a position to call her 'Lola'! I should like to know," I exclaimed, hurling the "Indicateur des Chemins de Fer" on to the seat of a summer-house, built after the manner of a little Greek temple, "I should like to know what the deuce she means by it!"

"Hallo! Hallo! What the devil's the matter?" cried a voice; and I found I had disturbed from his slumbers an unnoticed Colonel of British Cavalry.

"A thousand pardons!" said I. "I thought I was alone, and gave vent to the feelings of the moment."

Colonel Bunnion stretched himself and joined me.

"That's the worst of this place," he said. "It's so liverish. One lolls about and sleeps all day long, and one's liver gets like a Strasburg goose's and plays Old Harry with one's temper. Why one should come here when there are pheasants to be shot in England, I don't know."

"Neither your liver nor your temper seem to be much affected, Colonel," said I, "for you've been violently awakened from a sweet sleep and are in a most amiable frame of mind."

He laughed, suggested exercise, the Briton's panacea for all ills, and took me for a walk. When we returned at dusk, and after I had had tea before the fire (for December evenings in Algiers are chilly) in one of the pretty Moorish alcoves of the lounge, my good humour was restored. I viewed our pursuit of Captain Vauvenarde in its right aspect—that of a veritable Snark-Hunt of which I was the Bellman—and the name "Lola" curled itself round my heart with the same grateful sensation of comfort as the warm China tea. After all, it was only as Lola that I thought of her. The name fitted her personality, which Brandt did not. Out of "Brandt" I defy you to get any curvilinear suggestion. I reflected dreamily that it would be pleasant to walk with her among the roses in the sunshine and to drink tea with her in dusky Moorish alcoves. I also thought, with an enjoyable spice of malice, of what the retired Colonels and elderly maiden ladies would have to say about Lola when she arrived. They should have a gorgeous time.

So light-hearted did I become that, the next evening, while I was dressing for dinner, I did not frown when the chasseur brought me up the huge trilingual visiting-card of Professor Anastasius Papadopoulos.

"Show the gentleman up," said I.

Rogers handed me my black tie and began to gather together discarded garments so as to make the room tidy for the visitor. It was a comfortable bed-sitting-room, with the bed in an alcove and a tiny dressing-room attached. A wood fire burned on the hearth on each side of which was an armchair. Presently there came a knock at the door. Rogers opened it and admitted Papadopoulos, who forthwith began to execute his usual manoeuvres of salutation. Rogers stood staring and open-mouthed at the apparition. It took all his professional training in imperturbability to enable him to make a decent exit. This increased my good humour. I grasped the dwarf's hand.

"My dear Professor, I am delighted to see you. Pray excuse my receiving you in this unceremonious fashion, and sit down by the fire."

I hastily completed my toilette by stuffing my watch, letter-case, loose change and handkerchief into my pockets, and took a seat opposite him.

"It is I," said he politely, "who must apologise for this untimely call. I have wanted to pay my respects to you since I arrived in Algiers, but till now I have had no opportunity."

"Allow me," said I, "to disembarrass you of your hat."

I took the high-crowned, flat-brimmed thing which he was nursing somewhat nervously on his knees, and put it on the table. He murmured that I was "*Sehr aimable.*"

"And the charming Monsieur Saupiquet, how is he?" I asked.

He drew out his gilt-embossed pocket-book, and from it extracted an envelope.

"This," said he, handing it to me, "is the receipt. I have to thank you again for regulating the debt, as it has enabled me to transact with Monsieur Saupiquet the business on which I summoned him from Toulon. He is the most obstinate, pig-headed camel that ever lived, and I believe he has returned to Toulon in the best of health. No, thank you," he added, refusing my offer of cigarettes, "I don't smoke. It disturbs the perfect adjustment of my nerves, and so imperils my gigantic combinations. It is also distasteful to my cats."

"You must miss them greatly," said I.

He sighed—then his face lit up with inspiration.

"Ah, signor! What would one not sacrifice for an idea, for duty, for honour, for the happiness of those we love?"

"Those are sentiments, Monsieur Papadopoulos," I remarked, "which do you infinite credit."

"And, therefore, I express them, sir," he replied, "to show you what manner of man I am." He paused for a moment; then bending forward, his hands on his little knees—he was sitting far back in the chair and his legs were dangling like a child's—he regarded me intently.

"Would you be equally chivalrous for the sake of an idea?"

I replied that I hoped I should conduct myself *en galant homme* in any circumstances.

"I knew it," he cried. "My intuition is never wrong. An English statesman is as fearless as Agamemnon, and as wise as Nestor. Have you your evening free?"

"Yes," I replied wonderingly.

"Would you care to devote it to a perilous adventure? Not so perilous, for I"—he thumped his chest—"will be there. But still *molto gefahrlich*."

His black eyes held mine in burning intensity. So as to hide a smile I lit a cigarette. I know not what little imp in motley possessed me that evening. He seemed to hit me over the head with his bladder, and counsel me to play the fool like himself, for once in my life before I died. I could almost hear him speaking.

"Surely a crazy dwarf out of a nightmare is more entertaining company than decayed Colonels of British Cavalry."

I blew two or three puffs of my cigarette, and met my guest's eager gaze.

"I shall be happy to put myself at your disposal," said I. "May I ask, without indiscretion—?"

"No, no," he interrupted, "don't ask. Secrecy is part of the gigantic combination. *En galant homme*, I require of you—confidence."

With an irresistible touch of mockery I said: "Professor Papadopoulos, I will be happy to follow you blindfold to the lair of whatever fire-breathing dragon you may want me to help you destroy."

He rose and grasped his hat and made me a profound bow.

"You will not find me wanting in courage, Monsieur. There is another small favour I would ask of you. Will you bring some of your visiting-cards?"

"With pleasure," said I.

At that moment the gong clanged loudly through the hotel.

"It is your dinner-hour," said the dwarf. "I depart. Our rendezvous—"

"Let us have no rendezvous, my dear Professor," I interposed. "What more simple than that you should do me the pleasure of dining with me here? We can thus fortify ourselves with food and drink for our adventure, and we can start on it comfortably together whenever it seems good to you."

The little man put his head on one side and looked at me in an odd way.

"Do you mean," he asked in a softened voice, "that you ask me to dine with you in the midst of your aristocratic compatriots?"

"Why, evidently," said I, baffled. "It's only an ordinary table d'hote dinner."

To my astonishment, tears actually spurted out of the eyes of the amazing little creature. He took my hand and before I knew what he was going to do with it he had touched it with his lips.

"My dear Professor!" I cried in dismay.

He put up a pudgy hand, and said with great dignity:

"I cannot dine with you, Monsieur de Gex. But I thank you from my heart for your generous kindness. I shall never forget it to my dying day."

"But——"

He would listen to no protests. "If you will do me the honour of coming at nine o'clock to the Cafe de Bordeaux, at the corner of the Place du Gouvernement, I shall be there. *Auf wiedersehen*, Monsieur, and a thousand thanks. I beg you as a favour not to accompany me. I couldn't bear it."

And, drawing a great white handkerchief from his pocket, he wiped his eyes, blew his nose, and disappeared like a flash through the door which I held open for him.

I went down to dinner in a chastened mood. The little man had not shown me before the pathetic side of the freak's life. By asking him to dinner as if he were normal I had earned his eternal gratitude. And yet, with a smile, which I trust the Recording Angel when he makes up my final balance-sheet of good and evil will not ascribe to an unfeeling heart, I could not help formulating the hope that his gratitude would not be shown by presents of China fowls sitting on eggs, Tyrolese chalets and bottles with ladders and little men inside them. I did not feel within me the wide charity of Lola Brandt; and I could not repress a smile, as I ate my solitary meal, at the perils of the adventure to which I was invited. I had no doubt that it bore the same relation to danger as Monsieur Saupiquet's sevenpence-halfpenny bore to a serious debt.

Colonel Bunnion, a genial little red-faced man, with bulgy eyes and a moustache too big for his body, who sat, also solitary, at the next table to mine, suddenly began to utter words which I discovered were addressed to me.

"Most amazing thing happened to me as I was coming down to dinner. Just got out of the corridor to the foot of the stairs, when down rushed something about three foot nothing in a devil of a top-hat and butted me full in the pit of the stomach, and bounded off like a football. When I picked it up I found it was a man—give you my word—it was a man. About so high. Gave me quite a turn."

"That," said I, with a smile, "was my friend Professor Anastasius Papadopoulos."

"A friend of yours?"

"He had just been calling on me."

"Then I wish you'd entreat him not to go downstairs like a six-inch shell. I'll have a bruise to-morrow where the crown of his hat caught me as big as a soup-plate."

I offered the cheerily indignant warrior apologies for my friend's parabolic method of descent, and suggested Elliman's Embrocation.

"The most extraordinary part of it," he interrupted, "was that when I picked him up he was weeping like anything. What was he crying about?"

"He is a sensitive creature," said I, "and he doesn't come upon the pit of the stomach of a Colonel of British Cavalry every day in the week."

He sniffed uncertainly at the remark for a second or two and then broke into a laugh and asked me to play bridge after dinner. On the two preceding evenings he and I had attempted to cheer, in this manner, the desolation of a couple of the elderly maiden ladies. But I may say, parenthetically, that as he played bridge as if he were leading a cavalry charge according to a text-book on tactics, and as I play card games in a soft, mental twilight, and as the two ladies were very keen bridge players indeed, I had great doubts as to the success of our attempts.

"I'm sorry," said I, "but I'm going down into the town to-night."

"Theatre? If so, I'll go with you."

The gallant gentleman was always at a loose end. Unless he could persuade another human being to do something with him—no matter what—he would joyfully have played cat's cradle with me by the hour—he sat in awful boredom meditating on his liver.

"I'm not going to the theatre," I said, "and I wish I could ask you to accompany me on my adventure."

The Colonel raised his eyebrows. I laughed.

"I'm not going to twang guitars under balconies."

The Colonel reddened and swore he had never thought of such a thing. He was a perjured villain; but I did not tell him so.

"In what my adventure will consist I can't say," I remarked.

"If you're going to fool about Algiers at night you'd better carry a revolver."

I told him I did not possess such deadly weapons. He offered to lend me one. The two Misses Bostock from South Shields, who sat at the table within earshot and had been following our conversation, manifested signs of excited interest.

"I shall be quite protected," said I, "by the dynamic qualities of your acquaintance, Professor Anastasius Papadopoulos, with whom I have promised to spend the evening."

"You had better have the revolver," said the Colonel. And so bent was he on the point, that after dinner he came to me in the lounge and laid a loaded six-shooter beside my coffee-cup. The younger Miss Bostock grew pale. It looked an ugly, cumbrous, devastating weapon.

"But, my dear Colonel," I protested, "it's against the law to carry fire-arms."

"Law—what law?"

"Why the law of France," said I.

This staggered him. The fact of there being decent laws in foreign parts has staggered many an honest Briton. He counselled a damnation of the law, and finally, in order to humour him, I allowed him to thrust the uncomfortable thing into my hip-pocket.

"Colonel," said I, when I took leave of him an hour later, "I have armed myself out of pure altruism. I shan't be able to sit down in peace and comfort for the rest of the evening. Should I accidentally do so, my blood will be on your head."

CHAPTER XII

The tram that passes the hotel gates took me into the town and dropped me at the Place du Gouvernement. With its strange fusion of East and West, its great white-domed mosque flanked by the tall minaret contrasting with its formal French colonnaded facades, its groupings of majestic white-robed forms and commonplace figures in caps and hard felt hats; the mystery of its palm trees, and the crudity of its flaring electric lights, it gave an impression of unreality, of a modern contractor's idea of Fairyland, where anything grotesque might assume an air of normality. The moon shone full in the heavens, and as I crossed the Place I saw the equestrian statue of the Duke of Orleans silhouetted against the mosque. The port, to the east, was quiet at this hour, and the shipping lay dreamily in the moonlight. Far away one could see the dim outlines of the Kabyle Mountains, and the vague melting of sea and sky into a near horizon. The undefinable smell of the East was in the air.

The Cafe de Bordeaux, which forms an angle of the Place, blazed in front of me. A few hardy souls, a Zouave or two, an Arab, a bored Englishman and his wife, and some French inhabitants were sitting outside in the chilliness. I entered. The cafe was filled with a nondescript crowd, and the rattle of dominoes rose above the hum of talk. In a corner near the door I discovered the top of a silk hat projecting above a widely opened newspaper grasped by two pudgy hands, and I recognised the Professor.

"Monsieur," said he, when I had taken a seat at his table, "if the unknown terrors which you are going to confront dismay you, I beg that you will not consider yourself bound to me."

"My dear Professor," I replied, "a brave man tastes of death but once."

He was much delighted at the sentiment, which he took to be original.

"I shall quote it," said he, "whenever my honour or my courage is called into question. It is not often that a man has the temerity to do so. Can I have the honour of offering you a whisky and soda?"

"Have we time?" I asked.

"We have time," he said, solemnly consulting his watch. "Things will ripen."

"Then," said I, "I shall have much pleasure in drinking to their maturity."

While we were drinking our whisky and soda he talked volubly of many things—his travels, his cats, his own incredible importance in the cosmos. And as he sat there vapouring about the pathetically insignificant he looked more like Napoleon III than ever. His eyes had the same mournful depths, his features the same stamp of fatality. Each man has his gigantic combinations—perhaps equally important in the eyes of the High Gods. I was filled with an immense pity for Napoleon III.

Of the object of the adventure he said nothing. As secrecy seemed to be a vital element in his fifteen-cent scheme, I showed no embarrassing curiosity. Indeed, I felt but little, though I was certain that the adventure was connected with the world-cracking revelations of Monsieur Saupiquet, and was undertaken in the interest of his beloved lady, Lola Brandt. But it was like playing at pirates with a child, and my pity for Napoleon gave place to my pity for my valiant but childish little friend.

At last he looked again at his watch.

"The hour his struck. Let us proceed."

Instinctively I summoned the waiter, and drew a coin from my pocket; and when the grown-up person and the small boy hobnob together the former pays. But Anastasius, with a swift look of protest, anticipated my intention. I was his guest for the evening. I yielded apologetically, the score was paid, and we went forth into the moonlight.

He led me across the Place du Gouvernement and struck straight up the hill past the Cathedral, and, turning, plunged into a network of narrow streets, where the poor of all races lived together in amity and evil odours. Shops chiefly occupied the ground floors; some were the ordinary humble shops of Europeans; others were caves lit by a smoky lamp, where Arabs lounged and smoked around the tailors or cobblers squatting at their work; others were Jewish, with Hebrew inscriptions. There were dark Arab cafes, noisy Italian wine-shops, butchers' stalls; children of all ages played and screamed about the precipitous cobble-paved streets; and the shrill cries of Jewish women, sitting at their doors, rose in rebuke of husband or offspring. Not many lights appeared through the shuttered windows of the dark, high houses. Overhead, between two facades, one saw a strip of paleness which one knew was the moonlit sky. Conversation with my companion being difficult—the top of his silk hat just reached my elbow— I strode along in silence, Anastasius trotting by my side. Many jeers and jests were flung at us as we passed, whereat he scowled terribly; but no one molested us. I am inclined to think that Anastasius attributed this to fear of his fierce demeanour. If so, he was happy, as were the simple souls who flouted; and this reflection kept my mind serene.

Presently we turned into a wide and less poverty-stricken street, which I felt sure we could have reached by a less tortuous and malodorous path. A few yards down we came to a dark *porte cochère*. The dwarf halted, crossed, so as to read the number by the gas lamp, and joining me, said:

"It is here. Have you your visiting-cards ready?"

I nodded. We proceeded down the dark entry till we came to a slovenly, ill-kept glass box lit by a small gas jet, whence emerged a slovenly, ill-kept man. This was the concierge. Anastasius addressed a remark to him which I did not catch.

"*Au fond de la cour, troisième a gauche,*" said the concierge.

As yet there seemed to be nothing peculiarly perilous about the adventure. We crossed the cobble-paved courtyard and mounted an evil-smelling stone staircase, blackened here and there by the occasional gas jets. On the third landing we halted. Anastasius put up his hand and gripped mine.

"Two strong men together," said he, "need fear nothing."

I confess my only fear was lest the confounded revolver which swung insecurely in my hip-pocket might go off of its own accord. I did not mention this to my companion. He raised his hat, wiped his brow, and rang the bell.

The door opened about six inches, and a man's dark-moustachioed face appeared.

"*Vous desirez, Messieurs?*"

As I had not the remotest idea what we desired, I let Anastasius be spokesman.

"Here is an English milord," said Anastasius boldly, "who would like to be admitted for the evening to the privileges of the Club."

"Enter, gentlemen," said the man, who appeared to be the porter.

We found ourselves in a small vestibule. In front of us was a large door, on the right a small one, both closed. At a table by the large door sat a dirty, out-of-elbows raven of a man reading a newspaper. The latter looked up and addressed me.

"You wish to enter the Club, Monsieur?"

I had no particular longing to do so, but I politely answered that such was my desire.

"If you will give your visiting-card, I will submit it to the Secretariat."

I produced my card; Anastasius thrust a pencil into my hand.

"Write my name on it, too."

I obeyed. The raven sent the porter with the card into the room on the right, and resumed the perusal of his soiled newspaper. I looked at Anastasius. The little man was quivering with excitement. The porter returned after a few minutes with a couple of pink oval cards which he handed to each of us. I glanced at mine. On it was inscribed: *Cercle Africain d'Alger. Carte de Member Honoraire. Une soiree.* And then there was a line for the honorary member's signature. The raven man dipped a pen in the ink-pot in front of him and handed it to me.

"Will you sign, Messieurs?"

We executed this formality; he retained the cards, and opening the great door, said:

"*Entrez, Messieurs!*"

The door closed behind us. It was simply a *tripot*, or gambling-den. And all this solemn farce of Secretariats and *cartes d'entree* to obtain admission! It is curious how the bureaucratic instinct is ingrained in the French character.

It was a large, ill-ventilated room, blue with cigarette and cigar smoke. Some thirty men were sitting or standing around a baccarat table in the centre, and two or three groups hung around *ecarte* tables in the corners. A personage who looked like a slightly more prosperous brother of the raven outside and wore a dinner-jacket, promenaded the room with the air of one in authority. He scrutinised us carefully from a distance; then advanced and greeted us politely.

"You have chosen an excellent evening," said he. "There are a great many people, and the banks are large."

He bowed and passed on. A dingy waiter took our hats and coats and hung them up. Anastasius plucked me by the sleeve.

"If you don't mind staking a little for the sake of appearances, I shall be grateful."

I whispered: "Can you tell me now, my dear Professor, for what reason you have brought me to this gaming-hell?"

He looked up at me out of his mournful eyes and murmured, "*Patienza, lieber Herr.*" Then spying a vacant place behind the chairs at the baccarat table, he darted thither, and I followed in his wake. There must have been about a couple of hundred louis in the bank, which was held by a dissipated, middle-aged man who, having once been handsome in a fleshy way, had run to fat. His black hair, cropped short, stood up like a shoebrush, and when he leaned back in his chair a roll of flesh rose above his collar. I disliked the fellow for his unhealthiness, and for the hard mockery in his puffy eyes. The company seemed fairly homogeneous in its raffishness, though here and there appeared a thin, aristocratic face, with grey moustache and pointed beard, and the homely anxious visage of a small tradesman. But in bulk it looked an ugly, seedy crowd, with unwashed bodies and unclean souls. I noticed an Italian or two, and a villainous Englishman with a face like that of a dilapidated horse. A glance at the table plastered with silver and gold showed me that they were playing with a five-franc minimum.

Anastasius drew a handful of louis from his pocket and staked one. I staked a five-franc piece. The cards were dealt, the banker exposed a nine, the highest number, and the croupier's flat spoon swept the table. A murmur arose. The banker was having the luck of Satan.

"He always protects me, the good fellow," laughed the banker, who had overheard the remark.

Again we staked, again the hands were dealt. Our tableau or end of the table won, the other lost. The croupier threw the coins in payment. I let my double stake lie, and so did Anastasius. At the next coup we lost again. The banker stuffed his winnings into his pocket and declared a *suite*. The bank was put up at auction, and was eventually knocked down to the same personage for fifty louis. The horse-headed Englishman cried "*banco*," which means that he would play the banker for the whole amount. The hands were dealt, the Englishman lost, and the game started afresh with a hundred louis in the bank. The proceedings began to bore me. Even if my experience of life had not suggested that scrupulous fairness and honour were not the guiding principles of such an assemblage, I should have taken little interest in the game. I am a great believer in the wholesomeness of compounding for sins you are inclined to by damning those you have no mind to. It aids the nice balance of life. And gambling is one of the sins I delight to damn. The rapid getting of money has never appealed to me, who have always had sufficient for my moderately epicurean needs, and least of all did it appeal to me now when I was on the brink of my journey to the land where French gold and bank notes were not in currency. I repeat, therefore, that I was bored.

"If the perils of the adventure don't begin soon, my dear Professor," I whispered, "I shall go to sleep standing."

Again he asked for patience and staked a hundred-franc note. At that moment the man sitting at the table in front of him rose, and the dwarf slipped swiftly into his seat. He won his hundred francs and made the same stake again. It was obvious that the little man did not damn gambling. It was a sin to which he appeared peculiarly inclined. The true inwardness of the perilous adventure began to dawn on me. He had come here to make the money wherewith he could further his gigantic combinations. All this mystery was part of his childish cunning. I hardly knew whether to box the little creature's ears, to box my own, or to laugh. I compromised with a smile on the last alternative, and baccarat being a dreary game to watch, I strolled off to the nearest *ecarte* table, and, to justify my presence in the room, backed one of the players.

Presently my attention was called to the baccarat table by a noise as of some dispute, and turning, I saw the gentleman in the dinner-jacket hurrying to what appeared to be the storm centre, the place where Anastasius was sitting. Suspecting some minor peril, I left the *ecarte* players, and joined the gentleman in the dinner-jacket. It seemed that the hand, which is played in rotation by those seated at each tableau or half-table, had come round for the first time to Anastasius, and objection had been taken to his playing it, on the score of his physical appearance. The dwarf was protesting vehemently. He had played baccarat in all the clubs of Europe, and had never received such treatment. It was infamous, it was insulting. The malcontents of the punt paid little heed to his remonstrances. They resented the entrusting of their fortunes to one whose chin barely rose above the level of the table. The banker lit a cigarette and sat back in his chair with a smile of mockery. His attitude brought up the superfluous flesh about his chin and the roll of fat at the back of his neck. With his moustache *en croc*, and his shoebrush hair, I have rarely beheld a more sensual-looking desperado.

"But gentlemen," said he, "I see no objection whatever to Monsieur playing the hand."

"Naturally," retorted a voice, "since it would be to your advantage."

The raven in the dinner-jacket commanded silence.

"Gentlemen, I decide that, according to the rules of the game, Monsieur is entitled to play the hand."

"Bravo!" exclaimed one or two of my friend's supporters.

"*C'est idiot!*" growled the malcontents.

"*Messieurs, faites vos jeux!*" cried the croupier.

The stakes were laid, the banker looked around, estimating the comparative values of the two tableaux. Anastasius had backed his hand with a pile of louis. To encourage him, and to conciliate the hostile punt, I threw down a hundred-franc note.

"Les jeux sont faits? Rien ne va plus."

The banker dealt, two cards to each tableau, two to himself. Anastasius, trembling with nervous excitement, stretched out a palsied little fist towards the cards. He drew them towards him, face downwards, peeped at them in the most approved manner, and in a husky voice called for an extra card.

The card dealt face upwards was a five. The banker turned up his own cards, a two and a four, making a point of six. Naturally he stood, Anastasius did nothing.

"Show your cards—show your cards!" cried several voices.

He turned over the two cards originally dealt to him. They were a king and a nine, making the natural nine, the highest point, and he had actually asked for another card. It was the unforgivable sin. The five that had been dealt to him brought his point to four. There was a roar of indignation. Men with violent faces rose and cursed him, and shook their fists at him. Others clamoured that the coup was ineffective. They were not going to be at the mercy of an idiot who knew nothing of the game. The hand must be dealt over again.

"Jamais de la vie!" shouted the banker.

"Le coup est bon!" cried the raven in authority, and the croupier's spoon hovered over the tableau. But the horse-headed Englishman clutched the two louis he had staked. He was damned, and a great many other things, if he would lose his money that way. The raven in the dinner-jacket darted round, and bending over him, caught him by the wrist. Two or three others grabbed their stakes, and swore they would not pay. The banker rose and went to the rescue of his gains. There was screaming and shouting and struggling and riot indescribable. Those round about us went on cursing Anastasius, who sat quite still, with quivering lips, as helpless as a rabbit. The raven tore his way through the throng around the Englishman and came up to me excited and dishevelled.

"It is all your fault, Monsieur," he shrieked, "for introducing into the club a half-witted creature like that."

"Yes, it's your fault," cried a low-browed, ugly fellow looking like a butcher in uneasy circumstances who stood next to me. Suddenly the avalanche of indignation fell upon my head. Angry, ugly men crowded round me and began to curse me instead of the dwarf. Cries arose. The adventure began, indeed, to grow idiotically perilous. I had never been thrown out of doors in my life. I objected strongly to the idea. It might possibly hurt my body, and would certainly offend my dignity. I felt that I could not make my exit through the portals of life with the urbanity on which I had counted, if, as a preparatory step, I had been thrown out of a gambling-hell. There were only two things to be done. Either I must whip out my ridiculous revolver and do some free shooting, or I must make an appeal to the lower feelings of the assembly. I chose the latter alternative. With a sudden movement I slipped through the angry and gesticulating crowd, and leaped on a chair by one of the deserted *ecarte* tables. Then I raised a commanding arm, and, in my best election-meeting voice, I cried:

"*Messieurs!*"

The unexpectedness of the manoeuvre caused instant silence.

"As my friend and myself," I said, "are the cause of this unpleasant confusion, I shall be most happy to pay the banker the losses of the tableau."

And I drew out and brandished my pocket-book, in which, by a special grace of Providence, there happened to be a considerable sum of money.

Murmurs of approbation arose. Then the Englishman sang out:

"But what about the money we would have won, if that little fool had played the game properly?"

The remark was received with cheers.

"That amount, too," said I, "I shall be happy to disburse."

There was nothing more to be said, as everybody, banker and punt, were satisfied. The raven in the dinner-jacket came up and informed me that my proposal solved the difficulty. I besought him to make out the bill for my little entertainment as quickly as possible. Then I dismounted from my chair and beckoned to the dwarf, still sitting white and piteous, to join me. He obeyed like a frightened child who had been naughty. All his swagger and braggadocio were gone. His bosom heaved with suppressed sobs. He sat down on the chair I had vacated and buried his face on the *ecarte* table. We remained thus aloof from the crowd who were intent on the calculation at the baccarat table. At last the raven in the dinner-jacket arrived with a note of the amount. It was two thousand three hundred francs. I gave him the notes, and, taking Anastasius by the arm, led him to the door, where the waiter stood with our hats and coats. Before we could reach it, however, the banker, who had risen from his seat, crossed the room and addressed me.

"Monsieur," said he, with an air of high-bred courtesy, "I infinitely regret this unpleasant affair and I thank you for your perfect magnanimity."

I did not suggest that with equal magnanimity he might refund the forty-six pounds that had found its way from my pocket to his, but I bowed with stiff politeness, and made my exit with as much dignity as the attachment to my heels of the crestfallen Anastasius would permit.

Outside I constituted myself the guide, and took the first turning downhill, knowing that it would lead to the civilised centre of the town. The dwarf's roundabout route was characteristic of his tortuous mind. We walked along for some time without saying anything. I could not find it in my heart to reproach the little man for the expensiveness (nearly a hundred pounds) of his perilous adventure, and he seemed too dazed with shame and humiliation to speak. At last, when we reached, as I anticipated, the Square de la Republique, I patted him on the shoulder.

"Cheer up, my dear Professor," said I. "We both are acquainted with nobler things than the ins and outs of gaming-hells."

He reeled to a bench under the palm trees, and bursting into tears, gave vent to his misery in the most incoherent language ever uttered by man. I sat beside him and vainly attempted consolation.

"Ah, how mad I am! Ah, how contemptible! I dare not face my beautiful cats again. I dare not see the light of the sun. I have betrayed my trust. Accursed be the cards. I, who had my gigantic combination. It is all gone. Beautiful lady, forgive me. Generous-hearted friend, forgive me. I am the most miserable of God's creatures."

"It is an accident that might happen to any one," I said gently. "You were nervous. You looked at the cards, you mistook the nine for a ten, in which case you were right to call for another card."

"It is not that," he wailed. "It is the spoiling of my combination, on which I have wasted sleepless nights. A curse on my mad folly. Do you know who the banker was?"

"No," said I.

"He was Captain Vauvenarde, the husband of Madame Brandt."

CHAPTER XIII

You could have knocked me down with a feather. It is a trite metaphor, I know; but it is none the less excellent. I repeat, therefore, unblushingly— you could have knocked me down with a feather. I gasped. The little man wiped his eyes. He was the tearfullest adult I have ever met, and I once knew an Italian *prima donna* with a temperament.

"Captain Vauvenarde? The man with the shoebrush hair and the rolls of fat at the back of his neck? Are you sure?"

The dwarf nodded. "I set out from England to find him. I swore to the *carissima signora* that I would do so. I have done it," he added, with a faint return of his self-confidence.

"Well, I'm damned!" said I, in my native tongue.

I don't often use strong language; but the occasion warranted it. I was flabbergasted, bewildered, out-raged, humiliated, delighted, incredulous, and generally turned topsy-turvy. In conversation one has no time for so minute an analysis of one's feelings. I therefore summed them up in the only word. Captain Vauvenarde! The wild goose of my absurd chase! Found by this Flibbertigibbet of a fellow, while I, Simon de Gex, erstwhile M.P., was fooling about War Offices and regiments! It was grotesque. It was monstrous. It ought not to have been allowed. And yet it saved me a vast amount of trouble.

"I'm damned!" said I.

Anastasius had just enough English to understand. I suppose, such is mortal unregeneracy, that it is the most widely understood word in the universe.

"And I," said he, "am eternally beaten. I am trampled under foot and shall never be able to hold up my head again."

Whereupon he renewed his lamentations. For some time I listened patiently, and from his disconnected remarks I gathered that he had gone to the Cercle Africain in view of his gigantic combinations, but that the demon of gambling taking possession of him had almost driven them from his mind. Eventually he had lost control of his nerves, a cloud had spread over his brain, and he had committed the unspeakable blunder which led to disaster.

"To think that I should have tracked him down—for this!" he exclaimed tragically.

"What beats me," I cried, "is how the deuce you managed to track him down. Your magnificent intellect, I suppose"—I spoke gently and not in open sarcasm—"enabled you to get on the trail."

He brightened at the compliment. "Yes, that was it. Listen. I came to Algiers, the last place he was heard of. I go to the cafes. I listen like a detective to conversation. I creep behind soldiers talking. I find out nothing. I ask at the shops. They think I am crazy, but Anastasius Papadopoulos has a brain larger than theirs. I go to my old friend the secretary of the theatre, where I have exhibited the marvellous performance of my cats. I say to him, 'When have you a date for me?' He says, 'Next year.' I make a note of it. We talk. He knows all Algiers. I say to him, 'What has become of Captain Vauvenarde of the Chasseurs d'Afrique?' I say it carelessly as if the Captain were an old friend of mine. The secretary laughs. 'Haven't you heard? The Captain was chased from the regiment——'"

"The deuce he was!" I interjected.

"On account of something," said Anastasius. "The secretary could not tell what. Perhaps he cheated at cards. The officers said so.

"'Where is he now?' I ask. 'Why, in Algiers. He is the most famous gambler in the town. He is every night at the Cercle Africain, and some people believe that it belongs to him.' My friend the secretary asks me why I am so anxious to discover Captain Vauvenarde. I do not betray my secret. When I do not wish to talk I close my lips, and they are sealed like the tomb. I am the model of discretion. You, Monsieur, with the high-bred delicacy of the English statesman, have not questioned me about my combination. I appreciate it. But, if you had, though it broke my heart, I should not have answered."

"I am not going to pry into your schemes," I said, "but there are one or two things I must understand. How do you know the banker was Captain Vauvenarde?"

"I saw him several times in Marseilles with the *carissima signora*."

"Then how was it he did not recognise you to-night?"

"I was then but an acquaintance of Madame; not her intimate friend, counsellor, champion, as I am now. I did not have the honour of being presented to Captain Vauvenarde. I went to-night to make sure of my man, to play the first card in my gigantic combination—but, alas! But no!" He rose and thumped his little chest. "I feel my courage coming back. My will is stiffening into iron. When the *carissima signora* arrives in Algiers she will find she has a champion!"

"How do you know she is coming to Algiers?" I asked startled.

"As soon as I learned that Captain Vauvenarde was here," he replied proudly, "I sent her a telegram. 'Husband found; come at once.' I know she is coming, for she has not answered."

An idea occurred to me. "Did you sign your name and address on the telegram?"

He approached me confidentially as I sat, and wagged a cunning finger.

"In matters of life and death, never give your name and address."

As Professor Anastasius Papadopoulos was himself again, and as I began to sneeze—for the night was chilly—I rose and suggested that we might adjourn this conference till the morrow. He acquiesced, saying that all was not lost and that he still had time to mature his combinations. We crossed the road, and I hailed a cab standing by the Cafe d'Alger. I offered Anastasius to drive him to his hotel, but he declined politely. We shook hands.

"Monsieur," said he, "I have to make my heartfelt apologies for having caused you so painful, so useless, and so expensive an evening. As for the last aspect I will repay you."

"You will do no such thing, Professor," said I. "My evening has, on the contrary, been particularly useful and instructive. I wouldn't have missed it for the world."

And I drove off homewards, glad to be in my own company.

Here was an imbroglio! The missing husband found and, like most missing husbands, found to be entirely undesirable. And Lola, obviously imagining her summons to be from me, was at that moment speeding hither as fast as the *Marechal Bugeaud* could carry her. If I had discovered Captain Vauvenarde instead of Anastasius I would have anathematised him as the most meddlesome, crazy little marplot that ever looked like Napoleon the Third. But as the credit of the discovery belonged to him and not to me, I could only anathematise myself for my dilettanteism in the capacity of a private inquiry agent.

I went to bed and slept badly. The ludicrous scenes of the evening danced before my eyes; the smoke-filled, sordid room, the ignoble faces round the table, the foolish hullaballoo, the collapse of Anastasius, my melodramatic intervention, and the ironical courtesy of the fleshy Captain Vauvenarde. Also, in the small hours of the night, Anastasius's gigantic combinations assumed a less trivial aspect. What lunatic scheme was being hatched behind that dome-like brow? His object in taking me to the club was obvious. He could not have got in save under my protection. But what he had reckoned upon doing when he got there Heaven and Anastasius

Papadopoulos only knew. I was also worried by the confounded little pain inside.

On the following afternoon I went down to meet the steamer from Marseilles. I more than expected to find the dwarf on the quay, but to my relief he was not there. I had purposely kept my knowledge of Lola's movements a secret from him, as I desired as far as possible to conduct affairs without his crazy intervention. I was not sorry, too, that he had not availed himself of my proposal to visit me that morning and continue our conversation of the night before. The grotesque as a decoration of life is valuable; as the main feature it gets on your nerves.

I stood on the sloping stone jetty among the crowd of Arab porters and Europeans and watched the vessel waddle in. Lola and I, catching sight of each other at the same time, waved handkerchiefs in an imbecile manner, and when the vessel came alongside, and during the tedious process of mooring, we regarded each other with photographic smiles. She was wearing a squirrel coat and a toque of the same fur, and she looked more like a splendid wild animal than ever. Something inside me—not the little pain—but what must have been my heart, throbbed suddenly at her beauty, and the throb was followed by a sudden sense of shock at the realisation of my keen pleasure at the sight of her. A wistful radiance shone in her face as she came down the gangway.

"Oh, how kind, how good, how splendid of you to meet me!" she cried as our hands clasped. "I was dreading, dreading, dreading that it might be some one else."

"And yet you came straight through," said I, still holding her hand—or, rather, allowing hers to encircle mine in the familiar grip.

"Didn't you command me to do so?"

I could not explain matters to her then and there among the hustle of passengers and the bustle of porters. Besides, Rogers, who had come down with the hotel omnibus, was at my side touching his hat.

"I have ordered you a room and a private sitting-room with a balcony facing the sea. Put yourself in charge of me and your luggage in charge of Rogers and dismiss all thoughts of worry from your mind."

"You are so restful," she laughed as we moved off.

Then she scanned my face and said falteringly. "How thin and worn you look! Are you worse?"

"If you ask me such questions," said I, "I'll leave you with the luggage in charge of Rogers. I am in resplendent health."

She murmured that she wished she could believe me, and took my arm as we walked down the jetty to the waiting cab.

"It's good to hear your voice again," I said. "It's a lazy voice and fits in with the lazy South." I pointed to the burnous-enveloped Arabs sleeping on the parapet. "It's out of place in Cadogan Gardens."

She laughed her low, rippling laugh. It was music very pleasant to hear after the somewhat shrill cachinnation of the Misses Bostock of South Shields. I was so pleased that I gave half a franc to a pestilential Arab shoeblack.

"That was nice of you," she said.

"It was the act of an imbecile," I retorted. "I have now rendered it impossible for me to enter the town again. How is Dale?"

She started. "He's well. Busy with his election. I saw him the day before I left. I didn't tell him I was coming to Algiers. I wrote from Paris."

"Telling him the reason?"

She faced me and met my eyes and said shortly: "No."

"Oh!" said I.

This brought us to the cab. We entered and drove away. Then leaning back and looking straight in front of her, she grasped my wrist and said:

"Now, my dear friend, tell me all and get it over."

"My dear Madame Brandt—" I began.

She interrupted me. "For goodness' sake don't call me that. It makes a cold shiver run down my back. I'm either Lola to you or nothing."

"Then, my dear Lola," said I, "the first thing I must tell you is that I did not send for you."

"What do you mean? The telegram?"

"It was sent by Anastasius Papadopoulos."

"Anastasius?" She bent forward and looked at me. "What is he doing here?"

"Heaven knows!" said I. "But what he has done has been to find Captain Vauvenarde. I am glad he has done that, but I am deeply sorry he sent you the telegram."

"Sorry? Why?"

"Because there was no reason for your coming," I said with unwonted gravity. "It would have been better if you had stayed in London, and it will be best if you take the boat back again to-morrow."

She remained silent for a while. Then she said in a low voice:

"He won't have me?"

"He hasn't been asked," I said. "He will, as far as I can command the situation, never be asked."

On that I had fully determined; and, when she inquired the reason, I told her.

"I proposed that you should reunite yourself with an honourable though somewhat misguided gentleman. I've had the reverse of pleasure in meeting Captain Vauvenarde, and I regret to say, though he is still misguided, he can scarcely be termed honourable. The term 'gentleman' has still to be accurately defined."

She made a writhing movement of impatience.

"Tell me straight out what he's doing in Algiers. You're trying to make things easy for me. It's the way of your class. It isn't the way of mine. I'm used to brutality. I like it better. Why did he leave the army and why is he in Algiers?"

"If you prefer the direct method, my dear Lola," said I—and the name came quite trippingly on my tongue—"I'll employ it. Your husband has apparently been kicked out of the army and is now running a gambling-hell."

She took the blow bravely; but it turned her face haggard like a paroxysm of physical pain. After a few moments' silence, she said:

"It must have been awful for him. He was a proud man."

"He is changed," I replied gently. "Pride is too hampering a quality for a knight of industry to keep in his equipment."

"Tell me how you met him," she said.

I rapidly sketched the whole absurd history, from my encounter with Anastasius Papadopoulos in Marseilles to my parting with him on the previous night. I softened down, as much as I could, the fleshiness of Captain Vauvenarde and the rolls of fat at the back of his neck, but I portrayed the villainous physiognomies of his associates very neatly. I concluded by repeating my assertion that our project had proved itself to be abortive.

"He must be pretty miserable," said Lola.

"Devil a bit," said I.

She did not answer, but settled herself more comfortably in the carriage and relapsed into mournful silence. I, having said my say, lit a cigarette. Save for the clanging past of an upward or downward tram, the creeping drive up the hill through the long winding street was very quiet; and as we mounted higher and left the shops behind, the only sounds that broke the afternoon stillness were the driver's raucous admonition to his horses and the wind in the trees by the wayside. At different points the turns of the road brought to view the panorama of the town below and the calm sweep of the bay.

"Exquisite, isn't it?" I said at last, with an indicative wave of the hand.

"What's the good of anything being exquisite when you feel mouldy?"

"It may help to charm away the mouldiness. Beauty is eternal and mouldiness only temporal. The sun will go on shining and the sea will go on changing colour long after our pains and joys have vanished from the world. Nature is pitilessly indifferent to human emotion."

"If so," she said, her intuition finding the weakness of my slipshod argument, "how can it touch human mouldiness?"

"I don't know," said I. "The poets will tell you. All you have to do is to lie on the breast of the Great Mother and your heartache will go from you. I've never tried it myself, as I've never been afflicted with heartache."

"Is that true?" she asked, womanlike catching at the personal.

I smiled and nodded.

"I'm glad on your account," she said sincerely. "It's the very devil of an ache. I've always had it."

"Poor Lola," said I, prompted by my acquired instinct of eumoiriety. "I wish I could cure you."

"You?" She gave a short little laugh and then turned her head away.

"I had a very comfortable crossing," she remarked a moment later.

I gave her into the keeping of the manager of the hotel and did not see her again until she came down somewhat late for dinner. I met her in the vestibule. She wore a closely fitting brown dress, which in colour matched the bronze of her hair and in shape showed off her lithe and generous figure.

I thought it my duty to cheer her by a well-deserved compliment.

"Are you aware," I said, with a low bow, "that you're a remarkably handsome woman?"

A perfectly unnecessary light came into her eyes and a superfluous flush to her cheeks. "If I'm at least that to you, I'm happy," she said.

"You're that to the dullest vision. Follow the *maitre d'hotel*," said I, as we entered the *salle a manger*, "and I'll walk behind in reflected glory."

We made an effective entrance. I declare there was a perceptible rattle of soup-spoons laid down by the retired Colonels and maiden ladies as we passed by. Colonel Bunnion returned my nod of greeting in the most distracted fashion and gazed at Lola with the frank admiration of British Cavalry. I felt foolishly proud and exhilarated, and gave her at my table the seat commanding a view of the room. I then ordered a bottle of champagne, which I am forbidden to touch.

"It isn't often that I have the pleasure of dining with you," I said by way of apology.

"This is the very first time," she said.

"And it's not going to be the last," I declared.

"I thought you were going to ship me back to Marseilles to-morrow."

She laughed lazily, meeting my eyes. I smiled.

"It would be inhuman. I allow you a few day's rest."

Indeed, now she was here I had a curious desire to keep her. I regarded the failure of my eumoirous little plans with more than satisfaction. I had done my best. I had found (through the dwarf's agency) Captain Vauvenarde. I had satisfied myself that he was an outrageous person, thoroughly disqualified from becoming Lola's husband, and there was an end of the matter. Meanwhile Fate (again through the agency of Anastasius) had brought her many hundreds of miles away from Dale and had moreover brought her to me. I was delighted. I patted Destiny on the back, and drank his health in excellent Pommery. Lola did not know in the least what I meant, but she smiled amiably and drank the toast. It was quite a merry dinner. Lola threw herself into my mood and jested as if she had never heard of an undesirable husband who had been kicked out of the French Army. We talked of many things. I described in fuller detail my adventure with Anastasius and Saupiquet, and we laughed over the debt of fifteen sous and the elaborate receipt.

"Anastasius," she said, "is childish in many ways—the doctors have a name for it."

"Arrested development."

"That's it; but he is absolutely cracked on one point—the poisoning of my horse Sultan. He has reams of paper which he calls the dossier of the crime. You never saw such a collection of rubbish in your life. I cried over it. And he is so proud of it, poor wee mite." She laughed suddenly. "I should love to have seen you hobnobbing with him and Saupiquet."

"Why?"

"You're so aristocratic-looking," she did me the embarrassing honour to explain in her direct fashion. "You're my idea of an English duke."

"My dear Lola," I replied, "you're quite wrong. The ordinary English duke is a stout, middle-aged gentleman with a beard, and he generally wears thick knickerbockers and shocking bad hats."

"Do you know any?"

"Two or three," I admitted.

"And duchesses, too?"

I again pleaded guilty. In these democratic days, if one is engaged in public and social affairs one can't help running up against them. It is their fault, not mine.

"Do tell me about them," said Lola, with her elbows on the table.

I told her.

"And are earls and countesses just the same?" she asked with a disappointed air.

"Just the same, only worse. They're so ordinary you can't pick them out from common misters and missuses."

Saying this I rose, for we had finished our dessert, and proposed coffee in the lounge. There we found Colonel Bunnion at so wilful a loose end that I could not find it in my heart to refuse him an introduction to Lola. He manifested his delight by lifting the skirt of his dinner-jacket with his hands and rising on his spurs like a bantam cock. I left her to him for a moment and went over to say a civil word to the Misses Bostock of South Shields. I regret to say I noticed a certain frigidity in their demeanour. The well-conducted man in South Shields does not go out one night with a revolver tucked away in the pocket of his dress-suit, and turn up the next evening with a striking-looking lady with bronze hair. Such goings-on are seen on the stage in South Shields in melodrama, and they are the goings-on of the villain. In the eyes of the gentle ladies my reputation was gone. I was trying to rehabilitate myself when the chasseur brought me a telegram. I asked permission to open it, and stepped aside.

The words of the telegram were like a ringing box on the ears.

"Tell me immediately why Lola has joined you in Algiers. — KYNNERSLEY."

Not "Dale," mark you, as he has signed himself ever since I knew him in Eton collars, but "Kynnersley." Why has Lola joined you? Why have you run off with Lola? What's the reason of this treacherous abduction? Account for yourself immediately. Stand and deliver. I stood there gaping at the words like an idiot, my blood tingling at the implied accusation. The peremptoriness of it! The impudence of the boy! The wild extravagance of the idea! And yet, while my head was reeling with one buffet a memory arose and gave me another on the other side. I remembered the preposterous attitude in which Dale had found us when he rushed from Berlin into Lola's drawing-room.

I took the confounded telegram into a remote corner of the lounge, like a dog with a bone, and growled over it for a time until the humour of the situation turned the growl into a chuckle. Even had I been in sound health and strength, the idea of running off with Lola would have been absurd. But for me, in my present eumoirous disposition of mind; for me, a half-disembodied spirit who had cast all vain and disturbing human emotions into the mud of Murglebed-on-Sea; for me who had a spirit's calm disregard for the petty passions and interests of mankind and walked through the world with no other object than healing a few human woes; for me who already saw death on the other side of the river and found serious occupation in exchanging airy badinage with him; for me with an abominable little pain inside inexorably eating my life out and wasting me away literally and perceptibly like a shadow and twisting me up half a dozen times a day in excruciating agony; for me, in this delectable condition of soul and this deplorable condition of body, to think of running hundreds of miles from home with—to say the least of it—so inconvenient a creature as a big, bronze-haired woman, the idea was inexpressibly and weirdly comic.

I stepped into the drawing-room close by and drew up a telegram to Dale.

"Lady summoned by Papadopoulos on private affairs. Avoid lunacy save for electioneering purposes.—SIMON."

Then I joined Lola and Colonel Bunnion. She was lying back in her laziest and most pantherine attitude, and she looked up at me as I approached with eyes full of velvet softness. For the life of me I could not help feeling glad that they were turned on me and not on Dale Kynnersley.

Almost immediately the elder Miss Bostock came up to claim the Colonel for bridge. He rose reluctantly.

"I suppose it's no use asking you to make a fourth, Mr. de Gex?" she asked, after the subacid manner of her kind.

"I'm afraid not," I replied sweetly. Whereupon she rescued the Colonel from the syren and left me alone with her. I lit a cigarette and sat by her side. As she did not stir or speak I asked whether she was tired.

"Not very. I'm thinking. Do you know you've taught me an awful lot?"

"I? What can I have taught you?"

"The way people like yourself look at things. I'm treating Dale abominably. I didn't realise it before."

Now why on earth did she bring Dale in just at that moment.

"Indeed?" said I.

She nodded her head and said in her languorous voice:

"He's over head and ears in love with me and thinks I care for him. I don't. I don't care a brass button for him. I'm a bad influence in his life, and the sooner I take myself out of it the better. Don't you think so?"

"You know my opinions," I said.

"If I had followed your advice at first," she continued, "we needn't have had all this commotion. And yet I'm not sorry."

"What do you propose to do?" I asked.

"Before deciding, I shall see my husband."

"You shall do no such thing."

She smiled. "I shall."

I protested. Captain Vauvenarde had put himself outside the pale. He was not fit to associate with decent women. What object could she have in meeting him?

"I want to judge for myself," she replied.

"Judge what? Surely not whether he is eligible as a husband!"

"Yes," she said.

"But, my dear Lola," I cried, "the notion is as crazy as any of Anastasius Papadopoulos's. Of course, as soon as he learns that you're a rich woman, he'll want to live with you, and use your money for his gaming-hell."

"I am going to meet him," she said quietly.

"I forbid it."

"You're too late, dear friend. I wrote him a letter before dinner and sent it to the Cercle Africain by special messenger. I also wrote to Anastasius. I asked them both to see me to-morrow morning. That's why I've been so gay this evening."

At the sight of my blank face she laughed, and with one of her movements rose from her chair. I rose too.

"Are you angry with me?"

"I thought I had walked out of a nightmare," I said. "I find I'm still in it."

"But don't be angry with me. It was the only way."

"The only way to, or out of, what?" I asked, bewildered.

"Never mind."

She looked at me with a singular expression in her slumbrous eyes. It was sad, wistful, soothing, and gave me the idea of a noble woman making a senseless sacrifice.

"There is no earthly reason to do this on account of Dale," I protested.

"Dale has nothing to do with it."

"Then who has?"

"Anastasius Papadopoulos," she said with undisguised irony.

"I beg your pardon," I said rather stiffly, "for appearing to force your confidence. But as I first put the idea of joining your husband into your head and have enjoyed your confidence in the matter hitherto, I thought I might claim certain privileges."

As she had done before, she laid her hands on my shoulders—we were alone in the alcove—and looked me in the eyes.

"Don't make me cry. I'm very near it. And I'm tired to-night, and I'm going to have a hellish time to-morrow. And I want you to do me a favour."

"What is that?"

"When I'm seeing my husband, I'd like to know that you were within call—in case I wanted you. One never knows what may happen. You will come won't you, if I send for you?"

"I'm always at your service," I said.

She released my shoulders and grasped my hand.

"Good-night," she said, abruptly, and rushed swiftly out of the room, leaving me wondering more than I had ever wondered in my life at the inscrutable ways of women.

CHAPTER XIV

I am glad I devoted last night and the past hour this morning to bringing up to date this trivial record, for I have a premonition that the time is rapidly approaching when I shall no longer have the strength of will or body to continue it. The little pain has increased in intensity and frequency the last few days, and though I try to delude myself into the belief that otherwise I am as strong as ever, I know in my heart that I am daily growing weaker, daily losing vitality. I shall soon have to call in a doctor to give me some temporary relief, and doubtless he will put me to bed, feed me on slops, cut off alcohol, forbid noise and excitement, and keep me in a drugged, stupefied condition until I fall asleep, to wake up in the Garden of Prosperpine. Death is nothing; it is the dying that is such a nuisance. It is going through so much for so little. It is as bad as the campaign before a parliamentary election. It offends one's sense of proportion. In a well-regulated universe there would be no tedious process of decay, either before or after death. You would go about your daily avocation unconcerned and unwarned, and then at the moment appointed by an inscrutable Providence for your dissolution—phew!—and your clothes would remain standing for a surprised second, and then fall down in a heap without a particle of you inside them. If we have to die, why doesn't Providence employ this simple and sensible method? It would save such a lot of trouble. It would be so clean, so painless, so picturesque. It would add to the interest of our walks abroad. Fancy a stout, important policeman vanishing from his uniform—the helmet falling over the collar, the tunic doubling in at the belt, the knees giving way, and the unheard, merry laughter of the disenuniformed spirit winging its way truncheonless into the Empyrean.

But if you think you are going to get any fun out of dying in the present inconvenient manner, you are mistaken. Believe one who is trying.

I will remain on my feet, however, as long as my will holds out. In this way I may continue to be of service to my fellow creatures, and procure for myself a happy lot or portion. Even this morning I have been able to feel the throb of eumoiriety. A piteous letter came from Latimer, and a substantial cheque lies on my table ready to be posted. I wonder how much I have left? So long as it is enough to pay my doctor's bills and funeral expenses, what does it matter?

The last line of the above was written on December 21st. It is now January 30th, and I am still alive and able to write. I wish I weren't. But I will set down as plainly as I can what has happened in the interval.

I had just written the last word, seated at my hotel window in the sunshine, and enjoying, in spite of my uncheerful thoughts, the scents that rose from the garden, when I heard a knock at my door. At my invitation to enter, Anastasius Papadopoulos trotted into the room in a great state of excitement carrying the familiar bunch of papers. He put his hat on the floor, pitched the papers into the hat, and ran up to me.

"My dear sir, don't get up, I implore you. And I won't sit down. I have just seen the ever beautiful and beloved lady."

I turned my chair away from the table, and faced him as he stood blowing kisses with one little hand, while the other lay on his heart. In a flash he struck a new gesture; he folded his arms and scowled.

"I was with her. She was opening her inmost heart to me. She knows I am her champion. A servant came up announcing Monsieur Vauvenarde. She dismissed me. I have come to my patron and friend, the English statesman. Her husband is with her now."

I smiled. "Madame Brandt told me that she had asked for an interview."

"And you allow it? You allow her to contaminate her beautiful presence with the sight of that traitor, that cheat at cards, that murderer, that devil? Ah, but I will not have it! I am her champion. I will save her. I will save you. I will take you both away to Egypt, and surround you with my beautiful cats, and fan you with peacock's feathers."

This was sheer crackedness of brain. For the first time I feared for the little man. When people begin to talk that way they are not allowed to go about loose. He went on talking and the three languages he used in his jargon got clotted to the point of unintelligibility. He spoke very fast and, as far as I could understand, poured abuse on the head of Captain Vauvenarde, and continued to declare himself Lola's champion and my devoted friend. He stamped up and down the room in his tightly buttoned frock-coat from the breastpocket of which peeped the fingers of his yellow dogskin gloves. At last he stopped, and drawing a chair near the window perched on it with a little hop like a child. He held out his hand.

"Do you believe I am your friend?"

"I am sure of it, my dear Professor."

"Then I'll betray a sacred confidence. The *carissima signora* loves you. You didn't know it. But she loves you."

I stared for a moment at the dwarf as if he had been a reasonable being. Something seemed to click inside my head, like a clogged cog-wheel that had suddenly freed itself, and my mind went whirling away straight through the past few weeks. I tried to smile, and I said:

"You are quite mistaken."

"Oh, no," he replied, wagging his Napoleonic head. "Anastasius Papadopoulos is never mistaken. She told me so herself. She wept. She put her beautiful arms round my neck and sobbed on my shoulder."

I found myself reproving him gently. "You should not have told me this, my dear Professor. Such confidences are locked up in the heart of *un galant homme*, and are not revealed even to his dearest friend."

But my voice sounded hollow in my own ears, and what he said for the next few minutes I do not remember. The little man had told the truth to me, and Lola had told the truth to him. The realisation of it paralysed me. Why had I been such a fool as not to see it for myself? Memories of a hundred indications came tumbling one after another into my head—the forgotten glove, the glances, the changes of mood, the tears when she learned of my illness, the mysterious words, the abrupt little "You?" of yesterday. The woman was in love, deeply in love, in love with all the fervour of her big nature. And I had stood by and wondered what she meant by this and by that—things that would have been obvious to a coalheaver. I thought of Dale and I felt miserably guilty, horribly ashamed. How could I expect him to believe me when I told him that I had not wittingly stolen her affections from him. And her affections? *Bon Dieu!* What on earth could I do with them? What is the use of a woman's love to a dead man? And did I want it even for the tiny remainder of life?

Anastasius, perceiving that I paid but scant attention to his conversation, wriggled off his chair and stood before me with folded arms.

"You adore each other with a great passion," he said. "She is my Madonna, and you are my friend and benefactor. I will be your protection and defence. I will never let her go away with that infamous, gambling and murdering scoundrel. My gigantic combinations have matured. I bless your union."

He lifted his little arms in benediction. The situation was cruelly comical. For a moment I hated the mournful-visaged, posturing monkey, and had a wild desire to throw him out of the window and have done with him. I rose and, towering over him, was about to lecture him severely on his impertinent interference, when the sight of his scared face made me turn away with a laugh. What would be the use of reproaching him? He would only sit down on the floor and weep. So I paced the room, while he followed me with his eyes like an uncertain spaniel.

"Look here, Professor," said I at last. "Now that you've found Captain Vauvenarde, brought Madame Brandt and him together, and told me that she is in love with me, don't you think you've done enough? Don't you think your cats need your attention? Something terrible may be happening to them. I dreamed last night," I added with desperate mendacity, "that they were turned into woolly lambs."

"Monsieur," said the dwarf loftily, "my duty is here. And I care not whether my cats are turned into the angels of Paradise."

I groaned. "You are wasting a great deal of money over this affair," I urged.

"What is money to my gigantic combinations?"

"Tell me," I cried with considerable impatience. "What are your confounded combinations?"

He began to tremble violently. "I would rather die," said he, "than betray my secret."

"It's all some silly nonsense about that wretched horse!" I exclaimed.

He covered his ears with his hands. "Blasphemy! Blasphemy! Don't utter it!"

In another moment he was cowering on his knees before me.

"You, of all men, mustn't blaspheme. You whom I love like my master. You whom the divine lady loves. I can't bear it!" He continued to gibber unintelligibly.

He was stark mad. There was no question of it. For a moment I stood irresolute. Then I lifted him to his feet and patted his head soothingly.

"Never mind," said I. "I was wrong. It was a beautiful horse. There never was such a horse in the world. If I had a picture of him I would hang it up on the wall over my bed."

"Would you?" he cried joyfully. "Then I will give you one."

He trotted over to the bundle of papers that reposed in his hat on the floor, searched through them, and to my dismay handed me a faded, unmounted, and rather torn and crumpled photograph of the wonderful horse.

"There!" said he.

"I could not rob you of it," I protested.

"It will be my joy to know that you have it—that it is hanging over your bed. See—have you a pin? I myself will fix it for you."

While he was searching my table for pins the chasseur of the hotel came with a message from Madame Brandt. Would Monsieur come at once to Madame in her private room?

"I'll come now," I said. "Professor, you must excuse me."

"Don't mention it. I shall occupy myself in hanging the picture in the most artistic way possible."

So I left him, his mind apparently concentrated on the childish task of pinning the photograph of the ridiculous horse on my bedroom wall, and went with the most complicated feelings downstairs and through the corridors to Lola's apartments.

She rose to meet me as I entered.

"It's very kind of you to come," she said in her fluent but Britannic French. "May I present my husband, Monsieur Vauvenarde."

Monsieur Vauvenarde and I exchanged bows. I noticed at once that he wore the Frenchman's costume when he pays a *visite de ceremonie*, frock-coat and gloves, and that a silk hat lay on the table. I was glad that he paid her this mark of respect.

"I have had the pleasure of meeting you before, Monsieur," said he, "in circumstances somewhat different."

"I remember perfectly," said I.

"And your charming but inexperienced little friend—is he well?"

"He is at present decorating my room with photographs of Madame's late horse, Sultan," said I.

He was startled, and gave me a quick, sharp look. I did not notice it at the time, but I remembered it later. Then he broke into an indulgent laugh.

"The poor animal!" He turned to Lola. "How jealous I used to be of him! And how quickly the time flies. But give yourself the trouble of seating yourself, Monsieur."

He motioned me to a chair and sat down. He was a man of polished manner and had a pleasant voice. I guessed that in the days when he paid court to Lola, he had been handsome in his dark Norman way, and possessed considerable fascination. Evil living and sordid passions had coarsened his features, produced bagginess under the eyes and a shiftiness of glance. Idleness and an inverted habit of life were responsible for the nascent paunch and the rolls of fat at the back of his neck. He suggested the revivified corpse of a fine gentleman that had been unnaturally swollen. I had disliked him at the Cercle Africain; now I detested him heartily. The idea of Lola entering the vitiated atmosphere of his life was inexpressibly repugnant to me.

Contrary to her habit, Lola sat bolt upright on the stamped-velvet suite, the palms of her hands pressing the seat on either side of her. She caught the shade of disgust that swept over my face, and gave me a quick glance that pleaded for toleration. Her eyes, though bright, were sunken, like those of a woman who has not slept.

"Monsieur," said Vauvenarde, "my wife informs me that to your disinterested friendship is due this most charming reconciliation."

"Reconciliation?" I echoed. "It was quickly effected."

"*Mon Dieu*," he said. "I have always longed for the comforts of a home. My wife has grown tired of a migratory existence. She comes to find me. I hasten to meet her. There is nothing to keep us apart. The reconciliation was a matter of a few seconds. I wish to express my gratitude to you, and, therefore, I ask you to accept my most cordial thanks."

"It has always been a pleasure to me," said I very frigidly, "to place my services at the disposal of Madame Brandt."

"Vauvenarde, Monsieur," he corrected with a smile.

"And is Madame Vauvenarde equally satisfied with the—reconciliation?" I asked.

"I think Monsieur Vauvenarde is somewhat premature," said Lola, with a trembling lip. "There were conditions—"

"A mere question of protocol." He waved an airy hand.

"I don't know what that is," said Lola. "There are conditions I must fix, and I thought the advice of my friend, Monsieur de Gex—"

"Precisely, my dear Lola," he interrupted. "The principle is affirmed. We are reconciled. I proceed logically. The first thing I do is to thank Monsieur de Gex—you have a French name, Monsieur, and you pronounce it English fashion, which is somewhat embarrassing—But no matter. The next thing is the protocol. We have no possibility of calling a family council, and therefore, I acceded with pleasure to the intervention of Monsieur. It is kind of him to burden himself with our unimportant affairs."

The irony of his tone belied the suave correctitude of his words. I detested him more and more. More and more did I realise that the dying eumoirist is capable of petty human passions. My vanity was being sacrified. Here was a woman passionately in love with me proposing to throw herself into another man's arms—it made not a scrap of difference, in the circumstances, that the man was her husband—and into the arms of such a man! Having known me to decline—etcetera, etcetera! How could she face it? And why was she doing it? To save herself from me, or me from herself? She knew perfectly well that the little pain inside would precious soon settle that question. Why was she doing it? I should have thought that the first glance at the puffy reprobate would have been enough to show her the folly of her idea. However, it was comforting to learn that she had not surrendered at once.

"If I am to have the privilege, Monsieur," said I, "of acting as a family council, perhaps you may forgive my hinting at some of the conditions that doubtless are in Madame's mind."

"Proceed, Monsieur," said he.

"I want to know where I am," said Lola in English. "He took everything for granted from the first."

"Are you willing to go back to him?" I asked also in English.

She met my gaze steadily, and I saw a woman's needless pain at the back of her eyes. She moistened her lips with her tongue, and said:

"Under conditions."

"Monsieur," said I in French, turning to Vauvenarde, "forgive us for speaking our language."

"Perfectly," said he, and he smiled meaningly and banteringly at us both.

"In the first place, Monsieur, you are aware that Madame has a little fortune, which does not detract from the charm you have always found in her. It was left her by her father, who, as you know, tamed lions and directed a menagerie. I would propose that Madame appointed trustees to administer this little fortune."

"There is no necessity, Monsieur," he said. "By the law of France it is hers to do what she likes with."

"Precisely," I rejoined. "Trustees would prevent her from doing what she liked with it. Madame has indeed a head for affairs, but she also has a woman's heart, which sometimes interferes with a woman's head in the most disastrous manner."

"Article No. 1 of the protocol. *Allez toujours*, Monsieur."

I went on, feeling happier. "The next article treats of a little matter which I understand has been the cause of differences in the past between Madame and yourself. Madame, although she has not entered the arena for some time, has not finally abandoned it." I smiled at the look of surprise on Lola's face. "An artist is always an artist, Monsieur. She is willing, however, to renounce it for ever, if you, on your side, will make quite a small sacrifice."

"Name it, Monsieur."

"You have a little passion for baccarat———"

"Surely, Monsieur," said he blandly, "my wife would not expect me to give up what is the mere recreation of every clubman."

"As a recreation pure and simple—she would not insist too much, but———" I shrugged my shoulders. I flatter myself on being able to do it with perfect French expressiveness. I caught, to my satisfaction, an angry gleam in his eye.

"Do you mean to say, Monsieur, that I play for more than recreation?"

"How dare I say anything, Monsieur. But Madame is prejudiced against the Cercle Africain. For a bachelor there is little to be said against it—but for a married man—you seize the point?" said I.

"*Bien*, Monsieur," he said, swallowing his wrath. "And Article 3?"

"Since you have left the army—would it not be better to engage in some profession—unless your private fortune dispenses you from the necessity."

He said nothing but: "Article 4?"

"It would give Madame comfort to live out of Algiers."

"*Moi aussi*," he replied rather unexpectedly. "We have the whole of France to choose from."

"Would not Madame be happier if she lived out of France, also? She has always longed for a social position."

"*Eh, bien?* I can give her one in France."

"Are you quite sure?" I asked, looking him in the eyes.

"Monsieur," said he, rising and giving his moustache a swashbuckler twist upward, "what are you daring to insinuate?"

I leaned back in my chair and fingered the waxed ends of mine.

"Nothing, Monsieur; I ask a simple question, which you surely can have no difficulty in answering."

"Your questions are the height of indiscretion," he cried angrily.

"In that case, before we carry this interview further, the Family Council and Madame would do well to have a private consultation."

"Monsieur," he cried, completely losing his temper. "I forbid you to use that tone to me. You are making a mock of me. You are insulting me. I bore with you long enough to see how much further your insolence would dare to go. I'm not to have a hand in the administration of my wife's money? I'm to forsake a plentiful means of livelihood? I'm to become a commercial traveller? I'm to expatriate myself? I'm to explain, too, the reasons why I left the army? I would not condescend. Least of all to you."

"May I ask why, Monsieur?"

"*Tonnerre de Dieu!*" He stamped his foot. "Do you take me for a fool? Here I am—I came at my wife's request, ready to take her back as my wife, ready to condone everything—yes, Monsieur, as a man of the world—you think I have no eyes, no understanding—ready to take her off your hands—"

I leaped to my feet.

"Monsieur!" I thundered.

Lola gave a cry and rushed forward. I pushed her aside, and glared at him. I was in a furious rage. We glared at each other eye to eye. I pointed to the door.

"*Monsieur, sortez!*"

I went to it and flung it wide. Anastasius Papadopoulos trotted into the room.

His entrance was so queer, so unexpected, so anti-climatic, that for the moment the three of us were thrown off our emotional balance.

"I have heard all, I have heard all," shrieked the little man. "I know you for what you are. I am the champion of the *carissima signora* and the protector of the English statesman. You are a traitor and murderer—"

Vauvenarde lifted his hand in a threatening gesture.

"Hold your tongue, you little abortion!" he shouted.

But Anastasius went on screaming and flourishing his bundle of papers.

"Ask him if he remembers the horse Sultan; ask him if he remembers the horse Sultan!"

Lola took him by the shoulders.

"Anastasius, you must go away from here—to please me. It's my orders."

But he shook himself free, and the silk hat which he had not removed fell off in the quick struggle.

"Ask him if he remembers Saupiquet," he screamed, and then banged the door.

A malevolent devil put a sudden idea into my head and prompted speech.

"*Do* you remember Saupiquet?" I asked ironically.

"Monsieur, meddle with your own affairs and let me pass. You shall hear from me."

The dwarf planted himself before the door.

"You shall not pass till you have answered me. Do you remember Saupiquet? Do you remember the five francs you gave to Saupiquet to let you into Sultan's stable? Ah! Ha! Ha! You wince. You grow pale. Do you remember the ball of poison you put down Sultan's throat?"

Lola started forward with flaming eyes and anguished face.

"You—you?" she gasped. "You were so ignoble as to do that?"

"The accursed brute!" shouted Vauvenarde. "Yes, I did it. I wish I had burned out his entrails."

Anastasius sprang at him like a tiger cat. I had a quick vision of the dwarf clinging in the air against the other's bulky form, one hand at his throat, and then of an incredibly swift flash of steel. The dwarf dropped off and rolled backwards, revealing something black sticking out of Vauvenarde's frock-coat—for the second I could not realise what it was. Then Vauvenarde, with a ghastly face, reeled sideways and collapsed in a heap on the ground.

CHAPTER XV

Of what happened immediately afterwards I have but a confused memory. I remember that Lola and I both fell on our knees beside the stabbed man, and I remember his horrible staring eyes and open mouth. I remember that, though she was white and shaky, she neither shrieked, went into hysterics, nor fainted. I remember rushing down to the manager; I remember running with him breathlessly through obscure passages of the hotel in search of a doctor who was attending a sick member of the staff. I remember the rush back, the doctor bending over the body, which Lola had partially unclothed, and saying:

"He is dead. The blade has gone straight through his heart."

And I have in my mind the unforgettable and awful picture of Anastasius Papadopoulos disregarded in a corner of the room, with his absurd silk hat on—some reflex impulse had caused him to pick it up and put it on his head—sitting on the floor amid a welter of documents relating to the death of the horse Sultan, one of which he was eagerly perusing.

After this my memory is clear. It was only the first awful shock and horror of the thing that dazed me.

The man was dead, said the doctor. He must lie until the police arrived and drew up the *proces-verbal*. The manager went to telephone to the police, and while he was gone I told the doctor what had occurred. Anastasius took no notice of us. Lola, holding her nerves under iron control, stood bolt upright looking alternately at the doctor and myself as we spoke. But she did not utter a word. Presently the manager returned. The alarm had not been given in the hotel. No one knew anything about the occurrence. Lola went into her bedroom and came back with a sheet. The manager took it from her and threw it over the dead man. The doctor stood by Anastasius. The end of a strip of sunlight by the window just caught the dwarf in his corner.

"Get up," said the doctor.

Anastasius, without raising his eyes from his papers, waved him away.

"I am busy. I am engaged on important papers of identification. He had a white star on his forehead, and his tail was over a metre long."

Lola approached him.

"Anastasius," she said gently. He looked up with a radiant smile. "Put away those papers." Like a child he obeyed and scrambled to his feet. Then, seeing the unfamiliar face of the doctor for the first time, he executed one of his politest and most elaborate bows. The doctor after looking at him intently for a while, turned to me.

"Mad. Utterly mad. Apparently he has no consciousness of what he has done."

He lured him to the sofa and sat beside him and began to talk in a low tone of the contents of the papers. Anastasius replied cheerfully, proud at being noticed by the stranger. The papers referred to a precious secret, a gigantic combination, which he had spent years in maturing. I shivered at the sound of his voice, and turned to Lola.

"This is no place for you. Go into your bedroom till you are wanted."

I held the door open for her. She put her hands up to her face and reeled, and I thought she would have fallen; but she roused herself.

"I don't want to break down—not yet. I shall if I'm left alone—come and sit with me, for God's sake."

"Very well," said I.

She passed me and I followed; but at the door I turned and glanced round the cheerful, sunny room. There, against the background of blue sky and tree tops framed by the window, sat Anastasius Papadopoulos, swinging his little legs and talking bombastically to the tanned and grizzled doctor, and opposite stood the correctly attired hotel manager in the attitude in which he habitually surveyed the lay-out of the table d'hote, keeping watch beside the white-covered shape on the floor. I was glad to shut the sight from my eyes. We waited silently in the bedroom, Lola sitting on the bed and hiding her face in the pillows, and I standing by the window and looking out at the smiling mockery of the fair earth. An agonising spasm of pain—a *momento mori*—shot through me and passed away. I thanked God that a few weeks would see the end of me. I had always enjoyed the comedy of life. It had been to me a thing of infinite jest. But this stupid, meaningless tragedy was carrying the joke too far. My fastidiousness revolted at its vulgarity. I no longer wished to inhabit a world where such jests were possible. . . . I had never seen a man die before. I was surprised at the swiftness and the ugliness of it. . . . I suddenly realised that I was smoking a cigarette, which I was quite unconscious of having lit. I threw it away. A minute afterwards I felt that if I did not smoke I should go crazy. So I lit another. . . . The ghastly silliness of the murder! . . . Colonel Bunnion's loud laugh rose from the terrace below, jarring horribly on my ears. A long green praying mantis that had apparently mounted on the bougainvillea against the hotel wall appeared in meditative stateliness on the window-sill. I picked the insect up absent-mindedly, and began to play with it. Lola's voice from the bed startled me and caused me to drop the mantis. She spoke hoarsely.

"Tell me—what are they going to do with him?"

I turned round. She had raised a crushed face from the pillows, and looked at me haggardly. I noticed a carafe of brandy and a siphon by the bedside. I mixed her a strong dose, and, before replying, made her drink it.

"They'll place him under restraint, that's all. He's not responsible for his actions."

"He did that once before—I told you—but without the knife—I wish I could cry—I can't—You don't think it heartless of me—but my brain is on fire—I shall always see it—I wish to God I had never asked him to come— Why did I? My God, why did I?—It was my fault—I wanted to see him— to judge for myself how much of the old Andre was left—there was good in him once—I thought I might possibly help him—There was nothing for me to do in the world—Without you any kind of old hell was good enough—That's why I sent for him—When he came, after a bit, I was afraid, and sent for you———"

"Afraid of what?" I asked.

"He asked me at once what money I had—Then there seemed to be no doubt in his mind that I would join him—We spoke of you—the friend who could advise me—He never said—what he said afterwards—I thought it kind of him to consent to see you—I rang the bell and sent the chasseur for you. I supposed Anastasius had gone home—I never thought of him. The poor little man was sweet to me, just like a dog—a silent, sympathetic dog—I spoke to him as I would to something that wouldn't understand— all sorts of foolish things—Now and then a woman has to empty her heart"—she shivered—her hands before her face.

"It's my fault, it's my fault."

"These things are no one's fault," I said gently. But just as I was beginning to console her with what thumb-marked scraps of platitude I could collect—the only philosophy after all, such is the futility of systems, adequate to the deep issues of life—the door opened and the manager announced that the police had arrived.

We went through the ordeal of the *proces-verbal.* Anastasius, confronted with his victim, had no memory of what had occurred. He shrieked and shrank and hid his face in Lola's dress. When he was forced to speak he declared that the dead man was not Captain Vauvenarde. Captain Vauvenarde was at the Cercle Africain. He, himself, was seeking him. He would take the gendarmes there, and they could arrest the Captain for the murder of Sultan of which his papers contained indubitable proofs. Eventually the poor little wretch was led away in custody, proud and smiling, entirely convinced that he was leading his captors to the arrest of Captain Vauvenarde. On the threshold he turned and bowed to us so low that the brim of his silk hat touched the floor. Then Lola's nerve gave way and she broke into a passion of awful weeping.

The *commissaire de police* secured the long thin knife (how the dwarf had managed to conceal it on his small person was a mystery) and the bundle of documents, and accompanied me to my room to see whether he had left anything there to serve as a *piece de conviction*. We found only the crumpled picture of the horse Sultan neatly pinned against my bedroom wall, and on the floor a ribbon tied like a garter with a little bell opposite the bow. On it was written "Santa Bianca," and I knew it was the collar of the beloved cat which he must have been carrying about him for a talisman. The *commissaire* took this also.

If you desire to know the details of the judicial proceedings connected with the murder of Andre Marie-Joseph Vauvenarde, ex-Captain in the Chasseurs d'Afrique, and the trial of Anastasius Papadopoulos, I must refer you to the Algerian, Parisian, and London Press. There you will find an eagerly picturesque account of the whole miserable affair. Now, not only am I unable to compete with descriptive verbatim reporters on their own ground, but also a consecutive statement, either bald or graphic, of the tedious horrors Lola Brandt and I had to undergo, would be foreign to the purpose of these notes, however far from their original purpose an ironical destiny has caused them to wander. You know nearly all that is necessary for you to know, so that when I am dead you may not judge me too harshly. The remainder I can summarise in a few words. At any rate, I have told the truth, often more naively than one would have thought possible for a man who prided himself as much as I did on his epicurean sophistication.

These have been days, as I say, of tedious horror. There have been endless examinations, reconstructions of the crime, exposures in daring publicity of the private lives of the protagonists of the lunatic drama. The French judges and advocates have accepted the account given by Lola and myself of our mutual relations with a certain mocking credulity. The Press hasn't accepted it at all. It took as a matter of course the view held by the none too noble victim. At first, seeing Lola shrug her shoulders with supreme indifference as to her own reputation, I cared but little for these insinuations. I wrote such letters to my sisters and to Dale as I felt sure would be believed, and let the long-eared, gaping world go hang. Besides, I had other things to think of. Physical pain is insistent, and I have suffered damnable torture. The pettiness of the legal inquiry has been also a maddening irritation. Nothing has been too minute for the attention of the

French judiciary. It seemed as though the whole of the evil gang of the Cercle Africain were called as witnesses. They testified as to Captain Vauvenarde's part proprietorship of the hell—as to wrong practices that occurred there—as to the crazy conduct of both Anastasius and myself on the occasion of my insane visit. Officers of the Chasseurs d'Afrique were compelled further to blacken the character of the dead man—he had been a notorious plucker of pigeons during most of his military career, and when at last he was caught red-handed palming the king at *ecarte*, he was forced to resign his commission. Arabs came from the slums with appalling stories. Even the stolid Saupiquet, dragged from Toulon, gave evidence as to the five-franc bribe and the debt of fifteen sous, and identified the horse Sultan by the crumpled photograph. Lola and I have been racked day after day with questions—some, indeed, prompted by the suspicion that Vauvenarde might have met his death directly by our hand instead of that of Anastasius. It was the Procureur-general who said: "It can be argued that you would benefit by the decease of the defunct." I replied that we could not benefit in any way. My sole object was to effect a reconciliation between husband and wife. "Will you explain why you gave yourself that trouble?" I never have smiled so grimly as I did then. How could I explain my precious pursuit of the eumoirous to a French Procureur-general? How could I put before him the point of view of a semi-disembodied spirit? I replied with lame lack of originality that my actions proceeded from disinterested friendship. "You are a pure altruist then?" said he. "Very pure," said I. . . . It was only the facts of the scabbard of the knife having been found attached to the dwarf's person beneath his clothes, and of certain rambling menaces occurring in his Sultan papers that saved us from the indignity of being arrested and put into the dock. . . .

During all this time I remained at the hotel at Mustapha Superieur. Lola moved to a suite of rooms in another hotel a little way down the hill. I saw her daily. At first she shrank from publicity and refused to go out, save in a closed carriage to the town when her presence was necessary at the inquiries. But after a time I persuaded her to brave the stare of the curious and stroll with me among the eucalyptus woods above. We cut ourselves off from other human companionship and felt like two lost souls wandering alone through mist. She conducted herself with grave and simple dignity. . . . Once or twice she visited Anastasius in prison. She found him humanely treated and not despondent. He thought they had arrested him for the poisoning of the horse, and laughed at their foolishness. As they refused to return him his dossier, he occupied himself in reconstructing it, and wrote pages and pages of incoherence to prove the guilt of Captain Vauvenarde. He was hopelessly mad. . . . The bond of pain bound me very close to Lola.

"What are you going to do with your life?" I asked her one day.

"So long as I have you as a friend, it doesn't greatly matter."

"You forget," I said, "that you can't have me much longer."

"Are you going to leave me? It's not because I have dragged you through all this dirt and horror. Another woman might say that of another man— but not I of you. Why are you going to leave me? I want so little—only to see you now and then—to keep the heart in me."

"Can't you realise, that what I said in London is true?"

"No. I can't. It's unbelievable. You can't believe it yourself. If you did, how could you go on behaving like anybody else—like me for instance?"

"What would you do if you were condemned to die?"

She shuddered. "I should go mad with fear—I——" She broke off and remained for some moments reflective, with knitted brow. Then she lifted her head proudly. "No, I shouldn't. I should face it like you. Only cowards are afraid. It's best to show things that you don't care a hang for them."

"Keep that sublime *je m'en fich'isme* up when I'm dead and buried," said I, "and you'll pull through your life all right. The only thing you must avoid is the pursuit of eumoiriety."

"What on earth is that?" she asked.

"The last devastating vanity," said I.

And so it is.

"When you are gone," she said bravely, "I shall remember how strong and true you were. It will make me strong too."

I acquiesced silently in her proposition. In this age of flippancy and scepticism, if a human soul proclaims sincerely its faith in the divinity of a rabbit, in God's name don't disturb it. It is *something* whereto to refer his aspirations, his resolves; it is a court of arbitration, at the lowest, for his spiritual disputes; and the rabbit will be as effective an oracle as any other. For are not all religions but the strivings of the spirit towards crystallisation at some point outside the environment of passions and appetites which is the flesh, so that it can work untrammelled: and are not all gods but the accidental forms, conditioned by circumstance, which this crystallisation takes? All gods in their anthropo-, helio-, thero-, or what-not-morphic forms are false; but, on the other hand, all gods in their spiritual essence are true. So I do not deprecate my prospective unique position in Lola Brandt's hagiology. It was better for her soul that I should occupy it. Even if I were about to live my normal life out, like any other hearty human, marry and beget children, I doubt whether I should attempt to shake my wife's faith in my heroical qualities.

This was but a fragment of one among countless talks. Some were lighter in tone, others darker, the mood of man being much like a child's balloon which rises or falls as the strata of air are more rarefied or more dense. Perhaps during the time of strain, the atmosphere was more often rarefied, and our conversation had the day's depressing incidents for its topics. We rarely spoke of the dead man. He was scarcely a subject for panegyric, and it was useless to dwell on the memory of his degradation. I think we only once talked of him deeply and at any length, and that was on the day of the funeral. His brother, a manufacturer at Clermont-Ferrand, and a widowed aunt, apparently his only two surviving relatives, arrived in Algiers just in time to attend the ceremony. They had seen the report of the murder in the newspapers and had started forthwith. The brother, during an interview with Lola, said bitter things to her, reproaching her with the man's downfall, and cast on her the responsibility of his death.

"He spoke," she said, "as if I had suggested the murder and practically put the knife into the poor crazy little fellow's hand."

The Vauvenardes must have been an amiable family.

"Before I came," she said a little while later, "I still had some tenderness for him—a woman has for the only man that has been—really—in her life. I wish I could feel it now. I wish I could feel some respect even. But I can't. If I could, it would lessen the horror that has got hold of me to my bones."

It was a torture to her generous soul that she could not grieve for him. She could only shudder at the tragedy. In her heart she grieved more for Anastasius Papadopoulos, and in so doing she was, in her feminine way, self-accusative of callous lack of human feeling. It was my attempt to bring her to a more rational state of mind that caused us to review the dead man's career, and recapitulate the unpleasing incidents of the last interview.

Of Captain Vauvenarde, no more. He has gone whither I am going. That his soul may rest in peace is my earnest prayer. But I do not wish to meet him.

Lola went tearless and strong through the horrible ordeal of the judicial proceedings. She said I gave her courage. Perhaps, unconsciously, I did. It was only when the end came that she broke down, although she knew exactly what the end would be. And I, too, felt a lump in my throat when they sentenced Anastasius Papadopoulos to the asylum, and I saw him for the last time, the living parody of Napoleon III, frock-coated and yellow-gloved, the precious, newly written dossier in his hand, as he disappeared with a mournful smile from the court, after bowing low to the judge and to us, without having understood the significance of anything that had happened.

In the carriage that took us home she wept and sobbed bitterly.

"I loved him so. He was the only creature on earth that loved me. He loved me as only a dog can love—or an angel."

I let her cry. What could I say or do?

These have been weeks of tedious horror and pain. With the exception of Colonel Bunnion, I have kept myself aloof from my fellow creatures in the hotel, even taking my meals in my own rooms, not wishing to be stared at as the hero of the scandal that convulsed the place. And with regard to Colonel Bunnion shall I be accused of cynicism if I say that I admitted him—not to my confidence—but to my company, because I know that it delighted the honest but boring fellow to prove to himself that he could rise above British prejudice and exhibit tact in dealing with a man in a delicate position? For, mark you, all the world—even those nearest and dearest to me as I soon discovered—believed that the wife of the man who was murdered before my eyes was my mistress. Colonel Bunnion was kind, and he meant to be kind. He was a gentleman for all his wearisomeness, and his kindness was such as I could accept. But I know what I say about him is true. Ye gods! Haven't I felt myself the same swelling pride in my broadmindedness? When a man is going on my journey he does not palter with truth.

Though I held myself aloof, as I say, from practically all my fellow creatures here, I have not been cut off from the outside world. My sisters, like this French court in Algiers, have accepted my statement with polite incredulity. Their letters have been full of love, half-veiled reproach, anxiety as to their social position, and an insane desire to come and take care of me. This I have forbidden them to do. The pain they would have inflicted on themselves, dear souls, would have far outweighed the comfort I might have gained from their ministrations. Then I have had piteous letters from Dale.

". . . Your telegram reassured me, though I was puzzled. Now I get a letter from Lola, telling me it's all off—that she never loved me—that she valued my youth and my friendship, but that it is best for us not to meet again. What is the meaning of it, Simon? For Heaven's sake tell me. I can't think of anything else. I can't sleep. I am going off my head. . . ."

Again. ". . . This awful newspaper report and your letter of explanation—I have them side by side. Forgive me, Simon. I don't know what to believe, where to turn. . . . I have looked up to you as the best and straightest man I know. You must be. Yet why have you done this? Why didn't you tell me she was married? Why didn't she tell me? I can't write properly, my head is all on a buzz. The beastly papers say you were living with her in Algiers—but you weren't, were you? It would be too horrible. In fact, you say you weren't. But, all the same, you have stolen her from me. It wasn't like you. . . . And this awful murder. My God! you don't know what it all means to me. It's breaking my heart. . . ."

And Lady Kynnersley wrote—with what object I scarcely know. The situation was far beyond the poor lady's by-laws and regulations for the upbringing of families and the conduct of life. The elemental mother in her battled on the side of her only son—foolishly, irrationally, unkindly. Her exordium was as correct as could be. The tragedy shocked her, the scandal grieved her, the innuendoes of the Press she refused to believe; she sympathised with me deeply. But then she turned from me to Dale, and feminine unreason took possession of her pen. She bitterly reproached herself for having spoken to me of Madame Brandt. Had she known how passionate and real was this attachment, she would never have interfered. The boy was broken-hearted. He accused me of having stolen her from him—his own words. He took little interest in his electioneering campaign, spoke badly, unconvincingly; spent hours in alternate fits of listlessness and anger. She feared for her darling's health and reason. She made an appeal to me who professed to love him—if it were honourably possible, would I bring Madame Brandt back to him? She was willing now to accept Dale's estimate of her worth. Could I, at the least, prevail on Madame Brandt to give him some hope—of what she did not know—but some hope that would save him from ruining his career and "doing something desperate"?

And another letter from Dale:

". . . I can't work at this election. For God's sake, give her back to me. Then I won't care. What is Parliament to me without her? And the election is as good as lost already. The other side has made as much as possible of the scandal. . . ."

The only letters that have not been misery to read have come from Eleanor Faversham. There was one passage which made me thank God that He had created such women as Eleanor—

"Don't fret over the newspaper lies, dear. Those who love you—and why shouldn't I love you still?—know the honourable gentleman that you are. Write to me if it would ease your heart and tell me just what you feel you can. Now and always you have my utter sympathy and understanding."

And this is the woman of whose thousand virtues I dared to speak in flippant jest.

Heaven forgive me.

After receiving Lady Kynnersley's appeal, I went to Lola. It was just before the case came on at the Cour d'Assises. She had finished luncheon in her private room and was sitting over her coffee. I joined her. She wore the black blouse and skirt with which I have not yet been able to grow familiar, as it robbed her of the peculiar fascinating quality which I have tried to suggest by the word pantherine. Coffee over, we moved to the window which opened on a little back garden—the room was on the ground floor—in which grew prickly pear and mimosa, and newly flowering heliotrope. I don't know why I should mention this, except that some scenes impress themselves, for no particular reason, on the memory, while others associated with more important incidents fade into vagueness. I picked a bunch of heliotrope which she pinned at her bosom.

"Lola," I said, "I want to speak to you seriously."

She smiled wanly: "Do we ever speak otherwise these dreadful days?"

"It's about Dale. Read this," said I, and I handed her Lady Kynnersley's letter. She read it through and returned it to me.

"Well?"

"I asked you a week or two ago what you were going to do with your life," I said. "Does that letter offer you any suggestion?"

"I'm to give him some hope—what hope can I give him?"

"You're a free woman—free to marry. For the boy's sake the mother will consent. When she knows you as well as we know you she will—"

"She will—what? Love me?"

"She's a woman not given to loving—except, in unexpected bursts, her offspring. But she will respect you."

She stood for a few moments silent, her arm resting against the window jamb and her head on her arm. She remained there so long that at last I rose and, looking at her face, saw that her eyes were full of tears. She dashed them away with the back of her hand, gave me a swift look, and went and sat in the shadow of the room. An action of this kind on the part of a woman signifies a desire for solitude. I lit a cigarette and went into the garden.

It was a sorry business. I saw as clearly as Lola that Lady Kynnersley desired to purchase Dale's immediate happiness at any price, and that the future might bring bitter repentance. But I offered no advice. I have finished playing at Deputy Providence. A madman letting off fireworks in a gunpowder factory plays a less dangerous game.

Presently she joined me and ran her arm through mine.

"I'll write to Dale this afternoon," she said. "Don't let us talk of it any more now. You are tired out. It's time for you to go and lie down. I'll walk with you up the hill."

It has come to this, that I must lie down for some hours during the day lest I should fall to pieces.

"I suppose I'll have to," I laughed. "What a thing it is to have the wits of a man and the strength of a baby."

She pressed my arm and said in her low caressing voice which I had not heard for many weeks: "I shouldn't be so proud of those man's wits, if I were you."

I knew she said it playfully with reference to masculine non-perception of the feminine; but I chose to take it broadly.

"My dear Lola," said I, "it has been borne in upon me that I am the most witless fool that the unwisdom of generations of English country squires has ever succeeded in producing."

"Don't talk rot," she said, with foolishness in her eyes.

She accompanied me bareheaded in the sunshine to the gate of my hotel.

"Come and dine with me, if you're well enough," she said as we parted.

I assented, and when the evening came I went. Did I not say that we were like two lost souls wandering alone in the mist?

It was only when I rose to bid her good-night that she referred to Dale.

"I wrote to him this afternoon," she announced curtly.

"You said you would do so."

"Would you like to know what I told him?"

She put her hands behind her back and stood facing me, somewhat defiantly, in all her magnificence. I smiled. Women, much as they scoff at the blindness of our sex, are often transparent.

"It's your firm determination to tell me," said I. "Well?"

She advanced a step nearer to me, and looked me straight in the eyes defiantly.

"I told him that I loved you with all my heart and all my soul. I told him that you didn't know it; that you didn't care a brass curse for me; that you had acted as you thought best for the happiness of himself and me. I told him that while you lived I could not think of another man. I told him that if you could face Death with a smile on your face, he might very well show the same courage and not chuck things right and left just because a common woman wouldn't marry him or live with him and spoil his career. There! That's what I told him. What do you think?"

"Heaven knows what effect it will have," said I, wearily, for I was very, very tired. "But why, my poor Lola, have you wasted your love on a shadow like me?"

She answered after the foolish way of women.

I have not heard from either Dale or Lady Kynnersley. A day or two ago, in reply to a telegram to Raggles, I learned that Dale had lost the election.

This, then, is the end of my *apologia pro vita mea*, which I began with so resonant a flourish of vainglory. I have said all that there is to be said. Nothing more has happened or is likely to happen until they put me under the earth. Oh, yes, I was forgetting. In spite of my Monte Cristo munificence, poor Latimer has been hammered on the Stock Exchange. Poor Lucy and the kids!

I shall have, I think, just enough strength left to reach Mentone—this place is intolerable now—and there I shall put myself under the care of a capable physician who, with his abominable drugs, will doubtless begin the cheerful work of inducing the mental decay which I suppose must precede physical dissolution.

I must confess that I am disappointed with the manner of my exit. I had imagined it quite different. I had beheld myself turning with a smile and a jest for one last view of the faces over which I, in my eumoirous career, had cast the largesse of happiness, and the vanishing with a gallant carelessness through the dusky portals. Instead of that, here am I sneaking out of life by the back door, covering my eyes for very shame. And glad? Oh, God, how glad I am to slink out of it!

I have indeed accomplished the thing which I set out to do. I have severed a boy from the object of his passion. What an achievement for the crowning glory of a lifetime! And at what a cost: one fellow-creature's life and another's reason. On me lies the responsibility. Vauvenarde, it is true, did not adorn this grey world, but he drew the breath of life, and, through my jesting agency, it was cut off. Anastasius Papadopoulos, had he not come under my malign influence would have lived out his industrious, happy and dream-filled days. Lesser, but still great price, too, has been paid. Jealous hatred, misery and failure for the being I care most for in the world, the shame of a sordid scandal to those that hold me dear, the hopeless love and speedy mourning of a woman not without greatness.

I have tried to make a Tom Fool of Destiny—and Destiny has proved itself to be the superior jester of the two, and has made a grim and bedraggled Tom Fool of me.

. . . I must end this. I have just fallen in a faint on the floor, and Rogers has revived me with some drops Hunnington had given me in view of such a contingency.

These are the last words I shall write. Life is too transcendentally humorous for a man not to take it seriously. Compared with it, Death is but a shallow jest.

CHAPTER XVI

It is many weeks since I wrote those words which I thought were to be my last. I read them over now, and laugh aloud. Life is more devilishly humorous than I in my most nightmare dreams ever imagined. Instead of dying at Mentone as I proposed, I am here, at Mustapha Superieur, still living. And let me tell you the master joke of the Arch-Jester.

I am going to live.

I am not going to die. I am going to live. I am quite well.

Think of it. Is it farcical, comical, tragical, or what?

This is how it has befallen. The last thing I remember of the old conditions was Rogers packing my things, and a sudden, awful, excruciating agony. I lost consciousness, remained for days in a bemused, stupefied state, which I felt convinced was death, and found particularly pleasant. At last I woke to a sense of bodily constriction and discomfort, and to the queer realisation that what I had taken for the Garden of Proserpine was my own bedroom, and that the pale lady whom I had so confidently assumed was she who, crowned with calm leaves, "gathers all things mortal with cold, immortal hands" was no other than a blue-and-white-vested hospital nurse.

"What the——" I began.

"Chut!" she said, flitting noiselessly to my side. "You mustn't talk." And then she poured something down my throat. I lay back, wondering what it all meant. Presently a grizzled and tanned man, wearing a narrow black tie, came into the room. His face seemed oddly familiar. The nurse whispered to him. He came up to the bed, and asked me in French how I felt.

"I don't know at all," said I.

He laughed. "That's a good sign. Let me see how you are getting on." He stuck a thermometer in my mouth and held my pulse. These formalities completed, he turned up the bedclothes and did something with my body. Only then did I realise that I was tightly bandaged. My impressions grew clearer, and when he raised his face I recognised the doctor who had sat on the sofa with Anastasius Papadopoulos.

"Nothing could be better," said he. "Keep quiet, and all will be well."

"Will you kindly explain?" I asked.

"You've had an operation. Also a narrow escape."

I smiled at him pityingly. "What is the good of taking all this trouble? Why are you wasting your time?"

He looked at me uncomprehendingly for a moment, and then he laughed as the light came to him.

"Oh, I understand! Yes. Your English doctors had told you you were going to die. That an operation would be fatal—so your good friend Madame Brandt informed us—but we—*nous autres Francais*—are more enterprising. Kill or cure. We performed the operation—we didn't kill you—and here you are—cured."

My heart sickened with a horrible foreboding. A clamminess, such as others feel at the approach of death, spread over my brow and neck.

"Good God!" I cried, "you are not trying to tell me that I'm going to live?"

"Why, of course I am!" he exclaimed, brutally delighted. "If nothing else kills you, you'll live to be a hundred."

"Oh, damn!" said I. "Oh, damn! Oh, damn!" and the tears of physical weakness poured down my cheeks.

"*Ce sont des droles de gens, les Anglais!*" I heard him whisper to the nurse before he left the room.

Belonging to a queer folk or not, I found the prospect more and more dismally appalling according as my mind regained its clarity. It was the most overwhelming, piteous disappointment I have ever experienced in my life. I cursed in my whimpering, invalid fashion.

"But don't you want to get well?" asked the wide-eyed nurse.

"Certainly not! I thought I was dead, and I was very happy. I've been tricked and cheated and fooled," and I dashed my fist against the counterpane.

"If you go on in this way," said the nurse, "you will commit suicide."

"I don't care!" I cried—and then, they tell me, fainted. My temperature also ran up, and I became lightheaded again. It was not until the next day that I recovered my sanity. This time Lola was in the room with the nurse, and after a while the latter left us together. Even Lola could not understand my paralysing dismay.

"But think of it, my dear friend," she argued, "just think of it. You are saved—saved by a miracle. The doctor says you will be stronger than you have ever been before."

"All the more dreadful will it be," said I. "I had finished with life. I had got through with it. I don't want a second lifetime. One is quite enough for any sane human being. Why on earth couldn't they have let me die?"

Lola passed her cool hand over my forehead.

"You mustn't talk like that—Simon," she said, in her deepest and most caressing voice, using my name somewhat hesitatingly, for the first time. "You mustn't. A miracle really has been performed. You've been raised from the dead—like the man in the Gospel——"

"Yes," said I petulantly, "Lazarus. And does the Gospel tell us what Lazarus really thought of the unwarrantable interference with his plans? Of course he had to be polite——"

"Oh, don't!" cried, Lola, shocked. In a queer unenlightened way, she was a religious woman.

"I'm sorry," said I, feeling ashamed of myself.

"If you knew how I have prayed God to make you well," she said. "If I could have died for you, I would—gladly—gladly——"

"But I wanted to die, my dear Lola," I insisted, with the egotism of the sick. "I object to this resuscitation. I say it is monstrous that I should have to start a second lifetime at my age. It's all very well when you begin at the age of half a minute—but when you begin at eight-and-thirty years——"

"You have all the wisdom of eight-and-thirty years to start with."

"There is only one thing more disastrous to a man than the wisdom of thirty-eight years," I declared with mulish inconvincibility, "and that is the wisdom he may accumulate after that age."

She sighed and abandoned the argument. "We are going to make you well in spite of yourself," she said.

They, namely, the doctor, the nurse, and Lola, have done their best, and they have succeeded. But their task has been a hard one. The patient's will to live is always a great factor in his recovery. My disgust at having to live has impeded my convalescence, and I fully believe that it is only Lola's tears and the doctor's frenzied appeals to me not to destroy the one chance of his life of establishing a brilliant professional reputation that have made me consent to face existence again.

As for the doctor, he was pathetically insistent.

"But you must get well!" he gesticulated. "I am going to publish it, your operation. It will make my fortune. I shall at last be able to leave this hole of an Algiers and go to Paris! You don't know what I've done for you! I've performed an operation on you that has never been performed successfully before. I thought it had been done, but I found out afterwards my English *confreres* were right. It hasn't. I've worked a miracle in surgery, and by my publication will make you as the subject of it famous for ever. And here you are trying to die and ruin everything. I ask you—have you no human feelings left?"

At the conclusion of these lectures I would sigh and laugh, and stretch out a thin hand. He shook it always with a humorous grumpiness which did me more good than the prospect of acquiring fame in the annals of the *Ecole de Medicine*.

Here am I, however, cured. I have thrown away the stick with which I first began to limp about the garden, and I discourage Lola and Rogers in their efforts to treat me as an invalid. Like the doctor, I have been longing to escape from "this hole of an Algiers" and its painful associations, and, when I was able to leave my room, it occurred to me that the sooner I regained my strength the sooner should I be able to do so. Since then my recovery has been rapid. The doctor is delighted, and slaps me on the back, and points me out to Lola and the manager and the concierge and the hoary old sinner of an Arab who displays his daggers, and trays, and embroideries on the terrace, as a living wonder. I believe he would like to put me in a cage and carry me about with him in Paris on exhibition. But he is reluctantly prepared to part with me, and has consented to my return in a few days' time, to England, by the North German Lloyd steamer. He has ordered the sea voyage as a finishing touch to my cure. Good, deluded man, he thinks that it is his fortuitous science that has dragged me out of the Valley of the Shadow and set me in the Garden of Life. Good, deluded man! He does not realise that he has been merely the tool of the Arch-Jester. He has no notion of the sardonic joke his knife was chosen to perpetrate. That naked we should come into the world, and naked we should go out is a time-honoured pleasantry which, as far as the latter part of it is concerned, I did my conscientious best to further; but that we should come into it again naked at the age of eight-and-thirty is a piece of irony too grim for contemplation. Yet am I bound to contemplate it. It grins me in the face. Figuratively, I am naked.

Partly by my own act, and partly with the help of Destiny (the greater jester than I) I have stripped myself of all these garments of life which not only enabled me to strut peacock-fashion in the pleasant places of the world, but also sheltered me from its inclemencies.

I had wealth—not a Rothschild or Vanderbilt fortune but enough to assure me ease and luxury. I have stripped myself of it. I have but a beggarly sum remaining at my bankers. Practically I am a pauper.

I had political position. I surrendered it as airily as I had achieved it; so airily, indeed, that I doubt whether I could regain it even had I the ambition. For it was a game that I played, sometimes fascinating, sometimes repugnant to my fastidious sense of honourable dealing, for which I shall never recapture the mood. Mood depends on conditions, and conditions, as I am trying to show, are changed.

I had social position. I did not deceive myself as to its value in the cosmic scheme, but it was one of the pleasant things to which I was born, just as I was born to good food and wines and unpatched boots and the morning hot water brought into my bedroom. I liked it. I suspect that it has fled into eternity with the spirit of Captain Vauvenarde. The penniless hero of an amazing scandal is not usually made an idol of by the exclusive aristocracy of Great Britain.

I had a sweet and loyal woman about to marry me. I put Eleanor Faversham for ever out of my life.

I had the devotion and hero-worship of a lad whom I thought to train in the paths of honour, love and happiness. In his eyes I suppose I am an unconscionable villain.

I have stripped myself of everything; and all because the medical faculty of my country sentenced me to death. I really think the Royal Colleges of Surgeons and Physicians ought to pay me an indemnity.

And not only have I stripped myself of everything, but I have incurred an incalculable debt. I owe a woman the infinite debt of her love which I cannot repay. She sheds it on me hourly with a lavishness which scares me. But for her tireless devotion, the doctor tells me, I should not have lived. But for her selfish forbearance, sympathy, and compassion I should have gone as crazy as Anastasius Papadopoulos. Yet the burden of my debt lies iceberg cold on my heart. Now that we are as intimate as man and woman who are still only friends can be, she has lost the magnetic attraction, that subtle mystery of the woman—half goddess, half panther—which fascinated me in spite of myself, and made me jealous of poor young Dale. Now that I can see things in some perspective, I confess that, had I not been under sentence of death, and, therefore, profoundly convinced that I was immune from all such weaknesses of the flesh, I should have realised the temptation of languorous voice and sinuous limbs, of the frank radiation of the animal enchanted as it was by elusive gleams of the spiritual, of the Laisdom—in a word, of all the sexual damnability of a woman which, as Francois Villon points out, set Sardanapalus to spin among the women, David to forget the fear of God, Herod to slay the Baptist, and made Samson lose his sight. Whether I should have yielded to or resisted the temptation is another matter. Honestly speaking, I think I should have resisted.

You see, I should still have been engaged to Eleanor Faversham. . . . But now this somewhat unholy influence is gone from her. She has lifted me in her strong arms as a mother would lift a brat of ten. She has patiently suffered my whimsies as if I had been a sick girl. She has become to me the mere great mothering creature on whom I have depended for custard and the removal of crumbs and creases from under my body, and for support to my tottering footsteps. The glamour has gone from before my eyes. I no longer see her invested in her queer splendour. . . .

My invalid peevishness, too, has accentuated my sensitiveness to shades of refinement. There is about Lola a bluffness, a hardihood of speech, a contempt for the polite word and the pretty conventional turning of a phrase, a lack of reticence in the expression of ideas and feelings, which jar, in spite of my gratitude, on my unstrung nerves. Her ignorance, too, of a thousand things, a knowledge of which is the birthright of such women as Eleanor Faversham, causes conversational excursions to end in innumerable blind alleys. I know that she would give her soul to learn. This she has told me in so many words, and when, in a delicate way, I try to teach her, she listens humbly, pathetically, fixing me with her great, gold-flecked eyes, behind which a deep sadness burns wistfully. Sometimes when I glance up from my book, I see that her eyes, instead of being bent on hers have been resting long on my face, and they say as clearly as articulate speech: "Teach me, love me, use me, do what you will with me. I am yours, your chattel, your thing, till the end of time."

I lie awake at night and wonder what I shall do with my naked life sheltered only by the garment of this woman's love, which I have accepted and cannot repay. I groan aloud when I reflect on the irremediable mess, hash, bungle I have made of things. Did ever sick man wake up to such a hopeless welter? Can you be surprised that I regarded it with dismay? Of course, there is a simple way out of it, and into the shadowy world which I contemplated so long, at first with mocking indifference and then with eager longing. A gentleman called Cato once took it, with considerable aplomb. The means are to my hand. In my drawer lies the revolver with which the excellent Colonel Bunnion (long since departed from Mustapha Superieur) armed me against the banditti of Algiers, and which I forgot to return to him. I could empty one or more of the six chambers into my person and that would be the end. But I don't think history records the suicide of any humorist, however dismal. He knows too well the tricks of the Arch-Jester's game. Very likely I should merely blow away half my head, and Destiny would give my good doctor another chance of achieving immortal fame by glueing it on again. No, I cannot think seriously of suicide by violent means. Of course, I might follow the example of one Antonios Polemon, a later Greek sophist, who suffered so dreadfully from gout that he buried himself alive in the tomb of his ancestors and starved to death. We have a family vault in Highgate Cemetery, of which I possess the key. . . . No, I should be bored and cold, and the coffins would get on my nerves; and besides, there is something suggestive of smug villadom in the idea of going to die at Highgate.

Lola came up as I was scribbling this on my knees in the garden.

"What are you writing there?"

"I am recasting Hamlet's soliloquy," I replied, "and I feel all the better for it."

"Here is your egg and brandy."

I swallowed it and handed her back the glass.

"I feel all the better for that, too."

As I sat in the shade of the little stone summer-house within the Greek portico, she lingered in the blazing sunshine, a figure all glorious health and supple curves, and the stray brown hairs above the brown mass gleamed with the gold of a Giotto aureole. She stood, a duskily glowing, radiant emblem of life against the background of spring greenery and rioting convolvulus. I drew a full breath and looked at her as if magnetised. I had the very oddest sensation. She seemed, in Shakespearean phrase, to rain influence upon me. As if she read the stirrings of my blood, she smiled and said:

"After all, confess, isn't it good to be alive?"

A thrill of physical well-being swept through me. I leaped to my feet.

"You witch!" I cried. "What are you doing to me?"

"I?" She retreated a step, with a laugh.

"Yes, you. You are casting a spell on me, so that I may eat my words."

"I don't know what you are talking about, but you haven't answered my question. It *is* good to be alive."

"Well, it is," I assented, losing all sense of consistency.

She flourished the egg-and-brandy glass. "I'm so glad. Now I know you are really well, and will face life as you faced death, like the brave man that you are."

I cried to her to hold. I had not intended to go as far as that. I confronted death with a smile; I meet life with the wriest of wry faces. She would have none of my arguments.

"No matter how damnable it is—it's splendid to be alive, just to feel that you can fight, just to feel that you don't care a damn for any old thing that can happen, because you're strong and brave. I do want you to get back all that you've lost, all that you've lost through me, and you'll do it. I know that you'll do it. You'll just go out and smash up the silly old world and bring it to your feet. You will, Simon, won't you? I know you will."

She quivered like an optimistic Cassandra.

"My dear Lola," said I.

I was touched. I took her hand and raised it to my lips, whereat she flushed like a girl.

"Did you come here to tell me all this?"

"No," she replied simply. "It came all of a sudden, as I was standing here. I've often wanted to say it. I'm glad I have."

She threw back her head and regarded me a moment with a strange, proud smile; then turned and walked slowly away, her head brushing the long scarlet clusters of the pepper trees.

CHAPTER XVII

The other day, while looking through a limbo of a drawer wherein have been cast from time to time a medley of maimed, half-soiled, abortive things, too unfitted for the paradise of publication, and too good (so my vanity will have it) for the damnation of the waste-paper basket, I came across, at the very bottom, the manuscript of the preceding autobiographical narrative, the last words of which I wrote at Mustapha Superieur three years ago. At first I carried it about with me, not caring to destroy it and not knowing what in the world to do with it until, with the malice of inanimate things, the dirty dog's-eared bundle took to haunting me, turning up continually in inconvenient places and ever insistently demanding a new depository. At last I began to look on it with loathing; and one day in a fit of inspiration, creating the limbo aforesaid, I hurled the manuscript, as I thought, into everlasting oblivion. I had no desire to carry on the record of my life any further, and there, in limbo, it has remained for three years. But the other day I took it out for reference; and now as I am holiday-making in a certain little backwater of the world, where it is raining in a most unholiday fashion, it occurs to me that, as everything has happened to me which is likely to happen (Heaven knows I want no more excursions and alarums in my life's drama), I may as well bring the narrative up to date. I therefore take up the thread, so far as I can, from where I left off.

Lola, having nothing to do in Algiers, which had grown hateful to us both, accompanied me to London. As, however, the weather was rough, and she was a very bad sailor, I saw little of her on the voyage. For my own part, I enjoyed the stormy days, the howling winds and the infuriated waves dashing impotently over the steamer. They filled me with a sense of conflict and of amusement. It is always good to see man triumphing over the murderous forces of nature. It puts one in conceit with one's kind.

At Waterloo I handed Lola over to her maid, who had come to meet her, and, leaving Rogers in charge of my luggage, I drove homeward in a cab.

It was only as I was crossing Waterloo Bridge and saw the dark mass of the Houses of Parliament looming on the other side of the river, and the light in the tower which showed that the House was sitting, that I began to realise my situation. As exiles in desert lands yearn for green fields, so yearned I for those green benches. In vain I represented to myself how often I had yawned on them, how often I had cursed my folly in sitting on them and listening to empty babble when I might have been dining cosily, or talking to a pretty woman or listening to a comic opera, or performing some other useful and soul-satisfying action of the kind; in vain I told myself what a monument of futility was that building; I longed to be in it and of it once again. And when I realised that I yearned for the impossible, my heart was like a stone. For, indeed, I, Simon de Gex, with London once a toy to my hand, was coming into it now a penniless adventurer to seek my fortune.

The cab turned into the Strand, which greeted me as affably as a pandemonium. Motor omnibuses whizzed at me, cabs rattled and jeered at me, private motors and carriages passed me by in sleek contempt; policemen regarded me scornfully as, with uplifted hand regulating the traffic, they held me up; pavements full of people surged along ostentatiously showing that they did not care a brass farthing for me; the thousands of lights with their million reflections, from shop fronts, restaurants, theatres, and illuminated signs glared pitilessly at me. A harsh roar of derision filled the air, like the bass to the treble of the newsboys who yelled in my face. I was wearing a fur-lined coat—just the thing a penniless adventurer would wear. I had a valet attending to my luggage—just the sort of thing a penniless adventurer would have. I was driving to the Albany—just the sort of place where a penniless adventurer would live. And London knew all this—and scoffed at me in stony heartlessness. The only object that gave me the slightest sympathy was Nelson on top of his column. He seemed to say, "After all, you *can't* feel such a fool and so much out in the cold as I do up here."

At Piccadilly Circus I found the same atmosphere of hostility. My cab was blocked in the theatre-going tide, and in neighbouring vehicles I had glimpses of fair faces above soft wraps and the profiles of moustached young men in white ties. They assumed an aggravating air of ownership of the blazing thoroughfare, the only gay and joyous spot in London. I, too, had owned it once, but now I felt an alien; and the whole spirit of Piccadilly Circus rammed the sentiment home—I was an alien and an undesirable alien. I felt even more lost and friendless as I entered the long, cold arcade (known as the Ropewalk) of the Albany.

I found my sister Agatha waiting for me in the library. I had telegraphed to her from Southampton. She was expensively dressed in grey silk, and wore the family diamonds. We exchanged the family kiss and the usual incoherent greetings of our race. She expressed her delight at my restoration to health and gave me satisfactory tidings of Tom Durrell, her husband, of the children, and of our sister Jane. Then she shook her head at me, and made me feel like a naughty little boy. This I resented. Being the head of the family, I had always encouraged the deferential attitude which my sisters, dear right-minded things, had naturally assumed from babyhood.

"Oh, Simon, what a time you've given us!"

She had never spoken to me like this in her life.

"That's nothing, my dear Agatha," said I just a bit tartly, "to the time I've given myself. I'm sorry for you, but I think you ought to be a little sorry for me."

"I am. More sorry than I can say. Oh, Simon, how could you?"

"How could I what?" I cried, unwontedly regardless of the refinements of language.

"Mix yourself up in this dreadful affair?"

"My dear girl," said I, "if you had got mixed up in a railway collision, I shouldn't ask you how you managed to do it. I should be sorry for you and feel your arms and legs and inquire whether you had sustained any internal injuries."

She is a pretty, spare woman with a bird-like face and soft brown hair just turning grey; and as good-hearted a little creature as ever adored five healthy children and an elderly baronet with disastrous views on scientific farming.

"Dear old boy," she said in milder accents, "I didn't mean to be unkind. I want to be good to you and help you, so much so that I asked Bingley"— Bingley is my housekeeper—"whether I could stay to dinner."

"That's good of you—but this magnificence——?"

"I'm going on later to the Foreign Office reception."

"Then you do still mingle with the great and gorgeous?" I said.

"What do you mean? Why shouldn't I?"

I laughed, suspecting rightly that my sisters' social position had not been greatly imperilled by the profligacy of their scandal-bespattered brother.

"What are people saying about me?" I asked suddenly.

She made a helpless gesture. "Can't you guess? You have told us the facts, and, of course, we believe you; we have done our best to spread abroad the correct version—but you know what people are. If they're told they oughtn't to believe the worst, they're disappointed and still go on believing it so as to comfort themselves."

"You cynical little wretch!" said I.

"But it's true," she urged. "And, after all, even if they were well disposed, the correct version makes considerable demands on their faith. Even Letty Farfax—"

"I know! I know!" said I. "Letty Farfax is typical. She would love to be on the side of the angels, but as she wouldn't meet the best people there, she ranges herself with the other party."

Presently we dined, and during the meal, when the servants happened to be out of the room, we continued, snippet-wise, the inconclusive conversation. Like a good sister Agatha had come to cheer a lonely and much abused man; like a daughter of Eve she had also come to find out as much as she possibly could.

"I think I must tell you something which you ought to know," she said. "It's all over the town that you stole the lady from Dale Kynnersley."

"If I did," said I, "it was at his mother's earnest entreaty. You can tell folks that. You can also tell them Madame Brandt is not the kind of woman to be stolen by one man from another. She is a thoroughly virtuous, good, and noble woman, and there's not a creature living who wouldn't be honoured by her friendship."

As I made this announcement with an impetuosity which reminded me (with a twinge of remorse) of poor Dale's dithyrambics, Agatha shot at me a quick glance of apprehension.

"But, my dear Simon, she used to act in a circus with a horse!"

"I fail to see," said I, growing angry, "how the horse could have imbued her with depravity, and I'm given to understand that the tone of the circus is not quite what it used to be in the days of the Empress Theodora."

A ripple passed over Agatha's bare shoulders, which I knew to be a suppressed shrug.

"I suppose men and women look at these things differently," she remarked, and from the stiffness of her tone I divined that the idea of moral qualities lurking in the nature of Lola Brandt occasioned her considerable displeasure.

"I hope——" She paused. There was another ripple. "No. I had better not say it. It's none of my business, after all."

"I don't think it is, my dear," said I.

Rogers bringing in the cutlets ended the snippet of talk.

It was not the cheeriest of dinners. I took advantage of the next interval of quiet to inquire after Dale. I learned that the poor boy had almost collapsed after the election and was now yachting with young Lord Essendale somewhere about the Hebrides. Agatha had not seen him, but Lady Kynnersley had called on her one day in a distracted frame of mind, bitterly reproaching me for the unhappiness of her son. I should never have suspected that such fierce maternal love could burn beneath Lady Kynnersley's granite exterior. She accused me of treachery towards Dale and, most illogically, of dishonourable conduct towards herself.

"She said things about you," said Agatha, "for which, even if they were true, I couldn't forgive her. So that's an end of that friendship. Indeed, it has been very difficult, Simon," she continued, "to keep up with our common friends. It has placed us in the most painful and delicate position. And now you're back, I'm afraid it will be worse."

Thus under all Agatha's affection there ran the general hostility of London. Guilty or not, I had offended her in her most deeply rooted susceptibilities, and as yet she only knew half the imbroglio in which I was enmeshed. Over coffee, however, she began to take a more optimistic view of affairs.

"After all, you'll be able to live it down," she said with a cheerful air of patronage. "People soon forget. Before the year is out you'll be going about just as usual, and at the General Election you'll find a seat somewhere."

I informed her that I had given up politics. What then, she asked, would I do for an occupation?

"Work for my living," I replied.

"Work?" She arched her eyebrows, as if it were the most extraordinary thing a man could do. "What kind of work?"

"Road-sweeping or tax-collecting or envelope-addressing."

She selected a cigarette from the silver box in front of her, and did not reply until she had lit it and inhaled a puff or two.

"I wish you wouldn't be so flippant, Simon."

From this remark I inferred that I still was in the criminal dock before this lady Chief Justice. I smiled at the airs the little woman gave herself now that I was no longer the impeccable and irreproachable dictator of the family. Mine was the experience of every fallen tyrant since the world began.

"My dear Agatha, I've had enough shocks during the last few weeks to knock the flippancy out of a Congregational minister. In November I was condemned to die within six months. The sentence was final and absolute. I thought I would do the kind of good one can't do with a lifetime in front of one, and I wasted all my substance in riotous giving. In the elegant phraseology of high society I am stone-broke. As my training has not fitted me to earn my living in high-falutin ways, I must earn it in some humble capacity. Therefore, if you see me call at your house for the water rate, you'll understand that I am driven to that expedient by necessity and not by degradation."

Naturally I had to elaborate this succinct statement before my sister could understand its full significance. Then dismay overwhelmed her. Surely something could be done. The fortunes of Jane and herself were at my disposal to set me on my feet again. We were brother and sisters; what was theirs was mine; they couldn't see me starve. I thanked her for her affection—the dear creatures would unhesitatingly have let me play ducks and drakes with their money, but I explained that though poor, I was still proud and prized the independence of the tax-collector above the position of the pensioner of Love's bounty.

"Tom must get you something to do," she declared.

"Tom must do nothing of the kind. Let me say that once and for all," I returned peremptorily. "I've made my position clear to you, because you're my sister and you ought to be spared any further misinterpretation of my actions. But to have you dear people intriguing after billets for me would be intolerable."

"But what are you going to *do?*" she cried, wringing her hands.

"I'm going for my first omnibus ride to-morrow," said I heroically.

Upon which assertion Rogers entered announcing that her ladyship's carriage had arrived. A while later I accompanied her downstairs and along the arcade.

"I shall be so miserable, thinking of you, poor old boy," she said affectionately, as she bade me good-bye.

"Don't, I am going to enjoy myself for the first time in my life."

These were "prave 'orts," but I felt doleful enough when I re-entered the chambers where I had lived in uncomplaining luxury for fourteen years.

"There's no help for it," I murmured. "I must get rid of the remainder of my lease, sell my books and pictures and other more or less expensive household goods, dismiss Rogers and Bingley, and go and live on thirty shillings a week in a Bloomsbury boarding-house. I think," I continued, regarding myself in the Queen Anne mirror over the mantelpiece, "I think that it will better harmonise with my fallen fortunes if I refrain from waxing the ends of my moustache. There ought to be a modest droop about the moustache of a tax-collector."

The next morning I gave my servants a months' notice. Rogers, who had been with me for many years, behaved in the correctest manner. He neither offered to lend me his modest savings nor to work for me for no wages. He expressed his deep regret at leaving my service and his confidence that I would give him a good character. Bingley wept after the way of women. There was also a shadowy housemaidy young person in a cap who used to make meteoric appearances and whom I left to the diplomacy of Bingley. These dismal rites performed, I put my chambers into the hands of a house agent and interviewed a firm of auctioneers with reference to the sale. It was all exceedingly unpleasant. The agent was so anxious to let my chambers, the auctioneer so delighted at the chance of selling my effects, that I felt myself forthwith turned neck and crop out of doors. It was a bright morning in early spring, with a satirical touch of hope in the air. London, no longer to be my London, maintained its hostile attitude to me. If any one had prophesied that I should be a stranger in Piccadilly, I should have laughed aloud. Yet I was.

Walking moodily up Saint James's street I met the omniscient and expansive Renniker. He gave me a curt nod and a "How d'ye do?" and passed on. I felt savagely disposed to slash his jaunty silk hat off with my walking-stick. A few months before he would have rushed effusively into my arms and bedaubed me with miscellaneous inaccuracies of information. At first I was furiously indignant. Then I laughed, and swinging my stick, nearly wreaked my vengeance on a harmless elderly gentleman.

It was my first experience of social ostracism. Although I curled a contumelious lip, I smarted under the indignity. It was all very well to say proudly *"io son' io"*; but *io* used to be a person of some importance who was not cavalierly "how d'ye do'd" by creatures like Renniker. This and the chance encounters of the next few weeks gave me furiously to think. I knew that in one respect my sister Agatha was right. These good folks who shied now at the stains of murder with which my reputation was soiled would in time get used to them and eventually forget them altogether. But I reflected that I should not forget, and I determined that I should not be admitted on sufferance, as at first I should have to be admitted, into any man's club or any woman's drawing-room.

One day Colonel Ellerton, Maisie Ellerton's father, called on me. He used to be my very good friend; we sat on the same side of the House and voted together on innumerable occasions in perfect sympathy and common lack of conviction. He was cordial enough, congratulated me on my marvellous restoration to health, deplored my absence from Parliamentary life, and then began to talk confusedly of Russia. It took a little perspicacity to see that something was weighing on the good man's mind; something he had come to say and for his honest life could not get out. His plight became more pitiable as the interview proceeded, and when he rose to go, he grew as red as a turkey-cock and began to sputter. I went to his rescue.

"It's very kind of you to have come to see me, Ellerton," I said, "but if I don't call yet awhile to pay my respects to your wife, I hope you'll understand, and not attribute it to discourtesy."

I have never seen relief so clearly depicted on a human countenance. He drew a long breath and instinctively passed his handkerchief over his forehead. Then he grasped my hand.

"My dear fellow," he cried, "of course we'll understand. It was a shocking affair—terrible for you. My wife and I were quite bowled over by it."

I did not attempt to clear myself. What was the use? Every man denies these things as a matter of course, and as a matter of course nobody believes him.

Once I ran across Elphin Montgomery, a mysterious personage behind many musical comedy enterprises. He is jewelled all over like a first-class Hindoo idol, and is treated as a god in fashionable restaurants, where he entertains riff-raff at sumptuous banquets. I had some slight acquaintance with the fellow, but he greeted me as though I were a long lost intimate— his heavy sensual face swagged in smiles—and invited me to a supper party. I declined with courtesy and walked away in fury. He would not have presumed to ask me to meet his riff-raff before I became disgustingly and I suppose to some minds, fascinatingly, notorious. But now I was hail-fellow-well-met with him, a bird of his own feather, a rogue of his own kidney, to whom he threw open the gates of his bediamonded and befrilled Alsatia. A pestilential fellow! As if I would mortgage my birthright for such a mess of pottage.

So I stiffened and bade Society high and low go packing. I would neither seek mine own people, nor allow myself to be sought by Elphin Montgomery's. I enwrapped myself in a fine garment of defiance. My sister Jane, who was harder and more worldly-minded than Agatha, would have had me don a helmet of brass and a breastplate of rhinoceros hide and force my way through reluctant portals; but Agatha agreed with me, clinging, however, to the hope that time would not only reconcile Society to me, but would also reconcile me to Society.

"If the hope comforts you, my dear Agatha," said I, "by all means cherish it. In the meantime, allow me to observe that the character of Ishmael is eminently suited to the profession of tax-collecting."

During these early days of my return the one person with whom I had no argument was Lola. She soothed where others scratched, and stimulated where others goaded. The intimacy of my convalescence continued. At first I acquainted her, as far as was reasonably necessary, with my change of fortune, and accepted her offer to find me less expensive quarters. The devoted woman personally inspected every flat in London, with that insistence of which masculine patience is incapable, and eventually decided on a tiny bachelor suite somewhere in the clouds over a block of flats in Victoria Street where the service is included in the rent. Into this I moved with such of my furniture as I withdrew from the auctioneer's hammer, and there I prepared to stay until necessity should drive me to the Bloomsbury boarding-house. I thought I would graduate my descent. Before I moved, however, she came to the Albany for the first and only time to see the splendour I was about to quit. In a modest way it was splendour. My chambers were really a large double flat to the tasteful furnishing of which I had devoted the thought and interest of many years. She went with me through the rooms. The dining-room was all Chippendale, each piece a long-coveted and hunted treasure; the library old oak; the drawing-room a comfortable and cunning medley. There were bits of old china, pieces of tapestry, some rare prints, my choice collection of mezzotints, a picture or two of value—one a Lancret, a very dear possession. And there were my books—once I had a passion for rare bindings. Every thing had to me a personal significance, and I hated the idea of surrender more than I dared to confess even to myself. But I said to Lola:

"Vanity of vanities! All things expensive are vanity!"

Her eyes glistened and she slipped her arm through mine and patted the back of my hand.

"If you talk like that I shall cry and make a fool of myself," she said in a broken manner.

It is not so much the thing that is done or the thing that is said that matters, but the way of doing or saying it. In the commonplace pat on the hand, in the break in the commonplace words there was something that went straight to my heart. I squeezed her arm and whispered:

"Thank you, dear."

This sympathy so sure and yet so delicately conveyed was mine for the trouble of mounting the stairs that led to her drawing-room in Cadogan Gardens. She seemed to be watching my heart the whole time, so that without my asking, without my knowledge even, she could touch each sore spot as it appeared, with the healing finger. For herself she made no claims, and because she did not in any way declare herself to be unhappy, I, after the manner of men, took her happiness for granted. For lives there a man who does not believe that an uncomplaining woman has nothing to complain of? It is his masculine prerogative of density. Besides, does not he himself when hurt bellow like a bull? Why, he argues, should not wounded woman do the same? So, when I wanted companionship, I used to sit in the familiar room and make Adolphus, the Chow dog, shoulder arms with the poker, and gossip restfully with Lola, who sprawled in her old languorous, loose-limbed way among the cushions of her easy chair. Gradually my habitual reserve melted from me, and at last I gave her my whole confidence, telling her of my disastrous pursuit of eumoiriety, of Eleanor Faversham, of the attitude of Society, in fact, of most of what I have set down in the preceding pages. She was greatly interested in everything, especially in Eleanor Faversham. She wanted to know the colour of her eyes and hair and how she dressed. Women are odd creatures.

The weeks passed.

Besides ministering to my dilapidated spirit, Lola found occupation in looking after the cattery of Anastasius Papadopoulos, which the little man had left in the charge of his pupil and assistant, Quast. This Quast apparently was a faithful, stolid, but unintelligent and incapable German who had remained loyally at his post until Lola found him there in a state of semi-starvation. The sum of money with which Anastasius had provided him had been eked out to the last farthing. The cats were in a pitiable condition. Quast, in despair, was trying to make up his dull mind whether to sell them or eat them. Lola with superb feminine disregard of legal rights, annexed the whole cattery, maintained Quast in his position of pupil and assistant and informed the landlord that she would be responsible for the rent. Then she set to work to bring the cats into their proper condition of sleekness, and, that done, to put them through a systematic course of training. They had been thoroughly demoralised, she declared, under Quast's maladministration, and had almost degenerated into the unhistrionic pussies of domestic life. As for Hephaestus, the great ferocious tom, he was more like an insane tiger than a cat. He flew at the gate over which he used to jump, and clawed and bit it to matchwood, and after spitting in fury at the blazing hoop, sprang at the unhappy Quast as if he had been the contriver of the indignities to which he was being subjected. These tales of feline backsliding I used to hear from Lola, and when I asked her why she devoted her energies to the unproductive education of the uninspiring animals, she would shrug her shoulders and regard me with a Giaconda smile.

"In the first place it amuses me. You seem to forget I'm a *dompteuse*, a tamer of beasts; it's my profession, I was trained to it. It's the only thing I can do, and it's good to feel that I haven't lost my power. It's odd, but I feel a different woman when I'm impressing my will on these wretched cats. You must come one of these days and see a performance, when I've got them ship-shape. They'll astonish you. And then," she would add, "I can write to Anastasius and tell him how his beloved cats are getting on."

Well, it was an interest in her life which, Heaven knows, was not crowded with exciting incidents. Now that I can look back on these things with a philosophic eye, I can imagine no drearier existence than that of a friendless, unoccupied woman in a flat in Cadogan Gardens. At that time, I did not realise this as completely as I might have done. Because her old surgeon friend, Sir Joshua Oldfield, now and then took her out to dinner, I considered she was leading a cheerful if not a merry life. I smiled indulgently at Lola's devotion to the cats and congratulated her on having found another means whereby to beguile the *tedium vitae* which is the arch-enemy of content.

"I wish I could find such a means myself," said I.

I not only had the wish, but the imperative need to so do. To stand like Ajax defying the lightning is magnificent, but as a continuous avocation it is wearisome and unprofitable, especially if carried on in a tiny bachelor suite, an eyrie of a place, at the top of a block of flats in Victoria Street. Indeed, if I did not add soon to the meagre remains of my fortune, I should not be able to afford the luxury of the bachelor suite. Conscious of this, I left the lightning alone, after a last denunciatory shake of the fist, and descended into the busy ways of men to look for work.

Thus I entered on the second stage of my career—that of a soldier of Fortune. At first I was doubtful as to what path to glory and bread-and-butter I could carve out for myself. Hitherto I had been Fortune's darling instead of her mercenary, and she had most politely carved out my paths for me, until she had played her jade's trick and left me in the ditch. Now things were different. I stood alone, ironical, ambitionless, still questioning the utility of human effort, yet determined to play the game of life to its bitter end. What could I do?

It is true that I had been called to the Bar in my tentative youth, while I drafted documents for my betters to pull to pieces and rewrite at the Foreign Office; but I had never seen a brief, and my memories of Gaius, Justinian, Williams's "Real Property," and Austin's "Jurisprudence," were as nebulous as those of the Differential Calculus over whose facetiae I had pondered during my schooldays. The law was as closed to me as medicine. I had no profession. I therefore drifted into the one pursuit for which my training had qualified me, namely, political journalism. I had written much, in my amateur way, during my ten years' membership of Parliament; why, I hardly know—not because I needed money, not because I had thoughts which I burned to express, and certainly not through vain desire of notoriety. Perhaps the motive was twofold, an ingrained Puckish delight in the incongruous—it seemed incongruous for an airy epicurean like myself to spend stodgy hours writing stodgier articles on Pauper Lunacy and Poor Law Administration—and the same inherited sense of gentlemanly obligation to do something for one's king and country as made my ancestors, whether they liked it or not, clothe themselves in uncomfortable iron garments and go about fighting other gentlemen similarly clad, to their own great personal danger. At any rate, it complemented my work at St. Stephen's, and doubtless contributed to a reputation in the House which I did not gain through my oratory. I could therefore bring to editors the stock-in-trade of a fairly accurate knowledge of current political issues, an appreciation of personalities, and a philosophical subrident estimate of the bubbles that are for ever rising on the political surface. I found Finch of *The Universal Review*, James of *The Weekly*, and one or two others more than willing to give me employment. I put my pen also at the disposal of Raggles. It was as uplifting and about as mechanical as tax-collecting; but it involved less physical exertion and less unpleasant contact with my fellow creatures. I could also keep the ends of my moustache waxed, which was a great consolation.

My sister Agatha commended my courage and energy, and Lola read my articles with a glowing enthusiasm, which compensated for lack of exact understanding; but I was not proud of my position. It is one thing to stand at the top of a marble staircase and in a debonair, jesting fashion to fling insincere convictions to a recipient world. It is another to sell the same worthless commodity for money. I began, to my curious discomfort, to suspect that life had a meaning after all.

CHAPTER XVIII

One day I had walked from Cadogan Gardens with a gadfly phrase of Lola's tormenting my ears:

"You're not quite alive even yet."

I had spent most of the day over a weekly article for James's high-toned periodical, using the same old shibboleths, proclaiming Gilead to be the one place for balm, juggling with the same old sophistries, and proving that Pope must have been out of his mind when he declared that an honest man was the noblest work of God, seeing that nobler than the most honest man was the disingenuous government held up to eulogy; and I had gone tired, dispirited, out of conceit with myself to Lola for tea and consolation. I had not been the merriest company. I had spoken gloomily of the cosmos, and when Adolphus the Chow dog had walked down the room in his hind legs, I had railed at the futility of canine effort. To Lola, who had put forth all her artillery of artless and harmless coquetry in voice and gesture, in order to lure my thoughts into pleasanter ways, I exhibited the querulous grumpiness of a spoiled village octogenarian. We discussed the weather, which was worth discussing, for the spring, after long tarrying, had come. It was early May. Lola laughed.

"The spring has got into my blood."

"It hasn't got into mine," I declared. "It never will. I wonder what the deuce is the matter with me."

Then Lola had said, "My dear Simon, I know. You're not quite alive even yet."

I walked homewards pestered by the phrase. What did she mean by it? I stopped at the island round the clock-tower by Victoria Station and bought a couple of newspapers. There, in the centre of the whirlpool where swam dizzily omnibuses, luggage-laden cabs, whirling motors, feverish, train-seeking humans, dirty newsboys, I stood absently saying to myself, "You're not quite alive even yet."

A hand gripped my arm and a cheery voice said "Hallo!" I started and recognised Rex Campion. I also said "Hallo!" and shook hands with him. We had not met since the days when, having heard of my Monte Cristo lavishness, he had called at the Albany and had beguiled me into giving a thousand pounds to his beloved "Barbara's Building," the prodigious philanthropic institution which he had founded in the slums of South Lambeth. In spite of my dead and dazed state of being I was pleased to see his saturnine black-bearded face, and to hear his big voice. He was one of those men who always talked like a megaphone. The porticoes of Victoria Station re-echoed with his salutations. I greeted him less vociferously, but with equal cordiality.

"You're looking very fit. I head that you had gone through a miraculous operation. How are you?"

"Perfectly well," said I, "but I've been told that I'm not quite alive even yet."

He looked anxious. "Remains of trouble?"

"Not a vestige," I laughed.

"That's all right," he said breezily. "Now come along and hear Milligan speak."

It did not occur to him that I might have work, worries, or engagements, or that the evening's entertainment which he offered me might be the last thing I should appreciate. His head, for the moment, was full of Milligan, and it seemed to him only natural that the head of all humanity should be full of Milligan too. I made a wry face.

"That son of thunder?"

Milligan was a demagogue who had twice unsuccessfully attempted to get into Parliament in the Labour interest.

"Have you ever heard him?"

"Heaven forbid!" said I in my pride.

"Then come. He's speaking in the Hall of the Lambeth Biblical Society."

I was tempted, as I wanted company. In spite of my high resolve to out-Ishmael Ishmael, I could not kill a highly developed gregarious instinct. I also wanted a text for an article. But I wanted my dinner still more. Campion condemned the idea of dinner.

"You can have a cold supper," he roared, "like the rest of us."

I yielded. Campion dragged me helpless to a tram at the top of Vauxhall Bridge Road.

"It will do Your Mightiness good to mingle with the proletariat," he grinned.

I did not tell him that I had been mingling with it in this manner for some time past or that I repudiated the suggestion of its benign influence. I entered the tram meekly. As soon as we were seated, he began:

"I bet you won't guess what I've done with your thousand pounds. I'll give you a million guesses."

As I am a poor conjecturer, I put on a blank expression and shook my head. He waited for an instant, and then shouted with an air of triumph:

"I've founded a prize, my boy—a stroke of genius. I've called it by your name. 'The de Gex Prize for Housewives.' I didn't bother you about it as I knew you were in a world of worry. But just think of it. An annual prize of thirty pounds—practically the interest—for housewives!"

His eyes flashed in his enthusiasm; he brought his heavy hand down on my knee.

"Well?" I asked, not electrified by this announcement.

"Don't you see?" he exclaimed. "I throw the competition open to the women in the district, with certain qualifications, you know—I look after all that. They enter their names by a given date and then they start fair. The woman who keeps her home tidiest and her children cleanest collars the prize. Isn't it splendid?"

I agreed. "How many competitors?"

"Forty-three. And there they are working away, sweeping their floors and putting up clean curtains and scrubbing their children's noses till they shine like rubies and making their homes like little Dutch pictures. You see, thirty pounds is a devil of a lot of money for poor people. As one mother of a large family said to me, 'With that one could bury them all quite beautiful.'"

"You're a wonderful fellow," said I, somewhat enviously.

He gave an awkward laugh and tugged at his beard.

"I've only happened to find my job, and am doing it as well as I can," he said. "'Tisn't very much, after all. Sometimes one gets discouraged; people are such ungrateful pigs, but now and again one does help a lame dog over a stile which bucks one up, you know. Why don't you come down and have a look at us one of these days? You've been promising to do so for years."

"I will," said I with sudden interest.

"You can have a peep at one or two of the competing homes. We pop into them unexpectedly at all hours. That's a part of the game. We've a complicated system of marks which I'll show you. Of course, no woman knows how she's getting on, otherwise many would lose heart."

"How do the men like this disconcerting ubiquity of soap and water?"

"They love it!" he cried. "They're keen on the prize too. Some think they'll grab the lot and have the devil's own drunk when the year's up. But I'll look after that. Besides, when a chap has been living in the pride of cleanliness for a year he'll get into the way of it and be less likely to make a beast of himself. Anyway, I hope for the best. My God, de Gex, if I didn't hope and hope and hope," he cried earnestly, "I don't know how I should get through anything without hope and a faith in the ultimate good of things."

"The same inconvincible optimist?" said I.

"Yes. Thank heaven. And you?"

I paused. There came a self-revelatory flash. "At the present moment," I said, "I'm a perfectly convincible vacuist."

We left the tram and the main thoroughfare, and turned into frowsy streets, peopled with frowsy men and women and raucous with the bickering play of frowsy children. It was still daylight. Over London the spring had fluttered its golden pinions, and I knew that in more blessed quarters—in the great parks, in Piccadilly, in Old Palace Yard, half a mile away—its fragrance lingered, quickening blood already quickened by hope, and making happier hearts already happy. But here the ray of spring had never penetrated either that day or the days of former springs; so there was no lingering fragrance. Here no one heeded the aspects of the changing year save when suffocated by sweltering heat, or frozen in the bitter cold, or drenched by the pouring rain. Otherwise in these gray, frowsy streets spring, summer, autumn, winter were all the same to the grey, frowsy people. It is true that youth laughed—pale, animal boys, and pale, flat-chested girls. But it laughed chiefly at inane obscenity.

One of these days, when phonography is as practicable as photography, some one will make accurate records in these frowsy streets, and then, after the manner of the elegant writers of Bucolics and Pastorals, publish such a series of Urbanics and Pavimentals, phonographic dialogues between the Colins and Dulcibellas of the pavement and the gutter as will freeze up Hell with horror.

An anemic, flirtatious group passed us, the girls in front, the boys behind.

"Good God, Campion, what *can* you do?" I asked.

"Pay them, old chap," he returned quickly.

"What's the good of that?"

"Good? Oh, I see!" He laughed, with a touch of scorn. "It's a question of definition. When you see a fellow creature suffering and it shocks your refined susceptibilities and you say 'poor devil' and pass on, you think you have pitied him. But you haven't. You think pity's a passive virtue. It isn't. If you really pity anybody, you go mad to help him—you don't stand by with tears of sensibility running down your cheeks. You stretch out your hand, because you've damn well got to. If he won't take it, or wipes you over the head, that's his look-out. You can't work miracles. But once in a way he does take it, and then—well, you work like hell to pull him through. And if you do, what bigger thing is there in the world than the salvation of a human soul?"

"It's worth living for," said I.

"It's worth doing any confounded old thing for," he declared.

I envied Campion as I had envied no man before. He was alive in heart and soul and brain; I was not quite alive even yet. But I felt better for meeting him. I told him so. He tugged his beard again and laughed.

"I am a happy old crank. Perhaps that's the reason."

At the door of the hall of the Lambeth Ethical Society he stopped short and turned on me; his jaw dropped and he regarded me in dismay.

"I'm the flightiest and feather-headedest ass that ever brayed," he informed me. "I just remember I sent Miss Faversham a ticket for this meeting about a fortnight ago. I had clean forgotten it, though something uncomfortable has been tickling the back of my head all the time. I'm miserably sorry."

I hastened to reassure him. "Miss Faversham and I are still good friends. I don't think she'll mind my nodding to her from the other side of the room." Indeed, she had written me one or two letters since my recovery perfect in tact and sympathy, and had put her loyal friendship at my service.

"Even if we meet," I smiled, "nothing tragic will happen."

He expressed his relief.

"But what," I asked, "is Miss Faversham doing in this galley?"

"I suppose she is displaying an intelligent interest in modern thought," he said, with boyish delight at the chance I had offered him.

"*Touché*," said I, with a bow, and we entered the hall.

It was crowded. The audience consisted of the better class of artisans, tradesmen, and foremen in factories: there was a sprinkling of black-coated clerks and unskilled labouring men. A few women's hats sprouted here and there among the men's heads like weeds in a desert. There were women, too, in proportionately greater numbers, on the platform at the end of the hall, and among them I was quick to notice Eleanor Faversham. As Campion disliked platforms and high places in synagogues, we sat on one of the benches near the door. He explained it was also out of consideration for me.

"If Milligan is too strong for your proud, aristocratic stomach," he whispered, "you can cut and run without attracting attention."

Milligan had evidently just began his discourse. I had not listened to him for five minutes when I found myself caught in the grip which he was famous for fastening on his audience. With his subject—Nationalisation of the Land—and his arguments I had been perfectly familiar for years. As a boy I had read Henry George's "Progress and Poverty" with the superciliousness of the young believer in the divine right of Britain's landed gentry, and before the Eton Debating Society I had demolished the whole theory to my own and every one else's satisfaction. Later, as a practical politician, I had kept myself abreast of the Socialist movement. I did not need Mr. John Milligan, whom my lingering flippancy had called a son of thunder, to teach me the elements of the matter. But at this peculiar crisis of my life I felt that, in a queer, unknown way, Milligan had a message for me. It was uncanny. I sat and listened to the exposition of Utopia with the rapt intensity of any cheesemonger's assistant there before whose captured spirit floated the vision of days to come when the land should so flow with milk and money that golden cheeses would be like buttercups for the plucking. It was not the man's gospel that fascinated me nor his illuminated prophecy of the millennium that produced the vibrations in my soul, but the surging passion of his faith, the tempest of his enthusiasm. I had enough experience of public speaking to distinguish between the theatrical and the genuine in oratory. Here was no tub-thumping soothsayer, but an inspired zealot. He lived his impassioned creed in every fibre of his frame and faculties. He was Titanic, this rough miner, in his unconquerable hope, divine in his yearning love of humanity.

When he ended there was a dead silence for a second, and then a roar of applause from the pale, earnest, city-stamped faces. A lump rose in my throat. Campion clutched my knee. A light burned in his eyes.

"Well? What about Boanerges?"

"Only one thing," said I, "I wish I were as alive as that man."

A negligible person proposed a vote of thanks to Milligan, after which the hall began to empty. Campion, caught by a group of his proletariat friends, signalled to me to wait for him. And as I waited I saw Eleanor

Faversham come slowly from the platform down the central gangway. Her eyes fixed themselves on me at once—for standing there alone I must have been a conspicuous figure, an intruder from the gorgeous West—and with a little start of pleasure she hurried her pace. I made my way past the chattering loiterers in my row, and met her. We shook hands.

"Well? Saul among the prophets? Who would have thought of seeing you here!"

I waved my hand towards Campion. "We have the same sponsor." She glanced at him for a swift instant and then at me.

"Did you like it?"

"Have you seen Niagara?"

"Yes."

"Did you like it?"

"I'm so glad," she cried. "I thought perhaps——" she broke off. "Why haven't you tried to see me?"

"There are certain conventions."

"I know," she said. "They're idiotic."

"There's also Mrs. Faversham," said I.

"Mother is the dearest thing in life," she replied, "but Mrs. Faversham is a convention." She came nearer to me, in order to allow a freer passage down the gangway and also in order to be out of earshot of an elderly woman who was obviously accompanying her. "Simon, I've been a good friend to you. I believe in you. Nothing will shake my convictions. You couldn't look into my eyes like that if—well—you know."

"I couldn't," said I.

"Then why can't two honourable, loyal people meet? We only need meet once. But I want to tell you things I can't write—things I can't say here. I also want to hear of things. I think I've got a kind of claim—haven't I?"

"I've told you, Eleanor. My letters——"

"Letters are rubbish!" she declared with a laugh. "Where can we meet?"

"Agatha is a good soul," said I.

"Well, fix it up by telephone to-morrow."

"Alas!" said I; "I don't run to telephones in my eagle's nest on Himalaya Mansions."

She knitted her brows. "That's not the last address you wrote from."

"No," I replied, smiling at this glimpse of the matter-of-fact Eleanor. "It was a joke."

"You're incorrigible!" she said rebukingly.

"I don't joke so well in rags as in silken motley," I returned with a smile, "but I do my best."

She disdained a retort. "We'll arrange, anyhow, with Agatha."

Campion, escaping from his friends, came up and chatted for a minute. Then he saw Eleanor and her companion to their carriage.

"Now," said he a moment later, "come to Barbara and have some supper. You won't mind if Jenkins joins us?"

"Who's Jenkins?" I asked.

"Jenkins is an intelligent gas-fitter of Sociological tastes. He classes Herbert Spencer, Benjamin Kidd, and Lombroso as light literature. He also helps us with our young criminals. I should like you to meet him."

"I should be delighted," I said.

So Jenkins was summoned from a little knot a few yards off and duly presented. Whereupon we proceeded to Campion's plain but comfortably furnished quarters in Barbara's Building, where he entertained us till nearly midnight with cold beef and cheese and strenuous conversation.

As I walked across Westminster Bridge on my homeward way it seemed as if London had grown less hostile. Big Ben chimed twelve and there was a distinct Dick Whittington touch about the music. The light on the tower no longer mocked me. As I passed by the gates of Palace Yard, a policeman on duty recognised me and saluted. I strode on with a springier tread and noticed that the next policeman who did not know me, still regarded me with an air of benevolence. A pale moon shone in the heavens and gave me shyly to understand that she was as much my moon as any one else's. As I turned into Victoria Street, omnibuses passed me with a lurch of friendliness. The ban was lifted. I danced (figuratively) along the pavement.

What it portended I did not realise. I was conscious of nothing but a spiritual exhilaration comparable only with the physical exhilaration I experienced in the garden at Algiers when my bodily health had been finally established. As the body then felt the need of expressing itself in violent action—in leaping and running (an impulse which I firmly subdued), so now did my spirit crave some sort of expression in violent emotion. I was in a mood for enraptured converse with an archangel.

Looking back, I see that Campion's friendly "Hallo" had awakened me from a world of shadows and set me among realities; the impact of Milligan's vehement personality had changed the conditions of my life from static to dynamic; and that a Providence which is not always as ironical as it pleases us to assert had sent Eleanor Faversham's graciousness to mitigate the severity of the shock. I see how just was Lola's diagnosis. "You're not quite alive even yet." I had been going about in a state of suspended spiritual animation.

My recovery dated from that evening.

CHAPTER XIX

Agatha proved herself the good soul I had represented her to be.

"Certainly, dear," she said when I came the following morning with my request. "You can have my boudoir all to yourselves."

"I am grateful," said I, "and for the first time I forgive you for calling it by that abominable name."

It was an old quarrel between us. Every lover of language picks out certain words in common use that he hates with an unreasoning ferocity.

"I'll change it's title if you like," she said meekly.

"If you do, my dear Agatha, my gratitude will be eternal."

"I remember a certain superior person, when Tom and I were engaged, calling mother's boudoir—the only quiet place in the house—the osculatorium."

She laughed with the air of a small bird who after long waiting had at last got even with a hawk. But I did not even smile. For the only time in our lives I considered that Agatha had committed a breach of good taste. I said rather stiffly:

"It is not going to be a lovers' meeting, my dear."

She flushed. "It was silly of me. But why shouldn't it be a lovers' meeting?" she added audaciously. "If nothing had happened, you two would have been married by this time—"

"Not till June."

"Oh, yes, you would. I should have seen about that—a ridiculously long engagement. Anyhow, it was only your illness that broke it off. You were told you were going to die. You did the only honourable and sensible thing—both of you. Now you're in splendid health again—"

"Stop, stop!" I interrupted. "You seem to be entirely oblivious of the circumstances—"

"I'm oblivious of no circumstances. Neither is Eleanor. And if she still cares for you she won't care twopence for the circumstances. I know I wouldn't."

And to cut off my reply she clapped the receiver of the telephone to her ear and called up Eleanor, with whom she proceeded to arrange a date for the interview. Presently she screwed her head round.

"She says she can come at four this afternoon. Will that suit you?"

"Perfectly," said I.

When she replaced the receiver I stepped behind her and put my hands on her shoulders.

"'The mother of mischief,'" I quoted, "'is no bigger than a midge's wing,' and the grandmother is the match-making microbe that lurks in every woman's system."

She caught one of my hands and looked up into my face.

"You're not cross with me, Simon?"

Her tone was that of the old Agatha. I laughed, remembering the policeman's salute of the previous night, and noted this recovery of my ascendancy as another indication of the general improvement in the attitude of London.

"Of course not, Tom Tit," said I, calling her by her nursery name. "But I absolutely forbid your thinking of playing Fairy Godmother."

"You can forbid my playing," she laughed, "and I can obey you. But you can't prevent my thinking. Thought is free."

"Sometimes, my dear," I retorted, "it is better chained up."

With this rebuke I left her. No doubt, she considered a renewal of my engagement with Eleanor Faversham a romantic solution of difficulties. I could only regard it as preposterous, and as I walked back to Victoria Street I convinced myself that Eleanor's frank offer of friendship proved that such an idea never entered her head. I took vehement pains to convince myself Spring had come; like the year, I had awakened from my lethargy. I viewed life through new eyes; I felt it with a new heart. Such vehement pains I was not capable of taking yesterday.

"It has never entered her head!" I declared conclusively.

And yet, as we sat together a few hours later in Agatha's little room a doubt began to creep into the corners of my mind. In her strong way she had brushed away the scandal that hung around my name. She did not believe a word of it. I told her of my loss of fortune. My lunacy rather raised than lowered me in her esteem. How then was I personally different from the man she had engaged herself to marry six months before? I remembered our parting. I remembered her letters. Her presence here was proof of her unchanging regard. But was it something more? Was there a hope throbbing beneath that calm sweet surface to which I did not respond? For it often happens that the more direct a woman is, the more in her feminine heart is she elusive.

Clean-built, clean-hearted, clean-eyed, of that clean complexion which suggests the open air, Eleanor impressed you with a sense of bodily and mental wholesomeness. Her taste in dress ran in the direction of plain tailor-made gowns (I am told, by the way, that these can be fairly expensive), and shrank instinctively from the frills and fripperies to which daughters of Eve are notoriously addicted. She spoke in a clear voice which some called hard, though I never found it so; she carried herself proudly. Chaste in thought, frank in deed, she was a perfect specimen of the highly bred, purely English type of woman who, looking at facts squarely in the face, accepts them as facts and does not allow her imagination to dally in any atmosphere wherein they may be invested. To this type a vow is irrefragable. Loyalty is inherent in her like her blood. She never changes. What feminine inconsistencies she had at fifteen she retains at five-and-twenty, and preserves to add to the charms of her old age. She is the exemplary wife, the great-hearted mother of children. She has sent her sons in thousands to fight her country's battles overseas. Those things which lie in the outer temper of her soul she gives lavishly. That which is hidden in her inner shrine has to be wrested from her by the one hand she loves. Was mine that hand?

It will be perceived that I was beginning to take life seriously.

Eleanor must have also perceived something of the sort; for during our talk she said irrelevantly:

"You've changed!"

"In what way?" I asked.

"I don't know. You're not the same as you were. I seem to know you better in some ways, and yet I seem to know you less. Why is it?"

I said, "No one can go through the Valley of the Grotesque as I have done without suffering some change."

"I don't see why you should call it 'the Valley of the Grotesque.'"

I smiled at her instinctive rejection of the fanciful.

"Don't you? Call it the Valley of the Shadow, if you like. But don't you think the attendant circumstances were rather mediaeval, gargoyley, Orcagnesque? Don't you think the whole passage lacked the dignity which one associates with the Valley of the Shadow of Death?"

"You mean the murder?" she said with a faint shiver.

"That," said I, "might be termed the central feature. Just look at things as they happened. I am condemned to death. I try to face it like a man and a gentleman. I make my arrangements. I give up what I can call mine no longer. I think I will devote the rest of my days to performing such acts of helpfulness and charity as would be impossible for a sound man with a long life before him to undertake. I do it in a half-jesting spirit, refusing to take death seriously. I pledge myself to an act of helpfulness which I regard at first as merely an incident in my career of beneficence. I am gradually caught in the tangle of a drama which at times develops into sheer burlesque, and before I can realise what is going to happen, it turns into ghastly tragedy. I am overwhelmed in grotesque disaster—it is the only word. Instead of creating happiness all around me, I have played havoc with human lives. I stand on the brink and look back and see that it is all one gigantic devil-jest at my expense. I thank God I am going to die. I do die—for practical purposes. I come back to life and—here I am. Can I be quite the same person I was a year ago?"

She reflected for a few moments. Then she said:

"No. You can't be—quite the same. A man of your nature would either have his satirical view of life hardened into bitter cynicism or he would be softened by suffering and face things with new and nobler ideals. He would either still regard life as a jest—but instead of its being an odd, merry jest it would be a grim, meaningless, hideous one; or he would see that it wasn't a jest at all, but a full, wonderful, big reality. I've expressed myself badly, but you see what I mean."

"And what do you think has happened?" I asked.

"I think you have changed for the better."

I smiled inwardly. It sounded rather dull. I said with a smile:

"You never liked my cap and bells, Eleanor."

"No!" she replied emphatically. "What's the use of mockery? See where it led you."

I rose, half-laughing at her earnestness, half-ashamed of myself, and took a couple of turns across the room.

"You're right," I cried. "It led me to perdition. You might make an allegory out of my career and entitle it 'The Mocker's Progress.'" I paused for a second or two, and then said suddenly, "Why did you from the first refuse to believe what everybody else does—before I had the chance of looking you in the eyes?"

She averted her face. "You forget that I had had the chance of searching deep beneath the mocker."

I cannot, in reverence to her, set down what she said she found there. I stood humbled and rebuked, as a man must do when the best in him is laid out before his sight by a good woman.

A maidservant brought in tea, set the table, and departed, Eleanor drew off her gloves and my glance fell on her right hand.

"It's good of you to wear my ring to-day," I said.

"To-day?" she echoed, with the tiniest touch of injury in her voice. "Do you think I put it on to just please you to-day?"

"It would have been gracious of you to do so," said I.

"It wouldn't," she declared. "It would have been mawkish and sentimental. When we parted I told you to do what you liked with the ring. Do you remember? You put it on this finger"—she waved her right hand—"and there it has stayed ever since."

I caught the hand and touched it lightly with my lips. She coloured faintly.

"Two lumps of sugar and no milk, I think that's right?" She handed me the tea-cup.

"It's like you not to have forgotten."

"I'm a practical person," she replied with a laugh.

Presently she said, "Tell me more about your illness—or rather your recovery. I know nothing except that you had a successful operation which all the London surgeons said was impossible. Who nursed you?"

"I had a trained nurse," said I.

"Wasn't Madame Brandt with you?"

"Yes," said I. "She was very good to me. In fact, I think I owe her my life."

Hitherto the delicacy of the situation had caused me to refer to Lola no more than was necessary, and in my narrative I had purposely left her vague.

"That's a great debt," said Eleanor.

"It is, indeed."

"You're not the man to leave such a debt unpaid?"

"I try to repay it by giving Madame Brandt my devoted friendship."

Her eyes never wavered as they held mine.

"That's one of the things I wanted to know. Tell me something about her."

I felt some surprise, as Eleanor was of a nature too proud for curiosity.

"Why do you want to know?"

"Because she interests me intensely. Is she young?"

"About thirty-two."

"Good-looking?"

"She is a woman of remarkable personality."

"Describe her."

I tried, stumbled, and halted. The effort evoked in my mind a picture of Lola lithe, seductive, exotic, with gold flecks in her dusky, melting eyes, with strong shapely arms that had as yet only held me motherwise, with her pantherine suggestion of tremendous strength in languorous repose, with her lazy gestures and parted lips showing the wonderful white even teeth, with all her fascination and charm—a picture of Lola such as I had not seen since my emergence from the Valley—a picture of Lola, generous, tender, wistful, strong, yielding, fragrant, lovable, desirable, amorous—a picture of Lola which I could not put before this other woman equally brave and straight, who looked at me composedly out of her calm, blue eyes.

My description resolved itself into a loutish catalogue.

"It is not painful to you to talk of her, Simon?"

"Not at all. There are not many great-hearted women going about. It is my privilege to know two."

"Am I the other?"

"Who else?"

"I'm glad you have the courage to class Madame Brandt and myself together."

"Why?" I asked.

"It proves beyond a doubt that you are honest with me. Now tell me about a few externals—things that don't matter—but help one to form an impression. Is she educated?"

"From books, no; from observation, yes."

"Her manners?"

"Observation had educated them."

"Accent?"

"She is sufficiently polyglot to have none."

"She dresses and talks and behaves generally like a lady?"

"She does," said I.

"In what way then does she differ from the women of our class?"

"She is less schooled, less reticent, franker, more natural. What is on her tongue to say, she says."

"Temper?"

"I have never heard her say an angry word to or of a human creature. She has queer delicacies of feeling. For instance——"

I told her of Anastasius Papadopoulos's tawdry, gimcrack presents which Lola has suffered to remain in her drawing-room so as not to hurt the poor little wretch.

"That's very touching. Where does she live?"

"She has a flat in Cadogan Gardens."

"Is she in London now?"

"Yes."

"I should like very much to know her," she said calmly.

I vow and declare again that the more straightforward and open-eyed, the less subtle, temperamental, and neurotic are women, the more are they baffling. I had wondered for some time whither the catechism tended, and now, with a sudden jerk, it stopped short at this most unexpected terminus. It was startling. I rose and mechanically placed my empty tea-cup on the tray by her side.

"The wish, my dear Eleanor," said I, quite formally, "does great credit to your heart."

There was a short pause, marking an automatic close of the subject. Deeply as I admired both women, I shrank from the idea of their meeting. It seemed curiously indelicate, in view both of my former engagement to Eleanor and of Lola's frank avowal of her feelings towards me before what I shall always regard as my death. It is true that we had never alluded to it since my resurrection; but what of that? Lola's feelings, I was sure, remained unaltered. It also flashed on me that, with all the goodwill in the world, Eleanor would not understand Lola. An interview would develop into a duel. I pictured it for a second, and my sudden fierce partisanship for Lola staggered me. Decidedly an acquaintance between these two was preposterous.

The silence was definite enough to mark a period, but not long enough to cause embarrassment. Eleanor commented on my present employment. I must find it good to get back to politics.

"I find it to the contrary," said I, with a laugh. "My convictions, always lukewarm, are now stone-cold. I don't say that the principles of the party are wrong. But they're wrong for me, which is all-important. If they are not right for me, what care I how right they be? And as I don't believe in those of the other side, I'm going to give up politics altogether."

"What will you do?"

"I don't know. I honestly don't. But I have an insistent premonition that I shall soon find myself doing something utterly idiotic, which to me will be the most real thing in life."

I had indeed awakened that morning with an exhilarating thrill of anticipation, comparable to that of the mountain climber who knows not what panorama of glory may be disclosed to his eyes when he reaches the summit. I had whistled in my bath—a most unusual thing.

"Are you going to turn Socialist?"

"*Qui lo sa?* I'm willing to turn anything alive and honest. It doesn't matter what a man professes so long as he professes it with all the faith of all his soul."

I broke into a laugh, for the echo of my words rang comic in my ears.

"Why do you laugh?" she asked.

"Don't you think it funny to hear me talk like a two-penny Carlyle?"

"Not a bit," she said seriously.

"I can't undertake to talk like that always," I said warningly.

"I thought you said you were going to be serious."

"So I am—but platitudinous—Heaven forbid!"

The little clock on the mantelpiece struck six. Eleanor rose in alarm.

"How the time has flown! I must be getting back. Well?"

Our eyes met. "Well?" said I.

"Are we ever to meet again?"

"It's for you to say."

"No," she said. And then very distinctly, very deliberately, "It's for you."

I understood. She made the offer simply, nobly, unreservedly. My heart was filled with great gratitude. She was so true, so loyal, so thorough. Why could I not take her at her word? I murmured:

"I'll remember what you say."

She put out her hand. "Good-bye!"

"Good-bye and God bless you!" I said.

I accompanied her to the front door, hailed a passing cab, and waited till she had driven off. Was there ever a sweeter, grander, more loyal woman? The three little words had changed the current of my being.

I returned to take leave of Agatha. I found her in the drawing-room reading a novel. She twisted her head sideways and regarded me with a bird-like air of curiosity.

"Eleanor gone?"

Her tone jarred on me. I nodded and dropped into a chair.

"Interview passed off satisfactorily?"

"We were quite comfortable, thank you. The only drawback was the tea. Why a woman in your position can't give people China tea instead of that Ceylon syrup will be a mystery to me to my dying day."

She rose in her wrath and shook me.

"You're the most aggravating wretch on earth!"

"My dear Tom-Tit," said I gravely. "Remember the moral tale of Bluebeard."

"Look here, Simon"—she planted herself in front of me—"I'm not a bit inquisitive. I don't in the least want to know what passed between you and Eleanor. But what I would give my ears to understand is how you can go through a two hours' conversation with the girl you were engaged to—a conversation which must have affected the lives of both of you—and then come up to me and talk drivel about China tea and Bluebeard."

"Once on a time, my dear," said I, "I flattered myself on being an artist in life. I am humbler now and acknowledge myself a wretched bungling amateur. But I still recognise the value of chiaroscuro."

"You're hopeless," said Agatha, somewhat crossly. "You get more flippant and cynical every day."

CHAPTER XX

I went home to my solitary dinner, and afterwards took down a volume of Emerson and tried to read. I thought the cool and spacious philosopher might allay a certain fever in my blood. But he did nothing of the kind. He wrote for cool and spacious people like himself; not for corpses like me revivified suddenly with an overcharge of vital force. I pitched him—how much more truly companionable is a book than its author!—I pitched him across the room, and thrusting my hands in my pockets and stretching out my legs, stared in a certain wonder at myself.

I, Simon de Gex, was in love; and, *horribile dictu!* in love with two women at once. It was Oriental, Mormonic, New Century, what you will; but there it was. I am ashamed to avow that if, at that moment, both women had appeared before me and said "Marry us," I should have—well, reflected seriously on the proposal. I had passed through curious enough experiences, Heaven knows, already; but none so baffling as this. The two women came alternately and knocked at my heart, and whispered in my ear their irrefutable claims to my love. I listened throbbingly to each, and to each I said, "I love you."

I was in an extraordinary psychological predicament. Lola had remarked, "You are not quite alive even yet." I had come to complete life too suddenly. This was the result. I got up and paced the bird-cage, which the house-agents termed a reception-room, and wondered whether I were going mad. It was not as if one woman represented the flesh and the other the spirit. Then I might have seen the way to a decision. But both had the large nature that comprises all. I could not exalt one in any way to the abasement of the other. All my inherited traditions, prejudices, predilections, all my training ranged me on the side of Eleanor. I was clamouring for the real. Was she not the incarnation of the real? Her very directness piqued me to a perverse and delicious obliquity. And I knew, as I knew when I parted from her months before, that it was only for me to awaken things that lay virginally dormant. On the other hand stood Lola, with her magnetic seduction, her rich atmosphere, her great wide simplicity of heart, holding out arms into which I longed to throw myself.

It was monstrous, abnormal. I hated the abominable indelicacy of weighing one against the other, as I had hated the idea of their meeting.

I paced my bird-cage until it shrank to the size of a rat-trap. Then I clapped on my hat and fled down into the streets. I jumped into the first cab I saw and bade the driver take me to Barbara's Building. Campion suddenly occurred to me as the best antidote to the poison that had entered my blood.

I found him alone, clearing from the table the remains of supper. In spite of his soul's hospitable instincts, he stared at me.

"Why, what the——?"

"Yes, I know. You're surprised to see me bursting in on you like a wild animal. I'm not going to do it every night, but this evening I claim a bit of our old friendship."

"Claim it all, my dear de Gex!" he said cordially. "What can I do for you?"

It was characteristic of Campion to put his question in that form. Ninety-nine men out of a hundred would have asked what was the matter with me. But Campion, who all his life had given, wanted to know what he could co.

"Tell me fairy tales of Lambeth and idylls of the Waterloo Bridge Road. Or light your pipe and talk to me of Barbara."

He folded up the tablecloth and put it in the sideboard drawer.

"If it's elegant distraction you want," said he, "I can do better than that." He planted himself in front of me. "Would you like to do a night's real work?"

"Certainly," said I.

"A gentleman of my acquaintance named Judd is in the ramping stage of *delirium tremens*. He requires a couple of men to hold him down so as to prevent him from getting out of bed and smashing his furniture and his wife and things. I was going to relieve one of the fellows there now, so that he can get a few hours' sleep, and if you like to come and relieve the other, you'll be doing a good action. But I warn you it won't be funny."

"I'm in the mood for anything," I said.

"You'll come?"

"Of course."

"That's splendid!" he shouted. "I hardly thought you were in earnest. Wait till I telephone for some medicine to be sent up from the dispensary. I promised to take it round with me."

He telephoned instructions, and presently a porter brought in the medicine. Campion explained that it had been prescribed by the doctor attached to the institution who was attending the case.

"You must come and see the working of our surgery and dispensary!" he cried enthusiastically. "We charge those who can afford a sixpence for visit and medicine. Those who can't are provided, after inquiry, with coupons. We don't want to encourage the well-to-do to get their medical advice gratis, or we wouldn't be able to cope with the really poor. We pay the doctor a fixed salary, and the fees go to the general fund of the Building, so it doesn't matter a hang to him whether a patient pays or not."

"You must be proud of all this, Campion?" I said.

"In a way," he replied, lighting his pipe; "but it's mainly a question of money—my poor old father's money which he worked for, not I."

I reminded him that other sons had been known to put their poor old father's money to baser uses.

"I suppose Barbara is more useful to the community that steam yachts or racing stables; but there, you see, I hate yachting because I'm always sea-sick, and I scarcely know which end of a horse you put the bridle on. Every man to his job. This is mine. I like it."

"I wonder whether holding down people suffering from *delirium tremens* is my job," said I. "If so, I'm afraid I shan't like it."

"If it's really your job," replied Campion, "you will. You must. You can't help it. God made man so."

It was only an hour or two later when, for the first time in my life, I came into practical touch with human misery, that I recognised the truth of Campion's perfervid optimism. No one could like our task that night in its outer essence. For a time it revolted me. The atmosphere of the close, dirty room, bedroom, kitchen, dining-room, sitting-room, bathroom, laundry— all in one, the home of man, wife and two children, caught me by the throat. It was sour. The physical contact with the flesh of the unclean, gibbering, shivering, maniacal brute on the foul bed was unutterably repugnant to me. Now and again, during intervals of comparative calm, I was forced to put my head out of the window to breathe the air of the street. Even that was tainted, for a fried-fish shop across the way and a public-house next door billowed forth their nauseating odours. After a while access to the window was denied me. A mattress and some rude coverings were stretched beneath it—the children's bed—on which we persuaded the helpless, dreary wife to lie down and try to rest. A neighbour had taken in the children for the night. The wife was a skinny, grey-faced, lined woman of six-and-twenty. In her attitude of hopeless incompetence she shed around her an atmosphere of unspeakable depression. Although I could not get to the window, I was glad when she lay down and spared me the sight of her moving fecklessly about the room or weeping huddled up on a broken-backed wooden chair and looking more like a half-animated dish-clout than a woman.

The poor wretch on the bed was a journeyman tailor who, when sober, could earn fair wages. The cry of the wife, before Campion awed her into comparative silence, was a monotonous upbraiding of her husband for bringing them down to this poverty. It seemed impossible to touch her intelligence and make her understand that no words from her or any one could reach his consciousness. His violence, his screams, his threats, the horrors of his fear left her unmoved. We were there to guard her from physical danger, and that to her was all that mattered.

In the course of an hour or so the nausea left me. I felt braced by the grimness of the thing, and during the paroxysms I had no time to think of anything but the mechanical work in hand. It was all that Campion and I, both fairly able-bodied men, could do to keep the puny little tailor in his bed. Horrible shapes menaced him from which he fought madly to escape. He writhed and shrieked with terror. Once he caught my hand in his teeth and bit it, and Campion had some difficulty in relaxing the wretch's jaw. Between the paroxysms Campion and I sat on the bed watching him, scarcely exchanging a word. The wife, poor creature, whimpered on her mattress. It was not a pleasant vigil. It lasted till the grey dawn crept in, pitilessly intensifying the squalor of the room, and until the dawn was broadening into daylight. Then two of Campion's men from Barbara's Building arrived to relieve us. Before we went, however, the neighbour who had taken charge of the children came in to help the slatternly wife light a fire and make some tea. I have enjoyed few things more than the warm, bitter stuff which I drank out of the broken mug in that strange and depressing company.

I went out into the street with racked head and nerves and muscles. Campion kept his cloth cap in his hand, allowing the morning wind to ruffle his shaggy black hair, and drew a long breath.

"I think the worst is over now. As soon as he can be moved, I'll get him down to the annexe at Broadstairs. The sea air will pull him round."

"Isn't it rather hopeless?" I asked.

He turned on me. "Nothing's hopeless. If you once start the hopeless game down here you'd better distribute cyanide of potassium instead of coals and groceries. I've made up my mind to get that man decent again, and, by George, I'm going to do it! Fancy those two weaklings producing healthy offspring. But they have. Two of the most intelligent kids in the district. If you hold up your hands and say it's awful to contemplate their upbringing you're speaking the blatant truth. It's the contemplation that's awful. But why contemplate when you can do something?"

I admitted the justice of the remark. He went on.

"Look at yourself now. If you had gone in with me last night and just stared at the poor devil howling with D.T. in that filthy place, you'd have come out sick and said it was awful. Instead of that, you buckled to and worked and threw off everything save our common humanity, and have got interested in the Judds in spite of yourself. You'll go and see them again and do what you can for them, won't you?"

I was not in a merry mood, but I laughed. Campion had read the intention that had vaguely formulated itself in the back of my mind.

"Of course I will," I said.

We walked on a few steps down the still silent, disheartening street without speaking. Then he tugged his beard, half-halted, and glanced at me quickly.

"See here," said he, "the more sensible people I can get in to help us the better. Would you like me to hand you over the Judd family *en bloc*?"

This was startling to the amateur philanthropist. But it is the way of all professionals to regard their own business as of absorbing interest to the outside world. The stockbroking mind cannot conceive a sane man indifferent to the fluctuations of the money market, and to the professional cricketer the wide earth revolves around a wicket. How in the world could I be fairy godfather to the Judd family? Campion took my competence for granted.

"You may not understand exactly what I mean, my dear Campion," said I; "but I attribute the most unholy disasters of my life to a ghastly attempt of mine to play Deputy Providence."

"But who's asking you to play Deputy Providence?" he shouted. "It's the very last idiot thing I want done. I want you to do certain definite practical work for that family under the experienced direction of the authorities at Barbara's Building. There, do you understand now?"

"Very well, I'll do anything you like."

Thus it befell that I undertook to look after the moral, material, and spiritual welfare of the family of an alcoholic tailor by the name of Judd who dwelt in a vile slum in South Lambeth. My head was full of the prospect when I awoke at noon, for I had gone exhausted to sleep as soon as I reached home. If goodwill, backed by the experience of Barbara's Building, could do aught towards the alleviation of human misery, I determined that it should be done. And there was much misery to be alleviated in the Judd family. I had no clear notion of the means whereby I was to accomplish this; but I knew that it would be a philanthropic pursuit far different from my previous eumoirous wanderings abut London when, with a mind conscious of well-doing, I distributed embarrassing five-pound notes to the poor and needy.

I had known—what comfortable, well-fed gentleman does not?—that within easy walking distance of his London home thousands of human beings live like the beasts that perish; but never before had I spent an intimate night in one of the foul dens where the living and perishing take place. The awful pity of it entered my soul.

So deeply was I impressed with the responsibility of what I had undertaken, so grimly was I haunted by the sight of the pallid, howling travesty of a man and the squeezed-out, whimpering woman, that the memory of the conflicting emotions that had driven me to Campion the night before returned to me with a shock.

"It strikes me," I murmured, as I shaved, "that I am living very intensely indeed. Here am I in love with two women at once, and almost hysterically enthusiastic over a delirious tailor." Then I cut my cheek and murmured no more, until the operation was concluded.

I had arranged to accompany Lola that afternoon to the Zoological Gardens. This was a favourite resort of hers. She was on intimate terms with keepers and animals, and her curious magnetism allowed her to play such tricks with lions and tigers and other ferocious beasts as made my blood run cold. As for the bears, they greeted her approach with shrieking demonstrations of affection. On such occasions I felt the same curious physical antipathy as I did when she had dominated Anastasius's ill-conditioned cat. She seemed to enter another sphere of being in which neither I nor anything human had a place.

With some such dim thoughts in my head, I reached her door in Cadogan Gardens. The sight of her electric brougham that stood waiting switched my thoughts into another groove, but one running oddly parallel. Electric broughams also carried her out of my sphere. I had humbly performed the journey thither in an omnibus.

She received me in her big, expansive way.

"Lord! How good it is to see you. I was getting the—I was going to say 'the blind hump'—but you don't like it. I was going to turn crazy and bite the furniture."

"Why?" I asked with masculine directness.

"I've been trying to educate myself—to read poetry. Look here"—she caught a small brown-covered octavo volume from the table. "I can't make head or tail of it. It proved to me that it was no use. If I couldn't understand poetry, I couldn't understand anything. It was no good trying to educate myself. I gave it up. And then I got what you don't like me to call the hump."

"You dear Lola!" I cried, laughing. "I don't believe any one has ever made head or tail out of 'Sordello.' There once was a man who said there were only two intelligible lines in the poem—the first and the last—and that both were lies. 'Who will, may hear Sordello's story told,' and 'Who would, has heard Sordello's story told.' Don't worry about not understanding it."

"Don't you?"

"Not a bit," said I.

"That's a comfort," she said, with a generous sigh of relief. "How well you're looking!" she cried suddenly. "You're a different man. What have you been doing to yourself?"

"I've grown quite alive."

"Good! Delightful! So am I. Quite alive now, thank you."

She looked it, in spite of the black outdoor costume. But there was a dash of white at her throat and some white lilies of the valley in her bosom, and a white feather in her great black hat poised with a Gainsborough swagger on the mass of her bronze hair.

"It's the spring," she added.

"Yes," said I, "it's the spring."

She approached me and brushed a few specks of dust from my shoulder.

"You want a new suit of clothes, Simon."

"Dear me!" said I, glancing hastily over the blue serge suit in which I had lounged at Mustapha Superieur. "I suppose I do."

It occurred to me that my wardrobe generally needed replenishing. I had been unaccustomed to think of these things, the excellent Rogers and his predecessors having done most of the thinking for me.

"I'll go to Poole's at once," said I.

And then it struck me, to my whimsical dismay, that in the present precarious state of my finances, especially in view of my decision to abandon political journalism in favour of I knew not what occupation, I could not afford to order clothes largely from a fashionable tailor.

"I shouldn't have mentioned it," said Lola apologetically, "but you're always so spick and span."

"And now I'm getting shabby!"

I threw back my head and laughed at the new and comical conception of Simon de Gex down at heel.

"Oh, not shabby!" echoed Lola.

"Yes, my dear. The days of purple and fine linen are *vorbei*. You'll have to put up with me in a threadbare coat and frayed cuffs and ragged hems to my trousers."

Lola declared that I was talking rubbish.

"Not quite such rubbish as you may think, my dear. Shall you mind?"

"It would break my heart. But why do you talk so? You can't be—as poor—as that?"

Her face manifested such tragic concern that I laughed. Besides, the idea of personal poverty amused me. When I gave up my political work I should only have what I had saved from my wreck—some two hundred a year—to support me until I should find some other means of livelihood. It was enough to keep me from starvation, and the little economies I had begun to practise afforded me enjoyment. On the other hand, how folks regulated their balance-sheets so as to live on two hundred a year I had but a dim notion. In the course of our walk from Barbara's Building to the Judds the night before I had asked Campion. He had laughed somewhat grimly.

"I don't know. I don't run an asylum for spendthrift plutocrats; but if you want to see how people live and bring up large families on fifteen shillings a week, I can show you heaps of examples."

This I felt would, in itself, be knowledge of the deepest interest; but it would in no way aid me to solve my own economic difficulty. I was always being brought up suddenly against the problem in some form or another, and, as I say, it caused me considerable amusement.

"I shall go on happily enough," said I, reassuringly. "In the meantime let us go and see the lions and tigers."

We started. The electric brougham glided along comfortably through the sunlit streets. A feeling of physical and spiritual content stole over me. Our hands met and lingered a long time in a sympathetic clasp. Whatever fortune held in store for me here at least I had an inalienable possession.

For some time we said nothing, and when our eyes met she smiled. I think she had never felt my heart so near to hers. At last we broke the silence and talked of ordinary things. I told her of my vigil overnight and my undertaking to look after the Judds. She listened with great interest. When I had finished my tale, she said almost passionately:

"Oh, I wish I could do something like that!"

"You?"

"Why not? I came from those people. My grandfather swept the cages in Jamrach's down by the docks. He died of drink. He used to live in one horrible, squalid room near by. I remember my father taking me to see him when I was a little girl—we ourselves weren't very much better off at that time. I've been through it," she shivered. "I know what that awful poverty is. Sometimes it seems immoral of me to live luxuriously as I do now without doing a hand's turn to help."

"*Chacun a son metier*, my dear," said I. "There's no need to reproach yourself."

"But I think it might be my *metier*," she replied earnestly, "if only I could learn it."

"Why haven't you tried, then?"

"I've been lazy and the opportunity hasn't come my way."

"I'll introduce you to Campion," I said, "and doubtless he'll be able to find something for you to do. He has made a science of the matter. I'll take you down to see him."

"Will you?"

"Certainly," said I. There was a pause. Then an idea struck me. "I wonder, my dear Lola, whether you could apply that curious power you have over savage animals to the taming of the more brutal of humans."

"I wonder," she said thoughtfully.

"I should like to see you seize a drunken costermonger in the act of jumping on his wife by the scruff of the neck, and reduce him to such pulp that he sat up on his tail and begged."

"Oh, Simon!" she exclaimed reproachfully. "I quite thought you were serious."

"So I am, my dear," I returned quickly, "as serious as I can be."

She laughed. "Do you remember the first day you came to see me? You said that I could train any human bear to dance to whatever tune I pleased. I wonder if the same thought was at the back of your head."

"It wasn't. It was a bad and villainous thought. I came under the impression that you were a dangerous seductress."

"And I'm not?"

Oh, that spring day, that delicious tingle in the air, that laughing impertinence of the budding trees in the park through which we were then driving, that enveloping sense of fragrance and the nearness and the dearness of her! Oh, that overcharge of vitality! I leaned my head to hers so that my lips nearly touched her ear. My voice shook.

"You're a seductress and a witch and a sorcerer and an enchantress."

The blood rose to her dark face. She half closed her eyes.

"What else am I?" she murmured.

But, alas! I had not time to answer, for the brougham stopped at the gates of the Zoological Gardens. We both awakened from our foolishness. My hand was on the door-handle when she checked me.

"What's the good of a mind if you can't change it? I don't feel in a mood for wild beasts to-day, and I know you don't care to see me fooling about with them. I would much rather sit quiet and talk to you."

With a woman who wants to sacrifice herself there is no disputing. Besides, I had no desire to dispute. I acquiesced. We agreed to continue our drive.

"We'll go round by Hampstead Heath," she said to the chauffeur. As soon as we were in motion again, she drew ever so little nearer and said, in her lowest, richest notes, and with a coquetry that was bewildering on account of its frankness:

"What were we talking of before we pulled up?"

"I don't know what we were talking of," I said, "but we seem to have trodden on the fringe of a fairy-tale."

"Can't we tread on it again?" She laughed happily.

"You have only to cast the spell of your witchery over me again."

She drew yet a little nearer and whispered: "I'm trying to do it as hard as I can."

An adorable softness came into her eyes, and her hand instinctively closed round mine in its boneless clasp. The long pent-up longing of the woman vibrated from her in waves that shook me to my soul. My senses swam. Her face quivered glorious before me in a black world. Her lips were parted. Careless of all the eyes in all the houses in the Avenue Road, St. John's Wood, and in the head of a telegraph boy whom I only noticed afterwards, I kissed her on the lips.

All the fulness and strength of life danced through my veins.

"I told you I was quite alive!" I said with idiotic exultation.

She closed her eyes and leaned back. "Why did you do that?" she murmured.

"Because I love you," said I. "It has come at last."

Where we drove I have no recollection. Presumably an impression of green rolling plain with soft uplands in the distance signified that we passed along Hampstead Heath; the side thoroughfare with villa residences on either side may have been Kilburn High Road; the flourishing, busy, noisy suburb may have been Kilburn: the street leading thence to the Marble Arch may have been Maida Vale. To me they were paths in Dreamland. We spoke but little and what we did say was in the simple, commonplace language which all men use in the big crises of life.

There was no doubt now of my choice. I loved her. Love had come to me at last. That was all I knew at that hour and all I cared to know.

Lola was the first to awake from Dreamland. She shivered. I asked whether she felt cold.

"No. I can't believe that you love me. I can't. I can't."

I smiled in a masterful way. "I can soon show you that I do."

She shook her head. "I'm afraid, Simon, I'm afraid."

"What of?"

"Myself."

"Why?"

"I can't tell you. I can't explain. I don't know how to. I've been wrong—horribly wrong. I'm ashamed."

She gripped her hands together and looked down at them. I bent forward so as to see her face, which was full of pain.

"But, dearest of all women," I cried, "what in the world have you to be ashamed of?"

She paused, moistened her lips with her tongue, and then broke out:

"I'll tell you. A decent lady like your Eleanor Faversham wouldn't tell. But I can't keep these things in. Didn't you begin by saying I was a seductress? No, no, let me talk. Didn't you say I could make a man do what I wanted? Well, I wanted you to kiss me. And now you've done it, you think you love me; but you don't, you can't."

"You're talking the wickedest nonsense that ever proceeded out of the lips of a loving woman," I said aghast. "I repeat in the most solemn way that I love you with all my heart."

"In common decency you couldn't say otherwise."

Again I saw the futility of disputation. I put my hand on hers.

"Time will show, dear. At any rate, we have had our hour of fairyland."

"I wish we hadn't," she said. "Don't you see it was only my sorcery, as you call it, that took us there? I meant us to go."

At last we reached Cadogan Gardens. I descended and handed her out, and we entered the hall of the mansions. The porter stood with the lift-door open.

"I'm coming up to knock all this foolishness out of your head."

"No, don't, please, for Heaven's sake!" she whispered imploringly. "I must be alone—to think it all out. It's only because I love you so. And don't come to see me for a day or two—say two days. This is Wednesday. Come on Friday. You think it over as well. And if it's really true—I'll know then—when you come. Good-bye, dear. Make Gray drive you wherever you want to go."

She wrung my hand, turned and entered the lift. The gates swung to and she mounted out of sight. I went slowly back to the brougham, and gave the chauffeur the address of my eyrie. He touched his hat. I got in and we drove off. And then, for the first time, it struck me that an about-to-be-shabby gentleman with a beggarly two hundred a year, ought not, in spite of his quarterings, to be contemplating marriage with a wealthy woman who kept an electric brougham. The thought hit me like a stone in the midriff.

What on earth was to be done? My pride rose up like the *deux ex machina* in the melodrama and forbade the banns. To live on Lola's money—the idea was intolerable. Equally intolerable was the idea of earning an income by means against the honesty of which my soul clamoured aloud.

"Good God!" I cried. "Is life, now I've got to it, nothing but an infinite series of dilemmas? No sooner am I off one than I'm on another. No sooner do I find that Lola and not Eleanor Faversham is the woman sent down by Heaven to be my mate than I realise the same old dilemma—Lola on one horn and Eleanor replaced on the other by Pride and Honour and all sorts of capital-lettered considerations. Life is the very Deuce," said I, with a wry appreciation of the subtlety of language.

Why did Lola say: "Your Eleanor Faversham?"

I had enough to think over for the rest of the evening. But I slept peacefully. Light loves had come and gone in the days past; but now for the first time love that was not light had come into my life.

CHAPTER XXI

"The Lord will find a way out of the dilemma," said I confidently to myself as I neared Cadogan Gardens two days after the revelatory drive. "Lola is in love with me and I am in love with Lola, and there is nothing to keep us apart but my pride over a matter of a few ha'-pence." I felt peculiarly jaunty. I had just posted to Finch the last of the articles I had agreed to write for his reactionary review, and only a couple of articles for another journal remained to be written in order to complete my literary engagements. Soon I should be out of the House of Bondage in which I had been a slave, at first willingly and now rebelliously, from my cradle. The great wide world with its infinite opportunities for development received my liberated spirit. I had broken the shackles of caste. I had thrown off the perfumed garments of epicureanism, the vesture of my servitude. My emotions, once stifled in the enervating atmosphere, now awake fresh and strong in the free air. I was elemental—the man wanting the woman; and I was happy because I knew I was going to get her. Such must be the state of being of a dragonfly on a sunny day. And—shall I confess it?—I had obeyed the dragon-fly's instinct and attired myself in the most resplendent raiment in my wardrobe. My morning coat was still irreproachable, my patent leather boots still gleamed, and having had some business in Piccadilly I had stepped into my hatter's and emerged with my silk hat newly ironed. I positively strutted along the pavement.

For two days I had not seen her or heard from her or written to her. I had scrupulously respected her wishes, foolish though they were. Now I was on my way to convince her that my love was not a moment's surge of the blood on a spring afternoon. I would take her into my arms at once, after the way of men, and she, after the way of women, would yield adorably. I had no doubt of it. I tasted in anticipation the bliss of that first embrace as if I had never kissed a woman in my life. And, indeed, what woman had I kissed with the passion that now ran through my veins? In that embrace all the ghosts of the past women would be laid for ever and a big and lusty future would make glorious beginning. "By Heaven," I cried, almost articulately, "with the splendour of the world at my command why should I not write plays, novels, poems, rhapsodies, so as to tell the blind, groping, loveless people what it is like?

"Take me up to Madame Brandt!" said I to the lift-porter. "Madame Brandt is not in town, sir," said the man.

I looked at him open-mouthed. "Not in town?"

"I think she has gone abroad, sir. She left with a lot of luggage yesterday, and her maid, and now the flat is shut up."

"Impossible!" I cried aghast.

The porter smiled. "I can only tell you what has happened, sir."

"Where has she gone to?"

"I couldn't say, sir."

"Her letters? Has she left no address to which they are to be forwarded?"

"Not with me, sir."

"Did she say when she was coming back?"

"No, sir. But she dismissed her cook with a month's wages, so it seems as though she was gone for a good spell."

"What time yesterday did she leave?"

"After lunch. The cabman was to drive her to Victoria—London, Chatham and Dover Railway."

"That looks like the 2.20 to Paris," said I.

But the lift-porter knew nothing of this. He had given me all the information in his power. I thanked him and went out into the sunshine a blinking, dazed, bewildered and piteously crushed man.

She had gone, without drum or trumpet, maid and baggage and all, having dismissed her cook and shut up the flat. It was incredible. I wandered aimlessly about Chelsea trying to make up my mind what to do. Should I go to Paris and bring her back by main force? But how did I know that she had gone to Paris? And if she was there how could I discover her address? Suddenly an idea struck me. She would not have left Quast and the cattery in the same unceremonious fashion to get on as best they might. She would have given Quast money and directions. At any rate, he would know more than the lift-porter of the mansions. I decided to go to him forthwith.

By means of trains and omnibuses I arrived at the house in the little street off Rosebery Avenue, Clerkenwell, where the maker of gymnastic appliances had his being. I knocked at the door. A grubby man appeared. I inquired for Quast.

Quast had left that morning in a van, taking his cages of cats with him. He had gone abroad and was never coming back again, not if he knew it, said the grubby man. The cats were poison and Quast was a low-down foreigner, and it would cost him a year's rent to put the place in order again. Whereupon he slammed the door in my face and left me disconsolate on the doorstep.

The only other person with whom I knew Lola to be on friendly terms was Sir Joshua Oldfield. I entered the first public telephone office I came to and rang him up. He had not seen Lola for a week, and had heard nothing from her relating to her sudden departure. I went sadly home to my bird-cage in Victoria Street, feeling that now at last the abomination of desolation had overspread my life.

Why had she gone? What was the meaning of it? Why not a line of explanation? And the simultaneous disappearance of Quast and the cats—what did that betoken? Had she been summoned, for any reason, to the Maison de Sante, where Anastasius Papadopoulos was incarcerated? If so, why this secrecy? Why should Lola of all people side with Destiny and make a greater Tom Fool of me than ever? This could be no other than the final jest.

I do not care to remember what I did and said in the privacy of my little room. There are things a man locks away even from himself.

I was in the midst of my misery when the bell of my tiny flat rang. I opened the door and found my sister Agatha smiling on the threshold.

"Hallo!" said I, gazing at her stupidly.

"You're not effusive in your welcome, my dear Simon," she remarked. "Won't you ask me to come in?"

"By all means," said I. "Come in!"

She entered and looked round my little sitting-room. "What a pill-box in the sky! I had no idea it was as tiny as this. I think I shall call you Saint Simon Stylites."

I was in no mood for Agatha. I bowed ironically and inquired to what I owed the honour of the visit.

"I want you to do me a favour—a great favour. I'm dying to see the new dances at the Palace Theatre. They say they dance on everything except their feet. I've got a box. Tom promised to take me. Now he finds he can't. I've telephoned all over the place for something uncompromising in or out of trousers to accompany me and I can't get hold of anybody. So I've come to you."

"I'm vastly flattered!" said I.

She dismissed my sarcasm with bird-like impatience.

"Don't be silly. If I had thought you would like it, I should have come to you first. I didn't want to bore you. But I did think you would pull me out of a hole."

"What's a hole?" I asked.

"I've paid for a box and I can't go by myself. How can I? Do take me, there's a dear."

"I'm afraid I'm too dull for haunts of merriment," said I.

She regarded me reproachfully.

"It isn't often I ask you to put yourself out for me. The last time was when I asked you to be the baby's godfather. And a pretty godfather you've been. I bet you anything you don't remember the name."

"I do," said I.

"What's it then?"

"It's—it's——" I snapped my fingers. The brat's name had for the moment gone out of my distracted head. She broke into a laugh and ran her arm through mine.

"Dorcas."

"Yes, of course—Dorcas. I was going to say so."

"Then you were going to say wrong, for it's Dorothy. Now you *must* come—for the sake of penance."

"I'll do anything you please!" I cried in desperation, "so long as you'll not talk to me of my own affairs and will let me sit as glum as ever I choose."

Then for the first time she manifested some interest in my mood. She put her head to one side and scanned my face narrowly.

"What's the matter, Simon?"

"I've absorbed too much life the last few days," said I, "and now I've got indigestion."

"I'm sorry, dear old boy, whatever it is," she said affectionately. "Come round and dine at 7.30, and I promise not to worry you."

What could I do? I accepted. The alternative to procuring Agatha an evening's amusement was pacing up and down my bird-cage and beating my wings (figuratively) and perhaps my head (literally) against the bars.

"It's awfully sweet of you," said Agatha. "Now I'll rush home and dress."

I accompanied her down the lift to the front door, and attended her to her carriage.

"I'll do you a good turn some day, dear," she said as she drove off.

I rather flatter myself that Agatha had no reason to complain of my dulness at dinner. In my converse with her I was faced by various alternatives. I might lay bare my heart, tell her of my love for Lola and my bewildered despair at her desertion; this I knew she would no more understand than if I had proclaimed a mad passion for a young lady who had waited on me at a tea-shop, or for a cassowary at the Zoo; even the best and most affectionate of sisters have their sympathetic limitations. I might have maintained a mysterious and Byronic gloom; this would have been sheer bad manners. I might have attributed my lack of spontaneous gaiety to toothache or stomach-ache; this would have aroused sisterly and matronly sympathies, and I should have had the devil's own job to escape from the house unpoisoned by the nostrums that lurk in the medicine chest of every well-conducted family. Agatha, I knew, had a peculiarly Borgiaesque equipment. Lastly, there was the worldly device, which I adopted, of dissimulating the furnace of my affliction beneath a smiling exterior. Agatha, therefore, found me an entertaining guest and drove me to the Palace Theatre in high good humour.

There, however, I could resign my role of entertainer in favour of the professionals on the stage. I sat back in my corner of the box and gave myself up to my harassing concerns. Young ladies warbled, comic acrobats squirted siphons at each other and kicked each other in the stomach, jugglers threw plates and brass balls with dizzying skill, the famous dancers gyrated pyrotechnically, the house applauded with delight, Agatha laughed and chuckled and clapped her hands and I remained silent, unnoticed and unnoticing in my reflective corner, longing for the foolery to end. Where was Lola? Why had she forsaken me? What remedy, in the fiend's name, was there for this heart torture within me? The most excruciating agonies of the little pain inside were child's play to this. I bit my lips so as not to groan aloud and contorted my features into the semblance of a smile.

During a momentary interval there came a knock at the box door. I said, "Come in!" The door opened, and there, to my utter amazement, stood Dale Kynnersley—Dale, sleek, alert, smiling, attired in the very latest nicety of evening dress affected by contemporary youth—Dale such as I knew and loved but six months ago.

He came forward to Agatha, who was little less astounded than myself.

"How d'ye do, Lady Durrell? I'm in the stalls with Harry Essendale. I tried to catch your eye, but couldn't. So I thought I'd come up." He turned to me with frank outstretched hand, "How do, Simon?"

I grasped his hand and murmured something unintelligible. The thing was so extraordinary, so unexpected that my wits went wandering. Dale carried off the situation lightly. It was he who was the man of the world, and I the unresourceful stumbler.

"He's looking ripping, isn't he, Lady Durrell? I met old Oldfield the other day, and he was raving about your case. The thing has never been done before. Says they're going mad over your chap in Paris—they've given him medals and wreaths and decorations till he goes about like a prize bull at a fair. By Jove, it's good to see you again."

"You might have taken an earlier opportunity," Agatha remarked with some acidity.

"So I might," retorted Dale blandly; "but when a man's a born ass it takes him some time to cultivate sense! I've been wanting to see you for a long time, Simon—and to-night I just couldn't resist it. You don't want to kick me out?"

"Heaven forbid," said I, somewhat brokenly, for the welcome sight of his face and the sound of his voice aroused emotions which even now I do not care to analyse. "It was generous of you to come up."

He coloured. "Rot!" said he, in his breezy way. "Hallo! The curtain's going up. What's the next item? Oh, those fool dogs!"

"I adore performing dogs!" said Agatha, looking toward the stage.

He turned to me. "Do you?"

The last thing on earth I desired to behold at that moment was a performing animal. My sensitiveness led me to suspect a quizzical look in Dale's eye. Fortunately, he did not wait for my answer, but went on in a boyish attempt to appease Agatha.

"I don't despise them, you know, Lady Durrell, but I've seen them twice before. They're really rather good. There's a football match at the end which is quite exciting."

"Oh, the beauties!" cried Agatha over her shoulder as the dogs trotted on the stage. I nodded an acknowledgment of the remark, and she plunged into rapt contemplation of the act. Dale and I stood at the back of the box. Suddenly he whispered:

"Come out into the corridor. I've something to say to you."

"Certainly," said I, and followed him out of the box.

He thrust his hands into his pockets and looked at me with the defiant and you-be-damned air of the young Briton who was about to commit a gracious action. I knew what he was going to say. I could tell by his manner. I dreaded it, and yet I loved him for it.

"Why say anything, my dear boy?" I asked. "You want to be friends with me again, and God knows I want to be friends again with you. Why talk?"

"I've got to get if off my chest," said he, in his so familiar vernacular. "I want to tell you that I've been every end of a silly ass and I want you to forgive me."

I vow I have never felt so miserably guilty towards any human being as I did at that moment. I have never felt such a smug-faced hypocrite. It was a humiliating position. I had inflicted on him a most grievous wrong, and here he was pleading for forgiveness. I could not pronounce the words of pardon. He misinterpreted my silence.

"I know I've behaved rottenly to you since you've been back, but the first step's always so difficult. You mustn't bear a grudge against me."

"My dear boy!" I cried, my hand on his shoulder, touched to the heart by his simple generosity, "don't let us talk of grudges and forgiveness. All I want to know is whether you're contented?"

"Contented?" he cried. "I should just think I am. I'm the happiest ass that doesn't eat thistles!"

"Explain yourself, my dear Dale," said I, relapsing into my old manner.

"I'm going to marry Maisie Ellerton."

I took him by the arm and dragged him inside the box.

"Agatha," said I, "leave those confounded dogs for a moment and attend to serious matters. This young man has not come up to see either of us, but to obtain our congratulations. He's going to marry Maisie Ellerton."

"Tell me all about it," said Agatha intensely interested.

A load of responsibility rolled off my shoulders like Christian's pack. I looked at the dog football match with the interest of a Sheffield puddler at a Cup-tie, and clapped my hands.

An hour or so later after we had seen Agatha home, and Dale had incidentally chucked Lord Essendale (the phrase is his own), we were sitting over whisky and soda and cigars in my Victoria Street flat. The ingenuousness of youth had insisted on this prolongation of our meeting.

He had a thousand things to tell me. They chiefly consisted in a reiteration of the statement that he had been a rampant and unimagined silly ass, and that Maisie, who knew the whole lunatic story, was a brick, and a million times too good for him. When he entered my humble lodging he looked round in a bewildered manner.

"Why on earth are you living in this mouse-trap?"

"Agatha calls it a pill-box. I call it a bird-cage. I live here, my dear boy, because it is the utmost I can afford."

"Rot! I've been your private secretary and know what your income is."

I sighed heavily. I shall have to get a leaflet printed setting out the causes that led to my change of fortune. Then I can hand it to such of my friends as manifest surprise.

Indeed, I had grown so used to the story of my lamentable pursuit of the eumoirous that I rattled it off mechanically after the manner of the sturdy beggar telling his mendacious tale of undeserved misfortune. To Dale, however, it was fresh. He listened to it open-eyed. When I had concluded, he brought his hand down on the arm of the chair.

"By Jove, you're splendid! I always said you were. Just splendid!"

He gulped down half a tumbler of whisky and soda to hide his feelings.

"And you've been doing all this while I've been making a howling fool of myself! Look here, Simon, you were right all along the line—from the very first when you tackled me about Lola. Do you remember?"

"Why refer to it?" I asked.

"I must!" he burst in quickly. "I've been longing to put myself square with you. By the way, where is Lola?"

"I don't know," said I with grim truthfulness.

"Don't know? Has she vanished?"

"Yes," said I.

"That's the end of it, I suppose. Poor Lola! She was an awfully good sort you know!" said Dale, "and I won't deny I was hit. That's when I came such a cropper. But I realise now how right you were. I was just caught by the senses, nothing else; and when she wrote to say it was all off between us my vanity suffered—suffered damnably, old chap. I lost the election through it. Didn't attend to business. That brought me to my senses. Then Essendale took me away yachting, and I had a quiet time to think; and after that I somehow took to seeing more of Maisie. You know how things happen.

And I'm jolly grateful to you, old chap. You've saved me from God knows what complications! After all, good sort as Lola is, it's rot for a man to go outside his own class, isn't it?"

"It depends upon the man—and also the woman," said I, beginning to derive peculiar torture from the conversation.

Dale shook his wise head. "It never comes off," said he. After a pause he laughed aloud. "Don't you remember the lecture you gave me? My word, you did talk! You produced a string of ghastly instances where the experiment had failed. Let me see, who was there, Paget, Merridew, Bullen. Ha! Ha! No, I'm well out of it, old chap—thanks to you."

"If any good has come of this sorry business," said I gravely, "I'm only too grateful to Providence."

He caught the seriousness of my tone.

"I didn't want to touch on that side of it," he said awkwardly. "I know what an infernal time you had! It must have been Gehenna. I realise now that it was on my account, and so I can never do enough to show my gratitude."

He finished his glass of whisky and walked about the tiny room.

"What has always licked me," he said at length, "is why she never told me she was married. It's so curious, for she was as straight as they make them. It's devilish odd!"

"Yes," I assented wearily, for every word of this talk was a new pain. "Devilish odd!"

"I suppose it's a question of class again."

"Or sex," said I.

"What has sex to do with being straight?"

"Everything," said I.

"Rot!" said Dale.

I sighed. "I wish your dialectical vocabulary were not so limited."

He laughed and clapped me on the shoulder.

"Still the same old Simon. It does my heart good to hear you. May I have another whisky?"

I took advantage of this break to change the conversation. He had told me nothing of his own affairs save that he was engaged to Maisie Ellerton.

"Heavens!" cried he. "Isn't that enough?"

"An engagement isn't an occupation."

"Isn't it, by Jove?" He laughed boyishly. "I manage, however, to squeeze in a bit of work now and then. The mater has always got plenty on hand for me, and I do things for Raggles. He has been awfully decent. The first time I met him or any of the chiefs after the election I was in a blue funk. But no one seemed to blame me; they all said they were sorry; and now Raggles is looking out for a constituency for me to nurse for the next General Election. Then things *will* hum, I promise you!"

He waved his cigar with the air of a young paladin about to conquer the world. In spite of my own depression, I could not help smiling with gladness at the sight of him. With his extravagantly cut waistcoat, his elaborately exquisite white tie, his perfectly fitting evening clothes, with his supple ease of body, his charming manner, the preposterous fellow made as gallant a show as any ruffling blade in powder and red-heeled shoes. He had acquired, too, an extra touch of manhood since I had seen him last. I felt proud of him, conscious that to the making of him I had to some small degree contributed.

"You must come out and lunch with Maisie and me one day this week," said he. "She would love to see you."

"Wait till you're married," said I, "and then we'll consider it. At present Maisie is under the social dominion of her parents."

"Well—what of it?"

"Just that," said I.

Then the truth dawned on him. He grew excited and said it was damnable. He wasn't going to stand by and see people believe a lot of scandalous lies about me. He had no idea people had given me the cold shoulder. He would jolly well (such were his words) take a something (I forget the adjective) megaphone and trumpet about society what a splendid fellow I was.

"I'll tell everybody the whole silly-ass story about myself from beginning to end," he declared.

I checked him. "You're very generous, my dear boy," said I, "but you'll do me a favour by letting folks believe what they like." And then I explained, as delicately as I could, how his sudden championship could be of little advantage to me, and might do him considerable harm.

In his impetuous manner he cut short my carefully-expressed argument.

"Rubbish! Heaps of people I know are already convinced that I was keeping Lola Brandt and that you took her from me in the ordinary vulgar way—"

"Yes, yes," I interrupted, shrinking. "That's why I order you, in God's name, to leave the whole thing alone."

"But confound it, man! I've come out of it all right, why shouldn't you? Even supposing Lola was a loose woman—"

I threw up my hand. "Stop!"

He looked disconcerted for a moment.

"We know she isn't, but for the sake of argument—"

"Don't argue," said I. "Let us drop it."

"But hang it all!" he shouted in desperation. "Can't I do something! Can't I go and kick somebody?"

I lost my self-control. I rose and put both my hands on his shoulders and looked him in the eyes.

"You can kick anybody you please whom you hear breathe a word against the honour and purity of Madame Lola Brandt."

Then I walked away, knowing I had betrayed myself, and tried to light a cigar with fingers that shook. There was a pause. Dale stood with his back to the fireplace, one foot on the fender. The cigar took some lighting. The pause grew irksome.

"My regard for Madame Brandt," said I at last, "is such that I don't wish to discuss her with any one." I looked at Dale and met his keen eyes fixed on me. The faintest shadow of a smile played about his mouth.

"Very well," said he dryly, "we won't discuss her. But all the same, my dear Simon, I can't help being interested in her; and as you're obviously the same, it seems rather curious that you don't know where she is."

"Do you doubt me?" I asked, somewhat staggered by his tone.

"Good Heaven's, no! But if she has disappeared, I'm convinced that something has happened which I know nothing of. Of course, it's none of my business."

There was a new and startling note of assurance in his voice. Certainly he had developed during the past few months. What I had done, Heaven only knows. Misfortune, which is supposed to be formative of character, seemed to have turned mine into pie. How can I otherwise account for my not checking the lunatic impulse that prompted my next words.

"Well, something has happened," said I, "and if we're to be friends, you had better know it. Two days ago, for the first time, I told Madame Brandt that I loved her. This very afternoon I went to get her answer to my question—would she marry me?—and I found that she had disappeared without leaving any address behind her. So whenever you hear her name mentioned you can just tell everybody that she's the one woman in the whole wide world I want to marry."

"Poor old Simon," said Dale. "Poor old chap."

"That's exactly how things stand."

"Lord, who would have thought it?"

"How I've borne with you talking about her all this evening the devil only knows," I cried. "You've driven me half crazy."

"You should have told me to shut up."

"I did."

"Poor old Simon. I'm so sorry—but I had no idea you had fallen in love with her."

"Fallen in love!" said I, losing my head. "She's the only woman on God's earth I've ever cared for. I want her as I've wanted nothing in the universe before."

"And you've come to care for her as much as that?" he said sympathetically. "Poor old Simon."

"Why the devil shouldn't I?" I shouted, nettled by his "poor old Simons."

"Lola Brandt is hardly of your class," said Dale.

I broke out furiously. "Damn class! I've had enough of it. I'm going to take my life into my own hands and do what I like with it. I'm going to choose my mate without any reference to society. I've cut myself adrift from society. It can go hang. Lola Brandt is a woman worth any man's loving. She is a woman in a million. You know nothing whatever about her."

The last words were scarcely out of my mouth when an echo from the distance came and, as it were, banged at my ears. Dale himself had shrieked them at me in exactly the same tone with reference to the same woman. I stopped short and looked at him for a moment rather stupidly. Then the imp of humour, who for some time had deserted me, flew to my side and tickled my brain. I broke into a chuckle, somewhat hysterical I must admit, and then, throwing myself into an arm-chair, gave way to uncontrollable laughter.

The scare of the unexpected rose in Dale's eyes.

"Why, what on earth is the matter?"

"Can't you see?" I cried, as far as the paroxysms of my mirth would let me. "Can't you see how exquisitely ludicrous the whole thing has been from beginning to end? Don't you realise that you and I are playing the same scene as we played months ago in my library, with the only difference that we have changed roles? I'm the raving, infatuated youth, and you're the grave and reverend mentor. Don't you see? Don't you see?"

"I can't see anything to laugh at," said Dale sturdily.

And he couldn't. There are thousands of bright, flame-like human beings constituted like that. Life spreads out before them one of its most side-splitting, topsy-turvy farces and they see in it nothing to laugh at.

To Dale the affair had been as serious and lacking in the fantastic as the measles. He had got over the disease and now was exceedingly sorry to perceive that I had caught it in my turn.

"It isn't funny a bit," he continued. "It's quite natural. I see it all now. You cut me out from the very first. You didn't mean to—you never thought of it. But what chance had I against you? I was a young ass and you were a brilliant man of the world. I bear you no grudge. You played the game in that way. Then things happened—and at last you've fallen in love with her—and now just at the critical moment she has gone off into space. It must be devilish painful for you, if you ask me."

"Oh, Dale," said I, shaking my head, "the only fitting end to the farce would be if you wandered over Europe to find and bring her back to me."

"I don't know about that," said he, "because I'm engaged, and that, as I said, gives me occupation; but if I can do anything practicable, my dear old Simon, you've only got to send for me."

He pulled out his watch.

"My hat!" he exclaimed. "It's past two o'clock."

CHAPTER XXII

I am a personage apart from humanity. I vary from the kindly ways of man. A curse is on me.

Surely no man has fought harder than I have done to convince himself of the deadly seriousness of existence; and surely before the feet of no man has Destiny cast such stumbling-blocks to faith. I might be an ancient dweller in the Thebaid struggling towards dreams of celestial habitations, and confronted only by grotesque visions of hell. No matter what I do, I'm baffled. I look upon sorrow and say, "Lo, this is tragedy!" and hey, presto! a trick of lightning turns it into farce. I cry aloud, in perfervid zeal, "Life is real, life is earnest, and the apotheosis of the fantastic is not its goal," and immediately a grinning irony comes to give the lie to my credo.

Or is it that, by inscrutable decree of the Almighty Powers, I am undergoing punishment for an old unregenerate point of view, being doomed to wear my detested motley for all eternity, to stretch out my hand for ever to grasp realities and find I can do nought but beat the air with my bladder; to listen with strained ear perpetually expectant of the music of the spheres, and catch nothing but the mocking jingle of the bells on my fool's cap?

I don't know. I give it up.

Such were my thoughts on the morning after my interview with Dale, when I had read a long, long letter from Lola, which she had despatched from Paris.

The letter lies before me now, many pages in a curious, half-formed foreign hand. Many would think it an ill-written letter—for there are faults of spelling and faults of grammar—but even now, as I look on those faults, the tears come into my eyes. Oh, how exquisitely, pathetically, monumentally, sublimely foolish! She had little or nothing to do with it, poor dear; it was only the Arch-Jester again, leading her blindly away, so as once more to leave me high and dry on the Hill of Derision.

". . . My dear, you must forgive me! My heart is breaking, but I know I'm doing right. There is nothing for it but to go out of your life for ever. It terrifies me to think of it, but it's the only way. I know you think you love me, dear; but you can't, you can't *really* love a woman so far beneath you, and I would sooner never see you again than marry you and wake up one day and find that you hated and scorned me. . . ."

Can you wonder that I shook my fist at Heaven and danced with rage?

". . . Miss Eleanor Faversham called on me just a few minutes after you left me that afternoon. We had a long, long talk. Simon, dear, you must marry her. You loved her once, for you were engaged, and only broke it off because you thought you were going to die; and she loves you, Simon, and she is a lady with all the refinement and education that I could never have. She is of your class, dear, and understands you, and can help you on, whereas I could only drag you down. I am not fit to black her boots. . . ."

And so forth, and so forth, in the most heartrending strain of insensate self-sacrifice and heroic self-abasement. The vainest and most heartless dog of a man stands abashed and helpless before such things in a woman.

She had not seen or written to me because she would not have her resolution weakened. After the great wrench, succeeding things were easier. She had taken Anastasius's cats and proposed to work them in the music-halls abroad and send the proceeds to be administered for the little man's comfort at the Maison de Sante. As both her name and the Papadopoulos troupe of cats were well known in the "variety" world, it would be a simple matter to obtain engagements. She had already opened negotiations for a short season somewhere abroad. I was not to be anxious about her. She would have plenty of occupation.

". . . I am not sending you any address, for I don't want you to know where I am, dear. I shan't write to you again unless I scribble things and tear them up without posting. This is final. When a woman makes such a break she must do it once and for all. Oh, Simon, when you kissed me two days ago you thought you loved me; but I know what the senses are and how they deceive people, and I had only just caught your senses on that spring afternoon, and I made you do it, for I had been aching, aching for months for a word of love from you, and when it came I was ashamed. But I should have been weak and shut my eyes to everything if Miss Faversham had not come to me like God's good angel. . . ."

At the fourth reading of the letter I stopped short at these words. God's good angel, indeed! Could anything have been more calculated to put a man into a frenzy? I seized my hat and stick and went in search of the nearest public telephone office. In less than ten minutes I had arranged an immediate interview with Eleanor Faversham at my sister Agatha's, and in less than half an hour I was pacing up and down Agatha's sitting-room waiting for her. God's good angel! The sound of the words made me choke with wrath. There are times when angelic interference in human destinies is entirely unwarrantable. I stamped and I fumed, and I composed a speech in which I told Eleanor exactly what I thought of angels.

As I had to wait a considerable time, however, before Eleanor appeared, the raging violence of my wrath abated, and when she did enter the room smiling and fresh, with the spring in her clear eyes and a flush on her cheek, I just said: "How d'ye do, Eleanor?" in the most commonplace way, and offered her a chair.

"I've come, you see. You were rather peremptory, so I thought it must be a matter of great importance."

"It is," said I. "You went to see Madame Brandt."

"I did," she replied, looking at me steadily, "and I have tried to write to you, but it is more difficult than I thought."

"Well," said I, "it's no use writing now, for you've managed to drive her out of the country."

She half rose in her chair and regarded me with wide-blue eyes.

"I've driven her out of the country?"

"Yes; with her maid and her belongings and Anastasius Papadopoulos's troupe of performing cats, and Anastasius Papadopoulos's late pupil and assistant Quast. She has given up her comfortable home in London and now proposes to be a wanderer among the music-halls of Europe."

"But that's not my fault! Indeed, it isn't."

"She says in a letter I received this morning bearing no address, that if you hadn't come to her like God's good angel, she would have remained in London."

Eleanor looked bewildered. "I thought I had made it perfectly clear to her."

"Made what clear?"

She blushed a furious red. "Can't you guess? You must be as stupid as she is. And, of course, you're wildly angry with me. Aren't you?"

"I certainly wish you hadn't gone to see her."

"Was it merely to tell me this that you ordered me to come here?" she asked, with a touch of anger in her voice, for however much like God's good angels young women may be, they generally have a spirit of their own.

I felt I had been wanting in tact; also that I had put myself—through an impetuosity foreign to what I had thought to be my character—in a foolish position. If I replied affirmatively to her question, she would have served me perfectly right by tossing her head in the air and marching indignantly out of the room. I temporised.

"In order to understand the extraordinary consequences of your interview, I should like to have some idea of what took place. I know, my dear Eleanor," I continued as gently as I could, "I know that you went to see her out of the very great kindness of your heart—"

"No, I didn't."

I made a little gesture in lieu of reply. There was a span of silence. Eleanor played with the silky ears of Agatha's little Yorkshire terrier which had somehow strayed into the room and taken possession of her lap.

"Don't you see, Simon?" she said at last, half tearfully, without taking her eyes off the dog, "don't you see that by accusing me in this way you make it almost impossible for me to speak? And I was going to be so loyal to you."

A tear fell down her cheek on to the dog's back, and convicted me of unmitigated brutality.

"What else could you be but loyal?" I murmured. "Your attitude all through has shone it."

She flashed her hand angrily over her eyes, and looked at me. "And I wanted to be loyal to the end. If you had waited and she had waited, you would have seen. As soon as I could have conveyed it to you decently, I should have shown you——Ah!" She broke off, put the Yorkshire terrier on the sofa beside her, and rose with an impatient gesture. "You want to know why I called on Lola Brandt? I felt I had to know for myself what kind of woman she was. She was the woman between us—you and me. You don't suppose I ceased to care for you just because what we thought was a fatal illness broke off our engagement! I did care for you. I cared for you—in a way; I say 'in a way'—I'll tell you why later on. When we met here the last time do you think I was not moved? I knew your altered position would not allow you to suggest a renewal of the engagement so I offered you the opportunity. Do you remember? But I could not tell whether you still cared for me or whether you cared for the other woman. So I had to go and see her. I couldn't bear to think that you might feel in honour bound to take me at my word and be caring all the time for some one else. I went to see her, and then I realised that I didn't count. Don't ask why. Women know these things. And I found that she loved you with a warmth and richness I'm incapable of. I felt I had stepped into something big and splendid, as if I had been a caterpillar walking into the heart of a red rose. I felt prim and small and petty. Until then I had never known what love meant, and I didn't feel it; I couldn't feel it. I couldn't give you a millionth part of what that woman does. And I knew that having lived in that atmosphere, you couldn't possibly be content with me. If you had waited, I should have found some means of telling you so. That's what I meant by saying I was loyal to you. And I thought I had made it clear to her. It seems I didn't. It isn't my fault."

"My dear," said I, when she had come to the end of this astonishing avowal, and stood looking at me somewhat defiantly and twisting her fingers nervously in front of her, "I don't know what in the world to say to you."

"You can tell me, at least, that my instinct was right."

"Which one? A woman has so many."

"That you love Lola Brandt."

I lifted my arms in a helpless gesture and let them drop to my sides.

"One is not one's own master in these things."

"Then you do?"

"Yes," said I in a low voice.

Eleanor drew a long breath, turned and sat down again on the sofa.

"And she knows it?"

"I have told her so."

"Then why in the world has she run away?"

"Because you two wonderful and divinely foolish people have been too big for each other. While you were impressed by one quality in her she was equally impressed by another in you. She departed, burning her ships, so as to go entirely out of my life for the simple reason, as she herself expresses it, that she was not fit to black your boots. So," said I, taking her left hand in mine and patting it gently, "between you two dear, divine angel fools, I fall to the ground."

A while later, just before we parted, she said in her frank way:

"I know many people would say I've behaved with shocking impropriety—immodestly and all that. You don't, do you? I believe half the unhappiness in life comes from people being afraid to go straight at things. Perhaps I've gone too straight this time—but you'll forgive me?"

I smiled and squeezed her hand. "My dear," said I, "Lola Brandt was right. You are God's good angel."

I went away in a chastened mood, no longer wrathful, for what could woman do more for mortal man than what Eleanor Faversham had attempted? She had gone to see whether she should stand against her rival, and with a superb generosity, unprecedented in her sex, she had withdrawn.

The magnanimity of it overwhelmed me. I walked along the street exalting her to viewless pinnacles of high-heartedness. And then, suddenly, the Devil whispered in my ear that execrated word "eumoiriety." It poisoned the rest of the day. It confirmed my conviction of the ironical designs of Destiny. Destiny, not content with making me a victim of the accursed principle in my own person, had used these two dear women as its instruments in dealing me fresh humiliation. Where would it end? Where could I turn to escape such an enemy? If I had been alone in green fields instead of Sloane Square, I should have clapped my hands to my head and prayed God not to drive me crazy. I should have cried wild vows to the winds and shaken my fist at the sky and rolled upon the grass and made a genteel idiot of myself. Nature would have understood. Men do these things in time of stress, and I was in great stress. I loved a woman for the first time in my life—and I was a man nearly forty. I wanted her with every quivering nerve in me. And she was gone. Lost in the vast expanse of Europe with a parcel of performing cats. Gone out of my life loving me as I loved her, all on account of this Hell-invented principle. Ye gods! If the fierce, pure, deep, abiding love of a man for a woman is not a reality, what in this world of shadows is anything but vapour? I grasped it tight, hugged it to my bosom—and now she was gone, and in my ears rang the derisive laughter of the enemy.

Where would it end? What would happen next? Nothing was too outrageously, maniacally impossible. I walked up Sloane Street, a street for which impeccable respectability, security of life and person, comfortable, modern, twentieth-century, prosperous smugness has no superior in all the smug cities of the earth, and I was prepared to encounter with a smile of recognition anything that the whirling brains of Bedlam had ever conceived. Why should not this little lady tripping along with gold chain-bag and anxious, shopping knit of the brow, throw her arms round my neck and salute me as her long-lost brother? Why should not the patient horses in that omnibus suddenly turn into griffins and begin to snort fire from their nostrils? Why should not that policeman, who, on his beat, was approaching me with the heavy, measured tread, suddenly arrest me for complicity in the Pazzi Conspiracy or the Rye House Plot? Why should not the whole of the decorous street suddenly change into the inconsequence of an Empire ballet? Why should not the heavens fall down and universal chaos envelop all?

The only possible reason I can think of now is that the Almighty Powers did not consider it worth while to go to quite so much trouble on my account.

This, however, gives you some idea of my state of mind. But though it lasted for a considerable time, I would not have you believe that I fostered it unduly. Indeed, I repudiated it with some disgust. I took it out, examined it, and finding it preposterous, set to work to modify it into harmony with the circumstances of my every-day life. Even the most sorely tried of men cannot walk abroad shedding his exasperation around like pestilence. If he does, he is put into a lunatic asylum.

If a man cannot immediately assuage the hunger of his heart, he must meet starvation with a smiling face. In the meantime, he has to eat so as to satisfy the hunger of his body, to clothe himself with a certain discrimination, to attend to polite commerce with his fellow man and to put to some fair use the hours of his day. I did not doubt but that by means of intelligent inquiry which I determined to pursue in every possible direction I should sooner or later obtain news of Lola. A lady with a troupe of performing cats could not for long remain in obscurity. True, I might have gone in gallant quest of her; but I had had enough of such fool adventures. I bided my time, consulted with Dale, who took up the work of a private detective agency with his usual zeal, writing letters to every crony who languished in the exile of foreign embassies, and corresponding (unknown to Lady Kynnersley) with the agencies of the International Aid Society, did what I could on my own account, and turned my attention seriously to the regeneration of the Judds.

As the affairs of one drunken tailor's family could not afford me complete occupation for my leisure hours, I began to find myself insensibly drawn by Campion's unreflecting enthusiasm into all kinds of small duties connected with Barbara's Building. Before I could realise that I had consented, I discovered myself in charge of an evening class of villainous-looking and uncleanly youths who assembled in one of the lecture-rooms to listen to my recollections of the history of England. I was to continue the course begun by a young Oxford man, who, for some reason or other, had migrated from Barbara's Building to Toynbee Hall.

"I've never done any schoolmastering in my life. Suppose," said I, with vivid recollections of my school days, "suppose they rag me?"

"They won't," said Campion, who had come to introduce me to the class.

And they did not. I found these five and twenty youthful members of the proletariat the most attentive, respectable, and intelligent audience that ever listened to a lecture. Gradually I came to perceive that they were not as villainous-looking and uncleanly as at first sight I had imagined. A great many of them took notes. When I came to the end of my dissertation on Henry VIII, I went among them, as I discovered the custom to be, and chatted, answering questions, explaining difficulties, and advising as to a course of reading. The atmosphere of trust and friendliness compensated for the lack of material sweetness. Here were young men pathetically eager to learn, grateful for every crumb of information that came from my lips. They reminded me of nothing more than the ragged class of scholars around a teacher in a mediaeval university. Some had vague dreams of eventually presenting themselves for examinations, the Science and Art Department, the College of Preceptors, the Matriculation of the University of London. Others longed for education for its own sake, or rather as a means of raising themselves in the social scale. Others, bitten by the crude Socialism of their class, had been persuaded to learn something of past movements of mankind so as to obtain some basis for their opinions. All were in deadly earnest. The magnetic attraction between teacher and taught established itself. After one or two lectures, I looked forward to the next with excited interest.

Other things Campion off-handedly put into my charge. I went on tours of inspection round the houses of his competing housewives. I acted as his deputy at the police court when ladies and gentlemen with a good record at Barbara's got into trouble with the constabulary. I investigated cases for the charity of the institution. In quite a short time I realised with a gasp that I had become part of the machinery of Barbara's Building, and was remorselessly and helplessly whirled hither and thither with the rest of the force of the driving wheel which was Rex Campion.

The amazing, the astounding, the utterly incredible thing about the whole matter was that I not only liked it, but plunged into it heart and soul as I had never plunged into work before. I discovered sympathies that had hitherto lain undreamed of within me. In my electioneering days I had, it is true, foregathered with the sons of toil. I had shaken the horny hands of men and the soap-suddy hands of women. I had flattered them and cajoled them and shown myself mighty affable, as a sensible and aspiring Parliamentary candidate should do; but the way to their hearts I had never found, I had never dreamed of seeking. And now it seemed as if the great gift had been bestowed on me—and I examined it with a new and almost tremulous delight.

Also, for the first time in all my life, I had taken pain to be the companion of my soul. All my efforts to find Lola were fruitless. I became acquainted with the heartache, the longing for the unattainable, the agony of spirit. The only anodyne was a forgetfulness of self, the only compensation a glimmer of a hope and the shadow of a smile in the grey and leaden lives around me.

On Whit Monday evening I was walking along the Thames Embankment on my way home from Waterloo Station, wet through, tired out, disappointed, and looking forward to the dry, soft raiment, the warm, cosy room, the excellent dinner that awaited me in my flat. I—with several others—had been helping Campion with his annual outing of factory girls and young hooligans. The weather, which had been perfect on Saturday, Sunday, and when we had started, a gay and astonishing army, at seven o'clock, had broken before ten. It had rained, dully miserable, insistently all day long. The happy day in the New Forest had been a damp and dismal fiasco. I was returning home, thinking I might walk off an incipient chill, as depressed as no one but the baffled philanthropist can be, when I perceived a tattered and dejected man sitting on a bench, a clothes-basket between his feet, his elbows on his knees, his head in his hands, and sobbing as if his heart would break. As the spectacle of a grown-up man crying bitterly in a public thoroughfare was somewhat remarkable, I paused, and then in order to see whether his distress was genuine, and also not to arouse his suspicions, I threw myself in an exhausted manner on the bench beside him. He continued to sob. At last I said, raising my voice:

"You seem to be pretty miserable. What's wrong?"

He turned bleared, yet honest-looking eyes upon me.

"The whole blasted show!" said he. "There's nothing right in it, s'welp me Gawd."

I gave a modified assent to the proposition and drew my coat-collar over my eyes. "Being wet through doesn't make it any better," said I.

"Who would ha' thought it would come down as it has to-day? Tell me that. It's enough to make a man cut his throat!"

I was somewhat surprised. "You're not in such a great distress just because it has been a rainy day!"

"Ain't I just!" he exclaimed. "It's been and gone and ruined me, this day has. Look 'ere, guv'nor, I'll tell you all about it. I've been out of work, see? I was in 'orspital for three months and I couldn't get nothing regular to do when I come out. I'm a packer by trade. I did odd jobs, see, and the wife she earned a little, too, and we managed to keep things going and to scrape together five shillings, that's three months' savings, against Whitsun Bank Holiday. And as the weather was so fine, I laid it all out in paper windmills to sell to the kids on 'Amstead 'Eath. And I started out this morning with the basket full of them all so fine and pretty, and no sooner do I get on the 'Eath than the rain comes down and wipes out the whole blooming lot, before I could sell one. Look 'ere!"

He drew a bedraggled sheet of newspaper from the clothes-basket and displayed a piteous sodden welter of sticks and gaudy pulp. At the sight of it he broke down again and sobbed like a child.

"And there's not a bite in the 'ouse, nor not likely to be for days; and I daren't go home and face the missus and the kids—and I wish I was dead."

I had already seen many pitiful tragedies during my brief experience with Campion; but the peculiar pitifulness of this one wrung my heart. It taught me as nothing had done before how desperately humble are the aspirations of the poor. I thought of the cosy comfort that awaited me in my own home; the despair that awaited him in his.

I put my hand in my pocket.

"You seem to be a good chap," said I.

He shrugged his shoulders. The consciousness of applauded virtue offered no consolation. I drew out a couple of half-crowns and threw them into the basket.

"For the missus and the kids," said I.

He picked them out of the welter, and holding them in his hand, looked at me stupidly.

"Can you afford it, guv'nor?"

At first I thought this remark was some kind of ill-conditioned sarcasm; but suddenly I realised that dripping wet and covered with mud from head to foot, with a shapeless, old, green, Homburg hat drooping forlornly about my ears, I did not fulfil his conception of the benevolent millionaire. I laughed, and rose from the bench.

"Yes. Quite well. Better luck next time."

I nodded a good-bye, and walked away. After a minute, he came running after me.

"'Ere," said he, "I ain't thanked yer. Gawd knows how I'm going to do it. I can't! But, 'ere—would you mind if I chucked a lot of the stuff into the river and told the missus I had sold it, and just got back my money? She's proud, she is, and has never accepted a penny in charity in her life. It's only because it would be better for 'er."

He looked at me with such earnest appeal that I saw that the saving of his wife's pride was a serious matter.

"Of course," said I, "and here's a few ha'pence to add to it, so as to give colour to the story."

He saw that I understood. "Thank you kindly, sir," said he.

"Tell me," said I, "do you love your wife?"

He gaped at me for a moment; obviously the question had never been put to him either by himself or anybody else. Then, seeing that my interest was genuine, he spat and scratched his head.

"We've been together twenty years," he said, in a low voice, emotion struggling with self-consciousness, "and I've 'ad nothing agin her all that time. She's a bloomin' wonder, I tell you straight."

I held out my hand. "At any rate, you've got what I haven't," said I. "A woman who loves you to welcome you home."

And I went away, longing, longing for Lola's arms and the deep love in her voice.

Now that I come to view my actions in some sort of perspective, it seems to me that it was the underlying poignancy of this trumpery incident—a poignancy which, nevertheless, bit deep into my soul, that finally determined the current of my life.

A short while afterwards, Campion, who for some time past had found the organisation of Barbara's Building had far outgrown his individual power of control, came to me with a proposal that I should undertake the management of the institution under his general directorship. As he knew of my financial affairs and of my praiseworthy but futile efforts to live on two hundred a year, he offered me another two hundred by way of salary and quarters in the Building. I accepted, moved the salvage of my belongings from Victoria Street to Lambeth, and settled down to the work for which a mirth-loving Providence had destined me from my cradle.

When I told Agatha, she nearly fainted.

CHAPTER XXIII

No sooner had I moved into Barbara's Building and was preparing to begin my salaried duties than I received news which sent me off post haste to Berlin. And just as it was not I but Anastasius Papadopoulos who discovered Captain Vauvenarde, so, in this case, it was Dale who discovered Lola.

He burst in upon me one day, flourishing a large visiting-card, which he flung down on the table before my eyes.

"Do you recognise that?"

It was the familiar professional card of the unhappy Anastasius.

"Yes."

"Do you see the last line?"

I read "London Agents: Messrs. Conto and Blag, 172 Maiden Lane, W.C." I looked up. "Well?" I asked.

"It has done the trick," said he triumphantly. "What fools we were not to have thought of it before. I was rooting out a drawer of papers and came across the card. You remember he handed us one all round the first day we met him. I put it away—I'm rather a methodical devil with papers, as you know. When I found it, I danced a hornpipe all round the room and went straight off to Conto and Blag. I made certain she would work through them, as they were accustomed to shop the cats, and I found I was right. They knew all about her. Wouldn't give her address, but told me that she was appearing this week at the Winter Garten at Berlin. Why that pudding-headed quagga, Bevan, at the Embassy, hasn't kept his eyes open for me, as he promised," he went on a while later, "I don't know! I can understand Eugen Pattenhausen, the owl-eyed coot who runs the International Aid Society, not doing a hand's turn to aid anybody—but Bevan! For Heaven's sake, while you're there call at the Embassy and kick him."

"You forget, my dear boy," said I, with a laugh, for his news had made me light-hearted, "you forget that I have entered upon a life of self-denial, and one of the luxuries I must deny myself is that of kicking attaches."

"I've a good mind to go with you and do it myself. But it'll keep. Do you know, it's rather quaint, isn't it?" he said, after a pause, as if struck by a luminous idea—"It's rather quaint that it should be I who am playing the little tin god on wheels for you two, and saying 'Bless you, my children.'"

"I thought the humour of the situation couldn't fail to strike you at last."

"Yes," said he, knitting his brows into an air of dark reflection "it is funny. Devilish funny!"

I dismissed him with grateful words, and in a flutter of excitement went in search of Campion, whom I was lucky to find in the building.

"I'm sorry to ask for leave of absence," said I, "before I've actually taken up my appointment; but I must do so. I am summoned at once to Berlin on important business."

Campion gave willing consent. "How long will you be away?"

"That depends," said I, with a smile which I meant to be enigmatic, but assuredly must have been fatuous, "upon my powers of persuasion."

I had bright thoughts of going to Berlin and back in a meteoric flash, bringing Lola with me on my return journey, to marry her out of hand as soon as we reached London. Cats and Winter Gartens concerned me but little, and of trifles like contracts I took no account.

"If you're there any time," said Campion, tugging thoughtfully at his black beard, "you might look into what the Germans are doing with regard to Female Rescue Work. You might pick up a practical tip or two for use down here."

What a thing it is to be a man of one idea! I gave him an evasive answer and rushed away to make the necessary preparations for my journey. I was absurdly, boyishly happy. No doubt as to my success crossed my mind. It was to be my final and triumphant adventure. Unless the High Powers stove a hole in the steamer or sent another railway train to collide with mine, the non-attainment of my object seemed impossible. I had but to go, to be seen, to conquer.

I arrived safely in Berlin at half-past seven in the evening, and drove to a modest hotel in the Kaiserstrasse, where I had engaged a room. My first inquiry was for a letter from Lola. To my disappointment nothing awaited me. I had telegraphed to her at the Winter Garten the day before, and I had written as well. A horrible surmise began to dance before me. Suppose Messrs. Conto and Blag had given Dale erroneous information! I grew sick and faint at the thought. What laughter there would be in Olympus over my fool journey! In great agitation I clamoured for a programme of the Winter Garten entertainment. The hotel clerk put it into my trembling hands. There was no mention of Madame Lola Brandt, but to my unspeakable comfort I saw the announcement:

"Professorin Anastasius Papadopoulos und ihre wunderbaren Katzen."

Lola was working the cats under the little man's name. That was why she had baffled the inquiries instituted by Dale and myself and had not received my telegram. I scribbled a hasty note in which I told her of my arrival, my love, and my impatience; that I proposed to witness the performance that evening, and to meet her immediately afterwards at the stage-door. This, addressed to the Professorin Anastasius Papadopoulos, I despatched by special messenger to the Winter Garten. After a hasty toilet and a more hurried meal, I went out, and, too impatient to walk, I hailed a droschky, and drove through the wide, cheery streets of Berlin. It was a balmy June evening. The pavements were thronged. Through the vast open fronts of the cafes one saw agglutinated masses of people just cleft here and there by white-jacketed waiters darting to and fro with high-poised trays of beer and coffee. Save these and the folks in theatres all Berlin was in the streets, taking the air. A sense of gaiety pervaded the place, organised and recognised, as though it were as much part of a Berliner's duty to himself, the Fatherland, and the Almighty to be gay when the labours of the day are over as to be serious during business hours. He goes through it with a grave face and enjoys himself prodigiously. Your Latin when he fills the street with jest and laughter obeys the ebullience of his temperament; your Teuton always seems to be conscientiously obeying a book of regulations.

I soon arrived at the Winter Garten and secured a stall near the stage. The vast building was packed with a smoking and perspiring multitude. In shape it was like a long tunnel or a long, narrow railway station, an impression intensified by a monotonous barrel roof. This was, however, painted blue and decorated with myriads of golden stars. Along one side ran a gallery where those who liked to watch the performance and eat a six-course dinner at the same time could do so in elaborate comfort. In the centre of the opposite side was the stage, and below it, grouped in a semi-circle, the orchestra. Beneath the starry roof hung long wisps of smoke clouds.

The performance had only just begun and Lola's turn was seventh on the list. I reflected that greater deliberation in my movements would have suited the maturity of my years, besides enabling me to eat a more digestible dinner. I had come with the unreasoning impatience of a boy, fully conscious that I was too early, yet desperately anxious not to be too late. I laughed at myself indulgently and patted the boy in me on the head. Meanwhile, I gave myself up with mild interest to the entertainment provided. It was the same as that at any music-hall, winter garden, or variety theatre the world over. The same brawny gentlemen in tights made human pyramids out of themselves and played football with the little boys and minced with their aggravating steps down to the footlights; the same red-nosed clown tried to emulate his dashing companion on the horizontal bars, pulling himself up, to the eternal delight of the audience, by the seat of his baggy breeches, and hanging his hat on the smooth steel upright; the same massive lady with the deep chest sang sentimental ballads; the same China-man produced warrens of rabbits and flocks of pigeons from impossible receptacles; the same half-dozen scantily clad damsels sang the same inane chorus in the same flat baby voices and danced the same old dance. Mankind in the bulk is very young; it is very easily amused and, like a child, clamours for the oft-repeated tale.

The curtain went down on the last turn before Lola's. I felt a curious suspense, and half wished that I had not come to see the performance. I shrank from finding her a million miles away from me, a new, remote creature, impersonal as those who had already appeared on the stage. Mingled with this was a fear lest she might not please this vast audience. Failure, I felt, would be as humiliating to me as to her. Agatha, I remembered, confessed to the same feeling with regard to myself when I made my first speech in the House of Commons. But then I had an incontrovertible array of facts and arguments, drawn up by an infallible secretary and welded into cunning verbiage by myself, which I learned off by heart. And the House, as I knew it would, had been half asleep. I couldn't fail. But Lola had to please three thousand wide-awake Berlin citizens, who had paid their money for entertainment, with no other equipment than her own personality and the tricks of a set of wretched irresponsible cats.

The orchestra struck up the act music. The curtains parted, and revealed the brightly polished miniature gymnasium I had seen at Anastasius's cattery; the row of pussies at the back, each on a velvet stand, some white, some tabby, some long-furred, some short-furred, all sitting with their forepaws doubled demurely under their chests, wagging their tails comically, and blinking with feline indifference at the footlights; a cage in a corner in which I descried the ferocious wild tomcat; and, busily putting the last touches to the guy ropes, the pupil and assistant Quast, neatly attired in a close fitting bottle-green uniform with brass buttons. Almost immediately Lola appeared, in a shimmering gold evening gown, and with a necklet of barbaric gold round her neck. I had never seen her so magnificently, so commandingly beautiful. I was conscious of a ripple of admiration running through the huge assembly—and it was a queer sensation, half pride, half angry jealousy. My immediate neighbors were emphatic in their praise. Applause greeted her. She smiled acknowledgments and, flicking the little toy whip which she carried in her hand, she began the act. First of all, the cats jumped from their stands, right-turned like a military line, and walked in procession round the stage. At a halt and a signal each pussy put its front paws on its front neighbour and the march began again. Then Lola did something with voice and whip, and each cat dropped on its paws, and as if by magic there appeared a space between every animal.

At a further word the last cat jumped over the one in front and over the one in front of that and so on until, having cleared the first cat, it leaped on to its stand where it began to lick itself placidly. Meanwhile, the penultimate cat had begun the same evolution, and then the ante-penultimate cat, until all the cats had cleared the front one and had taken their positions on their stands. The last cat, left alone, looked round, yawned in the face of the audience, and, turning tail, regained its stand with the air of unutterable boredom. The audience, delighted, applauded vehemently. I raised my hands as I clapped them, trying vainly and foolishly to catch Lola's eye.

At a tap of her whip a white angora and a sleek tabby jumped from the stands and took up their positions one at each end of a miniature tight-rope. Lola stuck a tiny Japanese umbrella in the collar of each and sent them forth on their perilous journey. When they met in the middle, they spat and caterwauled and argued spitefully. The audience shrieked. Then by a miracle the cats cleared each other and pursued their sedate and cautious ways to their respective ends of the rope. The next act was a team of a dozen rats drawing a tiled chariot driven by a stolid coal-black cat with green, expressionless eyes, down an aisle formed by the other cats who sat in solemn contemplation on their tails. There was no doubt of Lola's success. The tricks were as marvellous in themselves as their execution was flawless. During the applause I noticed her eagerly scanning the sea of faces. Her eyes seemed to be turned in my direction. I waved my handkerchief, and instinct told me that at last she recognised the point of pink and the flutter of white as me.

Then the stage was cleared of the gentle cats and the wire cage containing Hephaestus was pushed forward by Quast. He showed off the ferocious beast's quality by making it dash itself against the wires, arch its huge back, and shoot out venomous claws. Lola commanded him by sign to open the cage. He approached in simulated terror, Hephaestus uttering blood-curdling howls, and every time he touched the handle of the door Hephaestus sprang at him like a tiger with the tomcat's hateful hiss. At last, amid the laughter of the audience (for this was prearranged business), Quast suddenly refused to obey his mistress any more, and went and sat on the floor in the corner of the stage. Then Lola, with a glance of contempt at him for his poltroonery and a glance of confidence at the audience, opened the cage door and dragged the gigantic and malevolent brute out by the scruff of its neck and held it up like a rabbit, as she had done in Anastasius's cattery.

Suddenly her iron grip seemed to relax; she made one or two ineffectual efforts to retain it and the brute dropped to the ground. She looked at it for a second disconcerted as if she had lost her nerve, and then, in a horrible flash, the beast sprang at her face. She uttered piercing screams. The blood spurted from the ghastly claws. Quick as lightning Quast leapt forward and dragged it off. Lola clapped both hands to her eyes, and reeled and tottered to the wings, where I saw a man's two arms receive her. The last thing I saw was Quast kneeling on the beast on the floor mastering him by some professional clutch. Then there rang out a sharp whistle and the curtain went down with a run.

I rose, sick with horror, barely conscious of the gasping excitement that prevailed around me, and blindly groped my path through the crowded rows of folk towards the door. I had only proceeded half-way when a sudden silence made me turn, and I saw a man addressing the audience from the stage. Apparently it was the manager. He regretted to have to inform the audience that Madame Papadopoulos would not be able to conclude her most interesting performance that evening as she had unfortunately received injuries of a very grave nature. Then he signalled to the orchestra, who crashed into a loud and vulgar march with clanging brass and thundering drum. It sounded so cynically and hideously inhuman that I trampled recklessly over people in my mad rush to the exit.

I found the stage-door, where a knot of the performers were assembled, talking of the horrible accident. I pushed my way shiveringly through them, and tried to rush into the building, but was checked by a burly porter. I explained incoherently in my rusty German. I came for news of Madame Papadopoulos. I was her *Verlobter* I declared, with a gush of inspiration. Whether he believed that I was her affianced I know not, but he bade me wait, and disappeared with my card. I became at once the object of the curiosity of the loungers. I heard them whispering together as they pointed me out and pitying me. The cat had torn her face away said one woman. I put my hands over my ears so as not to hear. Presently the porter returned with a stout person in authority, who drew me into the stage-doorkeeper's box.

"You are a friend of Frau Papadopoulos?"

"Friend!" I cried. "She is to be my wife. I am in a state of horror and despair. Tell me what has happened."

Seeing my condition, he laid aside his official manner and became human. It was a dreadful accident, said he. The beast had apparently got its claws in near her eyes; but what were her exact injuries he could not tell, as her face was all over blood and she had fainted with the pain. The doctor was with her. He had telephoned for an ambulance. I was to be quite certain that she would receive every possible attention. He would give my card to the doctor. Meanwhile I was quite at liberty to remain in the box till the ambulance came. I thanked him.

"In the meantime," said I, "if you can let me have a word with Fraulein Dawkins, her maid, should she be in the theatre, or Quast her attendant, I should be grateful."

He promised and withdrew. The doorkeeper gave me a wooden chair, and there I sat for an unconscionable time, faint and dizzy with suspense. The chance words I had heard in the crowd, the manager's remark about the claws, the memory of the savage spring at the beloved face made me feel sick. Every now and then, as some doors leading to the stage swung open, I could hear the orchestra and the laughter and applause of the audience. Both Dawkins and Quast visited me. The former was in a helpless state of tears and hand-wringing. As she knew no word of German she could understand nothing that the doctors or others said. Madame was unconscious. Her head was tightly bandaged. That was all the definite information she had.

"Did Madame know I was in front to-night?" I asked.

"Oh, yes, sir! I think she had a letter from you. She was so pleased, poor dear Madame. She told me that you would see the best performance she had ever given."

Whereupon she broke down and was useless for further examination. Then Quast came. He could not understand how the accident had occurred. Hephaestus had never before tried to attack her. She had absolute mastery over him, and he usually behaved with her as gently as any of the other cats. With himself it was quite different. He was accustomed to Hephaestus springing at him; but then he beat him hard with a great stick until he was so sore that he could neither stand up nor lie down.

"I have always implored Madame to carry something heavier than that silly little whip, and now it's all over. She will never be able to control him again. Hephaestus will have to be killed, and I will be desolate. Ach, what a misfortune!"

He began to weep.

"Good God!" I cried; "you don't mean to say that you're sorry for the brute?"

"One can't help being fond of him. We have been for five years inseparable companions!"

I had no sympathy to fling away on him at that moment.

"How do you account for his spring at Madame to-night? That's all I want to know."

"She must have been thinking of something else when she grabbed him. For she missed her grip. Then he fell and was frightened, and she must have lost her nerve. Hephaestus knew it, and sprang. That is always the case when wild animals turn. All accidents happen like that."

His words filled me with a new and sickening dread.

"She must have been thinking of something else." Of what else but of my presence there? That stupid, selfish wave of the handkerchief! I sat gnawing my hands and cursing myself.

The ambulance arrived. Men hurried past my box. I waited again in agony of mind. At last the porter came and cleared the passage and doorway of loungers, and I heard the tread of footsteps and gruff directions. The manager and a man in a frock-coat and black tie, whom I recognised as the doctor, came down the passage, followed by two great men carrying between them a stretcher covered by a sheet on which lay all that I loved in life. Dawkins followed, weeping, and then came several theatre folk. I went outside and saw the stretcher put into the ambulance-van, and then I made myself known to the doctor.

"She has received very great injuries—chiefly the right cheek and eye. So much so that she needs an oculist's care at once. I have telephoned to Dr. Steinholz, of No. 4, Thiergarten, one of our ablest oculists, to receive her now into his clinique. If you care to do so, you are welcome to accompany me."

I drove through the gay, flaring streets of Berlin like a man in a phantasmagoria of horror.

CHAPTER XXIV

The first time they allowed me to see her was after many days of nerve-racking anxiety. I had indeed called at the clinique two or three times a day for news, and I had written short letters of comfort and received weirdly-spelt messages taken down from Lola's dictation by a nurse with an imperfect knowledge of English. These kept the heart in me; for the doctor's reports were invariably grave—possible loss of sight in the injured eye and permanent disfigurement their most hopeful prognostications. I lived, too, in a nervous agony of remorse. For whatever happened I held myself responsible. At first they thought her life was in danger. I passed nightmare days. Then the alarming symptoms subsided, and it was a question of the saving of the eye and the decent healing of the cheek torn deep by the claws of the accursed brute. When Quast informed me of its summary execution I felt the primitive savage arise in me, and I upbraided Quast for not having invited me to gloat over its expiring throes. How the days passed I know not. I wandered about the streets, looking into the windows of the great shops, buying flowers and fruit for Lola in eccentric quantities. Or sitting in beerhouses reading the financial pages of a German paper held upside down. I could not return to London. Still less could I investigate the German philanthropic methods of rescuing fallen women. I wrote to Campion a brief account of what had happened and besought him to set a deputy to work on the regeneration of the Judds.

At last they brought me to where Lola lay, in a darkened room, with her head tightly bandaged. A dark mass spread over the pillow which I knew was her glorious hair. I could scarcely see the unbandaged half of her face. She still suffered acute pain, and I was warned that my visit could only be of brief duration, and that nothing but the simplest matters could be discussed. I sat down on a chair by the left side of the bed. Her wonderful nervous hand clung round mine as we talked.

The first thing she said to me, in a weak voice, like the faint echo of her deep tones, was:

"I'm going to lose all my good looks, Simon, and you won't care to look at me any more."

She said it so simply, so tenderly, without a hint of reproach in it, that I almost shouted out my horrible remorse; but I remembered my injunctions and refrained. I strove to comfort her, telling her mythical tales of surgical reassurances. She shook her head sadly.

"It was like you to stay in Berlin, Simon," she said, after a while. "Although they wouldn't let me see you, yet I knew you were within call. You can't conceive what a comfort it has been."

"How could I leave you, dear," said I, "with the thought of you throbbing in my head night and day?"

"How did you find me?"

"Through Conto and Blag. I tried all other means, you may be sure. But now I've found you I shan't let you go again."

This was not the time for elaborate explanations. She asked for none. When one is very ill one takes the most unlikely happenings as commonplace occurrences. It seemed enough to her that I was by her side. We talked of her nurses, who were kind; of the skill of Dr. Steinholz, who brought into his clinique the rigid discipline of a man-of-war.

"He wouldn't even let me have your flowers," she said. "And even if he had I shouldn't have been able to see them in this dark hole."

She questioned me as to my doings. I told her of my move to Barbara's Building.

"And I'm keeping you from all that splendid work," she said weakly. "You must go back at once, Simon. I shall get along nicely now, and I shall be happy now that I've seen you again."

I kissed her fingers. "You have to learn a lesson, my dear, which will do you an enormous amount of good."

"What is that?"

"The glorious duty of selfishness."

Then the minute hand of the clock marked the end of the interview, and the nurse appeared on the click and turned me out.

After that I saw her daily; gradually our interviews lengthened, and as she recovered strength our talks wandered from the little incidents and interests of the sick-room to the general topics of our lives. I told her of all that had happened to me since her flight. And I told her that I wanted her and her only of all women.

"Why—oh, why, did you do such a foolish thing?" I asked.

"I did it for your good."

"My dear, have you ever heard the story of the tender-hearted elephant? No? It was told in a wonderful book published years ago and called 'The Fables of George Washington AEsop.' This is it. There was once an elephant who accidentally trod on the mother of a brood of newly-hatched chickens. Her tender heart filled with remorse for what she had done, and, overflowing with pity for the fluffy orphans, she wept bitterly, and addressed them thus: 'Poor little motherless things, doomed to face the rough world without a parent's care, I myself will be a mother to you.' Whereupon, gathering them under her with maternal fondness, she sat down on the whole brood."

The unbandaged half of her face lit up with a wan smile. "Did I do that?"

"I didn't conceive it possible that you could love me except for the outside things."

"You might have waited and seen," said I in mild reproof.

She sighed. "You'll never understand. Do you remember my saying once that you reminded me of an English Duke?"

"Yes."

"You made fun of me; but you must have known what I meant. You see, Simon, you didn't seem to care a hang for me in that way—until quite lately. You were goodness and kindness itself, and I felt that you would stick by me as a friend through thick and thin; but I had given up hoping for anything else. And I knew there was some one only waiting for you, a real refined lady. So when you kissed me, I didn't dare believe it. And I had made you kiss me. I told you so, and I was as ashamed as if I had suddenly turned into a loose woman. And when Miss Faversham came, I knew it would be best for you to marry her, for all the flattering things she said to me, I knew—"

"My dear," I interrupted, "you didn't know at all. I loved you ever since I saw you first lying like a wonderful panther in your chair at Cadogan Gardens. You wove yourself into all my thoughts and around all my actions. One of these days I'll show you a kind of diary I used to keep, and you'll see how I abused you behind your back."

Her face—or the dear half of it that was visible—fell. "Oh, why?"

"For making me turn aside from the nice little smooth path to the grave which I had marked out for myself. I regarded myself as a genteel semi-corpse, and didn't want to be disturbed."

"And I disturbed you?"

"Until I danced with fury and called down on your dear head maledictions which for fulness and snap would have made a mediaeval Pope squirm with envy."

She pressed my hand. "You are making fun again. I thought you were serious."

"I am. I'm telling you exactly what happened. Then, when I was rapidly approaching the other world, it didn't matter. At last I died and came to life again; but it took me a long time to come really to life. I was like a tree in spring which has one bud which obstinately refuses to burst into blossom. At last it did burst, and all the love that had been working in my heart came to my lips; and, incidentally, my dear, to yours."

This was at the early stages of her recovery, when one could only speak of gentle things. She told me of her simple Odyssey—a period of waiting in Paris, an engagement at Vienna and Budapest, and then Berlin. Her agents had booked a week in Dresden, and a fortnight in Homburg, and she would have to pay the forfeit for breach of contract.

"I'm sorry for Anastasius's sake," she said. "The poor little mite wrote me rapturous letters when he heard I was out with the cats. He gave me a long special message for each, which I was to whisper in its ear."

Poor little Anastasius Papadopoulos! She showed me his letters, written in a great round, flourishing, sanguine hand. He seemed to be happy enough at the Maison de Sante. He had formed, he said, a school for the cats of the establishment, for which the authorities were very grateful, and he heralded the completion of his gigantic combinations with regard to the discovery of the assassin of the horse Sultan. Lola and I never spoke of him without pain; for in spite of his crazy and bombastic oddities, he had qualities that were lovable.

"And now," said Lola, "I must tell him that Hephaestus has been killed and the rest are again idling under the care of the faithful Quast. It seemed a pity to kill the poor beast."

"I wish to Heaven," said I, "that he had been strangled at birth."

"You never liked him." She smiled wanly. "But he is scarcely to be blamed. I grew unaccountably nervous and lost control. All savage animals are like that." And, seeing that I was about to protest vehemently, she smiled again. "Remember, I'm a lion-tamer's daughter, and brought up from childhood to regard these things as part of the show. There must always come a second's failure of concentration. Lots of tamers meet their deaths sooner or later for the same reason—just a sudden loss of magnetism. The beast gets frightened and springs."

Exactly what Quast had told me. Exactly what I myself had divined at the sickening moment. I bowed my head and laid the back of her cool hand against it, and groaned out my remorse. If I had not been there! If I had not distracted her attention! She would not listen to my self-reproach. It had nothing to do with me. She had simply missed her grip and lost her head. She forbade me to mention the subject again. The misery of thinking that I held myself to blame was unbearable. I said no more, realising the acute distress of her generous soul, but in my heart I made a deep vow of reparation.

It was, however, with no such chivalrous feelings, but out of the simple longing to fulfil my life that I asked her definitely, for the first time, to marry me as soon as she could get about the world again. I put before her with what delicacy I could that if she had foolish ideas of my being above her in station, she was above me in worldly fortune, and thus we both had to make some sacrifices to our pride. I said that my work was found—that our lives could be regulated as she wished.

She listened, without saying a word, until I had finished. Then she took my hand.

"I'm grateful," she said, "and I'm proud. And I know that I love you beyond all things on earth. But I won't give you an answer till I'm up and about on my feet again."

"Why?" I insisted.

"Don't ask. And don't mention the matter again. You must be good to me, because I'm ill, and do what I say."

She smiled and fondled my hand, and cajoled a reluctant promise from me.

Then came days in which, for no obvious reason, Lola received me with anxious frightened diffidence, and spoke with constraint. The cheerfulness which she had hitherto exhibited gave place to dull depression. She urged me continually to leave Berlin, where, as she said, I was wasting my time, and return to my work in London.

"I shall be all right, Simon, perfectly all right, and as soon as I can travel, I'll come straight to London."

"I'm not going to let you slip through my fingers again," I would say laughingly.

"But I promise you, I'll swear to you I'll come back! Only I can't bear to think of you idling around a woman's sick-bed, when you have such glorious things to do at home. That's a man's work, Simon. This isn't."

"But it is a man's work," I would declare, "to devote himself to the woman he loves and not to leave her helpless, a stranger in a strange land."

"I wish you would go, Simon. I do wish you would go!" she would say wearily. "It's the only favour I've ever asked you in my life."

Man-like, I looked within myself to find the reason for these earnest requests. In casting off my jester's suit had I also divested myself of the power to be a decently interesting companion? Had I become merely a dull, tactless, egotistical bore? Was I, in simple, naked, horrid fact, getting on an invalid's delicate nerves? I was scared of the new picture of myself thus presented. I became self-conscious and made particular efforts to bring a little gaiety into our talk; but though she smiled with her lips, the cloud, whatever it was, hung heavily on her mind, and at the first opportunity she came back to the ceaseless argument.

In despair I took her nurse into my confidence.

"She is right," said the nurse. "You are doing her more harm than good. You had better go away and write to her daily from London."

"But why—but why?" I clamoured. "Can't you give me any reason?"

The nurse glanced at me with a touch of feminine scorn.

"The bandages will soon be removed."

"Well?" said I.

"The sight of one eye may be gone."

"I know," said I. "She is reconciled to it. She has the courage and resignation of a saint."

"She has also the very common and natural fears of a woman."

"For Heaven's sake," I cried, "tell me plainly what you mean."

"We don't quite know what disfigurement will result," said the nurse bluntly. "It is certain to be very great, and the dread of your seeing her is making her ill and retarding her recovery. So if you have any regard for her, pack up your things and go away."

"But," I remonstrated, "I'm bound to see her sooner or later."

The nurse lost patience. "Ach! Can't you get it into your head that it is essential it should be later, when she is strong enough to stand the strain and has realised the worst and made her little preparations?"

I accepted the rebuke meekly. The situation, when explained, was comprehensible to the meanest masculine intelligence.

"I will go," said I.

When I announced this determination to Lola she breathed a deep sigh of relief.

"I shall be so much happier," she said.

Then she raised both her arms and drew my head down until our lips met. "Dear," she whispered, still holding me, "if I hadn't run away from you before I should run away now; but it would be silly to do it twice. So I'll come to London as soon as the doctor will let me. But if you find you don't and can't possibly love me I shan't feel hurt with you. I've had some months, I know, of your love, and that will last me all my life; and I know that whatever happens you'll be my very dear and devoted friend."

"I shall be your lover always!" I swore.

She shook her head and released me. A great pity welled up in my heart, for I know now why she had forbidden me to speak of marriage, and in some dim way I got to the depth of her woman's nature. I realised, as far as a man can, how the sudden blasting of a woman's beauty must revolutionise not only her own attitude towards the world, but her conception of the world's attitude towards her. Only a few weeks before she had gone about proudly conscious of her superb magnificence. It was the triumphant weapon in her woman's armoury, to use when she so chose. It had illuminated a man's journey (I knew and felt it now) through the Valley of the Shadow. It had held his senses captive. It had brought him to her feet. It was a charm that she could always offer to his eyes. It was her glory and her pride to enhance it for his delectation. Her beauty was herself. That gone, she had nothing but a worthless soul to offer, and what woman would dream of offering a man her soul if she had no casket in which to enshrine it? If I had presented this other aspect of the case to Lola, she would have cried out, with perfect sincerity:

"My soul! You get things like mine anywhere for twopence a dozen."

It was the blasting of her beauty that was the infinite matter. All that I loved would be gone. She would have nothing left to give. The splendour of the day had ceased, and now was coming the long, long, dreary night, to meet which with dignity she was nerving her brave heart.

The tears were not far from my eyes when I said again softly:

"Your lover always, dear."

"Make no promises," she said, "except one."

"And that is?"

"That you will write me often until I come home."

"Every day."

So we parted, and I returned to London and to my duties at Barbara's Building. I wrote daily, and her dictated answers gave me knowledge of her progress. To my immense relief, I heard that the oculist's skill had saved her eyesight; but it could not obliterate the traces of the cruel claws.

The days, although fuller with work and interests, appeared long until she came. I saw but little of the outside world. Dale, my sister Agatha, Sir Joshua Oldfield, and Campion were the only friends I met. Dale was ingenuously sympathetic when he head of the calamity.

"What's going to happen?" he asked, after he had exhausted his vocabulary of abuse on cats, Providence and Anastasius Papadopoulos. "What's the poor dear going to do?"

"If I am going to have any voice in the matter," said I, "she is going to marry me."

He wrung me by the hand enthusiastically and declared that I was the splendidest fellow that ever lived. Then he sighed.

"I am going about like a sheep without a leader. For Heaven's sake, come back into politics. Form a hilarious little party of your own—anything—so long as you're back and take me with you."

"Come to Barbara's Building," said I.

But he made a wry face, and said that he did not think Maisie would like it. I laughed and put my hand on his shoulder.

"My son, you have a leader already, and she has already tied a blue riband round your woolly neck, and she is pulling you wherever she wants to go. And it's all to the infinite advantage of your eternal soul."

Whereupon he grinned and departed to the sheepfold.

At last Lola came. She begged me not to meet her at the station, but to go round after dinner to Cadogan Gardens.

Dawkins opened the door for me and showed me into the familiar drawing-room. The long summer day was nearing its end, and only a dim twilight came through the open windows. Lola was standing rigid on the hearthrug, her hand shielding the whole of the right side of her face. With the free hand she checked my impetuous advance.

"Stop and look!" she said, and then dropped the shielding hand, and stood before me with twitching lips and death in her eyes. I saw in a flash the devastation that had been wrought; but, thank God, I pierced beneath it to the anguish in her heart. The pity—the awful, poignant pity—of it smote me. Everything that was man in me surged towards her. What she saw in my eyes I know not; but in hers dawned a sudden wonder. There was no recoil of shock, such as she had steeled herself to encounter. I sprang forward and clasped her in my arms. Her stiffened frame gradually relaxed and our lips met, and in that kiss all fears and doubts were dissolved for ever.

Some hours later she said: "If you are blind enough to care for a maimed thing like me, I can't help it. I shall never understand it to my dying day," she added with a long sigh.

"And you will marry me?"

"I suppose I've got to," she replied. And with the old pantherine twist of her body she slid from her easy-chair to the ground and buried her face on my knees.

And that is the end of my story. We were quietly married three weeks afterwards. Agatha, wishing to humour a maniac for whom she retained an unreasonable affection, came to the wedding and treated Lola as only a sweet lady could. But my doings passed her understanding. As for Jane, my other sister, she cast me from her. People who did these things, she maintained, must bear the consequences. I bore them bravely. It is only now that my name is beginning to be noised abroad as that of one who speaks with some knowledge on certain social questions that Jane holds out the olive branch of fraternal peace. After a brief honeymoon Lola insisted on joining me in Barbara's Building. A set of rooms next to mine was vacant, and Campion, who welcomed a new worker, had the two sets thrown into what house-agents term a commodious flat. She is now Lady Superior of the Institution. The title is Campion's, and for some odd feminine reason Lola is delighted with it.

Yes, this is the end of the story which I began (it seems in a previous incarnation) at Murglebed-on-Sea.

The maiming of Lola's beauty has been the last jest which the Arch-Jester has practised on me. I fancy he thought that this final scurvy trick would wipe Simon de Gex for ever out of the ranks of his rivals. But I flatter myself that, having snapped my fingers in his face, the last laugh has been on my side. He has withdrawn discomfited from the conflict and left me master of the ground. Love conquers all, even the Arch-Jester.

There are some who still point to me as one who has deliberately ruined a brilliant career, who pity me as one who has gone under, who speak with shrugged shoulders and uplifted eyebrows at my unfortunate marriage and my obscure and cranky occupation. The world, they say, was at my feet. So it was. But what the pitying critics lack the grace to understand is that better than to have it under one's feet is to have it, or that of it which matters, at one's heart.

I sit in this tiny hotel by the sea and reflect that it is over three years since I awoke from death and assumed a new avatar. And since my marriage, what have been the happenings?

Dale has just been elected for the Fensham Division of Westmoreland, and he has already begun the line of sturdy young Kynnersleys, of which I had eumoirous dreams long ago. Quast and the cats have passed into alien hands. Anastasius Papadopoulos is dead. He died three months ago of angina pectoris, and Lola was with him at the end. Eleanor Faversham has married a Colonial bishop. Campion, too, has married—and married the last woman in the world to whom one would have thought of mating him—a frivolous butterfly of a creature who drags him to dinner-parties and Ascot and suppers at the Savoy, and holds Barbara's Building and all it connotes in vixenish detestation. He roars out the agony of his philanthropic spirit to Lola and myself, who administer consolation and the cold mutton that he loves. The story of his marriage is a little lunatic drama all to itself and I will tell it some day. But now I can only rough-sketch the facts. He works when he can at the beloved creation of his life and fortune; but the brain that would be inadequate to the self-protecting needs of a ferret controls the action of this masterful enthusiast, and his one awful despair in life is to touch a heart that might beat in the bosom of a vicious and calculating haddock. I only mention this to explain how it has come to pass that Lola and I are now all-powerful in Barbara's Building. It has become the child of our adoption and we love it with a deep and almost fanatic affection. Before Lola my influence and personality fade into nothingness. She is the power, the terror, the adoration of Lambeth. If she chose she could control the Parliamentary vote of the borough. Her great, direct, large-hearted personality carries all before it. And with it there is something of the uncanny. A feat of hers in the early days is by way of becoming legendary.

A woman, on the books of the Building, was about to bring a hopeless human fragment into a grey world. Lola went to see what aid the Building could provide. In front of the door lounged the husband, a hulking porter in a Bermondsey factory. Glowering at his feet lay a vicious mongrel dog—bull-terrier, Irish-terrier, mastiff—so did Lola with her trained eye distinguish the strains. When she asked for his wife in travail the chivalrous gentleman took his pipe from his mouth, spat, and after the manner of his kind referred to the disfigurement of her face in terms impossible to transcribe. She paid no attention.

"I'm coming upstairs to see your wife."

"If you pass that door, s'welp me Gawd, I'll set the dog on yer."

She paused. He urged the dog, who bristled and growled and showed his teeth. Lola picked the animal up, as she would have picked up a sofa cushion, and threw him across the street. She went to where he had fallen, ordered him to his feet, and the dog licked her hand. She came back with a laugh.

"I'll do the same to you if you don't let me in!"

She pushed the hulking brute aside. He resisted and laid hands on her. By some extraordinary tamer's art of which she had in vain tried to explain to me the secret, and with no apparent effort, she glided away from him and sent him cowering and subdued some feet beyond the lintel of the door. The street, which was watching, went into a roar of laughter and applause. Lola mounted the stairs and attended to the business in hand. When she came down the man was still standing at the threshold smoking an obfusticated pipe. He blinked at her as if she had been a human dynamo.

"Come round to Barbara's Building at six o'clock and tell me how she is."

He came on the stroke of six.

The fame of Lola spread through the borough, and now she can walk feared, honoured, unmolested by night or by day through the streets of horror and crime, which neither I nor any other man—no matter how courageous—dare enter at certain hours without the magical protection of a policeman.

Sunshine has come at last, both into this little backwater of the world by the sea and into my own life, and it is time I should end this futile record.

Yesterday as we lay on the sands, watching the waves idly lap the shore, Lola brought herself nearer to me with a rhythmic movement as no other creature form of woman is capable of, and looked into my eyes. And she whispered something to me which led to an infinite murmuring of foolish things. I put my arms round her and kissed her on the lips and on her cheek—whether the beautiful or the maimed I knew not—and she sank into a long, long silence. At last she said:

"What are you thinking of?"

I said, "I'm thinking that not a single human being on the face of the earth has a sense of humour."

"What do you mean?" she asked.

"Simply this," said I, "that what has occurred billions of billions of millions of times on the earth we are now regarding as the only thing that ever happened."

"Well," said Lola, "so it is—for us—the only thing that ever happened."

And the astounding woman was right.